C000021967

For testimonials from law enforcement,
visit Carolyn Arnold's website.

ALSO BY CAROLYN ARNOLD

Brandon Fisher FBI Series
Eleven
Silent Graves
The Defenseless
Blue Baby
Violated
Remnants
On the Count of Three
Past Deeds

Detective Madison Knight Series
Ties That Bind
Justified
Sacrifice
Found Innocent
Just Cause
Deadly Impulse
In the Line of Duty
Power Struggle
Shades of Justic
What We Bury
Life Sentence

McKinley Mysteries
The Day Job is Murder
Vacation is Murder
Money is Murder
Politics is Murder
Family is Murder
Shopping is Murder
Christmas is Murder
Valentine's Day is Murder
Coffee is Murder
Skiing is Murder
Halloween is Murder
Exercise is Murder

Matthew Connor Adventure Series
City of Gold
The Secret of the Lost Pharaoh
The Legend of Gasparilla and His Treasure

Standalone Title
Assassination of a Dignitary

CAROLYN ARNOLD

WHAT WE BURY

HIBBERT & STILES
PUBLISHING INC.

Hibbert & Stiles Publishing Inc.
www.hspubinc.com

This is a work of fiction. Names, characters, places, and incidents are the products of the author's imagination or are used fictitiously. Any resemblance to actual events, locales, or persons, living or dead, is entirely coincidental.

Names: Arnold, Carolyn, author.
Title: What We Bury / Carolyn Arnold.
Description: [London, Ontario] : Hibbert & Stiles Publishing Inc., [2020] | Series: Detective Madison Knight series ; [book 10]
Identifiers: ISBN 9781989706411 (paperback 4.25 x 7) | ISBN: 9781989706428 (paperback 5 x 8) | ISBN 9781989706435 (hardcover) | ISBN 9781989706404 (ebook)

WHAT
WE BURY

One

S he's dead."

Those two words brought Madison Knight to 982 Hillcrest Drive in the middle of a Saturday afternoon in March. It was a quiet neighborhood in the south end of Stiles, a city of about three hundred sixty thousand, and it had been her real estate agent, Estelle Robins, who'd called. When Madison saw the name on caller ID, she'd assumed Estelle had found the perfect place for Madison and her boyfriend, Troy Matthews. Boy, had she been mistaken.

Madison parked in the driveway, admiring the raised bungalow with its grayish-brown brick and beige siding. It couldn't be older than fifteen years. The front door was under a small overhang, and that's where Estelle was standing, her arms wrapped around herself as if she were cold, but the temperature today was unusually warm. Some of the more northern states would envy their spring-like weather in early March.

Madison got out of the car and approached Estelle. She was normally the picture of calm and put-togetherness, but her hair was frizzed around her heart-shaped face, and her eyes were wet and wide. Her brown eyeshadow was smudged beneath her right eye, but her mascara had stayed in place.

"Omigod, Madison. I didn't know who else to call, but you'll know what to do."

"You did the right thing." Madison was a Major Crimes detective with the Stiles Police Department. Troy could have tagged along, as he was also a detective for the department, but his primary role was leader of a SWAT team. Solving murders was her thing. "Where is she?"

"In the shed. I'll take you there." Estelle led the way to a side gate next to the garage. Her hand was shaking as she worked the latch.

Madison followed Estelle down a concrete sidewalk toward the backyard. "How did you find her?"

"There's supposed to be an open house." Estelle spoke over her shoulder. "I was making sure the property looked good." Estelle stopped and hoisted a chain-link gate at the end of the walk that was hinged on the fence and wedged against the brick of the garage.

To the right was a deck, and ahead was a manageable yard. The rear of the lot was framed by mature cedars and a chain-link fence. There was another gate back there, and it appeared open.

Estelle pointed to a shed with a concrete foundation and beige siding. It was about twelve feet wide and twenty feet long.

"She's in there." Estelle shivered. "I can't believe this is happening."

Madison laid a hand on her arm. "It's a lot to process, for sure, but I'm here now. You said you had an open house scheduled—"

"Oh." Estelle ran a hand through her hair, making it even more frizzy. The extension of her arm revealed a beautiful big-faced watch, which she consulted. "It's scheduled to start in fifteen minutes. I wasn't thinking… There are still signs around the neighborhood."

Madison nodded. "I saw them on the way. They need to be taken down and the open house—"

"Canceled. Yes, I understand completely."

"Can you manage collecting the signs, or do you want help?"

Estelle rubbed the back of her neck. "I can handle it."

Madison nudged her head toward the house. "We'll also need to contact the homeowners and make them aware of the situation. I'll need to question them too."

Estelle chewed on her bottom lip. "I will call them."

"Okay, after you get the signs."

Estelle sniffled but stood tall, as if finding some strength. "I'll get the signs and come right back."

Madison headed across the lawn to the shed. The door was toward the rear of the building and next to a window. The handle had a keyhole. She gloved up and turned it. Unlocked. Had it been left that way or picked?

She stepped inside, immediately catching the stench of blood—something she didn't have much tolerance for despite her chosen profession. She swallowed roughly, and her stomach tossed, but she pushed forward.

She took her phone from her coat pocket and activated the flashlight to get a better look. The window let some light in, but the space was still immersed in shadows.

The beam went over stacked patio furniture, as well as shovels and garden tools that leaned against the wall and were laid out on a shelving unit. There were a couple large containers for cushions and garden pots in various shapes and sizes.

Madison edged farther inside, following drips of blood, and rounded a lawnmower.

And there she was. Jane Doe. Late forties, possibly fifties. Blank stare, pool of blood— Madison gazed at it. She was getting better at handling messy scenes, and she tamped down her visceral reaction as best she could, but it didn't help that she'd been battling with nausea lately anyhow.

She put a hand on her stomach, resembling, in a way, the dead woman, who had an arm cradled across her lower abdomen. Blood had seeped around her palms to the back of her hands and between her fingers. She'd been stabbed at least a few times, from the looks of it, each blow in the vicinity of her gut.

Doe's dress, casual—blue jeans, a light jacket unzipped, a gray T-shirt, black-heeled boots. Her makeup was artfully applied, and given the macabre circumstances, she was rather beautiful even in death. Her hair was wet—like her clothing—and spread around her head like a halo on a folded blue tarp. She must have been caught in last night's rain before seeking shelter from the storm. Aside from the tangible quality of death clinging to the air and the blood, it could almost be imagined that she'd slipped into the shed for a nap.

It was heartbreaking to think she'd died alone, bleeding, while rain beat against the metal roof. Had it hypnotized and soothed her as she drifted into darkness? Or had she fought for life?

There were no personal effects near the woman—no purse or phone—but her identification could be in her pockets. Madison wasn't going to go rummaging until she had backup.

No immediate sign of the murder weapon either.

Madison turned away and started making the necessary calls. Patrol officers to cordon off the property; her partner-on-the-job, Terry Grant, to assist her; Cole Richards, the medical examiner; and crime scene investigator and head of the forensics lab, Cynthia Baxter—or Baxter-Stanford now that she had married Lou Stanford, another Major Crimes detective.

She ended her last call, and the silence was deafening. Soon the property would be crawling with law enforcement and crime scene investigators. But for now, it was just her and Jane Doe.

Two

Officer Tendum sent me back." Terry Grant, Madison's partner who was three years younger than her thirty-six, was coming toward where she was standing next to the shed. Every one of his blond hairs lay perfectly in place, and his cheeks were flushed. She'd probably disturbed his run—something he chose to do for fun and exercise. To her, running was the devil's pastime.

He nudged his head to indicate the building. "The victim's in there?"

"Jane Doe, yep." She hated to think of the murdered as *victims*, detesting the assignment of a label to a once-living individual, loved by people.

She stepped aside for Terry to enter the building but stayed outside. "She's behind the lawnmower," she told him.

Terry poked his head through the doorway. "You're not coming?"

"No, I've seen her."

"You all right?"

"Yes, why wouldn't I be?" She raised her eyebrows. Her distaste was something she did her best to hide, but if she were honest with herself, she hadn't been too good at pulling it off.

"Uh-huh." Terry disappeared again.

She rolled her eyes and followed him.

"Estelle must have had quite a shock," he said.

"Yeah, you could say that." She came up next to Terry, who was standing at Doe's feet. "I didn't see any sign of the murder weapon, and given the blood drops leading from the doorway, I'd say Jane Doe walked in here."

Terry pointed a finger to the walls. "No spatter. This isn't where she was stabbed."

"I agree. We'll need to establish the primary." That being the scene of the crime. "The rain from last night would have washed away any blood outside leading to the shed, so it won't be easy. But I did notice something while I was waiting." Madison headed outside and gestured toward the back of the yard. "The gate's open. She might have come through there. She was stabbed and bleeding, seeking shelter—"

"Why not look or call for help?"

"Maybe she tried? She also could have been in a state of delirium and shock." Madison couldn't imagine anyone thinking rationally after being stabbed.

"Okay, well, if I remember the area right, there are some bars and restaurants a street south. Burnham Street. We may be looking at a date gone wrong."

Madison recalled Doe's dolled-up face and her apparel. "If that's the case, dating just got a whole lot less attractive."

"Hey, nothing like working a crime scene on Saturday afternoon," Cynthia Baxter-Stanford said, as she approached with her employee, Mark Adams. She went on. "Lou and I were just about to open a bottle of wine and watch a movie."

"Still in the honeymoon phase," Terry affirmed. "Before long you'll be fighting over who has the remote. He'll be drinking beer or whiskey; you'll be on your own with the wine…"

The way Terry spoke, a person would think he hated married life, but he loved his wife Annabelle and their eight-month-old daughter, Danielle, above all else.

"Guess time will tell." Cynthia winked at Madison.

Madison thought Cynthia's plans sounded like a lot more fun than what Madison had been up to before the call. She and Troy had been in a heated discussion about their future, specifically where they saw themselves living, but it seemed to be a cover for a topic they were avoiding. At least she was. She was confident he was going to propose at Cynthia's wedding a few weeks ago—just the way he'd been acting and looking at her. Even Cynthia thought for sure he was going to pop the question. But he still hadn't asked, and it left her feeling prickly and easily irritated. But whether he was responding to her energy or battling his own thoughts, he hadn't been too pleased when she said she had to leave.

Cynthia and Mark went into the shed and got to work, while Madison and Terry remained outside the door. They wanted to know if Jane Doe had a phone or ID in her pockets to start with, but they gave the investigators some space.

Several minutes later, Cynthia stepped out from the shed, a camera strapped around her neck. "There's something you're going to want to see."

Madison gave a curious glance at Terry and followed her friend inside, Terry at her heels.

Cynthia pointed at the pool of blood on the left side of the body. Mark shone a flashlight on the area.

"What am I looking at?" Madison crouched down.

"Right there. See it?" Cynthia swooped a fingertip over an area of blood. "It's rather faint to the naked eye, but—" she lifted her camera and held it so that Madison and Terry could see the screen "—it shows up quite clear in a photo."

"Is that…" Madison squinted at the screen.

"Letters written in blood?" Cynthia said.

"Yep. And given the caked blood under the index fingernail of her right hand, I'd say she wrote it herself."

"GB." Madison straightened up, placed her hands on her hips. "What does it stand for?"

Terry took out his phone, pecked on it. "GB can stand for gigabyte, Great Britain…"

Madison looked at her partner. "Just a guess, but I think Doe had something—or someone—else in mind. Maybe the first two letters of her killer's name or their initials?"

"So she knew her killer?" Terry volleyed back. "We're leaping to that."

"I'm just spitballing, Terry, and keeping an open mind."

"Since when?" he shoved out with a chuckle.

Madison met Cynthia's gaze, and her friend said, "He does have a point."

"Very funny, you two." Madison said. "But let's focus on the case, not me. Any sign of forced entry?"

Mark walked over and put the beam of a flashlight on the doorframe and handle. "Doesn't look like it, and I'd say the lock wasn't picked. No scratches in the metal other than the normal wear and tear that comes with sticking a key in and out over time."

"We'll ask the homeowners if they leave it unlocked. Do we have an ID?"

"I was just getting ready to check her pockets before…" Mark shot a look at Terry, then asked Cynthia, "You have all the pictures you need of her before I proceed?"

Cynthia nodded her go-ahead.

Mark lowered near the body, aware of the placement of his feet, and slipped a gloved hand into Doe's jacket pocket. "Nothing in this one." He rummaged in the other one and pulled out a balled-up tissue, lip balm, and a piece of paper. He was about to put the items into a clear evidence bag.

"Wait," Madison said. "Anything written on it?"

Mark dropped the tissue and balm into the bag, then took the paper in both hands and unfolded it. Madison stepped closer and could see the page was lined and whole, probably removed from a small notebook. She read what was there.

"The name Alan Lowe and a number." She took out her phone and placed the call. The line rang while Terry and Cynthia watched her. Mark went on to check Doe's jean pockets, front and back.

Madison's call was shuffled to voicemail, and in the greeting, Lowe announced himself as a financial adviser with Stiles Investment and Savings. Madison was familiar with the bank. Lowe was a new name to her. "Mr. Lowe, this is Detective Madison Knight with the Stiles PD. Please give me a call when you get this message." She rattled off her number and ended the call. Best to keep things vague for now. "It's a banker," she said. "The number either rang through to his desk extension or his cell phone. Hard to say."

Mark resumed full height. "Nothing in the pockets of her jeans."

"Also, no purse, wallet, or phone," Cynthia added.

"Guess it's official. Meet Jane Doe." Madison sighed. She'd hoped the name was only a temporary assignment, but it seemed it would be hanging around a bit longer.

Three

I'm also not seeing any personal effects or jewelry on her person," Madison observed. "No earrings, necklace, rings, or watch."

"Maybe we're looking at a mugging." Terry shrugged his shoulders.

Really, until they had more to go on, it was far too soon to lean heavily in any one direction. Cynthia and Mark went back to processing the scene. Mark placed yellow, numbered markers and a ruler beside each drop of blood, and Cynthia took a photo.

Madison nudged Terry's arm. "Let's go see if the homeowners are here yet."

"Sure."

"We'll leave you guys to it," Madison said. "Keep us posted if you find anything."

"Always do," Cynthia responded in a singsong voice that caused Madison to smile. She might have the slight tendency to micromanage.

Madison and Terry were just exiting as Cole Richards had a leg lifted to enter. The medical examiner's assistant, Milo, was behind him.

"You're leaving just when I arrived?" Richards smiled at her, the expression showcasing his white teeth and crinkling the dark skin around his eyes.

"Don't worry. I'll be back." Madison returned the smile, thankful that things between them had finally returned to normal. A couple years ago, Madison had pried into his personal life, exposing an old, yet still-painful wound, and another time not long after that, she'd questioned one of his rulings.

"I have no doubt." Richards laughed, and he and Milo proceeded inside.

Madison and Terry were making their way to the back door, and Officer Higgins was coming toward them. Higgins had been her training officer when she first joined the Stiles PD.

"What is it, Chief?" Madison accepted his desire not to advance rank, but it didn't stop her from using her affectionate nickname for him. After all, if Higgins had wanted to be police chief, he could have been.

"Just wanted to let you know that the Bernsteins are ready to speak with you, whenever you're ready."

"The Bernsteins?" Madison asked.

"Oh, figured you knew. The homeowners. Oliver and Rhea. They're in the house with Estelle."

"Good timing. We were just going to check on that."

Higgins started walking back in the direction of the house.

"Hey, Chief," she called out to him.

Higgins turned around. "You really need to stop calling me that."

"I don't see why."

"Probably because he's not the chief," Terry pointed out.

As if I don't know that... Troy's sister, Andrea Fletcher, had taken the post after the previous chief had retired.

"Are officers knocking on doors in the neighborhood yet?" she asked Higgins.

"Just getting started. I'll let you know if anything useful comes back."

"When they're finished on Hillcrest, it might not be a bad idea to have them canvass Burnham Street." He looked at her, some confusion in his eyes, and she turned and gestured to the open gate at the rear of the yard. "Terry and I were thinking she might have come through there."

"Okay. I'll make sure that happens."

"Good, and have them keep an eye out for the primary. It's not looking like she was killed here."

"You got it." Higgins took a step, stopped. "That all?"

"For now."

"All right, then. The Bernsteins are in the front sitting room. Just go through that door on the lower deck and up the stairs to the left."

"Thanks." His form disappeared through the side gate, and she turned to Terry. "Let's hope the Bernsteins can give us a name for Jane Doe."

Madison got the door for her and Terry. The place smelled of garlic, ground beef, and tomato sauce.

A man's voice carried down to the entry. "What's this going to do to our property value?"

She felt an instant dislike. Murder wasn't convenient for anyone, least of all the deceased, but it would seem the man was more concerned with his bottom line than the fact someone had died on his property.

The entry was more of a breezeway. It was a straight shot from the back door to the front. One set of stairs went down and another up. The walls of the staircases were open-sided with spindles that made it easy to see the spaces above and below. The stairs going down looked like they led to a large room, and up, to the sitting room Higgins had mentioned.

"Madison?" Estelle's head popped up over the top railing.

Madison wiped her feet on the mat, and Terry followed suit.

The upper level was beautiful. Glistening maple floors, large windows, and an open-concept floorplan. The sitting area was to the immediate right at the top of the stairs. A hallway veered to the left and likely led to a bedroom or two and a bathroom. And behind the living room was a dining area, the kitchen to the left of that.

Estelle's hair had been pulled back, the frizz smoothed out, and her makeup fixed. Knowing the woman as Madison did, she was a true professional and would have wanted to present a strong front for her clients.

"Madison," Estelle began, her gaze skipping over Madison to Terry. "This is Mr. and Mrs. Bernstein."

Sixty-somethings. Both with gray hair and faces so similar they could have been siblings rather than a married couple. They were trim and had mirroring expressions of shock. The woman's cheeks were flushed, and the man's body language was stiff and rigid. They were seated on a dark-blue couch.

"I'm Oliver," the man said, "and this is my wife, Rhea."

"I'm Detective Madison Knight, and this is my partner, Terry Grant."

"Also a detective," Terry added with some levity.

Estelle's gaze returned to Terry and she offered him a reserved smile.

"We have some questions for you…" Madison gestured toward an available cream-colored wingback chair.

"Absolutely. Sit wherever you'd like," Oliver told her.

She sat, and Terry dropped into another chair, first setting aside two throw pillows.

"We can imagine what a shock this must be," Madison said to start.

"It's shocking all right." Rhea blew out a breath and glanced at Estelle. "When Estelle told us what was in our shed..." She searched for her husband's hand, and he gave it to her.

"We can't show you a picture of her right now." Madison proceeded to describe Doe's looks. "Does that sound like someone you might know?"

"Could be." Oliver's voice was strained. "Hard to really tell without seeing— Do you have a name for us?"

"Unfortunately, there was no ID with her. Were you home last night?" They didn't have time of death yet, but it seemed safe to conclude Doe had died sometime during in the night, given the fact she was rain-soaked.

"I stepped out for some groceries about six and got home around seven," Oliver said. "Rhea was here, though. She made lasagna."

That explained the smells in the home.

"I was here all afternoon yesterday," Rhea volunteered. "Spent most of it downstairs in a recliner reading the latest Carolyn Arnold novel."

Madison pressed her lips into a tight smile. She'd never heard of the author, but that wasn't a surprise; her schedule didn't leave her much time to read.

"And from seven on?" Terry asked.

"We were here together." Oliver glanced at his wife and continued. "We watched Netflix until bed."

Madison glanced around the room, and there was no television.

"We watch it downstairs in our media room," Oliver said, seeming to notice Madison's search.

"What time did you go to bed?" Terry asked.

"Rhea went around nine thirty, and I fell asleep on the couch but staggered up to bed at around midnight."

Up. So the master bedroom must be down that hallway. Maybe if she wasn't there for a murder investigation, she would have appreciated a tour. "Did either of you hear or see anything in the night?"

"I didn't." Oliver accompanied his verbal answer with a shake of his head.

"And you, Mrs. Bernstein?" Madison prompted. "Maybe a noise in the wee hours?"

"Wee hours…" Rhea's blanched. "Come to think of it. I got up to use the washroom."

Madison leaned forward. "What time was this?"

"Oh, say about one in the morning. I can't remember exactly, but when you said, 'wee hours,' it sparked a memory. I heard a thump outside, but I was basically still asleep. Just figured it was nothing. The rain was lashing against the windows in the bedroom."

"You never looked out to see what it might have been?"

Rhea met her gaze. "I didn't. I'm sorry."

Madison ran through the possibilities in her head. The noise could have been Doe closing the shed door—then again, it could have been anything. "Do you normally keep your shed locked?"

"Never found a need to before." Oliver's eyes went downcast.

The Bernsteins had been fortunate not to have a break-in. They were only two blocks east and one north of the downtown core. There was a lot of petty theft in the area, including unlocked cars being riffled through for cash. "You probably know what I'm going to say." Madison smiled.

"That we should lock all our doors. Don't worry. We will now," Oliver said.

"One more question and we'll leave you for now," Madison began, "but is your back gate normally open or closed?" She recalled how it was sitting crooked on the hinges, and without getting a close look, it was hard to say if it was just a tricky gate that didn't latch.

"It should be closed," Rhea said tentatively.

"Okay, thank you." Madison walked over to the Bernsteins with her card. Rhea took it from her. "Call me if you have any questions or concerns. Or if you think of anything else that might help us with the case."

She and Terry saw themselves out through the rear door to the lower deck.

"So the Bernsteins didn't know her, or at least say they don't," Madison said. "But who really knows? It's not like we had a name to give them or a picture. I guess what I'm struggling with is why Doe went in their shed. And did she know it was sitting unlocked or just strike it lucky that way?"

"Let me consult my crystal ball…"

"Smart-ass." She punched him in the shoulder.

"Hey." Terry rubbed where she'd hit him. Sometimes their relationship was more like siblings than work partners.

"I'm just saying we've got to figure this out."

"This is where I'd say, 'no poop,' seeing as I don't swear." He smiled, but she rolled her eyes and shook her head. Her "brother" certainly had a way with words.

Four

On the way to the back gate, Madison ducked into the shed to see if Richards had anything to share. Cynthia and Mark were still kicking around, and Milo was next to Richards.

"I'd say she was stabbed." Richards laughed at his wise-guy answer to Madison's question about cause of death.

Madison shook her head. "I figured that much out myself. I was hoping for more details. How many stab wounds for instance?"

"Three, and given the angle, I'd say it is impossible she inflicted the injuries on herself."

It might seem ridiculous to think someone would stab themselves, but she'd come across it before. When she was a new detective, a man had been stabbed several times. The case was approached as attempted murder, but when the man woke from surgery, he'd admitted the entire thing had been a suicide attempt.

"Any idea what kind of instrument was used?" Madison stepped forward, and Richards looked at her as if to say *step back*. She stopped where she was but didn't retreat.

"That's where it's a little tricky. Of the three wounds, two look similar. They're more ragged than the third."

"You think different weapons were used?" Terry asked.

Richards met Terry's gaze. "It's possible. I'll know more once I get her back to the morgue."

"Don't even want to hazard a guess?" Madison smiled at the ME, but he wasn't one for spewing hypotheticals.

"Not this time, but nice try, Knight. I'd say her wounds are quite deep, though. Do you know where she was attacked?"

"Not yet," Madison said. "We think she might have come here on foot. Maybe from downtown."

Richards seemed to consider Madison's words, probably bringing up a map of the area in his head. "As I said, the stabs appear deep, but given their point of impact, it's possible the victim would have been alive for some time afterward."

"Giving her time to walk from point A— wherever that is—to here," Madison stated. "How long would she have had…after she was stabbed?" Her stomach roiled at the thought.

Richards glanced at the body. "I wouldn't say too long, but there's no absolute way of knowing. The mind and sheer will can be powerful."

It had obviously been long enough to get inside the shed and write GB in her blood. "Depending on where she came from, she probably didn't have much time to reach out for help." She looked at Terry. Still, one would think she would have tried, and it didn't explain why she came here. She kept circling back to thinking she had a connection to the Bernsteins.

"What's time of death looking like?" Terry asked Richards.

"Based on rigor, definitely over twelve hours ago." He held an open palm to Milo, and he dropped a thermometer in his hand. Richards pierced Doe's liver with it, and time ticked off on clocks the world over. After what felt like forever, Richards scribbled in a notebook and asked Milo for the temperature in the shed and for the averages in the past twenty-four hours. Eventually, Richards concluded, "She died between twelve and seventeen hours ago."

"Terry?" Let her partner calculate the math since he was so good at it.

"Between nine last night and two this morning," Terry kicked out.

Richards didn't say anything to Terry's conclusion, which meant it was right. Now they just needed to figure out what had brought Jane

Doe out during that time. Was it a date, business, or something else? Was she targeted, or was she simply in the wrong place at the wrong time? And what made her settle here, in this shed? Had it just been convenient and possibly on her way to her true destination? And where the hell had the stabbing happened?

Madison had one idea, and it was time to follow her gut.

Five

Madison left the shed and went to the back gate.

"You sure you don't want Cynthia and Mark back here first?" Terry called from behind her. "And you do realize even if Doe came this way, the chances of finding any proof—"

Madison held up her hand. "A little positivity would be nice."

"Who are you?"

She often wondered about that herself lately. She was teetering on the edge of obsession when it came to Troy and the lack of a proposal. She hadn't second-guessed her ability to read people since her ex-fiancé had broken her trust and slept with another woman over ten years ago.

She reached the gate, and it was open wide enough to pass through. She stepped onto a gravel driveway. It was banked by more cedar trees and scraggly bushes and ended at the sidewalk on Burnham Street. A uniformed officer was posted there, guarding the rear entrance to the property.

He dipped his head at them. She'd never seen him before.

She proceeded to walk carefully, cognizant of her footsteps, and stopped when she saw something in a section of dirt, clear of pebbles. A pointed toe. Small indentation for a heel. Doe's boot prints?

She glanced overhead. Large pine trees sheltered this section. Branches and foliage must have been enough to block the rain and preserve the prints. She placed her foot, suspended, next to the print. "I'd say size nine." She thought back to the woman, but she hadn't paid much attention to her feet except to notice she was wearing boots. "The direction shows the person going toward the gate. I'd wager Jane Doe came through here."

"You wanna make a bet?" Terry smiled at her.

They often made bets on the outcome or aspects of a case, and she was normally game, but she wasn't feeling like it today. She glanced over her shoulder at him. "I'll pass."

"And you do realize those prints could have been left by anyone. Maybe Mrs. Bernstein."

She shook her head and resumed scanning the ground. Sometimes it felt like her partner disagreed with her just for the sake of disagreeing.

"Oh. Look." She indicated her next find—little burgundy droplets.

Terry came up next to her, careful of his footing, too, and inspected them for himself. "Could be blood," he said.

"Could be? I think it's a sure thing. We need Crime Scene back here pronto."

Terry took off to notify Cynthia and Mark, and Madison gestured for the officer's attention. "In case we're gone before Crime Scene gets here," she started.

"Yes, ma'am?" He started walking toward her. She held up a hand.

"It's *Detective*, and be careful of your steps. I believe Jane Doe passed through here. But I need you to point out the print here—" Madison swirled the tip of her shoe over where it was "—and also, there appear to be blood droplets." She indicated those with her finger.

"I'll be sure to let the investigators know, ma—Detective."

She read his name tag. Harrison. He must have been a rookie. She sauntered slowly toward the sidewalk, scanning every inch as she went. She kept returning her gaze to the bushes. She'd manifest the murder weapon if she could, but the shrubbery wasn't giving up any secrets.

"Cynthia and Mark will be out shortly," Terry called from behind her. "They asked that we vamoose."

"They? I doubt Mark said that."

"Cynthia."

"That I believe." She started down the sidewalk, heading west toward downtown.

"Where are we going?" Terry caught up and kept pace with her.

"We're going to find out where she was stabbed."

"Based on your gut?"

"You know it."

"Come on, be real here, Maddy. If I didn't know you better, I'd say you just wanted to go for a walk."

"Here's what I'm thinking…" She ignored his jab. So what? She wasn't a fan of exercise; a lot of people weren't. "She was stabbed three times. Why stop there?"

"Ah…" Terry snapped his jaw shut. "No idea."

"I think it's possible her would-be killer got spooked or was interrupted and ran. And that tells me—"

"Jane Doe was attacked someplace public where other people could have come along."

"Uh-huh. Richards figured she died anywhere between nine last night and two this morning, and it's unlikely she could have walked too far with her injuries."

"She was probably attacked just down the street. Maybe near one of the bars or restaurants."

"That's how I see it."

"Okay, then, that takes us back to why she didn't seek help. And if there was an eyewitness or more, where are they now?"

She stopped walking, considered Terry's questions.

"Gotcha stumped?" He smiled.

"A little, yeah. *But*," she said, "just because the attacker got spooked doesn't mean someone was there. Could have just been a noise—" Her mind returned to Mrs. Bernstein's statement about waking up in the early hours and hearing something outside.

"Maddy?" Terry prompted.

"Rhea Bernstein told us that she heard a thump about one in the morning."

"So?"

"So I just assumed it was Doe closing the shed door or even nothing of importance, but what if Doe did seek help from the Bernsteins, and the thump Rhea heard had actually been Doe knocking on one of their doors?"

"Okay, but…" Terry let that dangle. "If Doe was attacked where people could potentially be around, you're telling me she never sought out their help? Or that no one saw her? That she walked to the Bernsteins with intention?"

"It's almost starting to seem like it. But that also brings to my attention that someone—homeowners even—along Burnham Street might have seen a woman hobbling along the sidewalk. But you also know what people can be like. They don't want to get involved and are fearful for their own safety. And as I had mentioned earlier, Doe wouldn't have been in a rational state of mind. She could have appeared intimidating."

"I get all that, but it's also possible Doe had a hard time finding help. People would have still been in the bars drinking. Assuming the thump Mrs. Bernstein heard about one in the morning is related to Doe."

"Yep, and that would leave the parking lots rather empty of people, as well as the alleyways that run between the bars and restaurants and behind, if I remember right." She resumed walking until she came to a public parking lot.

"What are you doing?"

"Assuming Doe had a vehicle and drove herself down here, she could have parked here." She waved a hand at a city sign that indicated no parking on either side of Burnham Street.

"And how do you intend to..." Terry's eyes skimmed the packed lot. It was going on four in the afternoon, and people were already venturing to the area for meals and drinks.

The sun winked off the windshields and had her reaching into her jacket pocket for her sunglasses. She came out empty-handed, but no surprise. She had a hard time hanging on to shades.

Terry had his on when she looked over at him.

She started, "We search the lot, see if—"

"One of the vehicles jumps out and says, 'I belong to a dead woman.'"

"Very funny."

"Jeez. Lighten up. What's wrong with you? It's Saturday, and if one of us would normally be griping about working—"

"My mood has nothing to do with working." She regretted the admission immediately. There was no way she was going to get into the tension in her relationship with Troy.

"Then, what?"

Terry had told her before that she was known to pry, but he was a pro himself. "We have a case to solve. Let's focus on that."

"Fine," he huffed. "If she was accosted in the parking lot, to me that supports the possibility that she was mugged. Think about it, she was about to get into her vehicle and her attacker confronts her. Maybe he or she left because they simply got what they wanted—her purse, phone, possibly jewelry."

"Okay, I can get behind that theory. But let's see if we can prove it."

He held eye contact, and it drilled in how different she was acting today, certainly not her usual self. Terry was typically the one telling her they needed proof.

"Actually…" Terry groaned. "If her attacker came at her when she was at her vehicle, they might have stolen it too. Then we'll have nothing to find."

She didn't want to entertain the idea, but it was possible. It could also explain why Doe was left to get away on foot—not that she would have been in any shape to drive. "Let's just spread out." She looked over the lot and noticed there were flyers stuck under the wipers of several vehicles. She snatched one. For some band playing that night at Luck of the Irish pub, which was the bar just next door. But it gave her an idea. "If Doe parked here, and assuming no one stole her vehicle—" she shot a seething look at Terry "—she would likely have a parking ticket on her hood. You go that way, and I'll start here."

Terry did as she asked, and she began with the row closest to her. After a few lanes, she was about to give up when she spotted a small slip stuck under the wiper of an older, gray sedan. She tore it off and yelled, "Jackpot!"

He whistled at the ticket. "Fifty bucks. Ouch."

She was more interested in the time stamps than the fine. "Doe—"

"You're assuming."

"Doe," she repeated, "parked here at eight last night and paid for four hours."

Terry bobbed his head side to side. "Lines up with the time-of-death window. Could be her car."

"I'd say it's a good bet—"

"Then—"

"No," she shot him down again. She wasn't in the mood to make wagers on the case. She was in the mood for answers, though. She pulled out her phone and called Higgins.

"Hey-lo," he answered.

"It's Madison, but I'm going to guess you knew that."

"Caller ID was a nifty invention."

"I need you to do something quick for me."

"Name it."

"Need you to run a plate number…" She gave him the tag.

"One second." The clicking of keys, then, "It's registered to a Chantelle Carson. Age forty-eight— Oh yeah, that's Jane Doe all right. I have her license photo in front of me. Blond, shoulder-length, gray eyes, round face, five eight. Where did you see the plate?"

"Her car's in the public lot on Burnham Street, just east of the bars and restaurants."

"I assume you had a good reason to be curious?"

"Taught by the best."

"Impressive."

She beamed and nodded at Terry. "We have her," she said to him. To Higgins, "Her next of kin? Address?" She put him on speaker for Terry's benefit. No one else was around.

"I'll shoot it all over to you," Higgins told her.

"Great. And if you could also get an officer over here to watch the car until it's processed and brought in?"

"You know it."

"And please let Richards know Doe's identity," she added.

"Absolutely."

With that, she hung up and smirked at Terry. "Turns out it was a good thing we went for a walk."

"I hate it when you brag."

Six

Madison cupped her eyes and squinted into the sedan's driver's-side window. It was immaculately kept. No dust on the dash or garbage within sight. It was possible Carson was the type who stuffed crap under her seat, though. Madison went around the car, repeating the process. "Wow, she keeps this thing clean."

"Not everyone treats their car like a garbage bin on four wheels."

"In your words, hardy-har. I'm too busy to—"

"An excuse. Everyone's busy."

She'd defend herself, but he was right. She had a horrible habit of tossing trash over her shoulder into the back seat. She wasn't quite as bad as she used to be because it drove Troy mad.

"So Carson came down here last night at eight," she started, "but then where did she go?" She looked toward the sidewalk.

"Again, a crystal ball would be helpful."

"Wouldn't it." She scanned the area. There were trees at the east end of the lot, separating it from the neighboring property, which was a house. The north side offered an optional entry point off Napoleon Avenue. "If she was attacked near here, why not head back to her car?"

"We don't know where her keys are. Maybe her attacker took them, leaving her without a way to get in her vehicle."

Madison chewed her bottom lip and stepped to the sidewalk, looked east. Nothing but houses. "What compelled her down the street as far as the Bernsteins'?" Her phone pinged with a text. A message from Higgins. "Next of kin is her ex-husband. Bill Carson. Higgins is sending more info to me via email, including his address. I also have Carson's phone number." They could potentially track it, but first, to even see if it was on, Madison called the number. She got a message that the line was no longer in service. She shared that with Terry as her phone beeped again. "And we have Carson's DMV picture."

"Not that we should be flashing that around until the ex-husband is notified."

She hated that he was right. "We can still ask around, using her description. Maybe someone saw the altercation?" She paused, taking in all the houses, and added, "Surely someone saw her stumbling along the sidewalk."

A police cruiser pulled into the lot, Higgins behind the wheel. He parked next to Carson's car and got out.

"I know I requested officers to canvass Burnham, but with her car being here, it's even more important that it gets done," Madison said.

Higgins nodded. "I get that. I'll update the officers who will be working the street about her car."

"Thank you," she said. "We'll leave this to you, then."

"Why?" Terry asked. "Where are we going?"

"To do some canvassing ourselves."

"Shouldn't we notify the ex—"

"Just amuse me for a minute." She proceeded west along Burnham Street.

The first establishment west of the public parking lot was Luck of the Irish. The pub was next to a restaurant Madison wouldn't return to or recommend. The service was slow, the food bland, and the prices ridiculous.

The laneway between the two businesses was just wide enough for one-way traffic. And only the select few were rewarded with parking at the backside of the pub and restaurant. Any delivery trucks bringing food and drink to the establishments would have had to park temporarily at the curb or go around to Napoleon Avenue.

Madison walked down the lane to the lot, and someone coughing got her attention. A man in his late forties/early fifties stood on a small stoop with cracked and crooked concrete steps outside a back door, a burning cigarette in hand.

He took a toke, exhaled. "Can I help you with something?"

Madison and Terry raised their badges.

"Detectives with the Stiles PD," she said, closing the distance between herself and the man. He didn't move except to take another drag on his smoke. "Were you in the area last night, say from about nine until two this morning?"

"Rather specific window." He flicked ash, took another hit. His eyes were beady and lazily drifted from her to Terry and back again.

She didn't want to get into the fact a woman was found dead not too far from there, especially without her next of kin being informed, but she wanted to probe some. He might have seen the attack. "Can you just answer my question?"

"I was working in the kitchen until ten. Headed out and went straight home." He extinguished his cigarette on a plate he held in his right hand.

"You didn't take any smoke breaks?" she asked.

"I did."

Madison wanted so badly to show him the DMV photo of Chantelle Carson but would follow protocol. "During your shift, did you happen to hear or see any altercations—either out here or maybe one that started inside the pub?" If the thump Mrs. Bernstein had heard was Carson, this man would have long been home by the time she was attacked, but until they had definitive reason to believe the noise was Carson, they had to consider the entire TOD window.

"I don't recall. Nothing out here anyway." He waved his cigarette over the lot. "If there was an argument out front, I might not have heard it."

"And nothing of that sort made it back to you in the kitchen?" She just wanted to be certain.

"Nope. Just a typical Friday. College kids out to get hammered."

"Did you notice any people in their forties in the crowd? I know you work in the kitchen, but you must pop into the dining room sometimes."

"There's usually some any given night. But like I said, no rumbles in the jungle." The man smiled at Terry.

"Okay," she said. "We might be around later."

"Whatever floats your boat, darlin'."

She left thinking that some people really were an acquired taste.

Terry walked the lot. She looked to the west of the pub, toward the restaurant and beyond it, to the back of the establishments within line of sight, of which there were several. Other businesses were across the street too. That also equated to a lot of dumpsters, and until they had a better way of knowing where the attack had taken place, searching all of them for the mere possibility of finding evidence didn't make sense.

"Let's head back," she said. "We'll talk to the Bernsteins now that we have Doe's real name and a photo." Given that the body was found on their property, an exception could be made.

"And the other bars and restaurants?"

"I'll have Higgins get officers to pay them a visit." She pulled her phone and keyed a quick text to that effect. "We'll also need to get ahold of the city for traffic-cam footage." She pointed just west of the pub and restaurant where Burnham intersected with Market Street. "It could give us something." She called her contact at the city but had to leave a message. She hung up and filled in Terry.

"Not much of a surprise with it being Saturday."

"Nope." It didn't mean that it wasn't frustrating. It was also frustrating that bars and restaurants along the stretch likely had security cameras but wouldn't hand them over without a warrant. And without something that confirmed Carson was indeed attacked in the immediate vicinity, no judge would approve the request.

Seven

By the time Madison and Terry walked through the Bernsteins' back gate, Richards and Milo were removing Carson's body from the outbuilding. The loss of life sank in Madison's gut. She would certainly do all she could to find that woman justice.

Madison hurried to catch up with them as they stopped at the entrance to the side gate. "When will you be conducting the autopsy?"

"Tomorrow morning," Richards said.

"More specifically?" She raised her brows and pressed her lips.

"Rather get it over and done, so let's say eight."

Eight, Sunday morning. She must have been delusional to think she'd get to sleep in. After all, she had the homicide case and her own business to take care of tonight.

"Did you hear me?" Richards prompted.

"I'll be there." Madison passed a side-glance at Terry, and he sighed. Though she wasn't sure why. He'd probably have gotten his run in by that time. People who ran *and* did mornings were a true enigma to her.

Richards and Milo saw themselves out with some help from a nearby officer who came along and got the gate.

She headed to the door off the lower deck, Terry following.

Estelle opened the door just as they reached it. Her complexion was ashen, and she was hugging herself.

"How are you doing?" Madison asked, though it seemed obvious her real estate agent wasn't doing that great.

"I don't know how you do this all the time." She gestured a hand toward the shed. "Dealing with dead bodies… Murder. Guess I like to live in my safe, little bubble."

Madison touched her arm. "Nothing wrong with that."

"I guess." A visible shiver tore through her.

"We need to speak with the Bernsteins again," Madison told her agent.

Estelle stepped back and let them inside.

Madison and Terry wiped their shoes on the mat and went up to the sitting room, Estelle in tow.

Oliver was walking from the kitchen with two steaming mugs, one of which he handed to Rhea, who was seated on the couch where she'd been before. She probably hadn't even left the spot.

Madison remained standing and said, "We have an identity on her now."

Rhea's breath caught, and she exhaled a jagged sigh.

"The woman was Chantelle Carson." Madison watched the Bernsteins' body language and facial tells. Slumped shoulders, wet eyes. "You knew her?"

Oliver's mouth set in a straight line, and he nodded.

Madison dropped into the chair she'd sat in the first time she talked to them. Her insides were quaking. She'd had a feeling there was a connection between Carson and the Bernsteins. "How?"

Oliver wrapped an arm around his wife's shoulders. "She helped us set up property insurance recently. Gave us a good deal too."

If Carson was in insurance and had written up the Bernsteins' policy, it would make sense that she'd know about the outbuilding. "What company does she work for?" They could get this from a report, but why wait?

"Southern Life," Oliver said.

Madison nodded. There was another thing they needed to clear up, though. "Mrs. Bernstein, you said that you heard a thump in the morning, around one o'clock?"

"That's right."

"Is it possible that someone had knocked on one of your doors?"

Rhea seemed to consider Madison's question. "I'm not sure."

"Would you mind if my partner and I conducted a little experiment?"

Rhea looked at her husband, back to Madison. "What is it?"

"I'd like you and I to go where you were when you heard the noise, and Detective Grant will knock on the different doors you have. Then you can tell me if any of them sound like what you heard that night." Madison realized there was the risk Rhea would confirm the sound out of desire rather than it actually being the noise, but it was worth a shot. Madison looked at Terry and nudged her head at him. "I'll call you once we're in position. Mrs. Bernstein?"

Rhea set her mug on the coffee table in front of her and led Madison down the hall to the master bedroom. Really, it was a suite with a small walk-in closet and a private bath complete with double sinks, jetted tub, and shower stall. A transom ran above three large windows on the back wall. To the right was an exterior door, and beside it, the entrance to the bathroom. That's where Rhea stopped.

"I was right here."

Madison called Terry on his cell phone and told him to knock on the door off the lower deck. She watched Rhea as Terry pounded in varying rhythms and heaviness. "Any of those sound like what you heard in the morning?"

Rhea's eyes were closed, and she shook her head.

"Try the door on the upper deck, Terry," Madison told him.

A few seconds later, Terry knocked on that door.

"That the sound?" Madison asked Rhea, and again she shook her head. "Okay, Terry. Thanks." She was disappointed as she had convinced herself Carson had tried to wake the Bernsteins for help.

"That! That right there," Rhea declared.

Madison looked out the window. Terry was climbing down the wooden staircase.

"I'm certain that's the noise I heard."

"Okay," Madison said to Rhea and stepped into the hall. In her phone to Terry, she added, "Mrs. Bernstein heard someone on the back stairs. Is there any sign of blood?" She thought she'd ask, but she wasn't too confident that the answer would be positive, given the rain.

"Not that I see," Terry replied, "but I'll have Cynthia and Mark take a look."

"Sounds good. You might as well come back in." Madison returned to Rhea.

She was looking at Madison with wide, wet eyes. "What does this mean?"

It would seem Carson had climbed the stairs to knock on the back door. There would be no easy way to tell the woman that Carson had likely tried to get their help, but she couldn't bring herself to lie either. She laid it out as kindly as she could.

"I could have..." Rhea sobbed, and Oliver entered the room.

Seeing him made Madison curious, though. "You didn't hear anything in the night, early this morning?" She'd asked him before but thought she would again.

"Once I'm asleep, I'm out," Oliver said.

"She tried to get us, Olie." Rhea put her arms around her husband, and he held on to her.

Madison told him it was likely that she'd knocked and the sound his wife had heard was Carson going back down the stairs.

Oliver's chin quivered, and he drew his wife tighter to himself.

"You can't blame yourselves for any of this. Do you hear me?" Madison asked.

The couple nodded.

"Please keep us informed." Oliver pulled back from his wife.

"I'll do my best, and call me if you need anything." With that, Madison saw herself through the house. She found Estelle sitting in the front room, staring off into space. "There's no reason you have to stay," Madison told her. "Officers will remain on the premises for a while yet."

The Bernsteins joined them. Terry was standing in the breezeway by the back door.

Madison gestured to him that she'd be there shortly.

Estelle's gaze went to the couple, and her brow pinched with concern. She glanced at Madison, but she didn't say anything.

"She's right, Estelle," Oliver said. "You can leave if you'd like."

"Thank you, Oliver, but I'm good to stay a bit longer." Estelle rubbed her arms.

Madison went out the front door with Terry, and they convened in the driveway. She noted that Terry had arrived in a department car, whereas she'd come in her own Mazda. "Want to follow me home? I'll drop off my car."

"Sure." Terry turned to leave.

"Actually, let's meet up at the station." Truth was she didn't want to run into Troy and possibly get sucked into a conversation. She just needed to keep moving with this case because the clock was ticking.

"That your final answer?" he teased.

"Yeah. And it would be great if you could pull the report on Carson so it's ready for when I arrive."

"Yes, your majesty." Terry smirked and bowed.

"Cut it out." She kept Terry around for several reasons, but he was certainly good for entertainment.

"You said that Higgins was sending it to you, though, didn't you?"

"Would be nice to see it on paper."

"Fine." He went on his way.

As she was pulling away from the house, she thought about how unpredictable life could be. Alive one minute, gone the next. She doubted anyone woke up thinking, *Today's the day I die*. Plans were always on the horizon, as if people preferred to play in a world without acknowledging death. It wasn't until it slapped them in the face that people were reminded of their mortality. Otherwise, most harbored fantasies of beating or outsmarting the Grim Reaper. But poor Chantelle Carson had failed, and Madison doubted she ever would have envisioned herself stabbed and bleeding out in a shed.

Eight

Madison beelined for her desk, her mind on the top right-hand drawer and her stash of Hershey's bars. If she just ate one, it should be enough to hold her for a while. It was going on six thirty, and despite the onset and offset of nausea, she could eat, just not anything too heavy. She rummaged in the drawer, pulled out a bar and tore the wrapper back.

"Why am I not surprised?" Terry was walking toward his desk, which faced hers.

"Never mind. Did you print the report?" She bit off some chocolate.

"No, I thought I'd just lay my head down, catch a couple winks while I waited on you."

"Your sarcasm is alive and well."

"I learn from the best. That's you, just in case you needed a clue."

"Very funny."

"Are you really eating a chocolate bar for dinner?"

She laughed. Terry, her food monitor. "I'm not sure why that would surprise you." They'd been partners going on eight years, and for that length of time, she'd always had a chocolate—more specifically, a Hershey's—addiction.

"I was hoping we'd stop somewhere, hit a drive-thru on the way to the ex-husband's—"

"Because that's so much healthier." She mumbled, "Vegetable," just before taking another bite of heaven.

"If that's what you have to tell yourself to soothe your conscience."

She scowled at him while her mouth was full of gooey milk chocolate. "Ymm," she moaned and closed her eyes.

"You really have a problem. You know that?"

"Whatev—" She chomped on another chunk. "Ymm."

Terry shook his head. "While you masticate that bar like a—"

She stopped chewing, her glare daring him to finish his sentence.

"In direct answer to your question, yes, I printed the background on Carson."

She finished her mouthful and looked at Terry. "And?"

"Carson got divorced eight months ago. She and her husband have had separate addresses for a couple years. He stayed in Deer Glen where the couple had lived together for twenty-seven years, and she moved to a house in Rosedale after their separation, until two months ago when she moved into an apartment in the east end."

Deer Glen and Rosedale were both high-end communities in the north end of Stiles. It was the type of suburbia that employed groundkeepers and maids.

"What made her move?" she asked.

"Not something the report tells us."

"Smart-ass. Was she fired or—"

"Not from what I can see. She started working at Southern Life around the time of her separation, and it looks like she was still there."

"Those reports aren't always up-to-date."

"Well, there's no way we can drop by and confirm her employment at this time on a Saturday."

"They're an insurance company, yes? So, what if a customer needs to make a claim? There has to be a twenty-four-hour, seven-day-a-week number."

"Sure, but it's not like anyone at the call center could verify Carson's employment. We'll need to wait until Monday and go into their local office."

She hated to concede that he was right. "What about her ex-husband, what does he do?"

"He's some bigwig manager with Stiles Insurance Company."

"They're huge."

"Yep. Boasted sales into the high eight figures last year."

"What I'm stuck on is...it seems the wife went to work for the competition. Because insurance was what she knew, or to stick it to her husband in some way? Where did she work before Southern Life?"

"For Stiles Insurance Company, but that's going back twenty-five years."

"And she was married for how long?"

"Twenty-three."

"You said they lived together for twenty-seven years, so that means she left her job..." She really hated math.

"It would have been around the same time as when they got married."

"Okay. Well, they must not have needed her money."

"I'd say not. Bill Carson doesn't need to work either. He has a net worth of eleven mil."

"All from selling insurance?"

Terry shook his head. "Family money. He inherited when his parents died. Bill would have been fifteen."

"Quite a fall for Chantelle Carson to go from living the lifestyle of the rich and famous to an apartment in the east end."

"I'd say."

"So, what took her there? You said she had a nice place in Rosedale even after they separated, yet she took a job almost right away. Maybe more to keep busy than for the money? We need to notify Bill Carson, but we also need to ask him some questions."

"I agree."

If she wasn't deeply rooted to her chair, she might have toppled over—Terry had actually agreed with her on something. "Did the couple have any kids?"

"Nope. And her parents are gone. But I've got Bill's address already in my phone, and I'd be happy to tell you where to go."

She stuffed a big piece of chocolate into her mouth and spoke. "I'm sure you would."

"Oh—" Terry moaned in disgust and held up a hand to block his view of her.

She got up, taking what was left of the bar, and headed to the station lot. She didn't know what she'd do without Terry in her life. He really was like the brother she never had, and it was so easy to get him riled up.

Nine

Madison was driving with Terry to Bill Carson's when her phone rang. She silently cursed. She'd escaped all talk with Sergeant Winston down at the station—a miracle—but she might have gotten excited too soon. She glanced at the caller ID. It wasn't Winston, but it was someone else she really didn't want to talk to right now.

"You going to get that?" Terry prompted from the passenger seat.

"Didn't think you liked it when I talked on the phone and drove."

"Since when does what I think stop you from doing anything?"

"Fair point." She'd smirk if her stomach wasn't clenched tight. With each trill of her phone, she felt stabbed with remorse. It was Troy, and she was ignoring him. She'd never done anything like that before. The ringing stopped, and she took a deep breath. "See, they'll get voicemail, leave a message…"

"Please tell me that you didn't just ignore Winston."

"The guy might irritate the shit out of—sorry, *crap*—out of me, but I'm smart enough to take his calls."

"If it wasn't him, then who was it?"

She pulled into Carson's driveway, shut off the ignition, and got out of the car.

"So?" Terry was at her heels.

"Anyone ever tell you you're nosy?" She really wanted to tell her partner to mind his own business, but then he'd immediately go to her personal life, and she didn't want to shine the spotlight there.

The house was a gray-brick mansion with a two-story entrance and columns banking each side of the door. Large windows yawned into the night, and light from inside pooled out to the front lawn. Anyone in the front room would have been on stage, but no one was there now.

She pressed the doorbell and tapped a foot.

"It couldn't have been a business call," Terry said, prattling on. "If it was Cynthia or someone else from the lab or— Oh."

She pushed the ringer again, refusing to look at Terry.

"It was your mother?"

Good guess. She and her mother didn't see eye to eye on most things—most being marriage *and* babies.

"Was it—"

"It's none of your—"

The door cracked open, and a woman was standing there in a black-and-white maid's uniform.

Madison held up her badge. "Detectives Madison Knight and Terry Grant of the Stiles PD. We'd like to speak with William Carson."

The woman's brow pinched, and she looked back and forth between them.

"Bill Carson, ma'am," Terry said.

She slowly looked at Terry, and her face softened. "Yes, just one minute, please." She closed the door in their faces, and Madison glanced at Terry.

Madison said, "I just assumed that Bill was short for—"

"That's the problem with *assume*. You make an ass out of you and—"

The door opened again, and a trim man in his fifties stood there, dressed in formal slacks and a white, collared shirt. The top three buttons were undone, and his tie was loosened around his neck. He studied the two of them and slipped his hands into his pockets.

"Mr. Bill Carson?" she asked to confirm.

"That's me, and you are police detectives?"

"Yes. I'm Detective Knight, and this is Detective Grant." Madison gestured to Terry. "There's something we need to tell you. Do you have someplace we could sit?"

"Sure." He stepped back to let them inside.

A tiered chandelier dripped over the entry, its lights twinkling through the crystals and casting small rainbows on the walls. The flooring was travertine and polished to a high shine. She could use her missing sunglasses again.

"Someplace to sit?" she prompted Bill when he hadn't moved.

Bill Carson regarded them with curiosity but relinquished with a nod and led them to the "stage." He sat on a cream-colored sofa, and Madison and Terry dropped into two facing chairs.

"We have some bad news about your ex-wife, Chantelle." Madison stopped talking when a teenage girl entered the room. Madison glanced at Terry. He'd said that Bill and Chantelle didn't have children.

"Tiffany, I'll be with you in a minute," Bill told the girl, his voice stiff.

Tiffany let her gaze linger on Madison and then Terry, but eventually she left in the direction from which she'd come.

"Sorry about the interruption," Bill said, matching gazes with Madison.

"Beautiful girl," Madison began. "She's your—"

"Stepdaughter. Well, not legally yet, but I'm engaged to her mother. We all live here together, so I think of her as—" Bill waved a hand. "Never mind all that. You said you have bad news about Chantelle?"

"She was found stabbed to death this afternoon." Notifications were best delivered without any sugarcoating. The worst responsibility of the job, and she and Terry used to take turns, but lately it always seemed to be her.

Bill blew out a puff of air and leaned forward. "I don't know what to say." He met Madison's eyes, and his were full of tears. "When was she—" He pinched his nose, sniffled and dropped his hand.

"She was stabbed between nine last night and two this morning." Though if Carson had tried the Bernsteins' door, that timeline would more accurately be between midnight and one thirty. "From what we could see, you're her next of kin. Her parents are dead, and she didn't have any siblings, and you never had children together."

"No." Bill raked a hand through his hair and bit his bottom lip. "Not for the lack of trying. She wanted kids, but it just wasn't meant to be, I guess. She couldn't have them, and she was devastated by that."

"Is that what led to your separation and eventual divorce?" Madison was trying to paint a picture of Chantelle Carson's life.

"It would be easier on me if I said yes, but it wouldn't be the truth. Maybe it curdled under the surface, existed in the words that went unspoken, but that time of our lives passed us by. I poured myself into work, and Chantelle managed the organization of numerous charity events and benefits."

"For business or…" Madison prompted.

"Personal interest. She took her responsibility toward the community seriously. She often said that we all need to do our part, and if we don't, we have no right to complain."

"Sounds like she was a smart woman," Terry interjected.

Bill looked at him. "She was."

"Then why did you end up getting divorced?" Madison asked.

Bill's face became hard angles and shadows. "I fell in love with Stephanie. I'd like to say it was because things between Chantelle and I were rough, but…"

Madison clenched her jaw. She'd learned the harsh truth that finding a faithful man was like sighting a unicorn. She wasn't as emotionally charged around the topic as she used to be, but it had taken years to move forward after finding her fiancé in bed with another woman. She knew of a few men who didn't stray. At least three—her father, Terry, and Troy—unless they had her fooled.

"It takes two," Terry said, responding in a far more diplomatic manner than she would have.

"It does," Bill said remorsefully. "I really do think part of what did us in was not being able to have children. It was like cancer killing us beneath the surface."

"I can appreciate that would have been difficult," Terry—the good cop—said.

"Is Stephanie here?" Madison asked.

Bill's gaze snapped to hers. "She's at work."

"And where's that?" Madison tossed back.

"Stiles Insurance." Bill glanced across the room, then back at Madison. "She was my boss."

That was a flip on the typical cliché that had the man falling in love with his female secretary.

Bill went on. "It was a little tense around the office at the beginning."

As much fun as this trip down memory lane might have been for Bill, Madison had some other lines of inquiry to make. "Chantelle got a job at Southern Life not long after you two separated. Do you know if she was still working there? We haven't had a chance to verify with the company."

"Unfortunately, we didn't keep in touch. I'm sure you can understand that would be awkward."

"You were married for twenty-three years," Madison countered, imagining that would afford some amicability. Then again, if Bill had cheated on Chantelle, Madison could understand if their connection completely fell apart, and it wasn't like they had kids to bring them together.

"We were, and the decision to stay out of each other's lives was a tough one, but it made it much easier to move on."

For her or you? Madison thought, although it would seem Bill had already left before the marriage dissolved.

"And I heard that she found someone," Bill continued.

Flapping jaws always followed in the wake of any breakup. "From whom?"

"Steph. She just mentioned it in passing, but she goes to the same gym as Lana—that's Lana Barrett, Chantelle's best friend since public school."

What a horrible picture he was painting of his ex's friend being buddies with his soon-to-be new wife. Talk about a spy in the ranks. "What's this guy's name?"

"Paul…I think." Bill knotted up his face.

"Paul. You think. We'll need to talk to this guy. You sure you don't know—"

"I don't, but Stephanie might. I don't think he would have done anything to hurt Chantelle. From what I heard, Chantelle was happy."

"Would you be able to reach your wife right now and just ask her quickly for his name?" Madison asked. "It might help us."

"I'll try her." Bill pulled his phone from a pocket and placed the call. "Hey, Steph… Just a quick question… I'll explain more when you get home. I know you're busy. But do you remember Chantelle's boyfriend's name?" Time passed, and Bill's face showcased shock and sadness, then landed on anger. "Told you, I'll explain once you're home." With that, he put his phone away. "She couldn't remember. And I'm in the doghouse because Steph has it in her head that I'm sitting here reminiscing."

"Do you do that often?" Madison latched on.

"No. Anyway, I'll straighten that out. But Lana would know the boyfriend's name for sure."

"Okay, just another question before we leave," Madison started. "You said you weren't in contact with Chantelle, but do you happen to know of anyone who might have wanted to harm her?"

"No. I can't imagine, honestly. Though she was what some might call a Goody Two-shoes. Always saw things black-and-white and made no secret of how she felt. It's why she was good at her job for the brief time she was at Stiles Insurance. She had no problem rejecting applicants."

"Why would they be rejected?" Madison asked.

"Well, when it comes to health or life insurance, a nurse goes out to a person's home and conducts an interview. That information is then reviewed before it's put through to different insurance companies. If a person's score is low… Say, for example, an applicant is very obese and looking for disability or critical care coverage. Statistically, overweight people are more of a health risk. A black-and-white assessment, to be sure, but there have to be some sort of guidelines in place. Anyway, Chantelle never had a problem telling people how things were."

Madison inched forward on her chair. "So she'd tell people they were rejected because of their weight?"

"Uh-huh. No qualms about it either."

"That must have made a lot of people angry."

"Absolutely. Some of them got out of control too. They really took it personally, but at the end of the day it wasn't Chantelle rejecting them; she knew what the company would approve and reject."

"She stopped the application process before it got all the way through?" Terry asked.

"That's right, and that was part of the job."

"You said, 'Some of them got out of control,'" Madison stated. "How's that?"

"Oh, threatening phone calls. They'd show up at the office with dead rats for her. It got pretty bad sometimes. I asked her to quit—we certainly didn't need the money—but she stayed on a little longer. It wasn't until one of the rejected applicants showed up at our door yelling for her, that I insisted she quit."

"Wow." Some people really took rejection hard. "How long ago was this?"

"Over twenty-some years ago."

Madison nodded. "One more thing. Do you have any idea what Chantelle might have meant by the letters GB?"

"In what context?"

"These letters were present where she was found." That's all Madison was prepared to give him.

"Well, in the world of insurance, GB would stand for group benefits." Bill raised his brows. "Does that help?"

"Guess we'll find out," Madison replied. Bill had discussed rejected personal applicants becoming enraged, but did someone behind a company have reason to want Chantelle Carson dead? It was a lead worth pursuing, but first, she and Terry would talk to the best friend and see what she had to say. Maybe they'd find out about the boyfriend while they were at it. In the least, he deserved to know what had happened to Chantelle. At most, he was the one that killed her. Both needed to be ruled out.

Ten

Before Madison and Terry left Bill Carson, she confirmed with him that Chantelle used to have a life insurance policy and a will. Whether she still did, and as to the current beneficiary, he couldn't say. Once in the car and heading to Lana Barrett's place, Madison gave Terry a side-glance, then tapped the wheel. "Carson's ex really didn't seem all that broken up about her death."

"I thought he was."

"I would have expected a little more emotion, given they were married for so long. I know they broke up a couple years ago, but you'd think there'd be more feeling there."

"Every relationship is different."

"I think I missed seeing your PhD." She flashed a quick smile at him.

"Ha-ha. I think he cared, but at the same time, the relationship was over, and people have to move on."

"As he pointed out," she mumbled as her thoughts went personal. What if what she had with Troy was over, washed up, played out? She had allowed herself to believe what she had with Troy was the real deal and would last. She'd even entertained marrying him, but— Her phone rang. She fished it out of her pocket and looked at the caller ID. Troy. She put it away without answering.

"Okay, now you have to talk to me." Terry angled his body toward her.

"What? Why?"

He pointed at her phone, obviously referring her rejected caller. "You could have sent them to voicemail, but you didn't—the thing's still ringing—which tells me you don't want whoever is calling to know you ignored their call. You just want them to think you couldn't answer."

She stopped at a red light, begging some greater being for this night to come to an end— or at least this conversation.

Terry went on. "It wasn't your mother, because I've seen you put her straight to voicemail, so that leaves one other person— Oh."

She glanced over at him. *Is my circle so small he can narrow it down to one person so quickly?* She took a deep breath as the last ring finished. Troy would be through to voicemail now.

"Everything all right with you and Troy?"

"All fine."

"Oh."

"Would you stop with the *oh*?" She pressed the gas, and they lurched forward through the intersection, nosing out the competition in the next lane.

"You guys fighting?"

"Not that it's any of your business."

"So…you are?"

She could have smacked herself in the forehead, but she glanced at him with narrowed eyes instead. "Just focus on the case. Bill Carson said that GB could stand for group benefits. Maybe she turned down some arrogant CEO who just couldn't handle it."

He leveled his gaze with hers, and she looked back out the windshield.

"I know you don't want to talk—"

"I do. About the case."

He muttered something as she turned into the lot for Barrett's apartment building.

She just needed Troy to step up and follow through with what he was going to do weeks ago. At least she'd bet her money on him planning to propose. Yet, day after day passed without one word about it. It was infuriating. She gripped the wheel tightly, her knuckles going white. She'd promised herself a long time ago to love with her whole heart, but she'd said nothing about sticking around if she wasn't getting the love she deserved in return.

***

Lana Barrett was a petite woman who could
easily fit into a suitcase. It was probably a good
thing other people couldn't read Madison's
mind. Chalk her psyche up to a hazard of the
job.

She and Terry were with Barrett in her living
room, which was a modest space, decorated
with a feminine touch. More throw pillows
than a department store, and most were floral.
Framed prints of Victorian-era houses in
the middle of fields with white picket fences
adorned the walls. There was a fresh bouquet of
daisies on the coffee table in front of the couch.
Their fragrance was potent. Madison pressed
her lips tightly together, willing her stomach
contents to calm.

"I can't believe she's dead. Murdered…"
Barrett's eyes were full of tears, but one had yet
to fall. She sat on the couch, tucked into herself,
small, grieving.

"Have you been friends for a long time?"
Madison asked, wanting to confirm what Bill
had told them.

"Since kindergarten." Barrett smiled, but the
expression faltered.

"Such a blessing to meet your best friend that
young." The girls Madison had been friends with
growing up weren't in her life anymore. Most

of them had moved away and gotten married. They all probably had a gaggle of kids by now.

"It was. We bonded over beating some boys."

Madison angled her head, smirked. "With your fists?"

Barrett shook her head. Though a smile toyed with her lips, the expression never birthed. "We would make castles in the sandbox at school. It sort of became a bit of a competition between the girls and the boys. Mostly between Chantelle and me and three guys in particular—Leslie, Kelly, and Taylor. All unisex names too—what are the odds?" She paused and attempted a smile again. "Chantelle was also my maid of honor. I'm divorced now. Have been for ten years. But we were there for each other through all of life's big events."

"So you were there for her through her separation from her husband and eventual divorce?" Madison asked.

"Yeah. She's suffered a lot in recent years."

"Do you know of anyone who might have wanted Chantelle dead?" Madison presented the textbook question.

Barrett shook her head. "Can't think of anyone off the top."

"What about the letters GB?" Madison said. "Do they mean anything to you?"

Barrett's forehead wrinkled in thought. Seconds later, she said, "Not that I can think of."

Madison said, "We understand that Chantelle was dating someone. A Paul somebody?"

"Saul Abbott, a while back, but that's been over for months. And, thank God. I thought he was scum from the start, but he seemed to make Chantelle happy. Turns out I was right—not that I wanted to be. There was no telling Chantelle, though. She fell hard and fast."

"Do you have his number, by chance?" Terry had his pen poised over his notepad.

"Nah, I don't, and I don't know where he went after moving out of Chantelle's house."

The back of Madison's neck tightened. "He lived with her?"

"Yep. The weasel wormed his way in, destroyed her life."

Madison had figured Barrett referred to the change in accommodation when she'd mentioned Carson suffered a lot in the past few years. Now it would seem she meant there was more. "When were they together? For how long?"

"Around the time of her divorce, and they were together a total of maybe five months. He moved into her house within their first month together. And can you believe she actually considered marrying him?"

Madison assembled the timeline in her head. Divorced eight months ago, together with Abbot for five, so they broke up three months ago. Two months ago, she moved into the east-end apartment. Madison had a feeling she knew where this was going but asked anyhow. "You said he destroyed her life. How?"

Barrett shook her head. "You know what? Forget scum. He was a shit. Plain and simple. He convinced her to add him to her bank accounts, credit card, and even to the mortgage on her house in Rosedale. He took out a second mortgage, emptied her accounts, racked up her credit card, and ran with the cash. He broke her heart, and he also destroyed her life. Literally. She had to sell her house in a buyer's marker. She still owed money on a place where she no longer lived." A few tears snaked down Barrett's cheeks, and she wiped them. "I offered for her to stay here, but she would prattle on about making her bed and needing to lie in it."

Madison hated that her suspicions had been right. "Guy sounds like a typical con artist. Did she report what he'd done?"

"No. She was embarrassed and devastated. And I tried to get her to file a police report, but she was so broken. She just wanted to move on and put it behind her. At least she didn't marry him, and apparently, he had it all set up too."

"All set up?" Terry asked. "The venue, the priest?"

Barrett snuffed out a bitter laugh. "Venue, yes. But that's a no to the priest. Saul didn't have a religious bone. Wow. Surprise. You know, I did try to warn her. I told her that guys like him don't fall for women like us. We're not old biddies, but we're not exactly cougars either."

"He's super good-looking?" Madison guessed.

"He is…and young. Twenty-five, or so he said. That's if anything he said was true. Blond, blue eyes. Speaking of…he was always holding eye contact to the point of it being uncomfortable."

"Lack of eye contact communicates a shadiness, but con men tend to overcompensate by peering into a person's eyes. They think it makes them seem more credible." The same applied to guilty suspects. "How tall was he?"

"I'd say about six feet."

"What about build?" Terry inquired.

"Fit. He definitely hit the weight room at the gym. Actually—" Barrett jumped up and went into another room, returning a moment later with a picture in a frame. "I keep meaning to put something new in here, but I've had it stuffed in my closet for a while now. Chantelle gave this to me." She handed the photo to Madison.

It showed Barrett and Carson with an attractive man. Madison pointed at him and glanced at Barrett.

"Yeah, that's Saul."

"Could I take this with us?" Madison asked.

"Sure. You don't think he ended up killing her?" Barrett's brow wrinkled.

"It's far too early to conclude anything," Madison replied. She was sure, though, that when she and Terry looked in the system, they wouldn't find Saul Abbott. Con men often used aliases. It might be beneficial to get what information they could from Barrett while they were here. "I'd like to revisit the marriage part. You said that Saul had arranged the venue. Where did he want the wedding to take place?"

"Just in a room at a local community center. He said he had a buddy, some guy named Carl Long, who could perform the ceremony. Supposedly, he obtained his marriage officiant license online."

Terry scribbled in his notepad.

Barrett went on. "Can you believe that Saul actually pitched it to Chantelle as an affordable way to tie the knot? Said they didn't need some big pompous ceremony with a bunch of people. Chantelle thought it sounded great. She never loved large gatherings."

Madison noted the discrepancy between what Barrett was telling them and the fact Bill Carson said Chantelle had organized large functions. Then again, she could have just stayed behind the scenes.

"He probably wanted it small because con men like to separate their marks from friends and loved ones," Terry pointed out.

"He's right," Madison said. "It makes their mark easier to control."

Barrett winced. "I hate to hear Chantelle referred to that way, but I know that's what she was to him. As you said—" she flicked a finger toward Terry "—he did like to separate her, at least keep an eye on her. We'd still get together, but always at her place where he would come into the room from time to time."

"But Chantelle never married him," Madison said. "What happened to break his spell?"

"She saw him kissing another woman, and she wouldn't hear any of his excuses. Around that time, she had credit problems rearing up."

"Did Chantelle start dating any other men more recently or have any disagreements with people? Maybe problems at work?" Madison asked.

"She swore off dating. She said men were nothing but trouble. And, yes, she was having problems at work. What they were exactly she wouldn't tell me much, other than she didn't trust her boss."

"Do you know anything about her having disgruntled customers?" Madison asked, her mind not far removed from GB—group benefits.

"Don't know."

"What's her boss's name?" Madison volleyed back.

"I can't remember right now."

"But she was still working at Southern Life?"

"She was." She let out a puff of air and wiped her cheeks. "I can't believe she's gone."

"We're sorry for your loss," Madison offered and stood, loathing what she had to say next.

"We'll need to you to identify Chantelle's body."
With Carson being divorced from Bill and their
lives being separate, it would be more suitable
for Barrett to handle this task.

"Wait, you don't know if—"

"We're quite certain it's her, but she wasn't
found with her ID," Madison said. "It's just for
the record."

"I'll do whatever I have to."

Madison handed her card to Barrett. "I'll have
Cole Richards—he's the medical examiner—
reach out to you to arrange a time. It will
probably happen within the next twenty-four
hours."

"Okay." A tear snaked down her cheek.

Madison and Terry saw themselves out. She
keyed a quick text to Richards with Barrett's
contact information and noted *for a formal
ID*, as she walked back to the car. Once inside,
she said to Terry, "We've got to find this Saul
Abbott, whoever he is."

"You think this con man guy killed her? I
mean, I can see motive for *Chantelle* to kill *him*
after what he put her through."

Madison gave Terry's words thought and
came up with one possibility. "Take a leap with
me—"

"When don't I?"

"Ha-ha. But what if Carson ended up
confronting him, and the situation got out of
hand?"

"You're right. That's a leap."

"Don't make me hit you." She smirked. "Is it really, though? If she was going to turn him into the police and expose him, he could have felt threatened and reacted to protect himself."

"Sure, but Barrett said Carson was broken."

"Only made her more desperate. Might not have wanted to get others involved, but that didn't mean she let it go. She wasn't afraid to reject people's insurance applications. That's what her ex told us. So she had a backbone in there."

"Several years ago anyway. Though, I guess a confrontation could have gotten out of hand. And maybe the purse was taken to make it look like a mugging."

She searched *Saul Abbott* on the laptop and had confirmation of her earlier fear. "No Saul Abbotts in Stiles. It's a fake name."

"Or he moved out of the area."

She locked eye contact with him. "Really? If he was in the area any length of time, which we know he was, I should be seeing something on him. A driver's license, a local address, but there's nothing. I'm confident that Saul Abbott isn't his real name. But we might be able to find him if we hunt down that guy who was going to marry them. Carl...what was it?"

Terry flipped through his notebook. "Carl Long."

"Assuming that name's not a work of fiction." She typed in the name. "There are a few. We'll just leave him for later. Right now, let's go by Carson's apartment and see what we can find."

"Works for me."

"We also have this." Madison held up the framed photo. "I'll get Cyn to run it through facial recognition software. If Saul Abbott has a record, we'll find him."

"Sounds good."

She started them out in the direction of Carson's apartment. The clock on the dash read *9:30 PM*. Carl would need to wait until tomorrow, because by the time she and Terry finished running through Carson's apartment and talking to her landlord, she'd need to call it a night. She had something else to take care of.

Eleven

Chantelle Carson's apartment building could have used some TLC. The eaves sagged, and the paint on the front door was chipped. Given the rundown exterior, Madison didn't hold much hope for a nicer interior.

Officer Harrison, who had been posted at the back entrance to the Bernsteins' property, was standing outside Carson's door. "Detectives," he said and added a smile. "The door's unlocked."

"Thanks." Good thing for his well-being he hadn't pulled out "ma'am" like he had earlier.

"I spoke to the building manager," Harrison said. "You know, when I got the key to the vic's apartment."

"Did you tell the manager that Chantelle Carson was murdered?" Madison drilled him with a glare.

"Uh, yes, ma'am."

And there it was! That word! She was only thirty-six, not fifty—the fact she probably had the better part of fifteen years on the officer aside. "Detective Knight," she seethed.

"Sorry, Detective, and should I have refrained from telling the manager?" Harrison looked from Madison to Terry, who shook his head.

"What's done is done," Terry told him.

She was too angry to speak. It would have been nice to see the manager's initial reaction to the news. "Please let the manager know we'd like to speak with—"

"Done," Harrison rushed out, standing tall and puffing out his chest. "I told him that detectives would be wanting to speak with him before the day's over. He said he'd get himself a coffee on account of the fact he's normally early to bed."

Madison took a deep breath, searched within for an ounce of patience. "And the man's name?"

"Theo Green, apartment 101, ma—"

She met his gaze, killing the *ma'am* on his tongue. She put on a pair of gloves and turned the door handle, letting herself and Terry inside.

A standing coatrack was positioned to the right of the door, the light switches behind it. Madison flicked them all on, revealing a compact, boxy space. There were some windows, their curtains drawn. Given the apartment's location on the north side of the building, the space was probably full of shadows even during the day.

The living room was straight ahead, sparsely decorated with cheap, possibly secondhand furniture. To the right of the entry was a galley-style kitchen with laminate counters and cabinetry faces and hardware that dated back to the sixties. The backsplash was a patterned tile illustrating weaved baskets with flowers on some, garlic bulbs on others.

But it wasn't just the dated decor and the cheap furnishings that made the place feel grimy; there was a strong chemical smell that seemed to be trying to hide a musty odor.

"Can't believe Carson went from homes in the north end to this." She was in a state of disbelief.

"Barrett said that Abbott destroyed her."

"Well, here's proof her finances took a hit. When the bank opens on Monday, we'll need to talk to that banker, Alan Lowe, the one named on the piece of paper from Carson's pocket."

Terry nodded.

Madison walked through the apartment. Things didn't get any better. A bathroom that had mold in the grout and a green toilet, sink, and tub. At least they matched.

A single bedroom that was barely big enough for a queen bed, dresser, and nightstand. A black-mold spot on the ceiling where there'd been a leak—or still was.

Madison grasped to find something good, but it was impossible. Even the building's location in the east end put it close to industrial buildings and the power generation plant. She never researched it but heard that living too close to one wasn't good for your health. Regardless, what seemed apparent was Chantelle Carson's life had taken a nosedive that led her to moving here. What Lana Barrett had told them appeared to be true, but they still had to prove this Saul Abbott character was responsible.

Madison glanced around the room, taking it in. For someone coming from money, Carson's bed didn't even have a headboard or footboard. It was just sitting on a wheeled metal frame. But the bed was made, a white duvet spread over it. There was a tower dresser, four drawers, of honey-colored wood and a mismatched nightstand. The latter held an alarm clock and a water glass on a coaster. That touch told Madison that Carson worked with what she had. Madison lifted the glass and noted how the water had evaporated and left rings on the inside. "This has been here for a day or two."

"We know she didn't make it home last night; maybe she wasn't here the night before either." Terry backed out of a closet he'd been in, holding a book.

"What is that?"

He thumbed through the pages. "Looks like a diary to me. Appears to be how she felt while going through her separation and divorce."

"We'll definitely want to take that with us." It could have been Carson's shrink who suggested she record her feelings and emotions, assuming she had one. Madison had been seeing one for a while now, something that had started as a mandatory requirement by her sergeant, but she'd continued seeing Dr. Tabitha Connor even after that time had passed. Her next appointment was this coming Monday.

"Not clear on how it will help solve her murder, but okay."

"Don't know until we take a closer look, do we?" She let her question sit and then added, "We discussed the possibility that Carson may have been planning to confront Abbott. Her intentions could be in that journal. Even if it doesn't cover Abbott, the journal might help us identify someone in her life with whom she had an issue or conflict."

Terry stuck his head back into the closet and reemerged with a shoebox. He lifted the lid and held it so Madison could see inside. "Looks like there are more journals."

"We'll take them all."

Madison returned to the living room. A sagging corduroy sofa, small flatscreen TV, and Blu-ray player. No stereo or sound system. A lidded ottoman served double duty as a coffee table and a storage container. A small bamboo tray sat on top of it with the TV remote and a box of tissues. Madison sat the tray on the couch and opened the ottoman. Inside was a laptop and its power cord. She removed both. They'd take them to Cynthia for her and her team to look over. There was also a small stack of bills from Stiles Wireless, a service provider for internet and cell phones. A customer herself and familiar with their invoices, Madison confirmed the billing was to Chantelle Carson and scanned down to see that Carson had Stiles Wireless manage both her internet and her phone. The account was current. She compared the phone number to the one she'd tried earlier that was disconnected. They were different.

She called Cynthia. When she answered, Madison gave her the new ten digits. "I'll need you to trace this when you get a chance. Might lead us to her phone, the crime scene, possibly her attacker."

"I'll get to it as soon as possible. Mark and I are just pulling into the lot at Carson's building."

"Thanks." Madison ended the call and updated Terry.

"Glad they're here. They can bag up the laptop, its cord, and the journals." He slipped into the kitchen and started opening cabinets.

Madison came up behind him. "Looking to fix yourself a snack?"

"Not a bad idea since it's well past dinner hour and you didn't stop anywhere for us to get food."

"My chocolate bar carried me over quite nicely." She realized that she'd had a few hours nausea-free. Maybe whatever bug she had was gone now.

"Huh," he grumbled and continued opening and closing doors. "Oh."

If I could take that one word away from him today… "What is it?"

He came out with a heap of envelopes. He fanned them. *Past Due* or *Final Notice* stamps adorned all of them, and none had been opened. Probably because she couldn't pay them, but she hadn't thrown them out either, so she must have had intentions to clear her debt.

"Poor lady," Madison lamented.

"Quite literally."

Madison rolled her eyes.

"Honey, I'm home," Cynthia called out.

"Trust me, you wouldn't want to live here." Madison proceeded to fill Cynthia and Mark in on the journals, laptop, and the Stiles Wireless bills. "There's also a bunch of past due notices—" Madison flicked a hand toward the kitchen counter where Terry had abandoned the pile of envelopes.

"Okay." Cynthia turned to Mark, who was behind her, and gestured for him to get to work.

"How did you make out with the back driveway at the Bernsteins', their upper deck, and Carson's car?"

Cynthia smirked and shook her head. To Terry, she said, "She doesn't give anyone much time to catch their breath."

"I know you live for this," Madison kicked out, aware her best friend loved her job.

"Nothing on the stairs or railing. The drops on the dirt were blood. Same type as Carson's, but it will take time to confirm DNA, as you know."

"And the shoeprint a match to her boots?" Madison asked.

"Could be."

"Anything in her car?"

"Yeah, found pictures of some guy in the glovebox."

"Some guy…" Slight goose bumps rose on Madison's arms.

"If I were to wager a guess, I'd say she was stalking him."

"And when were you going to fill me in on that?" Madison's tone was sharper than intended, but it felt like Cynthia had held back potentially important information.

"I am now." Cynthia moved past Madison.

"I'd like to see the pictures," Madison said.

"They've already been locked in evidence."

Madison talked herself down from lashing out at her friend. "There's someone who is of interest to the case."

"And when were you going to tell me?" Cynthia cocked her head and smiled.

"Trying to. Carson's ex was a con man. We still need to find him. The guy in the pictures… was he good-looking, blond?"

"Yeah," Cynthia said.

"Could be Saul Abbott." Madison looked at Terry.

"Who?" Cynthia asked.

"The someone who is of interest to the case, Cynthia. Keep up," Terry teased.

"You two have the ability to drive me crazy sometimes." Cynthia set out to join Mark in the collection of items and processing of the apartment.

Madison faced Terry. "So Carson was stalking Abbott."

"Sounds possible," he said slowly. "But it's still a leap from that to her winding up stabbed. Besides, remember GB. How does that connect to Abbott?"

Madison sighed and worried her lip. She had no idea. Yet.

Twelve

C hantelle was a nice enough lady, but…"
Theo Green, the building manager, seemed hesitant to say what he was thinking, as if it would somehow be speaking ill of the dead.

Madison and Terry were in his living room, sitting on a leather couch that smelled brand new, but thankfully overpowered the cacophony of other odors she'd concluded were inherent to the building itself. Green's apartment was a tad more spacious than Carson's but still dated and stinky. The walls were painted a neutral beige and were scuffed and dirty.

Green was a sixty-something single man with dark skin, a genuine smile, and a calm spirit. He was seated in a rocker recliner, and for a man used to going to bed early, his eyes were bright, and he seemed wide awake. Ah, the power of coffee.

It was just after ten by the time they'd knocked on his door and he'd opened it wide and welcomed them into his "humble home." She kept glancing at the plastic wall clock. For her other plans, she had to get into position preferably by eleven. Any later and she might as well wait until next week.

"I understand that this may be difficult for you," Madison began. "But whatever it is that you have to say about Chantelle, we need to hear it. No matter how bad it might sound." She wanted to add that he couldn't hurt her anymore but didn't think the older man needed a reminder that his tenant was dead.

Green fussed with the arm of his chair, appearing to tug at invisible threads. "She had a problem covering her rent."

"She wasn't living here long, was she?" Madison wanted him to tell them.

"Two months. She paid first and last, but she made it sound like scraping that together was an effort. Actually, she was a hundred bucks short, but I gave her an extension. She was supposed to make it up in the next few months, added to her rent. Guess that won't be happening now. But I feel for her. Life really seemed to have taken the wind out of her sails."

Madison licked her lips, pushed the cliché from mind. Her mother had murdered colloquialisms for her. "Did she ever tell you what had her down on her luck?" *Gah!* "You know, desperate?" Madison rephrased.

"No, she wasn't open about her personal life—at least not with me. Just appealed to my humanity to give her a break. She said she needed one."

Madison glanced at the clock again. She really had to get moving.

Green followed the direction of her gaze, then met her eyes. "She's really dead?"

"She is," Madison confirmed, even though Barrett hadn't officially ID'd Carson. Shock and disbelief were common in the wake of death in general, murder or otherwise. But with the former, people tended to have an extra hard time processing the fact that a life was snuffed out by another's hand.

"I was trying to get my head around how I was going to tell her that I'd have to evict her if she didn't get caught up. Guess that problem is solved." Green's voice was solemn, and there was a whisper of hope that testified he'd rather have that difficult conversation than the one he was having now.

Rationalization was another thing that came up after someone died, as if there was a hidden nugget of positivity to be found in the horror of loss. Theo Green, in Madison's opinion, was a man who sincerely cared about other people—even to his own detriment. And it was obvious he had a soft spot for the underdog. "We're sorry for your loss, Mr. Green."

He lifted his gaze to meet hers. "Just find who did this to her."

"That's our intention." She wasn't going to promise as much out loud, but she would find justice. It was a vow she made with every case.

Madison was behind the wheel again as she and Terry headed back to the station. She saw every minute turn over on the dash clock.

"I assume you want to see if we can find Carl Long tonight?" Terry asked, getting out of the car once she'd parked.

"Normally, I'd say yes, but—"

"Really?" Terry bugged his eyes out. "You're calling it a day already? It's not even midnight."

"Guess I'm learning from you that I need food and rest." She wasn't going to feign illness, and she certainly wasn't going to fill him on her plans.

"Hey, I'm not going to stand here arguing with you." He headed toward his van.

"We start early, though," she called after him.

"Eight. For the autopsy."

"Before eight so we're not late."

"You got it, boss."

She hustled toward her Mazda, and on the way, her phone rang. Troy. She couldn't avoid him forever.

"Hello," she answered after the third ring.

"I was starting to wonder if you dropped off the surface of the earth."

"I told you when I left that I was likely going to be late."

There was a pocket of silence that was painful for her. Lulls in conversations between them never used to be awkward. Now they seemed filled with assumptions about what the other was thinking and not saying.

"So the woman was murdered?"

Madison had given Troy the basics after Estelle's call. "Yeah, she was. I probably won't be home until really late if you want to go to bed without—"

"Yeah, no problem. Thanks for letting me know."

She took a deep breath. Before Troy, she easily let relationships go—no point to getting trapped by drama. She operated on the theory that if a relationship was work it wasn't worth the effort or meant to be. But with Troy, there was a damn part of her that wanted to fight, claw, scratch her way. Then, if it didn't meld, well, she'd have to rethink things. "I should have called you earlier or—"

"I tried calling."

She wasn't sure if his tone accused her of ignoring him or not. "Did you leave a voicemail?" She winced, guilt slicing through her for shifting the blame for the communication breakdown onto him.

"No. I figured you'd see my missed calls. You could have shot me a quick text."

She hesitated just a few seconds too long.

"Then again, I should know better. You're on a case and me, Hershey, everything else disappears. At least I know where I stand."

She pinched her eyes shut and clamped her mouth closed. Heat spiked through her. He didn't own her; they weren't even engaged, let alone married. And why should she have to explain the minutia of her day?

"Do you know when you'll be home?"

He rarely pushed her when she was working a case, and with the direct question, she was stabbed with sadness. For the sake of their relationship, she should head straight home but— "Probably about two, maybe earlier."

"Two? In the morning?"

"What do you want from me, Troy?" she spat. "It's a fresh case. You know the first twenty-four are important."

"Yeah, I know." He hung up.

Tears pooled in her eyes, and she cursed the warm liquid. She hated hiding this other side of her life from him, but it was for his own good. His claims of them being a team were nothing more than the offering of a kind man, saying the right thing, but not really intending any follow-through. And, sure they were a partnership, a united front—at least on some things. But he didn't quite get her obsession with ridding the police department of corrupt cops. He certainly wouldn't understand her using every spare second to gather intel before going to Internal Affairs. He'd tell her it was too dangerous or she was taking risks she didn't need to. What he didn't understand and maybe never would was that her vow to protect and serve the city of Stiles meant something to her down to her marrow. To start with, her vendetta against the Russian Mafia itself was personal; she blamed them for her grandfather's murder. To add to this, seeing her fellow officers betraying the badge drove her desire to serve justice even more. It was time for the mob and anyone on their payroll to live behind bars. It was the least of what they deserved.

Thirteen

Madison parked a few blocks away from Club Sophisticated. It was a downtown bar that had attracted people affiliated with the Russian Mafia in the past, and she was quite certain some previously unknown associates were still regulars, along with newfound corrupt cops. At least she had it on good authority.

About three weeks ago, she'd enlisted the help of friend and renowned reporter, Leland King, to investigate one cop she suspected of corruption. Dustin Phelps. King had captured photos inside the club of Phelps with another Stiles PD officer, Garrett Murphy. With them was Jonathan Wright, who was the right-hand man to Marcus Randall, a business tycoon in town suspected of crooked dealings, and a mystery woman. King bowed out after handing over the images because his mother's life was threatened. If he knew who the woman was, he hadn't said, and Madison had let it go, figuring she'd find it out for herself. She'd keep at it for a while longer, respecting King's decision, but uncovering the woman's identity was proving a bit difficult.

It was part of the reason why she was here after eleven at night, instead of being home with Troy and Hershey. It was also why she was dressed in black jeans, black shirt, and black hoodie—all of which she kept in the trunk of her Mazda. She'd checked her appearance in the pitted and smeared mirror of a gas station restroom after she changed, and it showed a woman about to commit a crime. After all, if duct tape, rope, and a knife were a murder kit, a black hoodie, shirt, and jeans were in the criminal handbook on what to wear. But she wasn't the one doing anything illegal.

She gave herself one last look in the rearview mirror before getting out of the car. Some of her short blond hair was poking out around her ears, and she tucked the strands out of sight. Now it was just her light complexion against the dark clothing.

She grabbed her camera from the trunk and set out for the rear of the club. Her reasoning was anyone involved with the Russians wouldn't leave by the front door. She'd find a spot to hide and snap pictures of anyone exiting.

She walked past other bars, and they appeared to be doing a good business. Looking through their windows, bodies were crammed and gyrating, and music thumped out to the sidewalk. She ducked down an alley that ran along the side of a jazz club. It ended at another alley that butted up to Club Sophisticated.

She ducked left, and the farther she walked, the stronger the stench of rotting garbage. She passed an overflowing dumpster. Its lid cocked, black bags hoisting it up. The reek had bile shooting up her throat. She snapped a hand over her mouth and swallowed roughly as she looked around for a good place to hide and take pictures. Most of the alley was exposed. Bags were piled next to the dumpster, and if she wedged herself behind them—

Fuck me, she thought, but the spot would offer the most concealment, and it was quite close to the back door.

She mumbled to herself as she set about getting into position. The garbage had her gagging again.

"Hey." It was a woman's voice. One Madison recognized—but from where? Regardless, maybe if she ignored her, she'd go away.

"I said, 'Hey,'" the woman repeated.

All wishful thinking apparently! She turned and wished she hadn't. She knew exactly who the woman was now. She'd clawed Madison during a previous investigation, and the woman also claimed to have "a gift" for seeing the future. *And things just keep getting better.*

The woman's gnarled face relaxed with seeming recognition but then contorted again. "You're that cop."

She resisted the urge to point out that for someone who could "see" things, the woman should have known who she was before Madison faced her. But she needed this woman's cooperation. She closed the distance between them. "I need you to keep quiet."

"Don't tell me what to do!"

"Shh." The woman recoiled, and Madison held up her hands. "I won't hurt you." Really, if anyone should be afraid—if history had a say— it was Madison.

"You homeless now?" The woman jutted out her chin and sneered. Even in the pale light, Madison noted that she had no teeth on the bottom, very few on top.

"No, but I'm—"

The back door of the club opened, and a woman came out. Slender, a few inches taller than Madison, probably about five eight. She had a swiftness to her steps and pulled the hood of her coat over her head and tucked her hands into her pockets. She didn't give the impression she saw Madison or the other woman. That could be what she wanted them to think, or it could be a matter of the homeless or perceived homeless being invisible to some.

But Madison noticed her. The mystery woman. Madison slammed the heel of her left boot into the ground. If she hadn't been stuck talking to "Claws," she'd have had another picture.

Madison felt a jabbing finger in her arm and pulled back.

"Why are you here?"

"Listen…" Madison took a few more steps closer to her intended roost—as disgusting as it was—and the woman moved with her. "I'm working a case, and I need you to leave."

"Oh, really. Not what I'm sensing."

"Then your senses are off."

The woman smacked her gums.

"Please, can you go somewhere else while I work? Just for a bit."

"For how long?"

Madison's gaze drifted to the door of the club. She prayed that no one else would come out while she was dealing with this impossible woman. "A couple hours at the most."

"'K, but then I'm back. That's where I sleep. Shelters me from the wind." She flicked a finger toward the area that Madison was going to use for concealment.

There were certainly people with far worse luck than she had.

Fourteen

A couple hours later, Madison could almost squeeze out the stench of the garbage—*almost*. Her stomach, though, was aware of the lingering potency.

It was probably about time for her to get moving anyhow. A quick look at her phone told her it was just after one in the morning. Her eyes were getting heavy, but she'd been up since about eight yesterday morning. Troy had an incessant need to clean the house every Saturday first thing, and he would keep the noise down, but the aroma of cleaners still found their way to their room and her nose. Come to think of it, her sense of smell was highly attuned these days. Whatever that was about.

The back door of Club Sophisticated swung open, and she lifted her camera. Blake Golden and Jonathan Wright. Seeing them made her hesitate, though, she shouldn't know why. Their presence here wasn't a huge surprise.

Madison had dated Golden for a while—that is, until she found out he put his defense-attorney skills to work for Dimitre Petrov, the Russian Mafia don.

Madison took a few pictures of the two men.

Wright was holding the door and peeked into the club, as if waiting on someone.

Madison adjusted her posture, sat up a little more. Still poised to hit the shutter button.

A man came through the doorway. Officer Dustin Phelps. Picture taken.

And another man. Officer Garrett Murphy. Image captured.

Her heart was racing. She didn't have the officers with a direct associate of the Mafia, but Golden and Wright could, by a stretch, be considered associates. It was disgusting to see her suspicions confirmed. Phelps and Murphy had taken an oath to serve and protect.

But things became even more difficult with Murphy. He'd been the best man at Cynthia's wedding, a last-minute stand-in. Madison would make certain he was corrupt before raising her concerns to her friend.

Golden and Wright went west, and Phelps and Murphy moved at a crawl in the opposite direction. Neither was saying anything, which was unfortunate.

The door swung open again.

"Are you coming or what?" Phelps called out to a man who'd just exited.

"Yes, Mom." The man's face, even in the dim lighting of the alley, mostly shadows, was familiar. It was Joel Phelps, Dustin's brother.

Madison couldn't see Dustin and Murphy, who were now blocked by the dumpster, but she no longer heard their footsteps. They must have been waiting for Joel.

Shortly after, their steps resumed, tapping off in an even rhythm, unlike Madison's heart. She'd had her suspicions about Joel before now, but it would seem they were confirmed. He, too, was corrupt. He worked as a freelance reporter and often contributed to the *Stiles Times*. Madison had been curious if he had somehow found out about King's poking around and been behind the threat on King's mother.

She'd love to pay Joel Phelps a visit, really get in his face, but there'd be no advantage. He'd just tip off his little brother, who would also inform Murphy. It would either make them burrow further underground or invoke retaliation.

She waited things out until she heard nothing other than the bass of the clubs before coming out of her hidey shithole. She started to move and stopped cold.

A scraping noise. *What the hell—*

She found the source and slapped a hand over her mouth to stifle a scream. A rat, the size of a small groundhog scurried out, its nose twitching, its beady eyes staring, and its throat making some dreadful squeak.

She flew from her hiding spot and performed a full-body shimmy. She wouldn't be able to shower long enough to wash tonight off, but before she'd have the luxury of even trying, she had a stop to make.

The storage building housed a couple hundred units of varying sizes. Madison had leased a small one. She walked through the maze of hallways; each section was motion-triggered to turn on lighting as she moved along. It put her in every spy movie ever written, and she felt like she might be getting in over her head. But she couldn't bring herself to turn her back on the corruption in her city, and she couldn't exactly come out with her mission to Troy. She just didn't think he'd fully understand her need.

She stopped outside unit 135, slipped the key into the padlock, and pushed up on the garage-style door. She pocketed the padlock. Thanks to common sense and those previously mentioned movies, she wasn't going to be careless enough to make it easy if a baddie was tailing her to lock her inside. They'd have to bring their own lock anyway. That thought did little to comfort her.

She stepped inside, facing the flood of guilt she always experienced from deceiving the people she loved. She worked to offset the chastisement with the justification that she was keeping them safe by housing anything related to her little side mission separate from them.

She flicked on a light and lowered the door, leaving it open just about a foot from the ground—another precaution.

The unit was about function not beauty. She had a shelving unit, corkboard, desk, chair, computer, and printer. She'd paid for all of it in cash, not that Troy was in the business of snooping through her purchases. But the money had come from her grandmother, which Madison felt was fitting. After all, if it wasn't for her grandfather taking down one of the Mafia's bookkeepers, he might still be alive today. Instead, Madison had never met him, and she'd lost her grandmother five years ago to a cancerous brain tumor.

Madison plugged her camera into the computer and transferred the pictures she'd taken. If anyone ever got ahold of it, they'd find nothing on the data card. She was quite sure coming up with a story to explain a camera in her trunk would be far easier than explaining why she had pictures of people coming out of Club Sophisticated, including fellow officers, depending on who was asking the question.

She brought up the images one at a time, zooming in and studying them. She paused on the photo of Blake Golden and Jonathan Wright. Wright had tailed her and Terry during the investigation into the murder of Randall's son, and she was quite certain that he was in cahoots with Petrov's right-hand men at the time. She'd also been quite sure that relationship had resulted in the murder of Ryan Turner, a friend of Randall's son, who was a threat to the business tycoon and possibly the Mafia. Ryan had died of an overdose—accidental, was the story—but Madison had never bought that. To her, though, Wright hanging out at Club Sophisticated was all the proof she needed that the guy was dirty—former Marine or not.

She stared at her photos for a while longer, then slumped in the chair. She was exhausted and frustrated. Really all these pictures proved was these men kept company with each other at a club, at least formerly haunted by the mob. She was going to need better if she was ever going to nail Phelps and Murphy.

But, if she could prove those cops were keeping company with the mob, that would be more than enough probative cause for an IA investigation. Maybe instead of trying to dig dirt on the officers directly, she should focus on the mystery woman.

She brought up the picture that Leland King had taken. She would have had another photo of the woman tonight if it hadn't been for Claws showing up. Madison zoomed in on her face. Beautiful, delicate features and brown eyes. But she was nameless. And it wouldn't matter how much staring Madison did, she couldn't conjure one up out of nowhere. She didn't have the "gift" Claws did.

She shut down her computer. It was time to call it a night and get under a showerhead.

Maybe when she woke up tomorrow morning, she'd have some grand epiphany about how to identify the mystery woman without involving Leland King.

Fifteen

Madison could stay this way forever. Shrouded in a fluffy comforter, her head on a soft pillow, the gentle snores of Hershey on his dog bed in the corner of the room. She was so tired, she felt drunk. Even with her eyes closed, her head was spinning. But she was aware of her surroundings, including Troy's hard body lying next to her, his warmth reaching out and closing the distance between them.

Her stomach clenched and heaved.

She jumped from bed and made it to the toilet just in time to puke her guts out. She sat on the ceramic floor afterward, getting as close as she could to the porcelain throne. She wasn't confident she didn't have any more offerings on board.

A soft knock on the door, followed by, "You all right, Bulldog?"

"Yeah, I'm—" She put her head over the bowl and purged again.

The door cracked open. She waved him away, but his steps came closer, and he put a hand on her shoulder. His touch soothed her, but she didn't want him seeing her this way. Nothing sexy about vomit.

"You can—" She was going to say "go," but she gagged. Chunks were lodged in her nose. She snatched a few squares of toilet paper and blew, using all her willpower not to spew again. She was really regretting the late night/early morning burger she'd picked up at a drive-thru on the way home.

"I'll be out there if you need me."

Yep, tried to warn ya!

The door clicked shut. Thankfully, with Troy on the other side.

She popped the TP in the toilet and flushed. She put her mind elsewhere, far from the smell lodged in her sinuses and the sour taste coating her tongue. Her resolve went to work. She had to pick herself up off the floor and get to the station to meet up with Terry for the autopsy.

She eventually convinced herself to move, her stomach calmer for the time being. She just hoped that feeling would last. After splashing cold water on her face, she met her eyes in the mirror. She really looked like shit. This was the first time the nausea had caused her to hurl. What was going on with her? She'd guess *pregnant* if she were talking about anyone else, but she and Troy took precautions. It had to just be some flu going around.

She made herself brush her teeth, coaxing herself that she'd feel far more human getting it done and over with it as fast as possible. She was in the middle of the process when her cell phone rang back in the bedroom. She poked her head out the door and mumbled around a mouthful of paste to Troy, "Can you get—"

"Hello," Troy said, and the ringing stopped.

She spat out the paste, rinsed, and spat some more, patted her face with the hand towel. She stepped into the hall and almost tripped on Hershey, who was lying right outside the bathroom door. "Good dog," she told him and hurried to the bedroom.

Troy was standing next to her nightstand, her phone to his ear, appearing to be having himself a good ol' chitchat. "She's not feeling well this morning."

She went to him and held out her hand, wiggling her fingers. "Phone."

"Here she is." Troy complied with her wishes.

"Hello," she said.

"You're not feeling well?" It was Terry.

She glared at Troy. "I'm fine."

Troy shook his head. He didn't smile easily, but she would describe the slight curl to his lips as nothing less than an expression of amusement. He was finding her ridiculous for wanting to deny how she felt, but Troy didn't know Terry as well as she did.

"Are you still coming in?" Terry asked.

"Yeah, just let me—" She caught the time on the alarm clock. *7:30 AM.* "Shit—"

"Really?"

"Sorry." She tried to censor her speech around him. "I'll meet you at the morgue."

"Okay." Terry didn't sound like he quite believed her.

She tossed her phone on the bed and went for her dresser. "You never should have told him I'm not feeling well," she said to Troy, who was hanging in the doorway. She looked over at him. "You hear…me?" The question broke up because she finally noticed him. How she hadn't before now—well, she must have been ill. He was standing there in boxers, chest bare, with his six-pack abs and muscular shoulders. Completing the picture was his tousled blond hair that begged for her fingertips.

He narrowed his eyes seductively and came over to her. "And why couldn't I tell him that? He's your partner."

"It's just not something we talk about."

"You're a strange one sometimes, you know."

"Thanks," she said drily.

"Don't take that the wrong way. I love that you're unique and you have these quirks, but—" he cupped her elbows in his big, strong, manly hands "—why can't he know you're not feeling well?"

"Why?" she pushed out. "Because he won't let it go. I had that cold a few weeks ago—you know, at the time of Cynthia's wedding."

"Sure…"

"Yeah, well, Terry has a way of making me feel worse."

"How?" His brow knotted.

"He just…" She rolled her hands not even sure how to put it into words. "He gets in my head. Psychosomatic."

"I see."

"Don't say it like you think I'm crazy."

"Well." He smiled and didn't hide the fact.

She nudged him in the shoulder but made the mistake of letting her palm lay flat against his bare flesh. She put her mouth on his and was ready to risk getting locked out of the autopsy when he pulled back.

"I thought you had to go," he said.

"What? No, I never said—"

He tucked some of her hair around her ear. "You told Terry you'd meet him at the morgue."

She let out a long sigh, also remembering last night when she'd hoped to greet a new day with a grand epiphany. That hadn't happened, and apparently sex wasn't happening either.

Sixteen

Madison hustled through the corridors to the morgue. She was moving so fast that her legs could barely keep up, and it had her torso leaning forward. She must have looked hilarious.

"Finally!" Terry flailed his arms when he saw her. He was positioned in the morgue doorway. "Standing here so Richards won't lock the doors, but I was starting to fear him coming along and pushing me into the hall."

"Oh, Terry, you scare easily." She smirked and entered the morgue. She went straight over to Cole Richards who was next to a gray slab where Chantelle Carson was draped with a white sheet from the breasts down. Her face appeared soft and relaxed, an observation Madison often made of the dead and found just as unusual every time. It often made her question if heaven or another spiritual plane did exist, but she didn't get too caught up in philosophy. Who could really say for sure?

"Good morning," she said.

"Morning." Richards didn't say anything about how close she was to being locked out, but his gaze and tone of voice certainly did. "I've reached out to the victim's friend, Lana Barrett," he said, "and she's coming in to make the formal ID this afternoon."

It was just procedure because Carson hadn't been found with identification, but they were certain she was the woman on the slab. Basically, if they didn't hear anything to the contrary from Richards, the ID held. In this instance, they'd proceed as if it was verified unless advised otherwise. "Okay, thanks."

Richards dipped his head. "All right, so I've done a preliminary. Lividity told me that she died lying on her back."

Lividity was how blood pooled to the lowest gravity points in a body after death. It was a good indicator of body position.

"She died in that shed, as we thought," Madison said.

"I believe that's safe to say."

Madison remembered the drops of blood leading from the door to where Carson had come to rest. "Do we know what items were used as a murder weapon yet?" She recalled Richards had thought a couple things could have been used.

"One weapon. A five-inch blade, non-serrated. Possibly a kitchen knife."

Madison glanced at Terry, back at Richards. "Sounds like you got that narrowed down."

Richards smiled and moved toward Carson. He lowered the sheet, exposing Carson's torso. The stab wounds had been cleaned but appeared raw. "As you know, I often x-ray the bodies before starting on the internal examination. Something turned up in the first wound."

"The first?" Madison asked, curious how he determined which came first.

Richards pointed with his gloved finger from one stab wound to the next and, as he went along, said, "One... Two... Three." He returned to number one.

She leaned over the body, the suspense killing her, but it was the smell of decomp that did her in. It shot straight up her nose and roiled her stomach. Bile started up her esophagus. How could she have anything left to puke? She stepped back and swallowed roughly.

Richards stopped all movement. "You all right?"

"Yeah...I..." She held up a finger and stared across the autopsy suite. She just needed to focus on the case and get the smell out of her— Another mouthful of bile, too much to swallow. *Shit! Shit!* She slapped one hand over her mouth and held up her index finger on the other hand. She hustled to the nearest sink and let it out. As she rinsed the basin and saw the last of her vomit go down the drain, any relief she felt physically was overridden by absolute embarrassment.

She turned slowly. Both men were watching her.

"Go ahead." She gestured toward Richards.

Richards didn't question her, didn't pry with his gaze. If only Terry worked that way; he was staring at her.

The ME pressed a finger next to wound one. "This is the cleaner cut as you can see. No hesitation marks." He paused and waited for Madison to nod in acknowledgment. He continued. "I collected this from the wound track." He grabbed a vial from a side table and held it up for Madison and Terry to see. A small silver object was inside.

"Looks like it could be the tip of the knife," Terry said.

"I'd say that it is. Stainless steel. And it's because it broke off in the first stab that the other two appear to have hesitation marks, but that was an error in judgment."

"So her attacker didn't hesitate?" Madison asked.

Richards shook his head. "Not that I see, and they also made the stabs in quick succession."

"Well, then, we just need to find a kitchen knife missing the tip," she tossed out and glanced at Terry.

"Yeah, that's all." Terry rubbed the back of his neck as he often did when he felt overwhelmed.

"Is there any way to tell from that what brand the knife was?"

"Not sure we could go that far with it, but the grade of stainless could be determined. Might even be able to narrow it down to type of knife, once we have something to compare it to anyway."

"The needle in the haystack," Terry lamented.

Madison ignored the cliché and continued. "The grade of stainless could tell us if it was a high-end knife, though?"

"Should."

"Then we'd have an idea of the wealth of our killer…to have that certain knife on hand," Madison concluded.

"Not really." Richards pressed his lips together. "Someone without much money could have been gifted an expensive knife set."

She nodded, and said, "Fine, I get that."

"And that's also making the assumption it's not your run-of-the-mill stainless steel, which it very well might be."

"Again, the needle in—" Terry clamped his mouth shut when she leveled her gaze on him.

"Were there any defensive wounds?" she asked.

"None."

"Her attacker could have surprised her," she suggested.

"Or she didn't have a chance to protect herself—with a waving knife coming at her and all," Terry countered with raised eyebrows.

"Or that," she conceded. "As for time of death, do you believe that—"

Richards nodded and set the vial back down. "I stand behind my original summation that she died between nine Friday night and two Saturday morning. Cause of death was a nicked artery." He pointed to wound three and continued. "The other two wounds, if they had been treated in time, are in nonlethal areas. If she had gotten help…"

"Except number three would have killed her anyway?" Madison wagered.

"It's possible if she got immediate help, surgery could have stayed the bleeding."

"Now we'll never know," Madison mumbled and licked her lips, feeling all pasty-mouthed. Gum would have been nice. "What does the angle of the wounds tell us about the height of the attacker?"

"Angled slightly upward, and I'd estimate her attacker would be no more than six feet."

Lana Barrett had described Saul Abbott as six foot. "It would seem she knew her attacker. It could explain her lack of defensive wounds. Maybe she never viewed them as a threat." Madison paused, mentally piecing together Carson's final moments. If Carson knew him or her, that meant the letters GB really could have been intended to identify her killer. If so, that seemed to eliminate Saul Abbot, but they didn't really know if that was his real name. Madison added, "And being stabbed by someone she trusted really would have put her into a state of shock." She glanced at Richards, who nodded in agreement. "The shock could have been what enabled her to walk to the Bernsteins."

"She would have been in delusional state, pumped with adrenaline. Though I don't hypothesize." Richards flashed her one of his toothy smiles, his pearly whites whiter than most people could hope for, even with a treatment.

She turned to her partner. "I think it's more important than ever to find out what GB stands for, and if it is a person, we might very well have our killer."

Seventeen

Madison and Terry stayed a while longer with Richards, but nothing seemed to come back as enlightening as the fact Chantelle Carson had likely known her attacker and wasn't the victim of a random mugging. They also dropped off the framed photo obtained from Lana Barrett to the lab, securing it in an evidence locker. Cynthia would probably be in later. If she hadn't been in a hurry last night, she would have run it up to Cynthia in Carson's apartment.

"We need to find Saul Abbott, like, yesterday." Madison huffed it back to her desk.

"Through this Carl Long guy?"

"That's the plan." She dropped into her chair.

"We could have started last night." He looked at her and held eye contact. "Surprised we didn't."

"I had to go home. Troy missed me."

"Uh-huh. For some reason, I think Mr. SWAT can manage on his own."

She turned on her monitor and started the search for Carl Long. She wanted to forget what Terry had just said. Because maybe he was right, and Troy could manage on his own. Maybe that's what he really wanted. Her stomach clenched as the results filled in on the screen. She scribbled down the addresses for the three Carl Longs in the city and said, "Let's go."

"So, what's going on with you?"

Madison had just pulled out of the station's lot and merged into traffic. "Nothing. I'm fine."

"Pfft. You're not fine. You've never been sick at an autopsy before."

"Just forget about it."

"Well, if you've got the flu, I don't want it." Terry shifted closer to the passenger door as if to emphasize his point.

"I don't have the flu." Not that she really had a clue what was going on. It seemed like everything—and nothing—churned her stomach these days.

"How long have you been feeling off?"

"I'm fine, Terry," she stamped out.

"Not sure about that. Troy said you were sick this morning."

She twisted her hands on the steering wheel. Troy hadn't understood why she didn't want Terry to know, but now she was dealing with it. "I'll be fine."

"Ah—" He held up a finger. "You will be, but you're not."

She kept her gaze straight ahead.

"I don't know how long you've been feeling sick—"

"I just ate something that didn't agree with me. That's all."

"Are you pregnant?"

She slammed the brakes at a yellow light, and the nose of the car dipped down. "No, I'm not pregnant."

"Whoa!" Terry held up his hands. "Okay, just a thought. Otherwise..." His face became shadowed.

"Otherwise what?"

"Remember when we were concerned about the mole on Annabelle's back?"

"From a few weeks ago? Yeah, I remember."

"Right. Okay, well, we thought it might be cancer."

"I remember that too."

He gave her this look that made her think he didn't find her insertion necessary and went on. "I did a lot of reading on the internet. You know, for common symptoms of cancer."

"You really shouldn't do that. It's not healthy."

"I'll tell you what's not healthy. Feeling like crap and doing nothing about it."

"It's noth—" She was prepared to downplay his concern again, to dismiss the way she felt, but then that one big C-word sank in. Her grandmother had died of a cancerous brain tumor. But Madison was fine. She didn't need a doctor to tell her. But what if she wasn't fine? What if she had cancer? Early detection was key to successful treatment. "I'll make an appointment with my doctor."

"There you go." Terry smiled, obviously pleased with himself.

She didn't know which was worse—not knowing the cause of her nausea or entertaining the possibility she might have cancer. Both served to make her feel awful, and the latter, afraid, and she didn't frighten easily.

Madison knocked on the door for Carl Long #1. A fifty-something answered in his boxers, not self-conscious about his appearance though maybe he should have been. He stank of stale beer—a putrid smell she never appreciated and an alcoholic beverage she could live without— and he had crumbs stuck in his chest hair. *Gak!*

It only took a few pointed questions to determine Carl Long #1 was not the Carl they were after.

Twenty minutes later, they were on the doorstep for Carl Long #2. Madison raised her hand to knock and hesitated, preparing herself for *what* might answer the door. She stalled long enough that Terry butted in and rapped his knuckles against the wood.

She glared at him.

"What? I would love to reclaim some of this weekend."

She knocked and kept it going.

"I'm coming!" a man yelled and flung the door open. Madison's hand was still raised. "What the hell is the damn rush?"

Madison pulled her detective's badge, and Terry followed her lead.

"Detectives Knight and Grant with the Stiles PD," she said, gesturing first to herself, then to Terry.

"Okay? What does that mean for me?" Carl Long #2 was obviously not swayed by the presence of law enforcement at his door. Either that or he was overcompensating. If Madison worked like Troy did, she'd have been armed with Carl Long's background before hitting his doorstep.

"It means that we have some questions for you, and we'd like the answers." She squared her shoulders and hardened her gaze.

"Doesn't everybody, sweetheart."

She bristled at his sexist retort. "We need to talk to you about your friend Saul Abbott." She ran with the assumption and made it sound like Saul was hurt or dead. Even though the name was an alias, a person close to Abbott would be familiar with it.

Carl's face went blank.

"Your friend Saul?" she prompted.

Still devoid of emotion. "I don't know anyone by that name. Why are you interested in this guy? Something happen to him?"

"Why would you care if you don't know him?" Madison eyed the opening in the doorway between Carl and the frame and brushed inside.

"Hey!" he called out.

She held up her hands. "I'll stay right here in the entry."

Long narrowed his eyes.

"It's just cold out there." She gave him a fake smile, which was painfully obvious given his withering expression in return. "You want to know what I think, Carl?"

"I don't really care," he deadpanned.

"I think you know Saul Abbott. I think you're really good friends with him."

"Listen, lady." He crossed his arms. "I don't know a Saul Abbott."

Madison caught a tattoo on his bicep, and she got a feeling. Lots of prison inmates got ink, and between that and his attitude toward them, she'd wager he spent some time behind bars. "You want to go back to jail? Keep lying to my face."

His eyes met hers, his mouth twitched, and he spun and flew out the door.

"Ah, shit!" She flailed her hands in the air. She hated it when they ran. The damn devil's pastime.

Terry was already down the front steps and to the sidewalk, well on his way to catching Carl Long #2. Might as well let her partner nab the guy. He's the one who loved running, after all.

She stepped out to the stoop and tapped a foot. Then stopped. A wave of nausea struck and had her rubbing her stomach. Could she really have cancer? What would she do? Poor Troy, her sister, her parents…

Terry returned holding Carl Long #2 by the back of his collar. "You wouldn't happen to have a pair of cuffs?" Terry said to her, even though he'd have his own.

She pulled hers out and handed them over.

"Thanks." Terry snapped them on Long's wrists.

Long howled. "You could take it a little easy."

Terry met her eyes, and he didn't say it out loud, but she got the message: *what's the fun in that?* She smiled. She'd really rubbed off on her partner.

Madison and Terry stood in the observation room looking at Carl Long. She was tapping a folder that contained his background against the palm of her right hand. She was already thoroughly familiar with his past, to the point that Troy would have been proud.

She headed next door to interrogation room two—technically labeled as *Interview* Room 2—Terry following.

Long was hunched forward, his shoulders rounded from a lifetime of poor posture. His potbelly, the result of poor eating habits. His greasy hair, poor hygiene. He wasn't much to look at, and he reeked of body odor, although Terry didn't seem to notice.

She wondered if an enhanced sense of smell was a symptom of cancer and tried to dismiss the panic in her chest. She had a job to focus on right now.

She slipped into the chair across from Long and opened the folder. "I know all there is to know about you. It's all right here." She patted the report.

Long didn't say anything.

Terry leaned against the wall behind Madison and jingled the change in his pocket, an unnerving technique he often utilized in the interview room.

She continued. "You went to Mitchell County Prison for break-and-enter when you were twenty-five. Served eleven years, and got out due to good behavior..." She paused there when Long's gaze flicked away.

"I shouldn't have gone to jail in the first place."

"Got out on good behavior about ten years ago," she finished. "You and a buddy smashed the window in a house and—"

"He made me. Not that anyone cares."

She could have said, "No one can make you do anything," but she wasn't that naive. There were people quite skilled at manipulating others. What Long told her, though, made her more convinced she'd found the Carl Long who was friends with Saul Abbott. The con man would make easy work of bending Long to his wishes. Long was a people pleaser.

She took out a copy of the photo Lana Barrett had given them and pushed it across the table. She said nothing but watched Long inspect it.

He flicked a finger toward the picture. "Who's this?"

Long wasn't going to win an acting award anytime soon. The dismissal was a vain attempt to cover up the recognition that lit in his eyes. It is often said the eyes are windows to the soul, and while Madison wasn't sure about that, they did have a way of saying a lot.

"You're sure you don't know that man?"

Long sniffed and didn't look back at the photo. "Never seen him before."

"Uh-huh."

"I don't care if you don't believe me."

"You should. That is unless you like the three squares a day at Mitchell County Prison. They must be tasty."

"Fine, I might know him," he mumbled.

"I didn't quite catch that." Madison angled her head and cupped her ear.

"I know him," Long repeated loud and clear.

"What's his real name?"

"If it's not Saul Abbott, I have no clue what it would be."

"Huh." Madison wasn't believing a word coming out of this man's mouth right now. "Who is he to you? It seems you have a great sense of loyalty toward him." She detected Long had something to lose if he exposed the extent of his relationship with Abbott. He could have been getting a kickback for the weddings—real and/or fake—that he performed for Abbott.

"He's just someone I know. Nothing much to it."

"Then you're not performing sham marriages for him?" she slapped out.

"No…no, of course not. I have my marriage officiant license."

She smirked. "Not denying the marriage part, though?"

Long tapped his fingers on the table. *Pat, pat, pat. Pat, pat, pat. Pat, pat, pat.*

"Not really a question," she said.

Long stopped tapping but said nothing.

Madison pulled a blown-up DMV photo of Chantelle Carson from the folder and tossed it across the table. "Do you know this woman?"

Long glanced at it and shook his head. "No."

"You're not young enough or anywhere near charming enough to play dumb and come off looking cute."

He scowled.

Her words might have been a little harsh, but they were on point as far as she was concerned. "How do you know her?"

"I just said *I don't know her.*" He spoke so slow that his four-worded claim came out sounding like four individual sentences. His eyes were flat, too, and she was leaning toward believing him.

"Well, your buddy Saul apparently knew her quite well," she began. "He was going to have you marry them."

"That's news to me."

"Do you know what Saul Abbott did to that woman?" Madison nudged her head toward the photo. Terry stopped jingling his change, and the room fell into a dense silence.

Long lowered his eyelids and shook his head.

She had a feeling he knew exactly what scheme Abbott was up to. Con men like that didn't just pull off something like this once and stop. There were probably other victims…and possibly after Carson. She had seen him kissing another woman. "Does Saul have a girlfriend currently?"

Long met her gaze, and the truth was reflected in them.

"Who?" she asked.

Terry started rattling his change again, and Long's gaze flicked past Madison to Terry.

She snapped her fingers to get Long's attention. "Who?" she repeated.

"No clue. Saul was always seeing someone, though."

Madison leaned across the table and pressed a finger to the photo of Carson. "That woman there, her name was Chantelle Carson."

"Was?" The word seemed to scratch from his throat.

"That's right. She was murdered. Stabbed three times. Know anything about that?"

He slowly shook his head and sat back in his chair, eyes wide and wet.

"I'm sure you can appreciate why we're interested in talking with Saul," she said after a few seconds.

"Not exactly. You think he killed her?"

She shrugged. "It's possible."

"Yeah, no, I don't think so."

"Saul's a con man. What's his real name anyhow? I'm sure you know." She thought she'd take another stab at wrestling it loose.

"I don't know, and that's the honest truth."

"Because you've been so honest up until this point," she volleyed back drily. "Your friend Saul ruined Chantelle financially, and, yes, we'd like to speak with him regarding Chantelle's murder. You said you didn't want to go jail. This is your chance to prove that. Just tell me where your buddy Saul is these days. Simple as that."

"I don't know."

She pushed her chair back, and its legs scraped against the floor. She stood and waved for Terry to join her.

Long reached his arms out. "Where are you go—"

"I'm leaving," she cut in.

"You can't just leave me here." His face knotted in panic.

"I can actually."

"On what grounds?" His voice reached a high octave.

"Obstruction of justice, for one. Possible accessory to murder. Probably conspiracy to commit fraud. I'm quite sure that you helped Saul with his con jobs by *marrying* him to women. Likely for a kickback. Give me time, and I'll get all the evidence I need against you."

Long rubbed his throat. "I honestly don't know where Saul is."

She took him in. "Here's the thing, Mr. Long. I hate liars, and you've lied to me. You first said you didn't know Saul, but it turns out you do. I really think you know where we could find Saul and just don't want to say. And that's fine. The city will be happy to have you for the night."

He sunk his head in his hands, and she and Terry left.

"You could have asked when he saw Abbott last," Terry said as they walked down the hall.

"I could have, but he's not ready to cooperate yet."

"Okay," Terry dragged out. "What do you suggest we do now?"

"I want to figure out how Long and Abbott first came into contact, and you noted his loyalty in there?" She jacked a thumb over her shoulder to indicate the interrogation room that was a good distance behind them now. They'd reached their desks. She dropped in her chair.

"I did. You even pointed it out to him."

"Right. He went away to prison for B&E."

"Yes, we know—"

She held up a hand to stay him. "He also committed that crime with someone. As he said, his buddy made him to do it. So who was his buddy?"

"All right, but Carl Long is forty-six. Saul Abbott is twenty-five."

Madison smirked. "He lied about his name, why not his age?"

"You saw his picture."

"I did, and some people can look a lot younger than their actual age." She was thinking she needed to have a better look at Saul's eyes. She pulled up the picture on her phone and enlarged it as much as she could, which wasn't much, and shook her head. No way of discerning maturity and experience from that photo. "Anyway, I think we really need to dig into Long's past. Who he committed the crime with to start."

"That being twenty-one years ago."

"Yeah, sure." She'd take his word for it, as she wasn't about to do the math.

"All right, let's get to work."

"Actually, I'm going to start on this," she said. "Could you follow up with Higgins on the canvassing officers and how they're making out? Also, maybe pop down to the lab, see if Cynthia's in yet and if she has anything for us."

"I can, but you sure you don't want to do that?"

"I'm good here."

Her partner held eye contact with her for a bit but ended up walking off. Usually she didn't miss an opportunity to talk with her friend, but she wasn't sure how she'd handle seeing her the day after spotting Garrett Murphy at Club Sophisticated. And, truth be told, her stomach was already churning.

Eighteen

Madison was reading the arrest record for Carl Long, including some of his lawyer's statements of defense. The house he'd entered belonged to his then-girlfriend's father. Long's attorney—doing what defense lawyers do—tried to minimize his part in the crime by saying that his girlfriend had told him to go to the house that night and enter through her window, only it was locked when Long showed up. Flimsy. And Long's defense fell further apart from there. One, an invitation to his girlfriend's room didn't explain his friend "tagging along." Two, it didn't provide a basis for the fact his friend had been armed with a KA-BAR knife. Three—and the most damaging—the girlfriend didn't back up Long's claim.

Madison pulled the background on Long's partner in crime, Peter Harris. Forty-five. Single. Currently employed by a car manufacturer in Stiles. She brought up his driver's license photo and slammed a palm on her desk. Unless the Saul

Abbott in the photo Lana Barrett had provided had undergone extreme cosmetic surgery, the likes of which would make Hollywood proud, Harris was not Abbott.

So how did Carl Long know Saul Abbott, whoever-he-was?

Her stomach rumbled, and a glance at the clock told her it was after one in the afternoon. She pulled out her drawer filled with the Hershey's bars and considered eating one, but chocolate was mostly all she was eating these days. She should eat something with protein, but that would mean leaving the station, and she'd like to get some things taken care of.

Another stab of hunger pain and she gave in, peeling back the wrapper on a bar. *Always heaven*, she thought as she chewed. All her chastisement from a few seconds ago were gone, melted like the chocolate on her tongue.

Besides, it was much easier to think with a full stomach. And if the candy was the only thing settling these days, then who was she to argue?

How does Carl Long know Saul Abbott?

The question repeated in her head as a constant droning. Eventually, the gist of an idea floated on the edges of her consciousness. Long was loyal and likely easy to control. He was an ex-con and would have probably learned some ways to beat the system while behind bars. If he was getting a kickback from Abbott, he wouldn't want to jeopardize his payday.

She returned to Long's background report. Listed under his place of work was *Self-Employed*. No details. It was hard to imagine that a person could make a living on performing wedding ceremonies alone, and he didn't have an actual business—it would have been noted. Previous employment was a body shop in the east end of town where Carl had started a few months after his release from prison and worked for seven years.

She googled Carl Long and got nothing besides a single, inactive social media account and some articles about the B&E.

So he was keeping a low profile. It was either because he reached the point in his life where he didn't see the value in keeping the world informed of his every move or because he was trying to live off the grid. At the least, she had a wedge that might work to get Carl Long to open up. But, for now, she'd let him stew in the drunk tank. It was surprising how cooperative and talkative a night in holding could make a person.

She tapped her foot, returning again to the question, how did Carl Long know Saul Abbott?

Not his partner in crime, she wrote on her notepad. Followed down the page by *Relative? Coworker?*... She tapped her pen. *Cellmate?*

She picked up her phone and placed the necessary calls. Weekend or not, it wouldn't matter. She requested a list of all the prisoners

Carl Long had shared a cell with. She was told it could take a bit to dig up those records.

More waiting. But she could go pay the body shop a visit on the off chance they'd be open on a Sunday and would have something to offer as to Abbott's identity or his whereabouts.

"Hey, so I've got updates." Terry was approaching with a cup of bullpen brew. With her delicate constitution, she couldn't even think about drinking one right now. She crumpled the wrapper of her bar and threw it into the garbage can under her desk, hoping Terry wouldn't notice. Too late. He angled his head and gave her his are-you-serious look.

"What's the news?"

Terry set his cup on the corner of her desk and flipped through his notebook. "The canvassing officers haven't found anything helpful. No one saw Carson on the street or heard anyone at their door in the night."

She wasn't surprised by this news, but still disappointed. "And…"

"Cynthia has submitted a request to Stiles Wireless for Carson's phone records."

"The trace on it?"

He shook his head. "No dice. So the phone's likely off and/or destroyed, wherever it is."

"Her laptop or journals… They tell us anything?"

Terry smirked, took a slow draw on his coffee, set the cup back on her desk. "Cynthia just got in about an hour ago and didn't make it home until the wee hours. Let's cut her some slack."

"So we don't have anything or…"

"It's a work in progress. She did say, however, that she was going to start running photos of Saul Abbott through facial rec software this afternoon. Might take a while for something to come back—if it does. As for the laptop, she said there are a lot of password-protected files."

"Ah." Madison sat up straighter. "That could indicate that Carson had something to hide."

"Quite possibly." He nudged his head toward her. "How did you make out? Taking a stab here—"

She groaned. Such a horrible play on words at any time, let alone when working a murder case with that cause of death. "Saul Abbott wasn't Long's partner in crime. It was some guy named Peter Harris." She went on to tell him about the body shop and her call to the prison.

"Huh." He fell quiet but held eye contact.

"You want to call it a day?" She wagered a guess.

"I was hoping to salvage some of my Sunday."

He probably wanted nothing more than to settle in with his wife and daughter. She thought of going home to Troy and Hershey, and while it held appeal, she was afraid she might come out and confront him about the lack of a proposal. And that was the last thing she wanted to do right now. "Go on," she told Terry.

"Really?"

She nodded. "Get out of here before I change my mind."

"See ya tomorrow." He tapped a hand on her shoulder and left. She imagined dust swirling in his haste to get out of there.

She pulled her phone from her pocket and stared at it. She should head home too. She could use her willpower and not attack Troy, or maybe the best thing would be to get everything, including how she was feeling, out in the open. She was just terrified she might not like his response. And there was at least one lead she might be able to follow today, Sunday or not. If that didn't pan out, there was still the matter of the mystery woman. Combined, she could probably be home in a few hours, in plenty of time for dinner, assuming she could stomach real food.

She brought up the text app, intent on telling Troy when he could expect her, her hands jittering, but found she had an unread message from him.

> *Called in. Probably won't be home until quite late. Pls confirm you rec'd msg. Hershey will need someone home. xo*

Of all the times for him to be called in for a job.

She stared at the hug and kiss. That small expression of love felt like a betrayal these days, as if mocking her. A single hug. A single kiss. Then again, Troy was never big on adding a string of them to any message. She was reading far too much into this. She was disappointed though. She was finally going to make time to spend with him, and he wasn't around.

But she looked at the time stamp on the message. His text had come in an hour ago, and Hershey would be fine for a bit longer. No need to put off her plans. Her day would just end differently than she'd imagined.

She keyed back, *Stay safe. Love you xo*

Those last two words locked in her brain as she put her phone back in her pocket. She did love that man, more than she should. Sure, she'd made a vow to love wholeheartedly, but it was made when she thought she was going to die a couple years ago. Surely it didn't count. There was something to be said about getting out of a relationship before it sucked you down like the *Titanic.*

Nineteen

Before heading out, Madison checked the operating hours for Chassis Worx, the body shop where Carl Long had worked after prison. She was in luck because they boasted hours of twenty-four seven, and that would probably make them the only garage open in Stiles on Sundays.

She drove over in her Mazda, figuring from there she'd go to her storage unit and proceed to see what she could muster up regarding the mystery woman's identity. That, of course, was somewhat dependent on what the people at Chassis Worx had to tell her. She promised, though, even if she got a solid lead on Saul Abbott, she'd have to leave it for another day. After all, Hershey would need her at home by the dinner hour.

A bell rang when she opened the front door of the shop. The bay doors were all shut, but through the windows, she could see some mechanics working away. None of them responded to her arrival, though, so she stuck her head through the doorway that connected the front office to the garage.

"Hello," she called out.

An air compressor came to life in response, and she was just about to round the first vehicle when a man approached from the back, wiping dirty, greasy hands on a rag.

"What can I do for you?" He squinted at her and let his gaze trail over her body.

She would have loved to push his eyes back in his skull. Instead, she drew her badge. "Detective Madison Knight."

"Ah." He groaned and looked away.

She'd had warmer receptions, but she'd certainly had cooler. "I'm here to ask about a former employee." The man's brows pinched like he was having a hard time hearing her. She continued, speaking louder. "Are you the manager?" She was going by her gut, but she anticipated a positive response.

"Yep. Luke Landers."

"Mr. Landers, do you have someplace private to talk?" *And quieter.*

He waved her through the door she'd come through, back into the front area and shut the door. Surprisingly, it buffered out the racket quite well.

"What employee?" he asked.

"Carl Long."

"Oh, I haven't heard that name in a while."

"I understand that he worked for you for seven years?"

"Yeah, but he left a few years ago now. He in some sort of trouble?"

"Hard to say yet." And *trouble* was a relative term. Guilty of murder? Unlikely. Abetting a murderer? Possibly. Playing a role in defrauding women and the government? Likely. "Why did he leave?" She knew it wasn't another job from the background report.

"Told me he found another job."

"Huh. Did you know where?"

"He didn't say; I didn't ask."

Madison nodded and brought up a photo of Saul Abbott on her phone and extended the screen for him to see. "Do you know that man?"

Landers studied it, eventually said, "Uh-huh."

Madison's heart raced. Maybe this was how they would find out Abbott's real name. "His name?"

"Oh, I should have been clearer." He looked from her phone to her eyes. "I recognize him."

All hope that had fired in her belly burned out. "Oh, well, maybe he worked for you while Carl did?" She certainly hadn't done any good hiding her disappointment.

"No," he said firmly and waved a hand. "But he was a friend of Carl's. He came around a couple times. Can't say I really liked the guy either. Gave me a bad feeling."

"In what way? Like he was violent or…"

"No, nothing like that, but he was shady. Just sort of twitchy. Didn't trust him."

"Okay, well, thank you for your time." She pulled her card and handed it to him. "If you happen to remember his name…"

"I won't. Don't think I ever heard it; otherwise, it would be in the vault." He tapped a finger to the top of his head.

Madison simply smiled at him and left. She'd discount the entire visit to the body shop as a waste of time, but she received another perspective on Abbott's character. All they'd been running on so far was what they'd heard from Lana Barrett. They knew Abbott was shady, but according to Landers, Abbott didn't strike him as a violent man. Either Landers didn't know how to read people—and their strongest person of interest in this case was going to be a dead end—or Abbott had changed.

Twenty

Madison pulled up to the storage facility and realized she rarely saw it in the light of day. She parked her Mazda around back, out of view of the road, just as a precaution. For the same reason, she kept checking over her shoulder as she made her way to her unit, unlocked the padlock, and entered.

She flipped on the light, lowered the door, and walked over to the desk. She waited for her computer to boot up and racked her brain for how she was going to broach the hunt for the mystery woman's identity. Ideas came to mind, but she didn't want to run with them unless necessary. One was to go back to Leland King and see if he did know her. He hadn't told her he did, but knowing the reporter the way she did, it wouldn't surprise her if he held that tidbit back—to protect her, his mother, himself. A second idea, even more crazy, was to visit the former police chief, Patrick McAlexandar, in prison. He was facing a murder charge and had ties with the Mafia—that wasn't in question—but if she wanted him to talk, she'd have to offer something, and she wasn't in the habit of making deals with criminals.

She logged in and opened the photo that Leland King had taken at Club Sophisticated: the one that showed Phelps, Murphy, Wright, and the mystery woman. Madison zoomed in on the woman's face. She'd learned a lot from watching Cynthia work over the years and made a copy of the file first, then she cropped the picture so it was just the woman and saved that image.

As the woman's eyes stared back at her, she was unmistakably the woman who had exited the club last night. If only Claws hadn't interrupted Madison's getting into position, she might have captured an even better shot, but this was what she had to work with, and it could be worse.

But as she stared at the face on her monitor, she felt something déjà vu-like. As if the woman were someone she knew or had known before, like the whisper of a memory she couldn't quite tack down.

"Who are you?" she asked out loud, and as her voice echoed back to her ears, she felt like she was going mad. Was she expecting an answer? Lunacy.

Dark hair, just past shoulder-length, and a petite, lean frame. She was well dressed in the photo that Leland had taken, as she was when Madison had seen her outside the club Saturday night. A wise assumption was she had money.

Madison's gut was screaming she was affiliated with the mob, but how to prove that? She could wait outside the club for her to leave and tail her, see where she went, and conduct a reverse-address search. Assuming, of course, the property where she'd be going would be under her name.

But one step at a time.

She brought up Google Images, clicked on the little camera icon in the search bar, and uploaded the new graphic she'd made with the woman's face only and waited on the results. She didn't need to wait long. A page worth of images came up and Madison studied each in turn. These women had similar faces, but none of them were her mystery woman.

She drummed her fingers on her desk. It was Sunday. The woman could return to the club tonight, and Madison could execute her idea to stalk her. But she had Hershey to care for. Still, the woman likely wouldn't be at the club until late again—if she did show. That would afford Madison plenty of time to go home, feed Hershey, hang around, and then head out.

Surely there had to be an easier way.

Her gaze stuck on the woman's face, and it clicked. There was another option that just occurred to her, but Cynthia wouldn't like it—not if Madison came right out and admitted who this woman was and why Madison was interested in her identity. But if she could somehow make Cynthia think the mystery woman was connected to the Carson case…

Cynthia did, after all, have facial recognition databases at her fingertips.

Madison headed to the station after calling Cynthia to confirm she was still there. Apparently not for much longer, but if Madison could "get her butt there yesterday," Cynthia would see what she could do.

She knocked on the lab's doorframe and kept going. Cynthia was sitting at her desk, a laptop in front of her.

Madison pointed to it. "Is that Carson's?"

"Yes. I'm seeing if I can crack the passwords." She swiveled and clapped her hands together between her knees.

"I'd say you're not having much luck."

"Thus far anyway. Grr."

Madison laughed. Forgetting, for the moment, about her friend's connection with Garrett Murphy.

"What is it that I can do for you? But make it quick." Cynthia smiled.

Madison handed her a data stick. "There's an image on there, and I need you to run it through facial rec."

"Okay." Cynthia narrowed her eyes. "Who is it?"

Madison had prepared herself for that question before heading over, and she had an answer. "If I knew that, I wouldn't need your help."

"Smart-ass." Cynthia giggled and stuck the drive into her computer. She brought up the image and turned to Madison, her eyes seeking a little more information.

"She's a person of interest." Not a lie and something Madison was comfortable in saying.

"Oh, is it someone you suspect of being that con man's new girlfriend? You think that maybe this girl killed Carson because she was jealous or something?" Cynthia raised her eyebrows.

"It's possible, right?" Madison tossed out and held eye contact with her friend until she nodded. *Is a lie by omission still a lie?*

"Absolutely. How you didn't kill Sovereign is beyond me."

Toby Sovereign had been her cheating fiancé. "So you'll help me—"

"Hey, yo." Garrett Murphy walked into the lab, and Cynthia got up to greet him with a friendly hug. Madison stood in front of the monitor. The last thing she needed was for him to see the woman, apparently an acquaintance of his, on the screen. Best case, there'd be a slew of uncomfortable questions. Worst case, she could put herself and possibly Cynthia in danger.

"Hey, Detective." Murphy gave her a weak wave to accompany his lame, detached greeting.

"Hi."

"You're coming over, right?" Cynthia asked Murphy. "Lou would be disappointed if you canceled."

"You bet. I'm just dropping in to confirm what time you want me there. I asked Lou, but he said you were here and to check with you. I guess he couldn't reach you."

"Sounds about right. I've been holed up in here, slaving away." Cynthia glanced at Madison.

"What time?" Murphy asked.

"Let's go with six. Sound good?"

"Works for me. See you in—" he consulted his wristwatch "—about an hour and a half. Bye, Detective." Murphy waved to Madison before turning to leave, and she was quite certain he was trying to see past her to the screen. But maybe it was just paranoia at work.

"That guy's clueless half the time, but I put up with him because of Lou," Cynthia said and returned to her desk as Madison shuffled to the side.

"Oh—" Murphy popped his head through the door.

Madison's heart hammered, and she tried to keep calm, but the mystery woman's face was right there.

"Does Lou have that beer I like?"

"How would I know?" Cynthia kicked back. "Call him for that."

"Bye." Murphy was gone again, and hopefully, for the foreseeable future.

Cynthia flailed her hands. "See what I mean? Clueless."

Madison had another word float to mind. *Corrupt.*

"So, yeah, if that's all you need, Maddy, I'll get it running through the databases. See if anything pops. She'll need to have a police record for something to come up, but you know that."

Madison pressed her lips and nodded. "Thank you. And speaking of popping, anything on Saul Abbott?"

Cynthia shook her head. "Nope. I'm going to try some other photos I have from Carson's collection and see if any of them work out better, but not today." She copied the image of the woman to her computer and removed the data stick. As she dropped it into her palm, Cynthia said, "Actually, you and Troy are more than welcome to come over as well. It's nothing fancy, just some burgers and weenies." She winked at the last word, Madison not missing the double entendre.

"I can't."

"Don't think about it or anything."

"No, it's just Troy's been called in, and I need to get home for Hershey."

"Bring him over."

Madison laughed. "Yeah, I'm sure Lou would love that. Dog crap in his manicured backyard."

Cynthia and Lou lived in a modest two-story home in the west end of the city that he'd owned before marrying her. It had a rather small yard, but it was Lou's pride and joy.

"True. Even if you picked it up…"

"Have fun." Madison stopped at the doorway on her way out and looked back at the monitor. The woman's face wasn't up anymore, but at twenty feet away, Madison couldn't clearly make out what was on the screen now. Hopefully, that meant that Murphy hadn't noticed his female friend when he popped his head in. She turned and left but couldn't help but feeling like she was turning her back on her friend in a metaphorical way. Madison didn't think Murphy had seen the woman's face, but if he had… No, she was being ridiculous to even consider he'd do anything to hurt Cynthia or Lou. Then again, if the man kept company with the mob, did he have qualms about anything?

Twenty-One

Madison stopped at a drive-thru and decided to give a cheeseburger another try. The way her stomach was tossing, it might have been a bad decision. It was just after five by the time she pulled into her driveway. Somehow seeing the empty spot where Troy's Expedition normally sat drilled in the fact she was on her own. For tonight? Or was it representative of her near future? Solitude was a familiar friend, but being with Troy this past year, she'd become domesticated. She enjoyed the companionship.

She let herself in, and Hershey jumped off the couch where he'd been sleeping and scrambled across the floor to her. He barked as if to say, "Hello," and she bent over and cupped his face, rubbed behind his ears.

"Hey, buddy. Hey. Wanna go cuddle?" She rushed over to the couch, which was within eyesight of the front door, and sat down. Hershey, the three-year-old and seventy-two-pound chocolate Lab, jumped up and sat with his front legs across her lap and his big head in her face. She wasn't a huge fan of dog kisses, a.k.a. slobber-infused licks. After all, she'd seen where that tongue went. Hershey kept a bit of distance and peered in her eyes while she petted him and soaked up his velvety-soft fur.

As she absorbed her canine's love and dished it back, there was a lot she could have been thinking about: the Carson case, the corrupt cops, the mob, the mystery woman, Cynthia, Troy, and the way life can change…the big C, but this second she wasn't bogged down with too much thought. She felt more in the moment than she had in a long time.

Flash back over three years, and who would have seen her with a dog? If it hadn't been for Terry gifting him to her for Christmas and swearing that he was the best thing for her, she never would have gotten herself a dog. The journey had been a little rough at first and a lot to balance, but now, well, she was a fur-baby momma.

A flash of mischievous bolted in Hershey's eyes, and that pink slip of his came out and got her from chin to forehead.

"Gak, gak." She sputtered and tried to put the images of him cleaning his nether regions out of her mind, but they were coming strong. As was the single patty, double cheese, and special sauce.

She shot up and ran down the hall. She again made it in time—barely.

Afterward, she wiped her face with a cool cloth and met her gaze in the mirror. What if she did have cancer? She closed her eyes and willed the fear away. She certainly couldn't just sit around in the house dwelling on her symptoms, and she knew better than to google them.

"So, what now?" Asked out loud as if the walls of the bathroom could hear and answer.

Hershey's claws clicked against the floor outside the door, and she had an idea. Hopefully, her stomach, now empty, would cooperate. She opened the door and said, "Hershey, wanna go for a walk?"

Hershey moaned and then barked. She smiled and leashed him up to make good on her promise to her canine baby.

Madison walked Hershey for a few blocks and let him set the pace. Thankfully, that was slow, and it suited her tender stomach fine. It was dusk when they set out, but the streetlights had buzzed to life when they turned around to head home. The breeze felt cool, and she was happy she wore her heavier jacket. But the shadows also had her feeling a chill.

She couldn't shake thoughts of Garrett Murphy showing up at the lab like that. What if he had seen the woman's picture? Goose bumps pricked her flesh, and a shiver tore through her. The wind felt like it carried eyes, and she still had some distance to cover before home. She was diligent and cognizant of her surroundings, but her imagination was morphing darkened objects into the forms of people. A backup generator or air conditioning unit was a hunched man. A lawn statue, a person coming toward her. A shrub, a face in the bramble.

She pulled out her phone, her heart beating fast. She needed a distraction to settle her mind. She called her sister Chelsea.

"Hey, sis," she said when Chelsea answered.

"Troy's out, and you're hungry, right? You should come over for dinner."

"I call and you assume I need you to feed me."

"Well, it's the dinner hour, so I might have assumed…"

Madison laughed, though she was a little offended. "Who's cooking?"

"Me."

Her sister was a wife and mother of three, and while she excelled in those roles, her culinary skills could use some work. Madison liked to think she was better in the kitchen. "Yeah, I'll be fine."

"Hey!"

Madison laughed. No need to tell Chelsea she'd already tried food and it had disagreed with her. "So, what's going on with you these days?" She hadn't spoken to her sister in a couple weeks. There were six years between them in age, Madison the elder, but it would seem Chelsea was most of the time. She just had her life so put together.

Something scurried across a person's lawn, and Hershey tugged, yanking Madison's arm out straight. She held the leash steady and projected the energy of her being the alpha. Hershey, it would seem, was jumping at shadows too. She picked up her pace.

"Nothing much," Chelsea said. "Life is rather dull at the moment. What about you? Anything exciting going on in the world of law enforcement?"

The fact Chelsea could still find enthusiasm for what Madison did touched her. Especially considering if anyone should detest Madison's job, her sister had that right. Because of Madison's poking around at the Russian Mafia, Chelsea had gotten caught up in the mess last December. A mob hit man had kidnapped her for the purpose of luring out Madison, which he accomplished, but it just hadn't paid off as he'd intended. Chelsea was still in therapy due to her days in captivity, but she was nothing if not resilient.

"Maddy?"

"Picked up a new murder case yesterday."

A few beats of silence, then, "That sounds wonderful."

Madison laughed at her sister's sarcasm. "It's what I do."

"And you're good at it. Just remember to live a little too. You've got that beautiful man, and he loves you."

"I know." The words were out, and Madison picked them apart. Did she know that anymore? Or was it merely something she wished for? Maybe she'd reached her expiry date and Troy was trying to find a gentle way of letting her go. But it was the hope, wistfulness, and anticipation in her sister's tone that was contagious. Madison hadn't told her that she thought Troy was going to propose. She didn't want Chelsea upset with him or to get excited about something that might never happen. Bad enough that her sister had once said Madison and Troy would make beautiful kids. Madison had booed that statement and asked that her sister never bring up children again. She wasn't exactly wired for motherhood. Besides, when would she have the time?

Madison walked up the concrete path to the front door of the Craftsman bungalow, a place she now called home, but it had taken a few months to change from "Troy's place." She'd even kept her apartment for a while after she'd moved in case their relationship crashed and burned.

"I'll let you get back to your exciting life," Madison said.

"Yeah, sure. First, finish up and mow down dinner. Then it's dishes and vacuuming. Wahoo."

"Fun times."

"I can hardly contain my excitement. Love you." With that, her sister hung up before Madison could reciprocate or say goodbye.

She let herself and Hershey into the house, wiped his paws with a towel near the front door, and freed him of the leash and collar. He headed straight for his water bowl. She went after him and filled up his food dish and pet the back of his head. "You're such a good boy."

He crunched away at his meal.

Now what? She'd never been good at sitting still. The clock on the wall showed it was just after six thirty. There were hours to go before showing up at Club Sophisticated would even make sense.

She returned to the front door, flipped on the outdoor light, and closed the curtains in the living room. She never relished being on display for her neighbors. When she turned, her gaze went down the hall to the master bedroom door. Her thoughts went to Troy. Had he planned to propose and then changed his mind? If so, there might be a ring around somewhere. But would he have left it in the house on the off chance she'd find it, or would he take it to work and hide it there or entrust it to a friend?

She hurried in the direction of the bedroom and straight to Troy's dresser.

She rooted through every drawer, setting aside his clothing carefully so as not to unfold any. She hated all stages of the laundry process, but Troy picked up the slack. If their relationship went south, she'd have to wash her own clothes again.

She finished searching all five drawers and… nada.

She stood back. Confused and clueless. But Troy would be too smart to hide the ring—if there was one—in their room. He'd have to know she might get suspicious and ruin the surprise. She tapped a finger to her chin. "Hmm."

Hershey sauntered into the room and looked up at her. She swore he was judging her.

"Don't you look at me like that."

But maybe he had every right. She should suspend the Easter-egg hunt altogether, but there was a buzzing in her brain that nattered mercilessly. If she could find a ring, she could at least prove to herself that she wasn't crazy for believing he was going to propose. After all, she was a detective and had always considered herself to have a knack for seeing people for who they were, not what they presented. She hated to think she couldn't read her own boyfriend.

But what if he turned up while she was in the middle of searching the house?

She pulled out her phone and checked his text. He had said he'd be home *quite late*.

That meant she had time, but did she really want to go through with a more in-depth search?

Twenty-Two

Madison had spent a couple hours snooping around. She'd rummaged through all the kitchen cupboards and drawers, the pantry, the guest room, in every nightstand and dresser they had. She returned to the kitchen, hands on hips, certain she was missing something. She was also exhausted, and it was only about eight o'clock. She wouldn't make it to stake out the club tonight if she didn't start caffeinating now.

She went to the coffeemaker and set about making a pot. Used filter dumped, new filter in. Next, coffee grounds, which were in—the freezer! She hadn't even thought to look there or in the fridge.

She moved around bags upon bags of frozen vegetables that Troy loved and two boxes of toaster waffles she loved.

No ring.

She closed the freezer door and looked in the fridge. Fresh vegetables and… She studied the packaging. Tofu. *Ick!* Definitely a Troy thing. She'd support his nutritional choices because it obviously did his body good, but she wouldn't be consuming that crap anytime soon.

The fridge came up empty too.

She reopened the freezer, grabbed the coffee, and started the machine. The smell alone was intoxicating. She dropped into a kitchen chair and inhaled.

Her phone rang. Caller ID told her it was Cynthia.

Madison answered. "You get a hit?"

"Whoa, slow down."

"Sorry," Madison backpedaled. But if she had an identity, that would eliminate the need to track the mystery woman at the club tonight.

"I wasn't calling about work, but no hits on the woman before I left."

"But it's still running?"

"Yes. So, what's up, girl?"

Madison smiled. "Thought you called me."

"I did, but you sound intense."

Her friend sounded like she'd been drinking wine.

"So…what are you doing?" Cynthia asked.

Madison hesitated to admit the truth, but this was Cynthia, her best friend, who knew that Madison had expected a proposal and how it was eating away at her. "I'm tearing the house apart looking for the ring."

"The— Oh."

"Yeah. I know I shouldn't be—"

"No, I totally understand. And Troy's not home so… Hey, I'll be right over, and we can look together."

"That's not necessary. I've looked every—"

"You find it, then?"

"No."

"Then you haven't looked everywhere. I'm quite sure he hid it around your place somewhere. On my way."

"I thought you guys had Garrett over tonight, and do you really think you should be driv—"

Click.

All righty then. At least her friend hadn't called it the lost proposal, as she'd dubbed it before. The term just came across so hopeless, as if the proposal would never happen. Madison preferred *delayed* to lost. At least it carried promise.

Madison could call Cynthia back, but if her friend answered, it would just be to say, "I'm on my way," before hanging up again. Cynthia had a way of latching on to something when she set her mind to it, much like Madison did.

Madison poured herself a cup of coffee and drank it slowly. Her stomach seemed to be handling the drink fine, so she took a second cup to the living room and watched some TV while she waited for Cynthia.

Despite the coffee, she nodded off to Hershey's snoring next to her on the couch with her hand on his neck, her fingers buried in his fur.

The doorbell rang, and it sounded like it was coming from the other side of the world. Madison opened her eyes. Characters in a sitcom were going on about quantum physics. She enjoyed the show when she could stay awake. More a statement about her than the show. She usually only dropped in front of the television when she was too tired for much else.

The time on the cable box told her it was nine thirty. She hadn't been asleep for that long, but Cynthia had taken her sweet time getting there.

The doorbell rang again, followed by knocking.

"Just a minute." She unlocked the dead bolt and swung the door open.

Cynthia was standing there in a coat over plaid pajama bottoms and holding a steaming pizza box and a bottle of red wine.

The food smelled delicious, but Madison would have to leave the wine alone if she was going to get to the club later.

"Thought you could use something to eat, and the men ate all the burgers and dogs." Cynthia handed the box to Madison, and her stomach rumbled with hunger. Tony's Pizzeria was stamped on the lid. They made the best pie in Stiles and surrounding area.

"See!" Cynthia jabbed a pointed finger to the logo. "Only the best, and it's fresh from the oven. Pepperoni, mushrooms, double cheese."

"Oh my god, you're an angel!" Madison held the box in one hand and threw her other arm around Cynthia. "Thank you, thank you, thank you."

She took the pizza to the kitchen, leaving Cynthia at the entry to shuck her shoes and coat.

"I guess I was right to assume you wouldn't be eating because you were home alone." Cynthia joined her in the kitchen.

Madison bit into a slice. Heaven. She could be offended that yet again she was underestimated to fend for herself, but if that opinion made people feed her, well, there were worse things. "The best pizza ever!"

Cynthia laughed and proceeded to pour two glasses of wine.

"Oh, just a little for me," Madison called out. "Speaking of… You're looking…um, relaxed. You didn't drive, did you?' She spoke around the bursting organism of flavor going on in her mouth.

"Please give me more credit than that. I took a cab."

"What's going on at your place anyway? Why leave?"

Cynthia tossed her head back and smiled. "Why leave? Let me see… The air is so thick with testosterone, I'm choking."

Madison chuckled and bit off more pizza. Sauce squeezed out the corner of her mouth, and she dabbed it with her fingertip.

Cynthia sat next to Madison, handed her a glass, and raised her own. "To being women."

Madison lifted her glass. "To being—"

"Correction. To finding that damn ring," Cynthia cut in just before their glasses met.

Madison could drink to that, so she did. Just a little. Then returned to devouring the pizza. By the end of the second slice, she finally seemed to surface and really take in her friend's wardrobe. A cotton pajama *set.* "You spending the night?"

"Nope. Just wanted to be comfortable." She fished herself a slice out of the box, and when finished, she shot to her feet. "Let's find that ring!"

"I don't know. Maybe I'm having a pang of conscience, but—"

"Nonsense. If you find the ring, it will put your mind at ease."

"It will?" Madison found fault with her friend's reasoning. She'd probably have more questions. Like was the proposal lost or simply delayed?

"Come on, let's finish what you started." She grinned at Madison, her hook baited.

"Fine." She closed the lid on the box and got up. "What did you tell Lou when you left?"

"That he and Garrett were driving me nuts, and I needed girl time." Cynthia's face fell somber. "I need to ask you this, but what are you going to do if there isn't a ring?"

Her friend certainly didn't hold back when she was drinking, and Madison didn't want to dwell on the possibility. Before she and Troy had gotten together, they had both been burned by love. He had a wife who had cheated on him with his best friend. She had her scum of a fiancé who she'd found in bed with another woman. She used to be fine with a level of commitment that kept them exclusive without the old-fashioned need to tie the knot. But these days, the tying of the knot was all she could think about. "I don't know," she admitted.

"Or what if you find out he was never going to propose? Are you going to ask him to mar—"

"What? No! I might be a modern woman, but he's gotta be the one to pop the question."

Cynthia held eye contact and eventually nodded. "I get that. I even respect that."

"I've already searched the house everywhere I could think of."

"You're sure you checked everywhere?"

"I'm pretty sure." Madison sighed and bit her bottom lip.

"Okay, he might not have hidden it in the house. You have a shed out back, right? Maybe it's in there? Oh, or in the garage?"

Madison went to the kitchen and through the door to the garage, flicking the light switch on the way. Then she stopped.

They didn't use the garage for their vehicles for a reason. They were also looking to up-size for a reason. Apparently, part of that reason was to have more space to house all Troy's crap.

"I never would have pegged Troy as a hoarder." Cynthia stood in the doorway, crossing her arms.

"The man isn't perfect." But Madison thought he was close to it, but if he broke her heart, she'd kill him. Possibly literally. No, she wouldn't… Yes, maybe… No…

"I don't think he would have hidden it out here. I mean—" Cynthia gestured around the clogged area "—how would he even get to it?"

"True that." Madison met her friend's gaze.

"Let's check the shed."

Madison grabbed the key, donned her coat and shoes, and Cynthia slipped into hers. Madison put the back light on, not that it reached the outbuilding, but it lit the patio. Hershey followed them outside, sniffed around, and did his thing.

Madison activated the flashlight on her phone and unlocked the shed. "It's not powered, so you might want to—"

Cynthia took out her phone and turned on its light.

They went inside and rooted through the cabinets and drawers. At least there was walking space, unlike the garage. Maybe if Troy moved some crap from the garage to the shed, she might be able to squeeze her Mazda 3 into the garage.

They searched for what felt like a long time. Eventually, Cynthia made the call.

"It's not here." She sounded almost as dejected as Madison felt. Every time a spot turned up empty, she doubted herself more. Maybe she didn't know him.

"Hey, wait." Cynthia perked up, her eyes sparking in the limited light of their phones. "You looked everywhere in the house, but by everywhere, did that include places you don't normally go? You tried the kitchen?"

"You're killing me."

Cynthia smiled. "The laundry room?"

Madison gripped Cynthia's forearm. "I didn't look there."

Both of them hurried back into the house, intent on beelining it for the laundry room, but Hershey wanted inside, and Madison had to stop to wipe his feet. "You go on ahead."

"You're sure?"

"Yeah." She cleaned Hershey off as quickly as she could make her hands work and caught up with Cynthia.

Cynthia was elbow deep in the cabinetry.

Madison didn't ask if she'd had any luck, because if her friend had, she'd have told her. Asking and being told something to the effect of "nothing yet" would have just burrowed a deeper hole in her heart.

Cynthia withdrew a lidded chest the size of a shoebox from one of the cabinets. She held it up to Madison as if to ask what was in there.

"Wouldn't have a clue. Open it." Madison stepped closer to her friend.

Cynthia braced to flip the lid. "Oh, I can't." She shoved the chest at Madison.

She took it and looked inside. A small box sat among other bric-a-brac.

Time stood still. Madison's breath froze. Her heart sped up.

She gave the chest back to Cynthia and took out the small box.

"Who's killing who? Open it," Cynthia urged.

Madison exhaled and cracked the lid, saw the contents, and snapped it shut again. She dropped the small box back into the chest. "Put it back. I never should have—"

Cynthia set the chest on the folding counter and opened the box. "Princess cut. Square shape. White gold." Cynthia met her gaze, and her eyes were watered up. "This ring is beautiful, Maddy."

But it isn't on my finger… Tears burned her eyes. She didn't know what she should be feeling or how to react. She was a mix of anger, happiness, shock, distrust, confusion. "Put it back," she said.

Cynthia did as Madison had asked. "What are you going to do?"

"I don't have a clue." Ironically, for all the emotions whirling through her, she felt numb, not knowing which one to latch on to, which one she felt more, which one she wanted to believe. Was her relationship with Troy over? The "lost proposal" the apt description?

"For what it's worth," Cynthia said gingerly, "he was going to ask you."

"Yeah. Was." Madison sniffled. "What made him change his mind?"

Cynthia pulled her into a hug, and Madison let herself cry. Just when she'd given herself over to believing she had the real deal with Troy, love slapped her in the face again.

Twenty-Three

Madison managed to convince Cynthia that she'd be fine and just needed to crawl into bed and get some sleep. But sleeping was the last thing she had on her mind. For one, between the coffee and that bloody ring on her mind, the Sandman wouldn't be visiting. And second, Cynthia had left in a cab just before eleven, so Madison should have time to get in position behind Club Sophisticated and see if the mystery woman showed up.

She parked her car a couple spaces down from where she had the night before and set out for the dumpster. So far, the pizza she'd eaten had stayed down, but she wasn't too confident it would remain that way if the garbage stank anything like it had last night.

She approached the back of the club and eyed the dumpster. Still overflowing and with a stack of the bags next to it, bigger than last night.

Joy, oh bliss.

Only thing in the positive column: there wasn't any sign of Claws. Maybe Madison's luck was turning.

But even with that thought, the ring flashed more dominantly in her mind and drilled home the fact that Troy hadn't proposed, and he might not ever. She tried to view the ring's presence being a promising thing, though. Surely if he had changed his mind entirely, he would have returned the ring. That is, unless it was final sale.

She took shallow breaths as she wedged herself next to the dumpster. Now life became a waiting game. Oh, how fitting, as it seemed to summarize her entire existence.

She pulled up her camera and looked through the lens periodically, more for something to do. For a long time, no one was exiting the club. Then the door finally opened.

Someone in a half-apron. Kitchen staff. Lighting up a cigarette.

The stench from the secondhand smoke carried across the night air and made her gag. It smelled so potent she would have thought the man was standing right next to her, not twenty feet away.

The man was fiddling with something on his cell phone, the screen's light bleeding into the night and casting him in its glow. Twentysomething. Black hair. Tanned complexion. Tattoos on his forearm. She could only distinguish darkened areas, not design. She snapped a few photos back to back. Once she got the images uploaded to her computer, she could zoom in and take a better look.

The door opened again. At first, she couldn't see who was there.

"Hey," the kitchen guy said.

The person at the door then fully emerged into the alley. Mystery woman.

But, shit, what was Madison going to do? If she came out of her hidey hole and followed her now, the smoker would see her.

The woman was making her way west, the same direction she'd left in the other night. She was wearing a different coat—cream-colored with a fur-lined hood. Expensive. It came to mid-thigh, and she was wearing black dress pants and pointy-heeled boots.

Madison watched as her form became smaller, then she turned her attention to the man. Still playing around on his phone. She had to decide whether to follow the woman or forego it until another night. She was already here, but if that man spotted her—and without knowing who he was—maybe it was too great a risk to take. But even if he saw her leave in the same direction as the woman, he wouldn't know who she was or that she was tailing her. She was being more paranoid than necessary.

She got out from behind the garbage, and at the first rustle of the bags, the man looked over.

"What the—" He shone his phone's light on her, and she turned her face downward, seeking obscurity under the hoodie.

She hustled along the alley to follow the woman, who was about a couple blocks in the distance. The woman turned left down a side street.

Madison pulled up the map of the area in her head. That would be Walnut Street.

She hurried her pace even more and cursed that she was starting to get close to a slow jog. But she had to be proactive, just in case the woman's picture didn't garner a hit in the facial rec databases. But if the mystery woman did pop up on facial rec and she was connected to the Mafia, how was she going to talk herself out of that one with Cynthia? She could just ease out by claiming, "Whoa, small world," or something like that, but would Cynthia buy it? Not likely.

Each step, she was mumbling expletives. At least she had her gun and her badge if worse came to worse tonight.

She rounded the corner on Walnut, and the woman was getting into a silver town car. Madison held out a hand to hail a cab. Something was working in her favor as one pulled over just as the town car was pulling away.

She got into the cab.

"Where to?" the driver asked.

Madison held up her badge. "I need you to follow the silver town car coming up on your left…but keep your distance."

"Aye, we don't want them to know we're following them."

"That's right. Do it right and there's a good tip in it for you."

"You got it." The driver smiled at her in the rearview mirror and merged into traffic, keeping a few car lengths back from their mark.

The town car made a right five streets west of Walnut, down First, and headed north. The farther they went, Madison concluded they must have been headed to one of the north-end, upper-crust neighborhoods. Her suspicion was confirmed when they pulled toward the gated community of Deer Glen.

"What would you like me to do now?" the driver asked her.

"Just pull up to the gate. I'll show them my badge."

"Will do." The man sounded far more excited than Madison felt. In honesty, her stomach was tossing, and her chest clenched with anxiety. If they messed up in any way and that woman knew they were following, depending on who she was, they could be in danger. And the driver was her responsibility.

"Like I said before, just keep your distance."

The driver pulled over and waited for the town car to go through the gate, then he rolled up. The trick was to have a decent amount of space between them and the town car but not so much that they lost track of their mark.

The security guard came over the speakers, and the driver announced his passenger as police.

There was a click, then the guard got out of the gatehouse and approached. Madison had her window down and her badge held up in preparation.

"Detective with Major Crimes, Stiles PD."

The guard was in his thirties, but his half-mast expression indicated he was bored with his job. He glanced at her badge and returned to his little gatehouse. The arm went up, and the taxi driver took them through. He stopped on the other side. He looked left, then right, then left.

"I don't see them," he said.

"I don't either." She was swearing in her head when she caught a vehicle's taillights several blocks down on the right. "Turn." She pointed in that direction, and the cabbie moved. "Maybe just a little faster," she suggested.

Her phone rang, cutting through the otherwise silent cab with the urgency of gunfire. Caller ID said it was Troy. She could avoid answering and he'd probably just conclude she was asleep, but she felt she owed him more than that, and he rarely called when he was working. She answered. "Everything all right?"

"Sure, except I'm curious why you're not home."

She saw the town car make a left and pointed erratically for the driver, but he was already on top of things.

"Madison?" Troy prompted.

"What? I…"

"Where are you? I'm home; you're not."

"Oh." She gulped. She hadn't even let his return factor into her decision to carry out this little rogue mission. "I'm following a lead," she pushed out, satisfied it wasn't exactly a lie, though he'd assume it had to do with the murder case. But could she really be held responsible for what he assumed?

"When will you be done?"

"I don't figure too long."

The garage door was lifting on one of the monster homes on the right side of the street. The light from inside spilled onto the drive, not that it was necessary. Landscape lighting had the house illuminated like a piece of artwork.

The town car pulled into the garage, and the door lowered.

The cabbie parked at the curb a few houses down. Far enough away? Hopefully.

"Ah, Troy, I've gotta go, but I'll be home soon." She didn't wait for his response and hung up.

She leaned forward on the bench seat and hunched down to get a good look out the window. Decided to slide over.

The place was palatial and had terra-cotta roof tiles and an arched double-door entry with columns.

"What do you want me to do now?" the cabbie asked.

Madison noted the number on the house they were parked in front of—4432—and that numbers decreased in the opposite direction from where the mystery woman had entered. That meant that it was likely 4438. "Just drive past at a normal speed and take me back to where you picked me up." She could have had him take her directly to her car, but she wanted some space between her and this little mission.

The cab was put into motion, and Madison watched closely to confirm the number as they passed the house. Worse case, she could confirm it with Google Maps, but she found the numbering in bold, black letters.

Any other time, she'd go into the station and run a reverse-address search, but with Troy already wondering where she was and her promise to be home soon, she'd follow through. But tonight, if she fell asleep, she'd be having dreams about 4438 Wedgewood Crescent and its mysterious occupant.

Twenty-Four

A **good sleep had been a hopeful wish.**
When Madison had returned home,
Troy was snoring and so was Hershey.
She got a lazy tail wag for a greeting. Between
thoughts of how she'd disappointed Troy again,
and finding the ring, and having the mystery
woman's address on her mind, she ended up
getting out of bed by six that morning. She even
successfully pulled it off without waking Troy.

She headed to the station, stopping for a
Starbucks caramel cappuccino and an impulse
buy of a cranberry muffin. Only because there
was a mix-up with the baker, they didn't have
anything chocolate. But maybe she should
expand her diet to include foods other than just
chocolate, burgers, and pizza. After all, she'd
finally shed some of the extra pounds she'd been
carrying around, and it would be nice if they
stayed lost.

She set her drink in the console and caught
a whiff as it passed under her nose. Normally

pleasant and something that would have her salivating, instead the smell had her stomach contracting into a raisin. She took a tentative sip and swallowed. That wasn't going to stay down, no way, no how. How frustrating! She'd been able to live with the nausea and dismiss it, but now it was greatly interfering with her life. She needed answers.

Her doctor's office wouldn't be open yet, but the minute it was, she'd be calling.

She parked in the station lot and went for her desk, carting her Starbucks with her. Sadly, the cappuccino was bound for a garbage can, but the fate of her muffin was still unknown. When she tossed her drink, she felt for Terry being around her when she was caffeine-free.

She set the brown bag with the muffin on her desk, not brave enough to try it just yet, and did a reverse-address search for 4438 Wedgewood Crescent through a website. Nada. She repeated the query in a police database. There she had a result in a second, not that it meant anything to her at face value. There were no names associated with the address, just a numbered business. The hairs rose on her arms. The Mafia set up dummy companies to manage their dealings.

She opened another database and keyed in the business number. Technically, it was a corporation, so the board members should be public knowledge, but there was only one associated name, and it wasn't a woman's. Staring back at her were two words that shook her to the core: Roman Petrov.

That was the name of Dimitre Petrov's biological father. But Roman was dead, wasn't he? Had the record not been updated, or had it been a mistake to think he was dead? If he was alive, did he have any physical tie to that house in the north end of the city? Did the woman live there, or was she visiting? Parking in the garage could indicate the former, but regardless, who was she to Roman: business associate, friend, or…relation?

Madison rubbed her arms, trying to fend off the chill in her veins.

"Hey."

She looked up to see Terry, but she was more looking through him, her mind so full of what she'd just uncovered.

"You all right?" he asked.

"Yeah, why wouldn't I—"

"You vomited at least a couple times yesterday."

Too much to hope he would have forgotten. "So far, everything's staying down." Not that she'd put anything in there—yet. She glanced at the brown bag. She'd try it later.

"Good. You ready to pull Carl Long into an interview room?"

She glanced at the wall clock: *8:20 AM.*

"Sounds like a plan," she said.

Neither of them made an immediate move to make that happen. Finally, Terry started to walk.

"Thanks," she said.

"Yep. That's what I'm here for, your Royal Highness," he teased and tossed out a smile.

She tried to return the expression but couldn't form one. Roman's name was still on her screen. It was a good thing Terry hadn't noticed, because she wouldn't even have known how to start explaining why.

After Terry had arranged to have Carl Long brought up from holding, Madison filled him in about Long's employment history and her visit to Chassis Worx yesterday. She also told him about his self-employed status, whatever that meant. She made a stop on the way to the interrogation room, but she and Terry entered together.

Long leaned forward with his head in his hands. He slowly lowered them and raised his eyes to glare at her. They were bloodshot, and his hair was sticking up. It was clear that he hadn't slept very well last night, and it was something she had counted on. Unless a person was drunk or high—and passed out as a result—most people in the tank never slept. She was expecting it would make him more forthcoming in the hopes he'd get out of there.

"You like coffee I assume?" She put a cup filled with bullpen brew in front of him.

Long scanned her face, glanced at the offering like it was a poisonous snake that would bite him. He peeled the plastic lid off and took a sip, obviously willing to take on any potential risk.

"It's not the best stuff, but it's better than nothing," she said.

Long closed his eyes as he took another sip.

"Just wondering if you feel more like talking today," she started.

He held the cup in both hands, cradling it, claiming it, owning it. "I said all I had to say yesterday."

Behind her, Terry started jingling his change. She glanced at him over a shoulder and said, "Huh. I thought for sure…" She swiveled and reached for Long's coffee and moved to stand.

"Stop!" Long cried out.

She did as he requested. He rolled his eyes. She raised her eyebrows, ticking off the passing seconds in her head.

"Fine, let's talk," he huffed.

"I visited your old employer, Luke Landers, yesterday," she started. "He told me that Saul showed up on occasion, that he was a friend of yours. What we don't know is how you know each other."

Long spun his cup. "Met him on the inside."

She thought of her call to the prison, but maybe that had been unnecessary. Though they still didn't have Abbott's real name. One thing at a time. "You were cellmates?" she wagered a guess.

Long slowly nodded.

Now she really wanted that list, but prison administrative offices didn't move fast, and they weren't easily motivated. "So…Saul's how old?" As she and Terry had touched on before, Abbott couldn't be twenty-five and have served at the same time as Long. Straight math—which she could do—told her that Abbott would have been at least fifteen as Long was getting out. Abbott had lied about his name and his age and withheld his past.

"No clue. We didn't exactly talk about that."

"What about real names?" she asked, trying again. Maybe Long would come clean today.

Terry paused the change jingling briefly, then restarted.

"He introduced himself to me as Saul Abbott." He hitched his shoulders. "If that's not his real name, I can't help you."

Surely, a guard would have called Abbott by his real name at some point, and Long would have overheard. But it was apparent that Long wasn't going to share that information if he had it. "When were you guys bunked together?"

Long's gaze snapped to hers as if taking insult at her comparing prison to a friendly sleepover. "For six months during the last year of my sentence. He got out before me." He paused there as if expecting Madison to interject with something, but she wasn't going to discourage him from talking. He drank some coffee, then continued. "I looked him up when I got out and we reunited."

Madison studied him. "Kind of hard to look up someone when you don't know their real name."

Long took a deep sigh. "Fine, he looked me up."

"Let's say I take your word," she said, not trusting him at all. "Why did he reach out to you?"

"I don't really know."

"Is his business a big source of your income?" She had her suspicions that was the case, as well as performing legitimate marriages.

"I don't know what you're talking about."

"Your record says you've been self-employed the last few years, but it doesn't say what you do, and there's no company registered to you." She clasped her hands on the table and leaned forward. "Do you report your earnings to the IRS?"

"Of course, I…" Long took a drink of his coffee, leaving the rest of his sentence unfinished.

"Uh-huh. They'd probably be interested to hear—"

Long held up his hands. "Fine. You want to know what I did for Saul? I married him to these women he'd meet. Not legally, though. But they had my valid license to see, and they'd feel hitched."

Madison was failing to see how a sham wedding would get Abbott access to these women's money, but how often did people inspect their marriage license to prove its authenticity? Usually people who took vows were in love, blinded. Like Carson, even without a "wedding," they'd sign over their money. "What happened when these women found out the marriage was fake?"

Long looked away and blush crept into his cheeks. He damn well should be ashamed—and held accountable.

"You are just as much part of the con and the fraud as Saul Abbott. You deserve to go back to prison."

"Please no."

She shrugged. "I don't see what other choice you're leaving us." She glanced back at Terry, and he shook his head in a way that communicated bad news for Long.

"I can tell you where you might find him."

"Might?" *Unbelievable.*

"He moves around."

I wonder why…

"When did you last see him?"

"Last week."

She peered into his eyes; he seemed to be telling the truth. She sat back. At least Saul was still in the area or had been a week ago. "Where did you see him?"

"He came to my house."

"For what purpose?" she asked, though she had a feeling she knew the reason.

"He was talking to me about staging another wedding."

Madison took a few seconds to cool her temper. Long didn't seem to have any qualms about playing his role in a crime. "Now Saul's with another woman?" He hadn't answered so much in words yesterday.

Long drank some of his coffee, then said, "Yeah."

He and Carson had only split up three months ago. Saul's proposals were plentiful but meaningless. All she wanted was one from Troy—one truly meaningful proposal. She pushed the thought from her mind and placed a hand over her stomach. "Do you know her name?"

He shook his head. "And I didn't meet her."

"You said you know where we might find him."

"I don't know if I should say."

"Way I see it, you best be telling us, because you're looking at prison time for your role in conning these women—"

"You can't prove that."

"Give her time," Terry said, pushing off the wall and coming over to the table.

Long's gaze flicked to Terry, back to Madison.

"What's it gonna be? As I've already said, I'm sure the IRS would be interested in you."

Long took a deep, heaving sigh.

"Need I also remind you that we're interested in speaking with Saul because one of the women he conned was murdered."

Long swallowed audibly. "I can't help you with that."

She leaned across the table. "Maybe you can't, but I feel you can. Where can we find Saul? And don't make me ask again."

Long worried his lip, spun his cup, met her gaze, and then gave her the location.

"Do you have a phone number for him?"

Long shook his head. "He'd just drop by."

She and Terry headed for the door.

"Wait," Long called out. "Can I go now?"

Madison looked at Terry, back to Long. "For now, but if Saul comes to you, you call me." She slapped her card on the table in front of him.

Twenty-Five

"Maddy."

Madison turned to see Troy. "Oh, hey there."

"I'll sign out a car and wait for you outside," Terry told her and carried on his way.

Troy shortened the distance between them, stopping so close she could feel his breath on her face.

"How's your day goin'?" she asked.

"Just getting started. Missed you this morning."

"Yeah, sorry, I just thought I'd get an early start."

"I know. You have that murder case."

"Uh-huh." And the Mafia and corrupt cops to bring down…

"And it's going all right?"

"We just caught another lead. That's where Terry and I are headed."

"And how are you feeling today?"

She hadn't puked yet. "Much better, but I really should get go—"

He leaned in and kissed her.

"Knight!" It was Sergeant Winston, and his bellow echoed down the hall.

Troy slowly pulled back, mischievousness painted all over his expression.

She shoved him in the chest. "Happy you're amused."

"Very." He laughed and left.

"I'd like a word," Winston said, "if you're not too busy with Romeo."

Troy saluted Winston and kept walking. She wished she had more leash to treat Winston that way. She spoke back enough and stood her ground when needed, but Troy didn't have to fear any professional repercussions. He didn't report to Winston, and his sister was the police chief. The fact Madison was dating the chief's brother didn't seem to carry the same weight.

Winston snarled, his gaze going past her. He must have caught Troy's gesture. "Where's Grant?"

"We're about to head out," she said. "Something I could do for you?"

"What do you think? You haven't filled me in on your current case."

"I haven't seen you around."

"Come with me." He led the way to his office, and she felt like a captive would have walking the plank on a pirate ship.

He parked behind his desk. She remained standing. "I really need to go. Terry's—"

"Sit," Winston barked, "and fill me in."

"Not much to say."

"Unbelievable." He shot bright red from his chin to the top of his balding head. "I thought I'd step back, let you roll with the case, figured you'd fill me in when you had something."

Since when did the man ever "step back"? Micromanaging was in his blood—for better or worse. And that trait was always worse when it was directed at her. "You sure that's what it was?"

"Excuse me?" Winston leaned forward, his elbows on the desk, his eyebrows pointing up like arrows.

"Never mind." She was dying to ask him where he'd been. Weekend or not, a fresh murder case should have had him in the office.

"That's what I thought. Fill me in."

"Female victim. Chantelle Carson, age forty-eight—"

"Yadda, yadda. Suspects? Leads?"

She glanced up to the ceiling, summoning a greater being for the patience to put up with this man. She'd heard her grandmother say no one was tested beyond what they could bear, but Winston was pushing the limits.

"Knight," he prompted.

"We're currently trying to track down her ex-boyfriend."

"You have reason to believe he killed her?"

"That part's not affirmative yet, but he's certainly a person of interest. We've found out he was a con man. He took Carson for everything, destroyed her life financially."

"And his motive for killing her?"

"Still trying to piece that together. But as I said, he's more a person of interest at this point."

"Okay, and that guy you held overnight?"

She filled him in on Carl Long and his working relationship with who they knew as Saul Abbott. "Guy's still bound for prison. Only a matter of time."

Winston scoffed. "Once proof is lined up maybe, but that would be for fraud. Not your department last I checked. But it would seem you have time on your hands." He leveled a look on her that didn't need words but got the message across. He was making a dig at her kissing Troy. She knew it wasn't appropriate to show displays of affection at work, and typically they didn't. Before she could say anything, he continued. "Clear this guy—the ex-boyfriend— or book him, but don't concern yourself with him being some con man."

Her earlobes sizzled with anger, and she balled her hands into fists behind her back. Winston had a way of operating within certain lines, and if any crime fell out of the purview, he could ignore it. But not her. "If he did this to Carson, he's taken other women's money and is apparently working one right—"

"No." He held up a hand. "Your job's to solve murder, Knight."

It took every bit of her willpower not to roll her eyes. As if she needed him to remind her what her job was!

Winston added, "You have concerns about fraud, forward his information to that department. Do we have an understanding?"

She turned, looked at the clock on the wall above the door, and started to leave.

"Knight, where are you—"

She stopped but didn't face him. "I have someplace I need to be."

Twenty-Six

The address that Long have given them for Abbott led them to a middle-class neighborhood where most houses were rented out. It was a redbrick structure that could handle a fresh coat of paint to the trim, and the eaves were in desperate need of replacement.

Madison knocked and footsteps padded toward the door. It creaked loudly as it was opened.

"Yes?" A woman in her late sixties, a head of white hair, stood there watching them with marked curiosity.

Madison held up her badge, and so did Terry. "We're Detectives Knight and Grant," she said. "We're looking for Saul Abbott. Would he be home?"

The woman clutched the fabric at the bosom of her shirt and looked past them. "I don't know… Who did you say you were looking for?"

There was faraway look in her eyes that spoke to possible Alzheimer's, but she seemed to be home alone—at least no caretaker had come to the door behind her—and she was dressed in a floral-pattern buttoned shirt and blue pants with an elastic waistband.

"Saul Abbott," Madison repeated.

"No one here by that name."

"And you are?"

"Mary Smith."

"How long have you lived here?" Madison asked.

"A while." The woman gave them a pleasant smile. "Time has a way of passing by."

"It does," Madison agreed, "but it could be helpful if you answered my question."

"I moved in last November."

Abbott would have moved into Carson's house… She flipped the pages of a calendar in her mind. It was March now, and Carson and Abbott started dating eight months ago; he moved in about a month after that. So seven months ago. That would make it August. It was possible the rental remained empty for a bit. First, they needed to confirm that Abbott had even lived there and Long hadn't lied to them. "Do you know who was here before you?"

Smith shook her head. "I'm sorry, dear."

"Could you give us the name and number for the landlord?" Madison took a stab at it being a rental.

Smith seemed to consider the question for several seconds. "One minute." She retreated down a hall behind her and called out, "You two stay right there."

"Yes, ma'am," Madison mumbled under her breath.

Smith returned a few minutes later and handed Terry a piece of lined paper with swirly handwriting on it.

He held it up and said, "Thank you."

"You're very welcome." Smith smiled and added, "I hope you find who you're looking for."

"Thank you."

The door was slowly closed in their faces.

Back in the car, Madison positioned her fingers over the keyboard of the on-board laptop. "Landlord's name and number?" she prompted Terry.

He gave her the name of Jerrod Stevens and his phone number.

She keyed it in. "All right. He's only a few blocks from here." She put the car into gear and took them to the landlord's house.

They were knocking on his front door about ten minutes later, and after the third time, it was obvious the landlord wasn't home. She turned on the stoop and looked over the street. The sun was shining brightly, and the sky was a rich blue. A gorgeous day for March. Even the temperature was mild. It was like the weather mocked her mood. She was with Terry, working the case, but her thoughts kept slipping to Troy and that ring he had hidden away in the laundry room. What had made him change his mind? Or was he just waiting for the perfect time? Somehow the latter assured her and lightened her heart, soothed her stomach. She could understand that Cynthia's wedding wasn't the ideal time for him to propose, but he'd had three weeks since then to ask her, and he hadn't.

The other thing killing her was seeing Roman Petrov's name attached to the address for the mystery woman, but it wasn't like she could sneak off and probe that any further right now.

She glanced back at the house, disappointed that Stevens wasn't home, but she and Terry weren't without leads. She glanced at the clock; it was going on eleven. "I think we should go talk to Carson's banker, Alan Lowe. According to Lana Barrett, Carson added Abbott to her bank accounts and her mortgage. He may have gone to the bank for this to happen. Lowe might have Abbott's details—"

"Except you're forgetting that by his nature he's a fraud. He very well could have provided fake ID with a fake address."

"God, this is frustrating."

"Since when does a lack of answers frustrate you?"

She glanced over at him ready to say, "Always," but he was smiling.

"All the time," he said in response to what had been a rhetorical question.

She waved him off. "Here's the thing, I believe Saul Abbott would have had to give the bank something in the way of identification to be added to Carson's account. We go have a talk with them, see if they'll let us look."

"Worth a try, I suppose, but can we stop for a bite to eat or a coffee? There's a Starbucks a couple blocks over."

She drove there, quite certain she wouldn't be able to stomach a coffee or a cappuccino. But if she went in and got their order, she'd have some time alone to call her doctor's office without Terry over her shoulder.

"I'll go in," she volunteered as she parked. "The usual drink?"

"Sounds good to me."

He loved hazelnut caps.

"And to eat?"

"Turkey breast and swiss on rye."

"You got it." She went inside the coffee shop and got in line, then placed her call to her doctor's office. She got through on the second ring and booked an appointment for four that afternoon. She should have just enough time to get from there to her shrink's by five. It could be pushing it, but Dr. Talmadge usually saw his patients right on the mark.

She got Terry's order and a chocolate chip muffin for herself, seeing as she'd left the cranberry muffin at the station. She handed Terry his coffee and sandwich and settled behind the wheel.

"Where's yours?" Terry held up his cup.

"I'm coffeed out, but I was hungry." That was the truth. Now if she could just keep it down...

"I'd say you're feeling better, but a coffee limit?" Terry took a sip of his drink, then said, "You're still not feeling well, are you?"

She sighed and smacked the sides of her hands on the steering wheel, stared out the windshield.

"I'll take that as a no."

"Terry." That's all she could get out, a warning, a plea to stop pressing her about her health, to stop worrying, to stop causing her to panic.

He raised his hands in surrender, which she caught out of her peripheral vision. "Excuse me for caring," he mumbled.

"I'm sure I'm fine. Everyone gets a little bug now and then. It's not the end of the world."

"But you made a doctor's appointment?" He started unwrapping his sandwich.

"I will," she said, hating herself for lying. It was one thing for Terry to follow up on her making an appointment and another for him to know when it was—he'd be persistent in finding out the results.

Twenty-Seven

I'm sorry, but Mr. Lowe is in a meeting with clients at the moment." Brittany, the woman who was seated behind the customer service counter of Stiles Investment and Savings, was in her early twenties and had a bright smile when they'd arrived. After Madison had introduced herself and Terry as police detectives, she became more reserved.

Madison tapped the edge of her badge on the counter, softly, just enough that Brittany's gaze went to Madison's hand. "When is he scheduled to be finished?"

"Fifteen minutes."

Normally, Madison wouldn't accept waiting, but if she did, then Alan Lowe might be more willing to cooperate and possibly even show them documents without requiring a warrant. Sometimes playing nice had advantages. "We'll wait. Please let him know we're here."

Brittany watched as Madison tucked her badge away and met Madison's eyes. "I will," she said.

"Thank you." Madison grabbed Lowe's card from a holder, then said, "We'll be right over there." She wiggled a finger in the direction of a small grouping of chairs positioned in the central area of the bank.

"Okay." Brittany smiled, or at least a small touch of one brightened her face.

Terry leaned in toward Madison and spoke low. "Impressive. You *can* be patient."

"There's that whole flies-with-honey thing." She rolled her eyes and took a seat. Her stomach tossed, but it was for hunger not nausea for a change. Terry had swallowed his sandwich in a few bites, and she started thinking about the chocolate chip muffin in the car. But she couldn't chance munching it down and having it come back to haunt her. In less than fifteen minutes, she'd be speaking with Alan Lowe in financial advising. She looked at his card.

Lowe's face had been slapped on there, and Madison held it for Terry to see. Lowe was thirtysomething and wearing wire-rimmed glasses with small lenses that seemed to get lost on his doughy, round face.

Madison crossed her legs and watched people in the bank go about their business. All different ages, body types, faces, but the more she observed, the more they blended.

"Detective Knight?" A man stepped toward them. His gaze was on Terry when he spoke.

"That's me." Madison stood.

"My apology for the assumption. I'm Alan Lowe." He extended his hand to her.

No glasses, and he'd shrunk since the photo was taken for his card. He had sunken cheekbones and defined jaw lines. His suit draped on his frame as if he'd misjudged his size, still thinking of himself as being bigger than he was.

"I've been watching my carbs," he said.

Madison feigned confusion at his remark. "What—"

"You're just looking at me surprised I don't look like my card." He pointed to the one in her hand. "I've been petitioning for new ones for a while now. I've lost a hundred pounds. Eating better and exercising thirty minutes, six days a week. It took me a year and a half to do it, but…" He let his words taper off to nothing.

"It's obvious the hard work and dedication paid off. Congratulations." It had taken her the equal amount of time to burn off the last stubborn twenty. Though her habit of consuming Hershey's bars had probably played a role in that. Still, his weight loss was impressive.

"Thank you." His gaze drifted to Terry again.

"Detective Grant," Terry said.

Lowe nodded. To Madison, he said, "I got your message and intended to call today. Guess that won't be necessary now." He looked at a young couple who had just sat down nearby. He smiled at them and went over. "Something's come up, and I'll just be a few minutes late for our meeting. If you'd like water or coffee, Brittany would be happy to get either for you."

The woman smiled and nodded. The man said, "Thank you."

Lowe returned to Madison and Terry. "All right, follow me." He took them into his office and gestured to two chairs across from his desk. After he got settled, he regarded them silently, apparently waiting for them to reveal the purpose of their visit.

"Unfortunately, we have some bad news about a former client of yours," Madison began. "Chantelle Carson was found murdered on Saturday."

Lowe let out a gasp. "Oh."

"We appreciate that must come as a shock," she said.

"You could say that. Wow."

"We found your name and number on a piece of paper in her pocket," Madison disclosed. "Do you know why she might have had that?"

"Ms. Carson has been a client of Stiles Investment and Savings for many years. For an exact length of time, I can look it up if you'd like." His eyes darted to the computer monitor.

"Please," Madison said, and Lowe proceeded to click on his keyboard.

After a few seconds, he looked up and said, "She's been with us for twenty-five years. Most of that with her husband and then in the last two years on her own."

"On her own," Madison started. "So no one else had access to her money?"

He peered at the monitor again. "Actually, Chantelle added someone by the name of Saul Abbott six months ago."

Just hearing this from the banker made it sink in that Abbott must have held real power over Carson. She'd invited him to move in after a month and added him to her accounts after two. Sad really.

Lowe sat back and frowned. He clasped his hands across his lap, his arms out as if to accommodate the extra weight he used to carry. "Not sure if I should say this, but the reason she probably had my number on her was that I've been working with her, trying to get her approved for some financing. She ran into some money problems and was trying to work out repayment."

"Money problems? Can you clarify?" Madison wanted to know what Lowe's take was on Carson's financial situation.

"Her bank accounts were tapped out, her credit card was maxed, and her mortgage went into default. She ended up selling her house, but for less than what she owed. I managed to get her loan for the balance of that amount— at least she wouldn't be saddled with the entire debt load."

Lowe was presenting himself a good guy—and he'd done a decent thing—but extending credit would have been in the best interest of the bank, more than concern about Carson. She was surprised, though, by how easily Lowe was parting with this information. "And this sort of activity was unusual for her? The maxed-out card, etcetera?"

"Absolutely. She always had money in her accounts, and she never carried a balance on her credit card."

"And when did that change?" Madison was quite sure she knew when but wanted to hear it from the banker.

"About four months ago."

"Only two months after Saul Abbott was given access to her money."

His gaze darted to the door. "I feel responsible in a way, and I couldn't help her."

Madison leaned forward. He'd already said he got her a loan, so he was hinting at something else. "Help her in what way?"

Lowe glanced at Terry, back to Madison. "Yeah, she, um, was in more recently and asked me all sorts of questions about the guy."

"Like what?"

"Mostly she wanted to know if I'd conducted a thorough credit check or background on him before adding him to the account."

"And did you?" Terry asked.

Lowe shook his head. "Since she was assuming the financial responsibility, I just needed her to sign off. That's all the bank requires, but I did insist on getting a photocopy of his driver's license."

Based on all those pictures in her car of Abbott and the locked files on her computer, she had to have been conducting some sort of investigation into the man. And to come to Lowe, she might have been feeling desperate. "Would we be able to take a look at it or make a copy?"

Lowe bit his bottom lip. "I could...with a warrant."

"Huh. Okay." It didn't take much to summon disappointment, as that was exactly how she felt.

"I'd like to show you, but...well, I could jeopardize my job." He looked appealingly to Terry, who nodded in understanding.

"No one needs to know," Madison interjected, stealing the banker's gaze. "And it might be a way you can help Ms. Carson." If all else failed, guilt trips often worked. She'd learned from the master—her mother.

"I don't—"

"Truly," she said. "We'll keep your name out of this." She didn't want to play dirty and point out that they could report him for an infraction of confidence just with the amount he'd told them already. It wouldn't get them any further, and it would be a bully move, but she'd resort to the threat if necessary.

Lowe's expression softened. "You sure about that?"

"You have my word," she said.

"Okay, give me a minute." He got up and left the office.

Terry leveled a look on her. "You shouldn't have promised him that."

"There's no reason his name even needs to come up. Besides, it's probably a fake license that won't get us anywhere." She hated to think that was likely, and because of the negative thinking, she wondered why they'd even come. But at least they had confirmed that Carson had been doing all she could to get information on Abbott. It would seem that she had planned on confronting him or reporting him.

Lowe returned to his office with a folder. He sat behind his desk again, opened the folder, and took out a sheet of paper, which he handed to Madison.

It was a color copy of a license. The photo was the face they were familiar with and attributed to Saul Abbott, but the address had him in Arkansas. She pointed this out to Lowe.

"I asked him about that. He said he hadn't a chance to update it yet."

Was it possible that Saul Abbott was his actual name, after all? There was something about seeing it in print that had doubt slipping in.

"When Mr. Abbott was here, do you remember what he was like with Ms. Carson?"

He rubbed his arms as if he were cold, but he was wearing a suit jacket and the temperature in his office hadn't dipped. "Do you think this man killed her?"

"Too early to say," Madison admitted. "But what was he like with her?"

"Very doting. Maybe *too* doting. Insincere. Sort of like how children are sometimes when they come in with their wealthy, elderly parents. All they see is money, and they'll say or do anything to get into their good graces."

Yet Lowe still hadn't conducted a background or credit check on Abbott—procedure aside. She had little tolerance for those who just did the required minimum.

"Can we have a copy of this?" Madison lifted the sheet a little higher.

"I'd prefer not."

"How about a picture?" she countered.

"Sure." Lowe pulled on his collar.

She took out her phone and snapped a photo. "Thank you." She gave him the sheet back.

Lowe put the photocopy back in the folder. "As you said, please don't tell anyone that I gave you that."

"I don't see any need to go there."

"Thank you."

"No. *Thank you.*" Madison stood, and Terry did the same. She made it to the door before turning around. "You might want to push for a new policy."

Lowe angled his head as if he didn't quite follow.

"If existing clients want another person or persons added to their accounts you should conduct due diligence regardless of what's protocol. It would protect your clients and the bank."

Lowe nodded slowly. His shoulders were sagging. She felt that he must be experiencing remorse, but he had only done what a client had asked of him and followed the procedure set in place. Sad to think that following the rules had contributed to the destruction of a woman's life.

Back in the department car, Madison plugged in the license number from the photo she'd taken of Abbot's ID into the laptop. The result was almost immediate. "Huh," she said. "The number was valid at one time, and it does tie back to a Saul Abbott. Definitely not the man we know by that name, though." She pointed to the image of a white-haired man.

"Never saw that coming."

"Me either." She pulled up another screen and searched *Saul Abbott* and the address in Arkansas. "Deceased twelve years." So much for her earlier moment of doubt that had her wondering if Saul Abbott was his real name. She went on. "The real Abbott's identity was stolen and used by whoever created the ID for Abbott.

Makes me wonder if our con man has ties to Arkansas."

"Unfortunately, without a real way to track the guy—and not knowing who he really is—that's something we'll probably need to pin for now."

"I know." She tapped the steering wheel.

"And we could be going down the wrong path entirely here," Terry said. "Abbott might have screwed Carson over, but it doesn't mean he killed her."

She took her muffin out of the paper bag and dug in.

"Southern Life next?" Terry asked.

She nodded with a mouthful, swallowed, then spoke. "We should notify them that Chantelle Carson is dead. And while we're there, we can try to figure out what problems she had at work, with her boss in particular."

"There's also the possibility that one of the applicants she rejected took it all too personally."

"That too." She swallowed a large chunk of muffin.

"You look like a snake eating a rat."

"Hmph." She finished her treat and tossed the bag into the back seat.

"Are you kidding me right now?"

She pulled out of the bank's parking lot, not inclined to respond to Terry.

"You're not going to defend yourself?" he said. "You're a pig."

She slammed the brakes at a red light.

"Whoa!" He gripped the dash.

"Has your wife not taught you that women detest being called pigs?"

"Okay, you're worse than a pig. They are actually rather clean animals so—" He silenced under her stare.

"I'll get the bag later. Right now, I don't want it underfoot."

"Yes, ma'am."

She growled and gunned the gas when the light changed green. Her partner didn't have a clue sometimes. Or maybe she could expand that and generalize it as men didn't have a clue.

Twenty-Eight

S outhern Life was housed in an industrial plaza in the south end of Stiles near the highway that stretched across most of the state from east to west. The building was a single-story with smoky-tinted glass.

The receptionist, a petite redhead about Madison's age, smiled at Madison and Terry when they entered.

Madison flashed her badge and gave a brief introduction, then said, "We'd like to speak with Chantelle Carson's boss."

The redhead's eyes beaded with tears. "Did something happen to her? I just felt it when she didn't show up this morning. I tried calling her but had to leave a message."

Someone other than Claws thinks they're clairvoyant...

"It would be best if we could speak with someone in management," Madison said.

The woman nodded and picked up her phone. "Mr. Rossi, I know you told me not to disturb you, but two detectives are here to speak with you." She spoke the latter part slowly, as if coming to grips with the implication of their presence. "No, I haven't heard from her.... Yes... Okay." She met Madison's gaze as she replaced the receiver to its cradle. Her hand was shaking the entire way. "Mr. Rossi will be out soon."

"Thank you." Madison wanted to ask her about Carson and the type of person she had been, but Rossi should hear about his employee before she rattled off inquiries. "What's Mr. Rossi's full name?"

The receptionist opened her mouth to answer, but it was a man's voice that interjected.

"Dean Franklin Rossi." A man swaggered toward them in a well-tailored suit. Designer label, if Madison were to guess. "You can follow me." He led them to a conference room that was fashionably appointed. While the exterior of the building didn't look like much, the furnishings were high-end and somewhat luxurious. The leather chairs around the table had thick cushions. Madison dropped into one, as did Terry and Rossi.

"My girl told me you are Stiles police detectives," Rossi said.

Madison took slight offense to him referring to the receptionist as "my girl," as if they'd suddenly fallen into the 1950s. Rossi was a good-looking man, about fifty, graying around his temples but in a graceful, charming way. He probably wasn't used to women rejecting him, and she pegged him as a womanizer, despite the fact he wore a wedding band. Maybe it was his chauvinistic nature that Carson had a problem with.

"I'm Detective Knight." Madison gestured to Terry. "He's Detective Grant."

Rossi butted his head toward Terry, returned his gaze to Madison.

There would be no more putting off the necessary conversation. She told him that Carson had been murdered over the weekend. He stared at her, his mouth slightly hanging open for a moment, then snapping shut. He rubbed his jaw. "I guess that's a good reason for not showing up to work."

Madison resisted her inclination to respond with something sharp. She'd seen all sorts of reactions to death and murder during her time as a cop. Rossi's was one she was familiar with—the shock that led to deflecting through humor.

"Do you know of anyone who might have wanted to harm her?" Madison asked.

Rossi shook his head. "I don't."

If he was going to reply with short snippets for their entire conversation, the interaction was going to be painful. "What about any clients who might have had an issue with her?"

"None that I'm aware of."

"She sometimes had to reject applicants though, I assume?" Terry said.

"Of course."

Madison reclaimed the lead. "I'm sure some people wouldn't take too kindly to that."

"There are a few nutcases that arise from time to time."

"Any recently for Ms. Carson?"

"Not that I'm aware of."

"And did she work any files for group benefits—setting them up or processing claims?" Madison's mind was on GB, the letters in blood.

"She didn't get into business accounts. Strictly handled individual applications."

GB might not have anything to do with group benefits, but it could still refer to a person's name or initials. "We'd like to get a copy of the files she was working recently, mostly interested in applicants she rejected," Madison requested.

"I can get that information for you. With a warrant."

"Consider it done." Madison leaned back in her chair. "What was Carson like?"

"Nice girl. Hard worker. She always did as I asked."

Again, with the word *girl* to describe a grown woman. At least he hadn't called her "my girl" like he had his receptionist. "You never had any problems with her? Disagreements?"

Rossi tugged on the lapels of his suit jacket.

"Mr. Rossi?" she prompted.

"Yeah? No. We worked well together."

Madison held her gaze on him, and he touched a hand to his left temple. He was nervous and uncomfortable. "You're sure you never—"

Rossi's eyes narrowed. "Okay, maybe we didn't always see things the same way."

Madison studied him and his awkward body language. Rossi was hiding something. "Where were you Friday night from nine o'clock until two Saturday morning?"

"Where was—" Rossi gulped. "You think that I…that I…"

"We're just crossing it off our list," she said. "We have certain procedures to follow and questions we need to ask."

"That was when she, uh…died?"

"Uh-huh," Madison said.

"Well, I had no reason to kill her."

"As I said, just procedure," she tossed out nonchalantly.

His eyes darted to Terry. "I was here."

"All that time?" she asked.

"Yes. I've been working on putting together an insurance package for a large corporation in town."

"Who?" she said.

"I'd rather not say if I don't have to."

She held his gaze and remained quiet.

Rossi continued. "Randall Investments."

She sank back in her chair. The city of Stiles was too small sometimes. Randall Investments was owned by Marcus Randall, Jonathan Wright's employer. "Is there anyone who can verify you were working Friday night through to Saturday morning?"

"Josie Hart."

"And who is Ms. Hart?" Madison asked.

"She's an intern here."

"Was it just the two of you here?"

"It was." Color rose in his cheeks, and he twisted the gold band on his wedding finger.

His body language confirmed the affair. At least he had the decency to feel shame. "You were sleeping with Ms. Hart on Friday night." Not a question.

"It's nothing. Just a brief tryst."

"Is that how your wife would describe it?" she fired back.

He grimaced. "I didn't mean for it to happen."

What was it with men and their seeming inability to keep it in their pants? Maybe marriage wasn't the path she wanted to go down. Possibly not even engagement. Just vows looming on the horizon had her ex-fiancé screwing another woman. Maybe men weren't meant for monogamy, and the prospect of settling down caused something to snap in them. If so, things with her and Troy really were fine as they stood. They were exclusive, but if it went up in flames, there was a lot less legal mess to sort out. But when she thought of her future, she couldn't imagine it without Troy next to her.

God, she was in deep. She cleared her throat. "We're going to need to speak with Ms. Hart."

"Josie's here today." He reached toward a phone in the center of the table. "Should I get her in here?"

"We'll want to speak with her, but alone," Madison said. "First, though, I'd like to know what sort of things you and Carson didn't agree on." She straightened her shoulders and locked eye contact with Rossi.

"Oh, okay." Rossi resettled back in his chair and sighed. "Where to start?"

Twenty-Nine

Madison watched Rossi for any tells of deception as he went on to explain that Carson was stubborn and opinionated and thought she knew more than he did. "Obviously, that bothered you?" she said.

"Damn right it did. I'm her boss. I'm actually the owner here." As he said that, pride inflated his chest. "I know what I'm doing."

"She questioned your work?" Terry leaned back.

"She didn't outright, but it was just…"

"Just?" Madison prompted.

"I caught her double-checking my work."

He had a way of saying a lot while saying nothing. "Specifically?"

Rossi drew his fingertip in circles on the table. "Claims I'd filed."

"Was it part of her job to review them, to ensure accuracy?" Madison inquired.

"Sure, when I asked her to," he said. "A second set of eyes never hurt." It was the slight twitch of his lips that said the opposite.

There was something about this guy Madison didn't trust, and it wasn't just the fact that he was a cheating scumbag. "I think we're ready to speak with Ms. Hart, if you could send her in?" Madison glanced at the door, giving further indication that this conversation was over.

"Ah, sure." Rossi tapped the table before getting up and leaving the room.

Madison looked at Terry. "I can see what Carson didn't like."

"Doesn't surprise me."

A few minutes later, a woman came into the room. She was mousy with dirty-blond hair and brown eyes, but they sparked with life. She wore stylish glasses that complemented the shape of her face. She had a sexy-librarian vibe coming off her. She probably swatted men away much like Cynthia had before settling down with Lou.

"Mr. Rossi said that you wanted to speak with me?"

"We do. Please." Madison gestured to a chair across from her, and Josie Hart acquiesced, but her movements were stiff and jerky, uncomfortable.

"He told me it's about last Friday night," Hart said.

"It is." Madison found it interesting that either Rossi hadn't mentioned Carson's murder or Hart was more focused on her affair with a married man. "Did he tell you why?"

Hart nodded and tucked a strand of hair behind her right ear. So it was the latter.

Not a single expression of sorrow over Carson's demise. "How long have you worked here?"

"Six months."

"Did you know Ms. Carson very well?"

She shook her head.

"Did you work with her on anything?"

"A little here and there. Mostly photocopying and whatnot that she needed done. Mostly I work alongside Mr. Rossi."

"I see."

Hart blushed.

Madison went on. "And what's the nature of your relationship with Mr. Rossi?"

"I'm pretty sure he told you."

Madison shrugged. "I'd like to hear your side."

"I'm sleeping with him and have been for a while."

She nodded, not quite able to find it in herself to point out their relationship meant nothing to Rossi. It didn't stop her from saying, "From what we've been told, Ms. Carson took issue with Mr. Rossi. Did it have something to do with the fact he's a married man but sleeping with his intern?"

Terry nudged his shoe against the side of hers. Her partner had a way of attempting to corral her when he thought she was being too blunt.

Hart jutted out her chin. "I wouldn't know what her issue was—or even if she had one. It's not like we spoke."

"Where were you last Friday night until two the next morning?" Madison asked, ignoring the snideness in the intern's voice.

"Here with Mr. Rossi working on an insurance proposal for Randall Investments."

Her reply came out as if it had been rehearsed. "Is that what Mr. Rossi told you to say?"

"No," she shot out. "I was here."

"And you worked on that proposal all night?" Madison pushed.

Hart's gaze flicked to Terry, back to Madison. "For most of it. And I see how you're looking at me, but he's an amazing man. His wife doesn't get him. She's always doing her own thing. Probably cheating on him."

"Is that what he told you?" Madison said.

Hart narrowed her eyes but didn't dispute Madison's allegation. "Neither of us had anything to do with Carson's death. We were both here."

Madison scanned the intern's face. An arrogant pride coated her features. She'd probably be a mistress all her life. This woman was everything Madison couldn't stand. "Stay in town, Ms. Hart." Madison stood.

"Whatever." Hart crossed her arms, giving the full image of a petulant child.

Before leaving Southern Life, Madison and Terry spoke with the redhead from the front desk. She described Carson as a gentle soul who didn't deserve to be screwed over and murdered. They also inquired as to the beneficiary noted on her life insurance and was told it was Saul Abbott. The address on file was for the house Carson had shared with him.

"I can't believe she didn't update her life insurance policy when they split," Madison said as she got into the department car.

"She must have overlooked it with everything else that happened."

"I can't believe it wasn't one of the first things she would have taken care of." Madison started the vehicle. "Anyway, all I know is whenever we catch up with Abbott, I'm going to strangle him. Carson had people who liked her, and she just thought she'd found Mr. Right. Look how that turned out." Somehow murder was always made worse when the victim had been a kind person. At least she felt even more responsible for making things right when that was the case. "We'll get the warrant paperwork started for Southern Life so we can see what Carson had been working on, but I also want to try Jerrod Stevens again. Maybe we'll find the landlord at home."

Thirty

It was two in the afternoon when Madison and Terry were getting out of the car at Jerrod Stevens's house. In a couple hours, she had two back-to-back appointments. She wasn't looking forward to either one and had considered canceling the one with her general practitioner. After all, her stomach hadn't kicked the muffin back out.

She knocked once, and footsteps headed toward the door.

A man stuck his head out and grimaced. "Cops or religion?"

He wasn't the first person to ask that question, but every time it happened, Madison wondered what it was about her and Terry that had people thinking they were on some sort of religious mission.

In response, both she and Terry held up their badges.

"Are you Jerrod Stevens?" Madison asked.

"The one and only, and thank God, because the world can only handle one of me." Stevens grinned and winked at her. "Come on in."

"We're Detectives Knight and Grant," she said, thinking she should record those words and simply hit play for the number of times she had to say it during an investigation. "We have some questions for you about a former tenant."

"Shoot."

She gave him the address in question. "Saul Abbott. We believe he rented from you before Mary Smith, who took over in November."

"All right, well, that's my property, but—" he scratched the back of his head with the fervor of a dog going after a flea "—I don't know that name."

She pulled up his picture on her phone and showed it to him.

"Nope, never seen him before. Doesn't mean he didn't drop around. I used to rent that place to a young woman. Maybe he was a friend of hers?"

"Do you know her name?" Madison asked.

"I'd have to go look at the records. My memory's not as good as it used to be."

"We'll wait," Madison assured him.

"All right…" He left them in the entry and headed toward the back of the home.

The part of the house they could see was tidy and compact with everything seeming to have its place. There was a mild odor that kept hitting her, but she couldn't quite pin its source. Her guess was something food related.

"Here we go…" Stevens was back, holding a ledger open. He drew a fingertip down the page, licked his finger and flipped to the next page. "Ah, here we go."

"Do you manage or own a lot of properties?" she asked.

"Five properties. Some are duplexes, and others, small apartments." He looked up from where he'd been in the book. "Here it is. Name's Shannon Keller."

"Do you know where Keller moved?" Maybe if they could find her, they'd find Abbott.

"I don't. I'm sorry."

"And she moved out when?" Madison's phone pinged with a text message, but she'd check it after they left.

"October."

That would make sense, as Mary Smith had told them she moved into the place in November. "And how long did you rent it to her?"

"A few years."

Madison nodded. "Do you have her phone number by chance?"

"Nah, sorry."

"Well, thank you for her name."

"Don't you mention it. I stand behind Stiles's finest." Stevens closed the book and tucked it under his right arm and waved his left hand.

She smiled at him. "Thank you," she repeated.

"No. *Thank you.*" Stevens shoved out his hand, nearly dropping the book in the process.

She shook his hand, then Stevens took Terry's.

"Thank you," he told Terry.

Terry just dipped his head, also smiling.

It felt like she was walking tall on the way back to the car. It had been far too long since the last time someone had expressed their gratitude for cops. Sadly, many people tended to judge the whole of law enforcement by the bad ones. Stevens's faith instilled an even greater desire to bring down the corrupt cops before they destroyed all she held dear.

She checked her phone, and the message was from Cynthia. "Looks like we have another lead." She filled Terry in after reading. "Cynthia received the phone logs from Stiles Wireless. One number called Carson fifty times in the week leading up to her murder. Cyn tracked it back to a John Clayton, here in Stiles." She put the car into gear.

Thirty-One

Just after three in the afternoon, and Madison's doctor's appointment was at four. She should probably let Terry tackle John Clayton on his own, but if necessary, she'd reschedule with her doctor. This was a solid lead, and she wanted to see the man face-to-face for herself, not hear about him from a second-hand account.

Clayton's criminal background was clean, but he was employed as a chef at the Pig King in the north end. The restaurant specialized in barbecued meat, primarily pork, as their name implied.

They drove to the place figuring that, with the time of day, they'd most likely find him in the kitchen.

Madison stepped inside and slowed her breathing. The smell of slow-roasting meat and sweet barbecue sauce was overpowering and flipped her stomach. She flashed her badge at the hostess and requested to speak with John

Clayton. The hostess nodded and went toward the back.

"John's busy. Is there something I can help you with?" It was the manager who ended up coming to see what she and Terry wanted. He was a potbellied, middle-aged man. The only thing going for him was a full head of hair.

"What you can help us with is getting Mr. Clayton," she said.

The manager sighed dramatically and opened his mouth, shut it, opened it. "Very well. I can spare him for no more than five minutes, though, and then he needs to get back to work. The crowds start rolling in just after five, and there's lots to prepare. Follow me." He took them back to the kitchen and shouted, "John!"

A large man, easily close to four hundred pounds, was chopping meat on a block. At the sound of his name, he suspended his cleaver in mid-strike. He squinted at Madison and Terry, his eyes small and beady and sunken in his face. "Who are you?" Obviously annoyed at the interruption and not in the mood to talk.

Well, too bad. "We're detectives with the Stiles PD, and we need to speak with you about Chantelle Carson."

The manager glanced from Madison to Clayton and slunk out of the room, seemingly not wanting to get involved in whatever this was about.

Clayton stared at Madison, and she could see his mind spinning and trying to decide whether he should run, but he wasn't exactly in the shape for it. Score for her.

He set down the cleaver and held up both his hands. "I'll stop calling her."

"Huh, it's only part of the reason we're here." Madison moved farther into the kitchen. "But why did you call her so much?"

Clayton's eyes darted from her to Terry to the door, and he started to move. He only got as far as the other side of the counter since she'd darted quickly to block him.

"Let's just talk. Okay?"

"I didn't do anything wrong. She did." He clenched his jaw and crossed his arms.

"How do you figure?"

"She rejected my application, and she wouldn't listen to reason."

"This was all about insurance?" Madison asked.

"Ah, yeah."

"So what? You intended to force her to hear what you had to say?" Madison said. "Fifty phone calls in the last week is a lot. Harassment."

"She just wouldn't listen," he spat.

"There would have been reasons you were rejected. What were they?" Madison wanted to get to the heart of his rage and take its temperature.

Clayton pressed his lips together like a fish and waved a hand down his body. "She gave me some scripted reply that I didn't qualify for critical care coverage because of my weight."

"That must have made you feel—"

"Pissed off? Yeah. I work in this kitchen eight hours a day, and I'm just fine. Do you see me panting?"

Surprisingly, she didn't. There was just a sheen of sweat on his forehead and face, but she probably looked the same. The kitchen was hot. "But this made you mad?"

"Sure. Now, maybe I shouldn't have called her so much, and I'll back off. Had no idea she was going to get the cops involved."

Madison stayed silent and walked around the counter, looking at the meat that Clayton had been chopping when they arrived. She held down the urge to gag at the sight of the pale flesh piled on the block.

"You really here because of the calls?" Clayton's cheeks went a bright shade of red— from his weight, the stress of their visit, or from fear of being found out.

"As I said, that's only part of it. Chantelle Carson was found murdered Saturday afternoon. Stabbed to death." Technically, she'd bled out, but if it hadn't been for the stabbing, she'd still be alive.

"She…She was…"

"Murdered," Madison stamped out. "And you called her right up until the day before her attack. You just said that being rejected made you 'pissed off.'"

"Sure did, but I— You think I killed her?"

Madison hitched a shoulder as if to say, *Why not?*

"No." Clayton shook his head. "My rejection was prejudice in action. I carry extra pounds, sure, but I have a clean bill of health. Check with my doctor. That's what I wanted her to do. Even the nurse who came to my house told me my blood pressure was spot-on. Denying me coverage is prejudice in action."

"Insurance is a business, based on statistics, and they have a right to refuse anyone they want." Madison recalled Bill Carson's comment about the system being nothing more than black-and-white. "You refused to accept they had that right. I mean, obviously. Harassing Ms. Carson. Where were you Friday night from nine until two Saturday morning?"

"I was here."

"If we spoke to your manager, he'll verify that you were here the entire time?"

Clayton gulped.

Madison scanned the kitchen and set her gaze on the knives, of which there were plenty. She walked over for a closer look. "Stainless steel blades?"

"Of...of course," Clayton stuttered.

"You wouldn't mind if we took one?" She leveled her gaze on him.

"You'd have to talk to Phil."

"Who's Phil?" she asked.

"The manager."

They hadn't gotten his name. Her eye landed on a few empty spots in a knife block. "You're missing a few already."

"Ah, yeah…" Clayton wiped his brow. "They wear down over time."

"Huh." Madison returned to Clayton's side. "When did you leave here Friday night?"

He scanned her face. "About eleven."

"Where did you go?" She swore she saw fresh beads of sweat forming. He was the right height for Carson's attacker, but would he have the physical ability to do the deed? Then again, he wasn't panting like one might expect with such an obese person.

"I went home. I was exhausted. I'd started at noon that day."

"Can anyone verify that you went home?" she asked.

"Ah, no, I live alone. Well, I have Sophie, but she's a cat."

"No landlord or neighbors who might have seen you?"

"Maybe?"

"Well, you're leaving us in a tough spot, Mr. Clayton. You'd have motive to want Ms. Carson dead—" she flailed a hand across the kitchen "—and access to an assortment of knives."

"Wait. You can't think that I…" He wiped his forehead again. "Just because I know how to work a knife?"

"Because you had motive. Did you miss that part? She denied your application for insurance, and unlike a rational person who just accepts that and moves on, you set out to harass her. You called her numerous times. Did you stalk her too?" Madison looked at Terry. "We should talk to her landlord and neighbors, see if they saw Clayton hanging around."

Clayton held up his hands. "Please…Okay, I was stupid. I…I may have followed her home once."

She'd heard enough. "You're coming downtown with us."

"No, please. Just listen to me."

"We will. Down at the station."

"I could lose my job."

"You should have thought of that before." Madison motioned for Terry to round up Clayton.

"Come on, Mr. Clayton," Terry said. "If you come without resisting, this will go a lot smoother."

They filled in the manager on their way out and were met with a lot of pleas and panic, but they had little choice but to take his head chef. And if Clayton had killed Carson, he wouldn't be returning any time soon. Getting the boss to hand over a knife for comparison was rather easy, and he didn't request a warrant.

Terry got Clayton into the back of the department car. It wasn't an official arrest yet, so no need to call in a cruiser. Outside the car, Madison spoke to Terry.

"I've got to leave him with you. As much as I hate to."

"Why?"

"I have that doctor's appointment." So much for keeping the time from him.

"By all means, then go. I can handle this, and I'll keep you posted."

"I'll join you at the station when I get out." She wasn't going to tell him she also had to see her shrink. Just let him think her general practitioner took longer to get her in.

"Fine by me. Go, take care of yourself."

She nodded and got into the driver's seat. She'd drive Terry and Clayton downtown and then head out, but she needed to hustle because the clock was ticking.

Thirty-Two

Madison was checking into her doctor's office at three fifty-five—five minutes to spare. Some might say she was late. She'd say she was right on time. She didn't even have to sit down before a nurse guided her to a room. That was a bonus, because she always cringed at the thought of sitting around a bunch of sick people with their runny noses and coughing and their kids touching everything with their sticky little fingers with no respect for boundaries.

She filled the nurse in on the purpose of the visit with the clear disclaimer that she was feeling better now but wanted to honor her appointment.

"Dr. Talmadge will be right with you," the nurse said and left.

Posters on the wall testified to the dangers of smoking, the importance of screening for breast cancer and how to go about self-testing, and how strokes were the silent killer. There were certainly a lot of ways to leave this world. All Madison knew was she wasn't ready to exit.

There was a knock, and the door inched open. Dr. Talmadge poked his head in, then entered the rest of the way. He closed the door behind him.

"Hello, Madison. It's been a long time since you were in."

"I'd say that's a good thing. No offense." She smiled and held up a hand.

"None taken." Talmadge came from England, and his voice still carried the beautiful English accent. She'd been seeing him since she was a little girl; he had another practice outside of Stiles, in the small town where she grew up. He put his clipboard on the counter, next to the sink. "So, what brings you here today?"

He could easily consult the nurse's notes, and Madison was sure he probably had, but as she liked to hear things from, say, a suspect's lips, he liked to hear his patients confirm their maladies.

"I'm actually feeling fine now."

He dropped onto a stool and smiled at her.

"What?" she asked.

"You're the same every time I see you. You obviously had something that brought you to me, but you always downplay whatever it is. Just tell me what prompted you to make the appointment."

"Fair enough. I've been feeling nauseous off and on for several days now. But today I was able to keep food down, and I'm much better."

"When did the nausea start?"

She'd been trying to figure that out but couldn't quite remember. "I'm not sure exactly, but it hung around for a few days."

"You mentioned keeping food down. Before today, you experienced vomiting?"

"Yesterday."

"I see." Talmadge wrote something on the pages attached to the clipboard.

She was afraid to ask what he meant by *I see*. It sounded so menacing. She cleared her throat and braved speaking anyhow. "My partner, at work," she clarified, "said that nausea can be a symptom of cancer."

He paused writing and met her eyes. "It can be a symptom of many things." He got off his stool. "I'd like to run some bloodwork, and we'll go from there. That okay?"

She turned her head for that next step. She didn't want to witness the process.

She felt the tiniest pinch—not her issue—but she'd made the mistake once of watching the vial fill with blood, swore she could feel it leaving her body. She never made that mistake again.

"All righty, all done."

She dared to look now. Talmadge pressed a cotton ball over the pinprick and slapped on a

Band-Aid. "You're quick," she said, appreciating that he hadn't delegated the task to a nurse, like most doctors would have.

"I didn't get this handsome and skilled in just a few years." He smiled and headed toward the door.

"When should I have the results?"

"A couple days, max. I'll call if there's anything to worry about."

She slipped off the examination table. "Do you think I have anything to worry about?"

Talmadge stopped next to the door, and he dipped his chin and said, "Worry is always a waste of time and energy." He held her gaze until she nodded.

Wise words, but much harder to implement. If only he'd given her something to go on besides a dose of adage, something more clinical and scientific. Maybe even assuaged her concerns about cancer, but he hadn't.

Thirty-Three

Madison left Talmadge's office and headed for Dr. Connor's. If traffic had cooperated, she'd have made it on time, but she turned up ten minutes late for her appointment.

She checked in and took a seat in Connor's waiting area. The office was essentially three spaces—one for reception, another for waiting, and then the therapy room. Each area felt intimate and was decorated in soft hues, probably to have a soothing effect on patients.

"Madison." Connor had come to collect her. If she had been with a patient, Madison never saw him or her leave.

"Hi." Madison stood and followed the doctor into her office.

Connor sank into her chair that looked far more comfortable than the couch, even with its throw pillows. Madison piled them to the side, except for one that she hugged to herself.

"What's happened since the last time I saw you? It's been over a month."

There wasn't so much judgment in Connor's tone or words as there was definite concern.

"Not a whole lot," Madison lied.

"Last time we spoke, you were battling with guilt over your sister's abduction." Connor's face was soft and motherly.

Madison gripped the pillow tighter, and after realizing it, she loosened her hold. "I've been very busy." Spoken as if that stopped the guilt from surfacing. It was her actions, her interference with the mob that had resulted in Chelsea's ordeal three months ago. Still, Madison refused to walk away—all because she couldn't ignore what was going on in her city.

"Often it's easier to keep busy than to face our feelings."

Madison stifled the urge to defend herself and insist that she had truly been busy, but maybe some of it had been self-inflicted busyness. Then again, she felt like if she didn't expose the corrupt cops, no one would. Most of the Stiles PD also believed the Mafia had left town when clearly that wasn't the case. Not with a house registered to a company attached to Roman Petrov.

"Madison?" Connor prompted.

"My mind just drifted. But I guess as long as people are killing each other…"

Connor crossed her long, slender legs. "We've discussed how important it is that you take care of yourself, Madison."

"I know."

"Are you?"

"I'm doing my best." Not a lie. She had gone to see Talmadge. But if she were really taking care of herself, she'd make time to rest and eat nutritional food at regular intervals, instead of leaving both things to chance.

"Share with me, please." Connor gestured with her gold pen.

"I just saw my family doctor before coming here."

"Oh?"

"It's nothing. I'm sure I'm fine. I already feel better."

"How were you feeling?"

"Sick. Off and on. Mostly on for several days."

"I see."

"What do you mean by that?"

"We've discussed this before, but when we don't properly process our emotions, they can surface as physical ailments. An easy example is stress. It often can give someone a kink in their neck or back pain. Most of us have been there before."

"Yep." Sergeant Winston gave her a headache every time she saw him.

Connor went on. "The guilt you mentioned feeling over your sister's abduction could be wreaking havoc. Making you feel ill…"

"I don't think it's about that."

"So you feel all better about the abduction? Don't feel it's your fault any longer?"

"I never said that."

Connor laid out both her hands, palms up, as if to say, *See?*

"I accept that I had a reason for doing what I did, for investigating the Mafia," she said, stamping down her feelings of regret that still crackled in her veins. "Chelsea is fine, is going to be more than fine."

"And what about you?" Connor's question sank like a weight on a bungee cord, due to fling up at any minute. "You had to kill a man," she said softly.

"It was self-defense." She hugged the pillow tighter. "Necessary." Something she never told anyone, not even Troy, was when it came to killing Constantine, she felt no regrets, no remorse. She was simply numb, indifferent, devoid of all emotion.

Connor held eye contact for a few seconds, then smiled reservedly. "It seems that you are feeling better."

"I am." Madison relaxed, but she wasn't fooled by Connor's new approach. The doctor was hoping Madison would let her guard down and start opening up about her feelings.

The clock on the wall ticked off the seconds, and Madison heard each one.

Connor uncrossed her legs. "How is your relationship with Troy?"

The question hit as a blow. "Fine."

Connor's lips twitched as if she was about to smile, but she didn't. "If I took away that word, how would you describe it?"

Madison smiled, though she doubted it touched her eyes. "Tense. At the moment."

"Why's that?"

She hugged the pillow tighter again but ended up tossing it to the end of the couch. "I thought he was going to propose a few weeks ago, but he didn't. Still hasn't."

"A few weeks ago? That was around the time of Cynthia's wedding, wasn't it?"

On her last visit, Madison had mentioned the upcoming nuptials. "Yeah. I actually thought he was going to ask that night."

"Do you want to marry him?"

"Of course I—" She snapped her mouth shut.

Connor grinned. "Have you asked him what he thinks of marriage?"

"I know he was burned by his first wife. She cheated on him, and he swore off marriage."

"But you think that's changed?"

Madison met Connor's gaze and nodded.

"What makes you think that?"

"I found a ring."

"Oh." A tiny word drawn out like it was four feet long.

"Yeah, and it's beautiful. I think he was going to propose, and he's changed his mind."

"Have you asked him about the ring?"

"I don't even know where to start." Truth: she wasn't sure her fragile heart could handle it if she brought up marriage and he shot her down. God, she hated being vulnerable!

"How about starting with, 'I found...'"

Madison shook her head. "He'd hate that. I know him well enough. He'd view it as a violation of his privacy."

"Okay, but may I ask, how do you know he doesn't still plan to ask? You did find the ring. Say, if he was going to propose but changed his mind altogether, why keep it? He would have returned it or pawned it, but from what I gather, he hid it."

"In a box in the laundry closet."

"Just going out on a limb here, but I'm guessing that's not someplace you would ordinarily go?"

"No." Madison smiled, not offended but rather impressed her shrink knew her so well. "You think he still plans to propose?"

"I don't have the answer to that." Connor smiled kindly, a twinkle in her eye.

What if Connor was right and he still did plan to propose? She'd been so temperamental with him lately, and maybe in retrospect, she'd been more aloof than he'd been. She was the one who had changed, not him. After all, she kept secrets and stayed out all hours of the day and night. She was doing her best to avoid any time alone with him. And it was killing her!

She sprung up from the couch.

"We have five minutes left," Connor said.

"I've gotta go." She rushed out the door and didn't turn back, but she called out, "Thank you," and kept going.

She had planned to meet up with Terry at the station, but Troy should be home from work. Let her partner handle the chef from the Pig King while she whisked Troy out for a nice dinner. They were past due for some time together.

She was driving home, and her phone rang. Caller ID showed on her car display and told her it was Terry. Madison answered. "I was going to call," she blurted out. "How's it going with Clayton?" There'd be plenty of time to bring up that she was heading home for the day.

"He lawyered up."

"Good sign the guy's probably guilty."

"So, what were you going to tell me? You said you were going to call? Was it just to ask questions that could wait until you got here?"

Voicing her decision to call it a day was a little tougher than she'd thought it would be. "Well, I was going to call it a day. Sounds like that might work out. Who knows when Clayton's lawyer's going to get there?"

A few beats, then, "Oh," coated with disappointment.

"You need me back?"

"I think you'll want to join me. I've discovered some things while reading Carson's journals. I mean, otherwise, I'd just be sitting here doing nothing pretty much. But she was some sort of whistleblower. Potentially anyhow. She mentioned her suspicions that her boss was guilty of insurance fraud, and she vowed to expose both him and Saul Abbott."

She stiffened at Terry's words and stopped for a red light. "Okay, Rossi said that Carson was double-checking his work. He wasn't pleased by that. Guess we now know why. He must have known she was going to report him."

"Still need proof, something solid," Terry said. "But what you'll really get excited about is Cynthia has unlocked the password-protected files on Carson's laptop. I thought you'd want to come back to the station and dig in with me. Carson didn't have anything specific documented about Rossi in her journals, but—"

"Could be in those files."

"Yeah, so are you coming back to the station? We can look at it together."

The light turned green. She hesitated long enough that the person behind her honked their car's horn and swerved around her.

"Maddy?" Terry prompted.

She had all these grandiose intentions of making things right with Troy—even if he didn't know they were falling apart. But her job was calling. Carson was asking for justice. And if there was any proof that Carson was going to expose her boss, Dean Rossi, he would have motive for murder.

She checked all her mirrors, and no one was there. She cranked the wheel and was just about to start into a U-turn from the outside lane.

The impact came quick and hard from behind and threw her forward. Just before everything went black, a pickup breezed past and she saw the driver's face. It was one she recognized.

Thirty-Four

Madison slowly opened her eyes. The light was blinding and pierced her skull. She closed them again.

"Madison?" A man's voice struck her ears like it was coming from another world.

She squinted, widening her eyes in increments as they adjusted to the light. Then she realized there was a plastic tube coming out of her mouth. It felt like she was choking. She clawed at whatever it was, and a warm hand stopped her. Troy's.

He reached for something next to her head and swept back some of her hair. "I'm so happy to see you again. Don't say anything. Just wait."

What was he talking about? What had happened? Where was she, and why was it so incredibly bright? Why couldn't she breathe right? She screamed in her head, and her pounding heart thumped a staccato rhythm.

A woman in a pale-blue uniform came into the room.

"She just woke up," Troy told her.

The woman fiddled with a machine next to the bed, and another person came into the room. A man in a white jacket. But she didn't have time for this—whatever this was. She had a job to do. She struggled to sit up. She had to get to the station. Terry. He had something for her to look at— She winced. Thinking too hard hurt, and her memory was nothing but little snippets attempting to come together to form a complete picture.

Rather firm hands held her in place. The woman in the pale-blue uniform on one side and the man in white on the other. Troy stood back now, his hands on her feet.

"Madison, I'm Dr. Hunt," the man in the white jacket said. "Nurse Vega is going to remove the breathing apparatus."

Breathing apparatus!

"When I say so, let out a deep breath, Madison," the nurse told her. "Blink twice if you hear me."

Madison blinked once. Twice. Her eyelids felt so heavy they just wanted to stayed shut.

The woman positioned herself over Madison's torso and put her hands in place to remove the tube. "Deep exhale now."

She did so, and the woman removed the tube. Madison could feel every inch of it coming up her throat and fought the gag reflex. Her throat was raw and dry.

"Wa...ter," she croaked out.

"Ice chips are the best we can do right now," the doctor said.

The nurse offered Madison a cup with ice chips, and she took one into her mouth.

"You were in a car accident," the doctor said.

A loud crunch. A force that lunged her forward, then back. The darkness.

He took out a stick from the pocket of his jacket and told her, "Follow this with your eyes." He moved it left to right, right to left, left to right. "Good, good." He went on to ask for her full name, birthday, Troy's name, what she did for a job, what year it was, the current president's name...so many questions. Eventually he stood back and smiled.

"Does that mean—" Troy's voice cracked. "Is she going to be okay?"

The doctor nodded. "It's early yet, but it's looking good that she'll make a full recovery."

Troy had resumed his spot next to her, and he had his one hand wrapped around hers. The other was on her shoulder. She sought out Troy's gaze, and when he looked into her eyes, she'd never seen him so pensive and anxious before. He looked like a mild breeze could knock his six-foot-four frame over.

"Wha...what happened?" She tried talking around the ice melting on her tongue.

"The accident caused your brain to swell, and to allow it time to heal, we put you into a medically induced coma," the doctor said. "We were worried for a while, but it would seem you have someone up there looking out for you." The doctor pointed toward the ceiling, and in Madison's foggy mind, it took a while to piece together that he was referring to God or a guardian angel. "You do have a few bruised ribs though."

That would explain why every breath was excruciating.

"They should heal up just fine," the doctor went on. "Just no marathons or intense exercise for the next while."

"No worries there," Troy said and winked at her. Madison's heart pinched, and she squeezed his hand. God, she loved that man, and he knew her so well.

"How long…have I…" She swallowed the melted ice. The cold of it was soothing to her throat.

"Better part of forty hours," Troy answered. "You had the accident on Monday night about six, and it's now Wednesday at eleven in the morning."

Wednesday?! Maybe this was all some horrible nightmare and she'd wake up in bed, warm and next to Troy.

"When should she be able to leave, Doctor?"

"Let's give it a couple more nights. We'll continue to monitor you," he said to Madison, "and if your vitals look good, you'll be free to go by Friday evening. I'm also sure you're anxious to know about your baby's well-being."

Baby! She must still be in a coma!

Troy stuttered, "She…she…she's *pregnant*?"

"You didn't know," the doctor concluded.

Madison was in complete shock. Troy was wide-eyed.

The doctor went on. "You're about six to eight weeks."

She pried her brain to think of her last cycle. She'd never been regular but— She gulped. It had been a while since her last period, but she was on birth control pills and was religious about taking them. How could she be pregnant?

The doctor glanced at the nurse, looked back at Madison and Troy, cleared his throat and said, "I see this is quite a surprise for the two of you. It's still early enough that if you wished to terminate the pregnancy, this could be done, but the sooner the better if that's the decision you're going to make."

Troy gripped her hand tighter.

"Well, we'll leave you two alone to talk," the doctor said, then looked at Troy. "Visiting hours are from noon until two if you want to have family and friends come in, but I recommend limiting the number of people who visit today. She's been through a lot and needs rest. And so do you."

"Thank you," Troy said, and the doctor and nurse left the room.

Troy looked at her. His mouth opened like he was going to say something a couple times, but nothing came out. His usual piercing green eyes had dulled and were a little bloodshot. His shoulders were sagged.

"How long…have…you…been here?" Her question came out in fragments.

"I've been by your side from the moment they let me."

Her gaze went to the chair he'd been sitting in when she'd woken up. "You—"

"My turn to ask a question." Hurt coated every word as if he'd been sliced by betrayal. He took her hand into both of his. "When were you going to tell me you're pregnant?"

She closed her eyes. The days of nausea and the vomiting, her sensitivity to smells, her inability to enjoy a cup of coffee… She should have known, but they took steps so pregnancy wouldn't happen. And though it had passed through her mind the other day, she'd dismissed it just as quickly as it had occurred. She was focused on her work—the murder investigation, bringing down corrupt cops, hindering the Mafia's operations…

"Maddy, please." Troy's voice ripped something inside of her, and she met his gaze again.

"I didn't know."

"That's why you were sick. Morning sickness." Troy put a hand through his hair. "We should have figured it out. But we take precautions. How—" He snapped his mouth shut.

Tears snaked down her cheeks. This was probably when he told her that he wasn't ready for a kid, that he didn't want a kid, that he didn't want to be with her, but he'd do what he could for the kid because he was that kind of man.

Seconds passed painfully.

"We're having a baby!" He cupped her face and kissed her lips. He pulled back and let out a holler. He went to the doorway and called down the hall. "I'm going to be a dad!"

What the hell? She laughed—and stopped from the pain in her throat and ribs.

He raced back to her. "I'm so happy."

"You're—" She couldn't speak. Personally, she was mortified and experiencing a myriad of emotions. Top of which was absolute panic. She'd never planned to be a mother. Kids weren't even on her radar.

"I'm so happy," he repeated. "And I love you."

She found herself smiling, caught up in his excitement and enthusiasm. Maybe between the two of them, they'd figure it out, make it work. Her stomach tossed—the pregnancy itself or nerves from being pregnant? After all, in about nine months, less some weeks, she'd be squeezing out a melon. Her body would never be the same. Her life would become about carpools and sports and—

"Did you hear me, Madison? I love you." He tapped another kiss on her lips.

"I love you, too." She attempted a smile, but she wanted to cry.

His face scrunched up. "You're not happy. You don't want this."

"It's…it's just a shock."

"Or a good surprise?" Another grin.

She slapped a hand toward him and winced from the pain of doing so. Probably one of the bruised ribs. "We don't even…have a…big enough house…for a kid."

"We can fix that. I'll call Estelle and get her seriously looking. What do you think? Four bedrooms? We'd have a couple spares. Could turn one into a home gym."

As she listened to Troy painting this glorious future of them together, raising their child, she could feel her freedom and independence slipping away. As much as she was happy that he loved her and would stand by her, she wished that time could be reversed. She wasn't sure she even wanted to consider what a baby would mean for her career and the badge she'd worked so hard for and valued so greatly.

Thirty-Five

Madison woke up to footsteps coming toward the bed.

"Hey, sis," Chelsea said.

Madison slowly opened her eyes. Her entire body ached, and she was more exhausted than she ever remembered being. *What I wouldn't do for a coffee*, she thought, then realized she'd have to cut back on caffeine—and wine!

Chelsea and her three nieces were standing on Madison's left while Troy kept vigil on the right. Madison glanced at him as if to remind him that they'd agreed not to tell anyone about the pregnancy until she passed her first trimester. Wow, her life was never going to be the same.

"Aunt Maddy." Chelsea's youngest, Brie, who was five, threw herself on Madison.

"Oh, sweetie." Chelsea pulled Brie back. "You have to be careful with Aunt Maddy. Hey, Troy."

"Hi." Troy smiled at her, and Chelsea returned a small one but kept her gaze on him for a bit. She seemed to suspect his good mood. Hopefully, she'd just credit it to Madison's return to the world of the conscious.

"Jim would have been here," Chelsea started, "but—"

"I understand," Madison assured her, finding her voice better than before, but her throat still hurt, and her mind was fuzzy. Jim, her brother-in-law, would be at work. She'd love to be working herself.

"You going to be okay, Auntie Maddy?" Brie's eyes were wide and wet.

Madison ran a hand over her head. "I'll be just fine, sweetie." Looking into her niece's little face had Madison putting a hand tenderly over her lower abdomen.

"You sure?" Brie's voice was a like a baby bird's, soft but chirping, insistent on answers.

"I am." Madison attempted a smile, but pain bolted through her.

"Make room for your sisters," Chelsea told Brie.

She obeyed her mother, and Marissa, the eldest, came over and kissed Madison on the forehead.

"Glad you're okay," Marissa said.

Marissa changed places with Lacey, and her third niece kissed her on the forehead too.

She was feeling so blessed to have these beautiful girls in her life. She'd always loved being an aunt and watching them grow into their own individuals. Marissa was always more mature than her years, like she housed the spirit of an old soul. Lacey was quiet, and Brie was the troublemaker. Fire sparked and crackled in her eyes.

Chelsea addressed Troy. "Did the doctor say how she is?"

"I'm right here," Madison said, managing to get it out in one breath. She hated being talked about like she wasn't there. Terry and Cynthia did it enough.

"Sorry." Chelsea laughed.

Brie was back at Madison's side and holding her hand.

"So?" Chelsea prompted.

Madison gestured for Troy to go ahead.

"She has a couple bruised ribs," Troy started. "They're going to keep her for observation until Friday, and if all looks good, she can go home."

Chelsea brushed a hand in Madison's hair. If Madison had been in any condition to hug, it was certain her younger sister would have squeezed her. "So lucky." She glanced at Troy. "Did you find the hit-and-run driver yet?"

Hit-and-run... Madison went cold.

"No." Troy stiffened and looked at Madison. "But you can rest assured I will."

"It's disgusting that someone would do that." Chelsea's tone was sharp and indignant.

Blurred images. A black smudge. A face. But whose? It wouldn't come into focus, just teetering on the edge of her consciousness. A searing pain buzzed in her temple. She put a hand there.

"Madison's car is a write-off," Troy said. "Whoever hit her had to inflict damage on their vehicle. Could be hurt themselves. We'll find them."

"A truck." In her head, she'd screamed, but her voice returned to her ears at the volume of a whisper.

Troy moved closer to her. "You saw who did this?"

"Yes. No. I don't know."

Chelsea offered a smile of sympathy.

"What do you remember?" Troy asked.

"Not much."

"A color of the vehicle maybe?"

"Black." Answered on instinct. The black smudge.

"Any plate? Even a partial?"

She shook her head, though she kept the movement small and deliberate, not in any hurry to find out what else hurt. It was the face haunting her—she knew the driver, but her mind wasn't cooperating.

"Anything else?" Troy asked.

There were several suspects who could be responsible. She and Terry could have gotten too close to Carson's killer. Then there was the mob, the mystery woman, Roman Petrov himself, and the corrupt cops. But she couldn't think about bringing all that up right now. Her mind was so groggy. "No."

"It's okay." Troy put a reassuring hand on her shoulder. "We'll figure it out. I'm going to call in about it being a black truck so people from the department know what we're looking for." Troy kissed her and left the room, his cell phone to his ear.

On his way out, Terry came in.

"There she is," he said. He was holding a bouquet of flowers in a vase.

"You didn't have to get me flowers," she said.

"I wanted to. Ah, where should I— Hi, Chelsea, girls."

"Hi," her nieces chorused.

"Hi, Terry," Chelsea said. "Here, give it to me."

Terry handed her the flowers, and Chelsea made room on the already crowded table in front of the window. Madison hadn't even noticed the smell until then or all the flowers around the room.

"Thanks," Madison said to Terry.

"Don't mention it." He stayed at the end of the bed, like he was afraid to get any closer. He met her gaze and pressed his lips, and she had a feeling.

"This isn't your fault."

"Logically, I know that, but if I didn't call you back to the station…" His voice petered out and disappeared.

"I was the one who—" Madison stopped talking there, a snippet of her memory seemed to have been misfiring. She couldn't remember...

Chelsea, Terry, and her nieces were all watching her.

"I'm just tired, guys."

"Yeah, we should get going," Chelsea said, holding out her hand toward Brie and flexing her fingers for her daughter to take it, which she did. "I'll stop by later," her sister said as the phone on the side table rang. Chelsea's eyes dipped to it. "I called Mom." Chelsea grabbed it and answered, "Madison Knight's room.... Yes, she's going to be just fine. Doctor's keeping her for a couple more days." Chelsea looked at Madison. "Yeah, here she is." She handed Madison the receiver and waved goodbye. Why did it feel like another hit-and-run?

"Hi, Mom," Madison said and mouthed *Sorry* to Terry.

"Sweetie, are you okay? You have bruised ribs and they put you in a coma, but you're fine now, right? Should I come up? I told your father we should get on the next plane—"

"I'm fine, Mom." She had to use a steely tone, or her message would go right over her mother's head. It still might. She tended to only hear what she wanted.

"You're sure you're—"

Madison rubbed her stomach, her thoughts on the baby growing inside her. The news would make her mother ecstatic, but she'd told Troy they'd wait to tell others, and she stood behind that. Anything could happen between now and delivery. "I'm fine, Mom. I promise."

"Okay, but if you want us there, we'll be on a plane immediately."

"I know, Mom." There was a time their relationship had been dicey. Every conversation was about Madison finding a man, settling down, having a family. That had finally eased up in recent months, and her mother even seemed to show Madison respect for what she had done to save Chelsea from the Russian Mafia hit man.

Terry dropped into the chair that Troy had vacated.

"Mom, I really should go. Terry's here."

"Okay." One word, and her mother sounded hurt.

"I can call you back later," Madison offered.

"Yes, okay, sweetie. Love you."

"Love you." Madison went to hang up, but the table was a little bit of a reach. "Terry—?"

"Yeah." He sprang into action and returned the receiver to the cradle. "Mothers, eh. So obsessed with how their daughters are after a serious accident."

She wanted to protest the serious part, but she had no recourse. Brain swelling, coma, bruised ribs. She was fortunate to be alive. Her fetus was fortunate. "I understand why she's concerned," she admitted. She was curious how Terry would react when he found she was pregnant. He'd probably be as excited as Troy, but he'd also find it extremely amusing. But enough thinking about that. "You catch Carson's killer yet?" She struggled to sit up and found she didn't have the strength. Her body was rebelling.

"Don't you worry about—"

"You know me better than that. You were telling me that Carson suspected her boss of insurance fraud." How could things from before the accident be so clear but the accident itself fuzzy? It hardly seemed fair. "Did you find any evidence?"

"Oh, yeah, we did. And Rossi will be going away for insurance fraud."

"But for the murder?"

Terry shook his head. "I pushed him hard, and his alibi holds."

"Did you get the files from Southern Life and see who Carson rejected?"

"We have the files, yes, but they still need to be worked through."

"Hey. I hope you're not talking about work. You should be getting rest." Cynthia flew into the room, nudged Terry out of the way. "Oh my God. Maddy, I got here as soon as I could. I'm sorry it wasn't sooner." She held out a teddy bear and angled him left and right as if he were dancing and defying gravity.

"Oh? For me?" Madison cooed dramatically. "You shouldn't have." She laughed but kept it shallow.

Cynthia grimaced. "You're in a lot of pain."

"You could say that, but nothing I can't handle."

"No, of course not. Bulldog can handle anything and everything." Troy swept up on her right and put an arm on the bed over her head.

"You know I don't—" Madison stopped talking when she looked up and met his gaze. His green eyes, though tired and bloodshot, still seemed to sizzle with life. She reached for his hand. She was going to point out yet again that she wasn't a huge fan of his nickname for her, but right now that man could call her whatever he wanted. She was carrying his baby. Even if she repeated that a million times it would feel surreal.

"On the way in a nurse told me visiting hours are over in a few minutes. How do they expect everyone to stop by—" She paused there and took in all the flowers. "I see people from the department have been by."

"Just you and Terry," Madison said.

"Lots of people were here, Maddy," Troy corrected. "You just didn't know. When the accident first happened, the waiting room was over capacity. Many had to wait outside due to regulations."

She smiled, feeling warm at people's concern for her well-being. "Sergeant Winston?"

"Yep, he was here." Troy pointed to a vase of daisies. "Those are from him."

"The sergeant bought me flowers. Wow, who would have thought I'd see the day?"

"Room for one more?" Andrea Fletcher entered the room, carrying an arrangement in a square vase consisting of flowers Madison didn't recognize.

"Hi." Madison smiled at her, the future aunt to her child, the current police chief.

"Oh, honey, how are you?" Andrea was always so immaculately put together. Small, pointed facial features accentuated with modestly applied makeup—pale-pink lipstick and muted brown eyeshadow. Her long, straight brown hair was pulled back into a ponytail, and bangs framed her face.

Tears pooled in Madison's eyes and she cursed herself, but exhaustion was also toying with her emotions. "I'm going to be fine." She bit back the urge to say the baby would be too. "Thank you for the flowers. They're beautiful."

"Not a problem at all." Andrea set them on a table, put a hand on her brother's shoulder, and acknowledged Cynthia and Terry with a dip of her head.

The nurse from before popped into the room. "Visiting time is over."

"Love you, Madison," Cynthia told her.

"Love you," she chorused back.

Terry waved goodbye and tried to sneak out. "Hey, I'll be calling," she told him. "Just because I'm in this bed doesn't mean I'm off the job."

"Ah, yes, it does," Troy said. "It's bad enough that you're working all the time. Saturday nights, Sundays…"

Her partner's gaze flicked to hers, and in that instant, she realized Terry had picked up on Troy's saying she'd worked Saturday night. Her partner knew she'd cut out on him Saturday night. Now he'd be curious why.

Andrea left, and the nurse said to Troy, "You, too, Mr. Matthews."

"I'd rather stay."

"I'll be fine, Troy," Madison said. "Go home and get some sleep."

He held eye contact with her for some time. "I'll be back first thing in the morning."

"I have no doubt."

"Okay." He kissed her, hugged her, and left. But if she knew that man at all, he wouldn't be crawling into bed; he'd be hunting down that black pickup, even if he had to search every garage and body shop in Stiles.

Thirty-Six

I t took a lot of convincing and negotiation, but Madison finally got Troy to leave her side and go into work the next day. By the time he'd left, it was nearing ten thirty, according to her cell phone. She'd spent enough hours in the hospital bed, but as long as she was stuck there, she could still do something.

She started with her voicemail, but it didn't hold much excitement. There was just one message from Dr. Talmadge's office telling her to call. She was certain it was to inform her she was pregnant, but life had served the news another way. She made the call anyway just to completely rule out any fears of cancer. It turned out they were just wanting to notify her of the pregnancy. *Just.* As if it wasn't going to change everything.

Next, she selected Terry from her contacts list. Surely, she could work the investigation from the hospital if she had to, but she'd at least like some updates.

Terry answered on the third ring. "Maddy?"

"I need you to bring me something to do. A laptop from the station, maybe some of Carson's journals or access to those files that were unlocked."

There was silence on his end.

"You there?"

"Yeah, but shouldn't you be resting?"

"Just get in here. I'm going mad." With that, she hung up, trusting that Terry would appease her and come in.

But what she really wanted was to get out of the hospital and back to her life. She adjusted her position and groaned in agony at the pain emanating from her ribs. They would have had her on medication, but due to the baby, it probably wasn't as high—or as powerful—a dose as would have been preferred.

And all she craved was a cup of hot coffee, regardless of whether or not she'd be able to keep it down. It was hard to focus in on how her stomach felt with her other injuries having her foremost attention.

She still couldn't remember too much about the accident. The images were only surfacing as blurred and disconnected. Beyond her conviction that it was a black truck, she couldn't recall much else—except for probably the most important factor. She'd recognized the driver. But every time she tried to concentrate and bring the face into focus, her head would throb.

She even tried to conjure all the potential players—the people who could have wanted her injured or worse. The same suspects kept recycling in her mind. Someone related to the Carson murder, the corrupt cops, the mob, or Roman Petrov himself.

Had he even died? It wasn't unthinkable that he'd staged his death, but why return to the same name? He was an arrogant bastard though, and his death had been on record for over twenty years. He might have supposed enough time had passed. A man like Roman could have many reasons for wanting to fake his death, but the foremost that Madison could think of was to escape prison. Again, it circled back to why use that name again? *If* this Roman Petrov was *the* Roman Petrov.

"Why can't you just sleep?" Terry entered the room with a laptop under his arm and a charging cable in hand.

"Oh, come on. Where's the fun in that?" She pushed the button on her bed to sit up straighter, changed her mind and angled it a bit more again. Gravity wasn't her friend right now.

"You know if Troy finds out—"

"He won't find out, and even if he does, he's not my boss."

Terry looked away.

"You're afraid of Troy."

He met her eyes and pinched his fingers on his free hand. "Just a little."

She laughed, then stopped abruptly and gripped her side. "You really—"

"You want me to leave?"

"Come on, don't be like that." She held out her hands to receive the laptop and the cord.

"Let me set it up right for you." He put the computer on the wheeled table used for her water and meals, then proceeded to hunt for an outlet, plugged it in, and tugged the charging end through the handle on the bed and wound it there. "Ready for when you need it. Just a feeling, but I'm sure you'll run the battery dry."

"Thank you."

"Uh-huh. Now, I better get going before a nurse gives me the boot."

"Oh, no, not until you update me."

Terry looked over his shoulder to the doorway, and Madison suspected he must have snuck past the nursing station. He took a deep breath that lifted his shoulders and sat in the chair to her right.

"How did things pan out with John Clayton and his knives?" she asked.

"He didn't do it. At least we can't put him in the area of the attack, and the knives from the Pig King and his apartment aren't a match for the stainless in Carson's wound."

"So you had to cut him loose."

"Yeah."

"Was the stainless steel ever linked to a specific brand of knife?"

"Nope. Just run-of-the-mill."

"Okay, well, we keep moving forward. Do we know the con man's real name yet?"

"You'd be the first to know…well, after me."

It was disappointing and frustrating it was taking so long to find Abbott. She'd checked her email just before her voicemail, and she still hadn't heard back from the prison on Long's cellmates. "And what about Shannon…" She couldn't bring her last name to mind.

"Shannon Keller. Nothing's turned up on her."

"Don't tell me it's another fake name? Did you try a reverse search using the address she rented from Stevens to see what name kicked back?"

"Yeah, and no luck. Just the landlord Jerrod Stevens."

"If we could find her, she could possibly lead us to Abbott."

"Yes," Terry dragged out, "but you're missing the part where I can't track her down."

Madison tried to think about how to go about finding this Shannon woman. "What if we got ahold of Keller's rent checks? Maybe the account's still active and the bank will have her number and her current address."

"Okay, I can give that a try." Terry pointed to the laptop. "I loaded all the unlocked files from Carson's hard drive that seem to pertain to Abbott."

"And nothing with his real name?"

Terry shook his head. "Not that I could find. I don't think that Carson uncovered that before she died."

"Huh," was all she said, but she was thinking that it might poke a hole in their theory of Carson confronting Abbott. Even if she had proof of his conning other women—if he had—there'd need to be a real name to charge him with the crimes.

"Anyway, I really need to go." Terry got up, was midway to the door and turned. "How are you doing anyway?"

"I'll be fine. You know it."

"Suppose I wouldn't expect anything else. Take care, and I'll stay in touch. I know you will." He smirked and left the room.

She turned on the laptop, and as she waited for the log-in screen, she recalled Terry's question about how she was doing. Honestly, she didn't want to give it too much thought. She was going to be a mother, and it didn't matter how many times that reality slammed into her consciousness, it was hard to process.

Having something else to occupy her mind was going to be a blessing.

She went to the file manager and got to work. There were several text files and quite a few JPEGs. She clicked on the first one and arrowed from one to the next. It was definitely Saul Abbott based on the picture Lana had provided them. The shots were taken at different times of day, in various locations that she couldn't readily identify. After she rolled through them, she put her attention on Carson's text documents. There were eleven files, and she started with a file called *Deceived*.

When it opened, Madison was faced with a list of names. A quick comparison told her they matched the file names. She guessed that *Deceived* was the master overview file with the others providing more individualized information. She scanned the women's names: Maria Barker, Melody Anderson, Natalie Reese, Margie Torres, Linda Chapman, Elizabeth Evans, Kathy Burke, Erica Murray, Hannah Wade, and Jane Maxwell.

Madison opened the file labeled *Reese*. As suspected, it was a background file on the woman. When she started dating Abbott, for how long, details of their relationship, how much he took her for. Reese had started seeing Abbott nine and a half years ago, not long after he got out of prison, according to Carl Long. Abbott hadn't wasted any time getting to work, but Madison wondered what had sent Abbott to prison in the first place.

The other files were much of the same information.

She read until her eyes got heavy and she couldn't resist closing them anymore. She slipped into a deep, dreamless slumber.

Thirty-Seven

Madison couldn't get out of the hospital fast enough. It was Friday evening, and she and Troy were still waiting on the final word from Dr. Hunt on whether she was clear to leave.

"I still can't believe that you've been working from your bed," Troy groaned.

He had discovered her yesterday, fast asleep, with the table and laptop still in front of her. He'd moved the computer to the farthest point on the nightstand. She'd have to get out of bed to reach it. Not a problem, but the fact that Troy stuck to her side was.

But even with him next to her for hours on end, she couldn't get herself to bring up the ring. It already felt like there was a sizzling, underlying tension between them, and she didn't feel like fanning it to spark. Troy also seemed to be avoiding the topic of the accident. Likely because he had no leads and didn't want to pressure her. Her memories of the accident weren't much clearer, but as Hunt told her, it was common for temporary amnesia in the case of traumatic injury. She just wished that she could conjure the driver's face. She couldn't shake the feeling that she knew who it was. In fact, she was sure of it. But the *who* continued to evade her.

"Then again," he went on, "I shouldn't be surprised, but I will be having a talk with Terry. Even Winston told you to rest and take all the time you need."

Sergeant Winston had dropped by again during visiting hours last night. Troy had been around to hear his admonition. Madison took Winston's words to mean that because she was a woman, he expected she'd be too weak to show up for days or weeks.

"So I called Estelle," Troy began. "I told her we're looking for a four-bedroom with a decent-size yard."

"Please tell me you didn't say anything about…" Madison couldn't bring herself to say *baby*. She'd had a couple days to come to grips with the pregnancy, but she still found that she was detached from the idea. There was a part of her mind that had shifted it into an alternate reality.

"No, of course not. We promised not to tell anyone until after your first trimester."

"That's right."

"Anyway, as soon as you're feeling up for it, she has a few places in mind for us to take a look at."

"Wonderful." She did her best to infuse as much excitement into the word as she could, but it came out sounding like someone was tugging down on it, sapping it of its typical mirth.

"You do still want that?" he asked, his normal confidence missing.

"Yes, of course." She put her hand on his forearm. She hoped as she peered into his eyes that he wouldn't ask the same question about the baby. It was going to change their lives, flip them upside down. And how she hated parents who blamed their children for everything— from being late for things to making their life more arduous. After all, they chose to have kids…or did they? There were probably a lot of mothers and fathers out there who had been in the same place as she and Troy with baby being a surprise. Troy had put it that way, and she thought how much better *surprise* sounded than *mistake*, which implied the child wasn't wanted. And everyone loved surprises. At least it had a more positive connotation to it. "How is Estelle, by the way?" she asked, trying to shift her thoughts from the baby.

"She's doing all right. She's worried about you."

Dr. Hunt came into the room, and Madison tried to read him as she sat straighter. It still hurt to move, but the drugs and rest must have been working because she wasn't in quite as much pain.

"All right, so I have all your test results back," he began. "I feel confident in releasing you, but you need to take it easy."

"When can I go back to work?" she blurted out.

The doctor smiled at Troy. "You were right."

"I have a case that needs my attention," she said, earning the doctor's gaze again.

"I'm sure Terry and others in the department can handle it," Troy said.

She faced him. "I don't want others to handle my case."

"You don't need to keep such a tight hold on—"

"I do," she ground out, her heart racing.

Troy shook his head and clenched his jaw.

"Remember the baby," the doctor said. "This is your first, and it's important to take good care of yourself, especially at the beginning. Or have you decided to terminate?"

Madison looked at Troy. "I'm keeping the baby." It was an instinctive response, even if it went against what she thought she wanted. There was a definitive line for her, though, between not necessarily wanting a child and aborting one.

Troy nodded and smiled. "I agree."

"Well then, congratulations to both of you."

"You said to take care of myself, but I can walk and move around?"

"Yes, of course. Just no running."

"No worry there." She smirked at Troy. "And I can also talk, right?" She had a purpose for the pointed questions.

"Yes, of course."

"Then I don't see why I can't do my job." She looked at Troy, not for permission, but ready to defend herself if need be. She had no intention of letting this baby run her life after she gave birth, and she certainly wasn't going to have it dictate everything while growing inside her.

"I see you're a police detective," Dr. Hunt said gingerly. "It's probably quite a stressful job."

"I've been doing it for a lot of years," she said, as if that made it easier.

The doctor glanced from her to Troy, back to her.

"There can be a lot of pressure," she admitted. "But I can manage."

"And if you can't?" Troy interjected.

She met his gaze, and his concern softened her core. "Then I'll pull back." At least that was what she'd said. She might be pregnant and on medication, but the driver of that pickup had put her in the hospital. What was their intent— to injure or to kill? She needed the answers, and she was more driven than ever to find them.

Thirty-Eight

The house smelled like a funeral home and looked like a flower shop. Chelsea and Cynthia came out of the kitchen and told her that casseroles were in the fridge and to call if there was anything she needed.

"I mean it," Cynthia repeated at the entry before leaving, and Madison had this horrible cinch in her chest. Her mind kept coming back to Garrett Murphy returning to the lab. What if he had noticed the mystery woman's face on Cynthia's monitor and felt threatened? Had he been the driver who struck her?

"Thanks," she said.

Troy closed the door behind her, and the house felt so quiet with them gone—except for her mind, which was whirling. She really could use Hershey's fur, but he wasn't there. "Where's Hershey?"

"At the kennel. I figured having him around might be too much for now."

She nodded, but Hershey never felt like any amount of work to her, and she missed the little guy. Troy must have been thinking he'd need to take care of her, and having Hershey there as well would be a lot. "You know I'm fine, right?"

Troy met her gaze, and in his eyes, she witnessed how exhausted he was.

"Never mind," she conceded. "You're probably right, and you've been through a lot too. You must have been scared."

"If I were you, I'd say something similar to 'more than I'd like to admit.'"

"Seriously? As if I'm the only one in our relationship who holds back their true feelings."

"I am one hundred percent open with you, Maddy. I have been from the beginning."

She wanted to contest his claim. The ring hidden away in the laundry closet proved he wasn't as open as he was trying to present himself. Then again, maybe he was still planning to pop the question. If so, why not after finding out about the baby? It would have been the perfect time to seal the commitment of their relationship, but maybe he didn't want to force it. Really, she could spin with all the hypotheticals.

He helped get her positioned on the couch with a pillow at her back and her legs along the length of the couch and over his lap. He started to rub her feet.

She closed her eyes. "You can do that forever."

"Then I'm not doing it right." He kneaded his knuckles a little harder into her soles.

"Ouch."

"You have a lot of tension down here for someone who's been lying on their ass for a few days."

At first, she heard *lying their ass off*. It was moments when she was alone with Troy that guilt ate her, gnawing her bones, sucking her marrow. She had never exactly lied to him. More like omissions or white lies, saying she was working. He'd think she meant a murder case, but his assumptions weren't her responsibility.

Troy stopped the foot massage, rested his hands on her shins, and let out a deep breath.

"You all right there?" she asked.

He smiled at her. An expression she used to nearly beg for him to show popped up often and easily since the baby news. His enthusiasm over their child made her feel like a charlatan.

"Things are going to change a lot around here," he said, confirming his mind was on the baby.

"They sure are." She wanted to amuse him and talk about their future, but she would rather close her eyes and plug her ears to the pregnancy. Nothing against the baby, but she'd never planned on being a mother. Maybe if she switched the subject… "No luck on finding the truck that hit me yet?" A throwaway question and a poor attempt at conversation. Troy would have told her if he'd had any news.

"Not yet. I have local collision centers and body shops on the lookout. Whoever struck you could have taken their truck outside the city though. Who knows? So…I was thinking I could order in some Chinese."

Apparently, he didn't want to talk about the lack of progress. "It's been a long time. But didn't Chelsea and Cynthia bring food?"

"They sure did." They met each other's eyes and laughed. She clutched her side.

It felt good not being the one on the receiving end of cooking insults for a change.

"I'll call." Troy patted her leg and got up from the couch. He paced the room as he placed their order.

While the thought of real food that didn't come from a hospital cafeteria sounded like heaven, she couldn't wait for life to return to a relative normal, even if that period would only last until the baby's arrival.

"Food should be here in forty minutes." He pocketed his phone and returned to the couch.

"Which means ten." Their local Chinese food restaurant was always at their door faster than their estimate.

"Interested in watching some TV?" He picked up the remote and flicked the television on without waiting for her answer. "Anything you want to watch, name it."

"*An Affair to Remember.*" She suggested the chick flick just for a reaction.

"Okay, anything but that."

She smiled. "I'm good with anything. But sports," she amended.

He found a sitcom they typically both enjoyed, and they settled in for at least the ten minutes Madison had predicted before there was a knock on the door.

Thirty-Nine

Being with Troy last night had felt like it had before Cynthia's wedding and the AWOL proposal. Too bad Madison's actions this morning might jeopardize everything. She'd slipped out of bed at a few minutes after four, careful not to wake Troy, who was breathing heavily, his mind playing somewhere in dreamland. If Hershey had been home, it would have been much more difficult to sneak out.

She took Troy's Expedition instead of a cab because she didn't want a driver hanging around for what she had planned. She just hoped Troy stayed asleep until she returned home.

It was still pitch black out when she drove to Garrett Murphy's house. She knew the addresses for Murphy and the Phelps brothers off the top of her head.

Murphy's was a bungalow. No garage. The driveway had a blue sedan parked at an angle. There was no pickup truck—black or any other color.

She tapped the wheel of the Expedition. What had she really expected—that the truck that hit her would be sitting there for the world to see? Maybe she was really losing it to think Murphy was behind the hit-and-run. Even if he saw the woman's picture on the Cynthia's monitor, it didn't mean he was homicidal. And while she could go into the station and confirm if Murphy or the Phelps brothers owned a black pickup, searching vehicle registrations would come with questions she didn't want to answer. If only she could put the truck in one of their driveways or garages and build her case from there.

She next drove to Dustin Phelps's place. It was a gorgeous home in a pricey neighborhood, but it went with the showy display and pretense Dustin liked to exhibit. He had his kids in expensive private schools and his mother in a Club Med retirement home. He was crooked, of that she was sure, but apparently had no qualms about flashing his blood money.

Dustin had a double-car garage and the driveway was empty. The pickup could have been in the garage. How was she supposed to—

She growled as the idea went through her head. The accident must have inflicted some damage if she thought she could just trespass. It was the type of neighborhood where everyone was preoccupied with their neighbors—time of day probably didn't matter—not out of concern but out of nosiness. They wanted to make sure everyone was following some list of imposed standards, such as how short to cut one's grass, how often, whether the yard was raked or the snow cleared, and when to put up Christmas lights and take them down. Everyone probably knew their neighbors' business.

Regardless, she parked a street over and cut the engine. Every step shot pain through her, but she pushed it aside, focused on her goal.

She reached Dustin's house and slunk up the driveway, thankful she'd had another black hoodie in her dresser to wear tonight. And at that thought, she gasped. Her car was a total write-off, but had the items in her trunk, her black clothing and camera, been handed over to Troy? He hadn't asked her about any of it, but she could have easily dismissed the clothing as being backup. The camera's presence could be a little harder to explain, but if it had made it back to him, at least there'd be no images for him to find on the memory card.

She made it to the garage. It had six rectangular windows across the top, but they were far too high for her to see through without a ladder.

She walked the side of the garage and found a man door. She put her hand on the knob, about to twist, but a place like this was probably wired with an alarm.

She should just leave. Hell, she could be on some surveillance video at this moment. Dustin Phelps could be inside watching her and laughing his ass off. But if he was, too late for her. She might as well keep going.

She went around to the back of the garage, through an unlocked gate, and found a window.

She leaned forward to peer inside, careful not to touch the window. She'd worked a case where a palm print on glass had factored into the investigation.

It was darker inside than it was outside. Though what did she expect? For it to be lit up? Her mind really wasn't working that great.

The window appeared easy to breach, but if she did, again there was risk of setting off an alarm. Heck, for all she knew, a rent-a-cop was on his way already.

How was she supposed to confirm whether he had the truck in the garage? She had to get inside.

She touched the windowpane, and a light turned on in the house to her left.

Shit! Shit! Shit!

Getting caught snooping was the last thing she wanted. She creeped around the side of the garage and hightailed it down the driveway and returned to the Expedition.

She got behind the wheel. Her head was pounding, and she should be in bed, following the doctor's orders to rest, but how could she

let whoever hit her just get away with it? She
had a third house she wanted to visit: the one
belonging to Joel Phelps, Dustin's brother.

She headed to his address.

She practically slammed the brakes when she
saw a black pickup in his drive. Goose bumps
crawled down her arms. Could this be the one
that hit her?

She parked a block away and walked, hoodie
up, head down. Every step she took was more
painful than the last, but she had to hurry and
get this over with, preferably while not being
spotted. She gripped her sides, her bruised ribs
throbbing.

Get this over with and get home, she coached
herself.

She went up Joel's driveway and rounded the
front of the truck. It had a chrome grille guard.

She pulled out her phone and ran its flashlight
over the nose of the vehicle. And there it was—a
speck of blue, barely noticeable, embedded in a
scratch mark on the grille guard. Could it be the
paint from her Mazda?

*A sudden impact. A loud crunch. Dizziness
and shock. A black smudge in the darkness. The
familiar face...* Her legs buckled beneath her,
and she reached for the truck to keep upright.
She was finally sure who had been behind the
wheel. She had seen him. And this truck had
been the one that hit her!

Her hands shook as she snapped pictures of the damage and license plate as quickly as possible. Finished, she hurried out of there, wincing through gritted teeth at the blinding pain from her ribs.

When she returned home, the house was silent. She changed in the second bedroom and tucked the clothing she'd worn out into a drawer of a nightstand and slipped into the master. She breathed with relief. It was quiet except for the sound of Troy's deep breathing. He was still asleep.

She got under the sheets and stared at the ceiling. No one was going to believe her when she told them who hit her vehicle and ran.

Forty

At some point Madison must have drifted off, because when she next opened her eyes, the sun was streaming in around the bedroom curtains. Her body was also extremely sore, and it felt like she went rounds in a ring with a professional boxer. Her early-morning sleuthing probably hadn't been the wisest decision, but it had paid off. It jogged her memory loose. She knew who the driver was and found the truck that hit her car.

She looked over to Troy's side of the bed, but he wasn't there. She touched the sheets, and they were cool, so he would have left a while ago.

She struggled out of bed. Every movement hurt, but staying put wasn't going to make anything better. She staggered down the hall, making a brief stop at the bathroom, then carried on to the living room.

"There she is." Troy was eating a bowl of cereal in front of the TV.

Have I fallen into the twilight zone? "Since when do you watch TV in the morning? And what time is it anyhow?"

"Just after nine." Troy muted the television and set his bowl on the coffee table; the spoon clattered against the ceramic. "And in answer to your other question... Since I have the day off work."

She didn't know what to touch on first—his unusual behavior of parking on the couch even on a day off or the fact he didn't have to go into work. "I thought you were scheduled for today?"

"I was, but I put in a request to take the weekend off. And considering all we've been through, my sergeant approved it. Besides, I need to take care of my girl." He got up and wrapped his arms around her, doing so gingerly, and kissed her.

"I don't need you to take care of me. I'm fine." She bit back the strong urge to wince as fire burned in her abdomen.

He pressed his lips and angled his head. "Sure seems like it."

"I mean it, Troy."

He held eye contact with her, and his eyes darkened. The slight frown also told her he liked the thought of taking care of her and hated being dismissed. But she was injured, not an invalid.

"What I really need is for the person who hit me to be held responsible," she said. It felt like an impossible riddle to sort out, knowing who struck her and how to communicate that to Troy. He'd ask questions she wouldn't want to answer, and she didn't know how to say it had been Garrett Murphy without disclosing her side mission..

"Don't think I'm not working on that from the couch. I have the guys still going by body shops."

By *guys* she was aware he meant his friends and the officers who reported to him on his SWAT team.

"And Terry came forward with some ideas too. People who surfaced in your murder investigation."

Right, she'd thought of that but must have failed to verbalize the list. The accident and medication were affecting her mind more than she'd like. "All cleared?"

"Yep." Troy grabbed his bowl and headed toward the kitchen. "Coffee?"

"I can get it myself." Whether she should be drinking it was another matter.

He spun. "As you keep telling me. Apparently, you don't need me for anything."

"Troy, that's not—"

He clenched his jaw.

"A coffee would be nice," she consented, "but I shouldn't."

"Well, it's a good thing I'm here to take care of you because I picked up some decaf after we found out about the baby."

He really was a keeper. "Thank you. That would be great."

"Just sit on the couch, and I'll bring it to you. That is, if you want."

She acquiesced. Maybe it wasn't so bad having someone take care of her.

A short time later, he returned with a glass of water, a coffee, a couple pills, and an apple on a tray. He set it on the table in front of her and sat next to her on the couch.

She pointed to the fruit and raised her eyebrows.

"I know you're not a fan of anything healthy, but you should start watching your diet."

She narrowed her eyes.

He held up a hand. "Not a comment about weight."

"Yeah, I thought you were smarter than that." She smiled at him.

"You just have to think about the baby now."

The baby… It wasn't a decision she could reverse or a purchase she could return. She'd accepted the pregnancy but hadn't yet embraced it. "You're right, and it's probably why I should tough out the pain." She flicked a finger toward the pills.

"The doctor said you're safe to take what he prescribed."

She nodded but didn't make a move for the medication.

"So…" Troy rubbed his hands together. "I was thinking we could binge Netflix all day. There seems to be a lot of hype out there about doing that. Maybe we should give it a go?"

"Not sure we're the binging type." Unless it was chocolate—that she could get behind.

"We could be today."

She should probably just leave all talk of the accident alone. After all, they had moved on, but it was hard to let it go when all she wanted to do was walk up to Garrett Murphy and strangle him. "We're not getting anywhere at all with finding the truck?"

Troy sighed. "There are over three hundred black pickups in Stiles. A make or model could help narrow that down." He watched her expectantly.

Could she tell him it was a GMC Sierra? That it was currently sitting in Joel Phelps's driveway? She could claim the memory resurfaced about make and model but giving its location would be impossible without coming clean about her actions that morning. But she couldn't let Murphy get away with what he'd done. She grabbed the pills and downed them with a swig of water.

"Maddy, if you know something you're not telling me, or suspect someone, please talk to me."

She met his gaze. Maybe she should just come clean.

"Maddy, I know you left the house."

"I…I… How?"

"I woke up, and you weren't in bed. I got up to check on you and noticed my Expedition was gone."

Just when she thought she got away with her little outing. "I did leave the house," she admitted.

"Where did you go?"

"That part…" She took a few deep breaths. "That part's a little tougher to explain."

"Seeing as we have all this newfound time on our hands…" He turned the TV off. After a few seconds of silence, he pushed out, "Tell me, Madison."

She bristled at the full expulsion of her name and his baritone. "I'm quite sure I remember the driver's face."

"What?" He shifted on the couch. "Do you know who it was?"

Tears pooled in her eyes.

"You do."

"I know this is going to sound crazy." To anyone other than her anyway. She'd already suspected this person was bad news before the hit-and-run. Maybe she should give Troy some credit. He knew of her suspicions about Dustin Phelps about a month ago; he'd even had a front-row seat to his bribing a witness to provide false testimony. He was there for her to correct the wrong.

"Maddy?"

"Garrett Murphy."

Troy remained quiet for several seconds, then, "He's a cop."

"I'm aware of that." *Not that he deserves the badge!*

"Why would he hit you?"

The question she feared he'd ask, but maybe she could just skirt around it. "I don't know."

Troy's forehead wrinkled up like he had a migraine and the light in the room was too bright. "And why hit you *and* run?"

"Again, I don't know."

"I'm going to ring his—" He went to get up, and she caught his arm and held him back. Her ribs bit, and she cried out in pain. He took her hand and stayed on the couch. "I'll just question him."

With his statement, her mind raised another concern. Maybe Troy would be safer knowing what he was potentially getting involved in, but then again, ignorance could protect him. "What if I told you I also remember the plate now…well, part of it." Technically the truth. The picture of the entire thing was on her phone, but she could recall the first few digits. She told him what they were, and he sprang from the couch.

"Where are you going?" she asked.

"You're all right here?"

"I'm fine, but—"

"I'm going to have a word with Murphy."

She got up and went to him. "But you're going to verify the plate first, right? Do your thing and go in prepared?" She felt her cheeks flush at her last question.

"Why? Do you think he was driving someone else's truck?" Troy sounded skeptical, not that she blamed him given the information he was going on.

"I mean, it's possible, right?" It just occurred to her now, but plates could be fake or switched. She should have taken a picture of the vehicle identification number, but it's not like she could have leaned over the truck's hood and peeked through the windshield like she could if it were a car. It was too high up.

"I guess so." Troy went down the hall, got dressed, and returned five minutes later. He stopped in front of her on the couch. "You sure you'll be—"

"I'm fine. And don't attack Murphy. I mean, I could have imagined it." Though she had no doubt it was him.

He scanned her eyes, and she hated what she saw in his. He was following the lead she'd provided but was fired more by emotion than conviction. "Okay." He kissed her cheek and headed for the door.

"Just be safe," she called out.

He stopped and turned. "I just want to put this to rest."

She could tell he still wasn't convinced Murphy was behind the hit-and-run. "Just keep in mind people can act out of character if it's to protect themselves." *Or their secrets,* she thought.

"I'll be fine." With that, he left.

Bless him for following up, even if he didn't fully believe her. The truth was in his eyes. He was appeasing her, but at the same time, he couldn't ignore what she was saying. If he had any clue that Murphy kept company with the mob and had run into her on purpose, he might kill the man. After all, Murphy could have not only killed her, but their baby.

Anger welled up inside of her. This had become very personal, and if she was going to protect her unborn child, she had to bring the whole lot down—and the sooner the better.

Forty-One

Madison grabbed the department laptop, ready to dig in. She needed to find out more about the numbered corporation connected to that Deer Glen neighborhood home and the Roman Petrov attached to it. She also wanted to get the mystery woman's identity once and for all. She'd just logged in, fingers poised over the keyboard ready to do some searches, when there was a knock on the door.

She answered and, at the sight of Terry, wished she was wearing something other than yoga pants and a sweatshirt. "What are you doing here?"

"Good morning to you, too." He brushed past her, holding a tray with two Starbucks coffee cups and a brown paper bag.

"I see you're at work already." He pointed to the laptop on the couch and backed out of his shoes.

"I am, but what are you doing here? It's Saturday."

"Ha-ha. Want to know the truth?" He handed her a cup, and she wished she could drink what he'd brought her. A caramel cappuccino—her favorite—and today it smelled divine. "I figured I'd catch you up before you harass me. More peaceful to be proactive," he added.

"Why start now?" She smiled at him and returned to the couch.

"Here. This is also for you." He gave her the bag.

"What is it?"

"Open it and find out." Before she got that far, he said, "A chocolate chip muffin."

"Ooh. Thank you." She pulled it from the bag and bit off a chunk from the top. When she lowered the baked good, her eyes landed on the apple, all shiny and healthy, staring back at her from the tray on the table. Judging her.

Terry sat on the couch beside her, unzipped his coat, and pulled out a folder. "I've got some big news."

"You put Carson's killer behind bars?" She would have loved to have played more of a role, but if Terry had apprehended Carson's murderer, she could focus on the mob and Murphy. Until the next murder case anyway.

"Not yet, but…" He removed a sheet from the file. "Meet Jake Elliott."

"And who's Jake—" She looked at the large photo of a man and recognized him instantly.

Terry took a drink of his Starbucks. "Meet our con man, previously known as Saul Abbott."

"How did you…" She skimmed the page and flipped it over. Double-sided, but only a partial background. "There's more that goes with this, right?"

"Yeah. In the folder." He made no move to retrieve the rest of the report.

"How did you find him? A hit with facial rec?"

Terry shook his head. "Unfortunately, for all the photos we had of him, none of them garnered a hit. But someone from the prison called looking for you and was told you were out. Their call got put through to me. Carl Long was cellmates with three men during his last year, one of whom was Jake Elliott." He took another draw on his drink.

There was a satisfaction that came with knowing his identity, but also a disappointment. "His name doesn't explain the GB written in blood."

"Unfortunately, no, and at this point, I'm still at a loss for its meaning."

"Still…" She sighed. "We need to find him and talk to him. You check out these addresses?"

He nodded. "No luck with any of them."

"Does Elliott have a phone we can trace?"

"None listed." Terry lifted his cup and took a big swallow.

"Huh. He probably uses a prepaid burner."

"I realize this guy's scum, but what would his motive be for killing Carson?"

"She has a lot on him," she said. "I only got started on the files you left me, but he conned ten women that Carson was aware of."

"Still, unless Elliott knew she was going to turn him in to the police, you'd think he'd want to stay clear of her."

"Yeah, but maybe Carson made that impossible. What did he go to prison for?"

"Get this. Assault."

"So he has a violent past." This wasn't boding well for his innocence and so much for Luke Landers's character testimony. "How long was his sentence?"

"Seven years."

"So the guy's not in his twenties now if he served some time alongside Carl Long." Even she could do that math. Long got out ten years ago and said Abbott/Elliott only beat him out by six months.

"Real age is thirty-eight. He was twenty-one when he went away."

She nodded. "Details of his crime?"

"He claimed self-defense, but it was bar fight that landed Elliott's opponent in the hospital with two broken legs."

"My God, we've got to find this guy. Where are we with tracking Shannon Keller?"

"I got a copy of a rent check from Stevens, and I've taken it to the bank, but they're not talking without a warrant. I didn't have you there to sweet-talk the clerk for information."

"Is the account still active?"

Terry shook his cup, likely to swirl the remaining liquid in hopes of it picking up some foam clinging to the sides. "Yes. I got that far, thank you very much. And the paperwork's started. Now we just wait."

Her mind was blank for other ways to track this guy down, but then she recalled the photos that Carson took. Surely among the hundreds of them, there was an area they could identify and stake out. She'd have to revisit them with a closer eye for any possible clues. She searched her memory for other angles of the case. "Did we ever get video footage from the city?" Another request that had fallen into a black hole. She never received a call back or an email.

"There was a hold up with it, but it should come through today." Terry set his cup on the table.

"Okay, so here's what I'm thinking. You review Carson's phone records. My interest is in the numbers she called in the last month. If she was going to confront Abbott—should I say, Jake Elliott—maybe she reached out to arrange a meetup. She could have played it nonchalant, like she missed him, and then brought up everything once they got together. And all this could be complete fabrication…" She was frustrated and had a headache.

"It's worth checking out. And you? I know you won't just be sitting around."

"I'll look at the pictures Carson took of Elliott. There has to be a clue in there somewhere as to his whereabouts." She was thinking it would have been nice if Carson had just documented these things, but then that would have made their job easy.

"All right. I'll keep you posted if I find anything." Terry got up.

"Thanks. Same here."

He pointed to her untouched cappuccino. "You feeling okay? I haven't seen you take a sip."

"Yep. We've just been busy talking."

"Okay," he said slowly and left. His empty cup remained on the table.

She got up and locked the door behind Terry. She was feeling torn and overwhelmed. She still intended to get Carson justice, but Madison could have been killed, along with her and Troy's baby. She could stick around home all day, doing her searches, and smacking into dead ends or she could follow through on one of her ideas. She could confront Murphy, but the situation called for some finesse, and she had sicced Troy on him. This left her free to pursue the Mafia angle, and she was quite sure that if it weren't for them, Murphy never would have done what he had. It was time to talk to Leland King and find out who the mystery woman was—once and for all. For her, for Troy, for their baby.

Forty-Two

Madison placed the call, arranged a meet in thirty minutes, and had a cab take her to the diner. She'd be early, but she'd also have time to select a table, hopefully in a corner and out of earshot of other patrons. She was seated in the same spot she had been a few weeks before when she'd met with Leland King about getting his help.

Leland walked through the doors, eyed her, and came over.

An attentive waitress was glued to his rear and handed out menus. "Can I get you started with coffees?"

"I'll have a ginger ale," she said and earned a quizzical look from King.

"I'll have a coffee. Black."

"You got it." The waitress winked at Leland.

"I shouldn't be here."

"I'm glad you are."

"Uh-huh. And I doubt I'll be staying long. What is it, Detective?"

There was a long history between the two of them, and the fact he addressed her by title said a lot. He was shut off and prepared to leave given the slightest provocation.

"I was in a bad hit-and-run earlier this week."

The waitress returned with their drinks and left.

Leland wrapped a hand around his mug but didn't take a sip. "You okay?"

"Just a couple bruised ribs." *Brain swelling, an induced coma, and oh! I'm pregnant!* But she wasn't getting into any of that. "I was lucky."

"What happened?"

"A truck slammed into the back of my car. Took off afterward."

He clenched his jaw, and his eyes glazed over, seeming to focus on nothing. "You haven't stopped looking into the corrupt cops or the mob." Not a question.

"You know I can't." She'd admit that much, but she wasn't going to get into how she'd intensified her efforts, even getting herself a headquarters of sorts.

"Well, I can't get involved. And you know why." He reluctantly met her gaze.

She held up a hand. "I know. I'm not asking you to. But I need to know if you found out something or know something you didn't share with me."

Leland took a long, slow draw on his coffee. "Just leave it alone, Maddy. Count your blessings that you walked away from the crash."

"Not a crash. A hit-and-run."

"Even more reason to let it go," he spat.

"I think they're feeling threatened."

"Sure. And you know what a wild animal does when it feels threatened? It kills."

"I lost nearly forty hours or so of my life to a coma. I'm done being Sleeping Beauty."

"If you keep pushing this, you could enter eternal rest."

"I know who hit me. I saw the driver."

Leland adjusted his posture, but he remained rigid and closed off.

"It was Garrett Murphy," she said.

He shook his head. "Don't know who that is."

"He's another corrupt officer I was going to have you investigate if…" She didn't need to finish. They both were aware of what followed *if*—if he hadn't received the threat against his mother. "He must have found out I was poking around, just as you were discovered looking into Phelps. I'm sure you know Dustin has a brother. His name is Joel, and he's a freelance writer for *Stiles Times*."

"I know him."

"I think he's the one who found out you were investigating his brother."

"I have no doubt. I already pieced that much together."

"Why didn't you say anything to me?"

"Because I thought you should leave it all the hell alone—both brothers, your efforts to ferret out corrupt cops, and your personal war on the Russians. And for the record, I still think you should."

"Well, I found the truck that hit me—"

"Why am I not surprised." Leland's knuckles were white around his mug.

"It was in Joel's driveway."

"But you saw this Murphy guy behind the wheel?"

"That's right. I'm just trying to figure out how to get him held accountable and find answers to some questions I have."

"I'll probably regret asking, but what are they?"

"In that picture you took, there was a woman. Shoulder-length brown hair. A lean, petite build. Do you know who she is?"

"Just walk away, Madison."

That firmed it up: he did know the woman's identity. "I followed her. She entered a house registered to a numbered company that tied back to Roman Petrov."

Leland's eyes flicked to hers, and his face became shadows. "It doesn't matter that I tell you to walk away, does it? You're not listening."

"He's still alive, isn't he?"

It seemed like several minutes before Leland spoke.

"He staged his death. He's in Russia, and that's about all I know. That and he makes his son Dimitre look like the tooth fairy. You don't mess with Roman." Leland's complexion paled in increments as he spoke. "Please, promise me you'll leave this alone." A genuine, heartfelt plea but one she couldn't honor.

"Leland, he's messed with me. If Murphy came after me because of the mob, the order came from somewhere higher up. We both know the mob doesn't make a habit of killing cops."

"Doesn't mean exceptions aren't made," he said somberly.

"That woman entered a house owned by him. Tell me who she is."

"I'll just tell you this. The mob is a family business."

A chill ran through her. "So she's his daughter, his lover, his—"

Leland shook his head. "His second cousin and star assassin. Tatiana Ivanova. You thought Constantine was a scary son of a bitch. Yeah, well she has him beat. And if she's in Stiles, something major is in the works. Guess you need to decide if bringing them down is worth the risk—and if you'll even survive long enough to do it."

She took a few deep breaths and put a hand on her stomach. She wasn't just gambling with her life anymore. Maybe she should leave it alone. If not for her sake, for her baby's.

Forty-Three

Madison watched King pull out of the diner's parking lot and took out her phone to call a cab, but it rang before she could get there. Caller ID told her it was Troy. He could be at their house. She answered, prepared to defend herself.

"Hey, how are you holding up?"

Guess he wasn't home. "Ah, good." She winced as a baby in the diner let out a loud wail, and she went outside. "Did you talk to Murphy?"

"Where are you?"

She opened her mouth, snapped it shut. There'd be no point in trying to convince him she was home. "Just stepped out."

"The doctor said—"

"I know what he said. That I can walk and talk, and I have a job to do."

"Is Terry there with you? Put him on the phone."

"Excuse me." She bristled at the implication that Terry had somehow become her caretaker in Troy's absence.

"I shouldn't have— Never mind."

"Murphy?" she prompted.

"He says he was home all night, Maddy." There was a solemnness to his voice that she didn't at all care for.

"Anyone able to verify that?"

"What am I supposed to do? Interrogate the guy? He's a fellow cop, Maddy. Why would he have hit you anyway?" He paused there, and the silence that filled the line told her he had his suspicions. How or why, she didn't yet know.

"I know what I saw, Troy," she said. "And you can't just close your mind to Murphy. He almost killed me and our baby." She was instantly struck with remorse for using their child as leverage. "He didn't, but…" she started to backpedal.

"Maddy." Troy sighed. "Murphy doesn't have a pickup truck. The partial you gave me ties back to Joel Phelps, Officer Phelps's brother. You and I need to talk, but I don't want to continue this conversation over the phone." His tone went dark and ominous. She was a fool to think she could keep her rogue mission from him forever. He was too smart. "You heard me, right? We need to—"

There was a beeping in her ear. "I've got another call coming in."

"Ignore it, Maddy, and meet me at home."

She looked at caller ID, and it was Terry. "I need to get this."

Troy hung up without saying another word.

I'm sorry, she said to him in her head and answered Terry's call.

"Just wanted to give you an update and check in, but I'm at your house and you're not. Where are you?"

"What's the update?" She appreciated that the men in her life cared about her welfare, but she was thirty-six-years old and more than capable of taking care of herself.

"Cynthia has the video from the city. I thought you might be up for watching it, but if you're not—"

"I'm good. Come get me?" She gave him the diner's name and address.

"Why are you there?"

"None of your business."

He remained silent. He'd been so kind with her, and the quiet infused her with guilt.

"I was hungry," she tossed out.

"Okay," he said. "I'll be there in five."

She bundled her jacket tighter to herself. Before now, she'd been too preoccupied to notice the cold breeze, but just standing there, it nipped at her bones. She shivered as she called Troy, intending to smooth things over. She landed in voicemail after only three rings. That meant one thing: he'd put her there.

Forty-Four

Madison sat on a stool in the forensics lab, munching on a Hershey's bar. She was already halfway finished when she looked at it with suspicion, curious about how much caffeine it might contain. She'd do what was necessary so Junior was healthy, but if she had to cut out chocolate along with coffee and wine, she might not have any friends left by the time the baby was born.

"What took them so long to get the video over here?" she asked Cynthia.

"The person who would normally take care of it was out sick with a bad cold."

"And no one else could forward the footage," Madison mumbled.

"No one else had access to their voicemail. Anyway, we have it now." Cynthia started the video, and it played on a wall-mounted TV that was connected to Cynthia's computer.

The feed showed from Market Street, looking down Burnham Street toward Luck of the

Irish pub and the public lot where Carson had parked. Potentially a great vantage point, but because of the rain, the feed wasn't too clear.

"I'm just going to forward closer to the time-of-death window." Cynthia proceeded to do just that.

"Actually, go until about eight. That's when Carson parked in the lot. Maybe we can see where she went from there."

"Got it." Cynthia forwarded and let it play when the time stamp in the bottom corner showed 7:58 PM. "How's that for precision?"

"Impressive." Terry smiled at Cynthia.

When the time stamp read 8:03 PM, Madison pointed at the screen. "There." Carson, identified by her clothing, was walking out of the lot to the sidewalk toward Market Street. "Can you pause and zoom in? Just to confirm it's her?"

"Sure." Cynthia did that.

"Unmistakably her," Terry said.

"Notice that she had a purse." Madison pointed toward the screen. "She also seems to be hugging it to herself."

"Nerves?" Terry suggested and shrugged. "Or she's protective of what's in it."

Madison bobbed her head at Cynthia, and she resumed the video. Carson's strides seemed determined, and her upper body angled forward as she went uphill. She stopped, turned around, and stood still for a few seconds before resuming her trek along the sidewalk.

Outside the pub, she looked up and then over her shoulders again—left then right, back left, right.

"She's nervous," Terry said. "Could have been for a date?"

Cynthia paused the video.

Madison shook her head. "I think she was there to confront Elliott. Either she called him and arranged to meet him, or she just knew he'd be there."

Terry faced her. "Assuming he was there."

"Right. I get that we might be off the mark with suspecting Elliott, but it's the fact we haven't been able to find him that bothers me. And if she was going to confront the con man who ripped her off, she'd probably want to do so in a public place."

"Because she feared him?" Terry shook his head at his own question. "No indication that she had or she would have said something in her files…or surely told her friend Lana that if anything happened to her to send the police to Abbott."

"Hit play again, please," Madison requested.

Cynthia did so, and Carson entered the pub.

"Now forward ahead to when she leaves," Madison said.

"You got it." Cynthia took them past ten, eleven, midnight… Still no sign of Carson exiting the front door. But at twelve forty-five Saturday morning, Carson emerged onto the sidewalk from the alley that led to the pub's parking lot, limping and hugging her arms around herself.

"No purse." Madison stiffened. "She must have been attacked in the back lot. We need the area searched for the murder weapon. She was stabbed somewhere behind the pub and restaurant."

"Right about where we were," Terry said.

"I didn't miss that," Madison replied.

"But you also know it's a week later. The knife used in the attack could be long gone," Terry started. "It and Carson's belongings could all be in the city dump."

"Or in the killer's possession," Madison countered, though Terry's theory was more likely.

Cynthia paused the video. "I'll get Mark on scene, and I'll go too."

"Well, someone needs to watch this video from earlier than eight until, say, two or later to see if there's any sign of Elliott or anyone else suspicious who comes up behind her." Madison hopped off the stool. "Shit."

"You okay?" Cynthia rushed over, and Madison held up a hand.

"I'm fine. I just keep forgetting that my body's against me at the moment."

"Hey, you're still alive," Cynthia shot back, driving home how lucky Madison had been— even if the entire event could have been avoided.

"I am." Her throat constricted from nerves as she spoke. She resisted the urge to put a hand over her stomach. She headed for the door with Terry.

"Madison, can we talk for a minute?" Cynthia asked.

"Ah, sure." Her heartbeat picked up speed and her palms went a little clammy. "I'll meet you in the lot," she told Terry, and he dipped his head in acknowledgment and was gone. She turned back to Cynthia and met a hardened expression. It was a look Madison was familiar with and normally came when her friend was concerned. "You don't have to worry about me, you know. The doctor told me I'll be fine." She reached out to touch Cynthia's shoulder, but she stepped back. "Something wrong?"

Cynthia crossed her arms, loosened them, let them drop. "I was terrified, Maddy. I thought that you might never wake up, that I lost you." Tears filled her eyes, and she sniffled.

"You didn't though."

"What is it with you?" Cynthia spun, sighed, turned around. "You think you're—what?— invincible, untouchable?"

"No—"

Cynthia held up a hand. "You must. Before I went on my honeymoon, before the wedding even, you were prying into the Mafia's affairs again. You had it in your head that the Stiles PD has corrupt cops."

"It's not in my head. It's a fact." Her heart was hammering, and it was suddenly feeling like her best friend was turning on her.

"Tell me you stopped pursuing this obsession of yours, that you've let it go."

Madison held her friend's gaze but said nothing.

Cynthia threw her arms in the air. "Yep, just as I thought. They did this to you. And let me guess—that woman whose picture you gave me has nothing to do with the Carson investigation."

Madison opened her mouth, unsure what to say, so snapped it shut.

"Uh-huh, as I suspected. You think she's tied up with the mob."

Know, thanks to Leland. "As far as the Stiles PD is concerned the mob's not even in town anymore."

Cynthia narrowed her eyes to slits. "Please. This is me you're talking to, not Stiles PD. They're in town still. I'm not blind, Maddy. And that's why I know here—" she laid a hand over her heart "—that your hit-and-run *accident* wasn't an accident. Do you really think it was?"

Madison hesitated but eventually shook her head.

"Good, at least you're not going to lie to my face about that."

She bristled. "What do you mean?"

"You used me," she spat. "Had me run her picture through facial rec databases."

"I never told you she was possibly connected to the Carson case. You assumed—"

"No." Cynthia shook her head. "You don't get to do that. And you have Troy, a man you supposedly love, running all over asking questions, interrogating people to find who did this to you. Have you bothered to tell him you think it's someone associated with the mob or even possibly a mob hit?" Cynthia crossed her arms again, this time tight, and she held the stance. Her gaze pierced through Madison's skull.

"I—"

"You don't need to answer my question. It was more rhetorical anyway. But tell me this: why was he asking Garrett Murphy where he was at the time of the..." Cynthia rolled her hand, as if not wanting to say accident one more time.

Cynthia was her best friend, her confidante, the person she went to when the world went sideways. She was the last person she'd ever want to hurt or have conflict with, but it seemed too late to avoid that. Her friend was far too smart for her own good. There was nothing Madison could say at this point, and even if she remained silent, Cynthia would probably connect the pieces: Madison's desire to bring down corrupt cops and Murphy being questioned for the hit-and-run...

Madison counted off the seconds in her head.

"Oh my God." Cynthia clamped a hand over her mouth, dropped it. "You think that… I can't believe this."

"I saw him."

"You saw him?" Cynthia spat.

Madison bristled and jutted out her jaw. "I did."

"Where?"

"As he drove past, just after… Before I passed out."

"How do you know you didn't just imagine it? See something you wanted to see?"

"Trust me, I never wanted to see his face!" She raised her voice, and Cynthia drew back.

"You know what? I'm glad you're okay. I really, truly am, Madison, but…" She swallowed roughly, and a few tears spilled down her cheeks. "Garrett is one of Lou's best friends."

"I know."

"But you still…" Her chest heaved. "You know what? We have work to do."

"Cyn."

"No." She waved over her head.

Madison stood there, watching her friend go to the closet for her coat and gather an evidence collection kit. Her heart was hurting so badly. First, Troy. Now, Cynthia. At least for now, Terry was on her side.

Forty-Five

After talking with Cynthia, which was nothing shy of an assault, Madison had tried reaching Troy again. She might not be able to set things right with Cynthia just yet, but she could try with him. He picked up just when she thought she was bound for voicemail purgatory.

"What is it, Maddy?"

"You want to talk. We'll talk."

"I said 'at home.' Face-to-face."

Her heart bumped off rhythm. His insistence that they talk at home had to be because, like Cynthia, he'd connected everything and figured out she was still looking into the mob. That would be preferable to him suggesting they go their separate ways for a while. But he wouldn't, would he? He'd promised her at the start of their relationship it would take her pissing him off a lot for him to walk. Surely now that she was carrying his child, he'd afford her even more leniency.

"So?" he said. "Are you headed home? I can be there in fifteen minutes."

She wasn't about to ask him where he'd been all this time, especially when she had to put him off for a bit. "I'm actually following a lead in the case I'm working on—" She paused at the distinct exhalation on Troy's end of the line. "What?"

"You should be home resting." His voice held concern and frustration.

"I'll wrap it up as fast as I can." Her entire body begged her to just go home and put her feet up.

"Just leave whatever it is to Terry and come home."

She reached the parking lot, and Terry was poised to toss her the keys for the sedan he'd signed out. He knew her preference was to drive rather than be chauffeured. He lowered his arms when he saw the phone at her ear.

"Maddy?" Troy prompted.

She was torn, but it only felt right that she saw this through as long as she could walk and function. "I have a job to do."

"Please don't be too long." Troy didn't sound pleased but resigned. "And don't get on my case if you find me settled in front of the TV when you get here."

"Oh, don't you dare." To her weary bones, parking on a couch sounded like bliss.

"Well, you're not here, so…" There was a tinge of playfulness in his voice, but it was tentative and fragile, almost as if awaiting reality to crush and destroy it.

"I'll be home in time for dinner." Last she knew, it was about two forty in the afternoon.

"Which is?"

"Time or food?"

"Suppose both."

"Since I'm the one who's working—"

"Nope, no way. You act like a healthy person, you're just as responsible for dinner as I am. Can't have it both ways. Off working during the day, invalid at night."

"One of those lovely casseroles it is, then."

"We'll talk when you get home. Not that you said when that was going to be."

"Gah. You know I'm not good with clocks."

"Amuse me."

She pulled her phone back and looked at the time in the upper left-hand corner. She'd lost twenty minutes; it was three o'clock on the mark. "Give me a couple hours, max."

"Wow. We'll be eating with old people."

"Elderly or mature adults…either term is a little more socially acceptable."

"Whatever, Maddy. We can always talk while dinner is in the oven."

Talk. Like a huge, looming storm threatening her life. She preferred the thought of watching TV, but said, "Sure, we can talk while we wait."

"Good. I love you."

"Love you, too." She hung up, and Terry tossed the keys. She reached out to catch them, and a blinding pain fired through her rib cage. The keys clattered to the concrete. "Son of a bitch!"

"Oh. Sorry." Terry winced. "I wasn't thinking." He retrieved the keys while she took slow, even-paced breaths. All her lungs wanted was to gulp oxygen. "Should I take you home?"

She couldn't speak. She couldn't move. Sparkles of white light were raining down in front of her vision. She stood there, tamping down her agony, talking herself through it, coaching herself from the ledge of defeat. "You…can…drive." She grimaced between each word.

"You got it." He nimbly jogged to the driver's door, and she waddled over to the passenger side.

She felt every bone of her spine as she lowered herself onto the seat.

"Just to clarify. I'm driving you…"

"To the pub." She pulled the seat belt across her lap and added, "Thank you."

"You're the most hardheaded person I know."

"Thank you again."

"Not necessarily a compliment," he mumbled and drove them to Luck of the Irish.

The entire way, he didn't say another word and neither did she. She was too busy concentrating on somehow lessening the spikes of pain still bolting through her.

Terry parked in the same lot that Carson had, after he confirmed there were no spaces left behind Luck of the Irish. There was no sign of Cynthia or Mark yet, but they'd be showing up soon.

The uphill walk to the pub was a little challenging and had Madison wishing she'd thought to bring another dosage of pills with her, but she wasn't about to let the pain win.

Terry got the door to the pub for her, and she stopped to read the sign posted next to it. On Fridays, they opened at noon and closed at three the next morning. It provided a good time frame for Cynthia to watch the video. That was assuming she was going to do that and not delegate the responsibility. Normally, it would be something Cynthia would take on herself, but she was more than ticked off at Madison. Though, surely she wouldn't let the personal conflict effect how she did her job.

For midafternoon, the place was bustling, and there were more people in there than could have parked out back. People were seated along the length of the long bar, which had to have twenty to thirty stools.

Madison wedged between a couple men, Terry behind her. A man in his thirties, wearing a change apron, smiled at them from behind the counter.

"What can I get ya?"

Madison could do hard liquor if it weren't for Peanut. *Peanut?* She withdrew her badge from her pocket and held it for the bartender. Terry mirrored her actions. The men to each side of her shuffled their stools over, giving them more room.

The bartender moved back. "I can get the manager for you."

"Actually, you might be able to help us," she said.

The man on her left got up and walked away. She watched after him, but he just found himself another spot at a table. Back to the bartender, she asked, "Were you working the night shift two Fridays ago?"

He shook his head.

"Did I hear you're looking for someone who worked two Friday nights ago?" A female server approached them, holding an empty tray in one hand.

How she'd overheard was a miracle. Between the music coming over the speakers and people's conversations, the place wasn't a library.

"That's right," Madison confirmed. "Were you?"

"I was."

Madison studied the young woman in front of her. Would she be the key to finding Jake Elliott?

Forty-Six

Madison asked the server if they could speak somewhere quieter, and she led her and Terry to a table in a shadowed corner. Not exactly private, but the music was decibels lower here. The server sat down so she was looking out over the restaurant, and Madison took the chair on her right. Terry sat across from the woman.

"I'm Detective Madison Knight, and this is Detective Terry Grant. What's your name?"

"Chloe Summers."

Madison pulled out her phone and brought up the DMV picture of Chantelle Carson. "Did you see her in here two Fridays ago?"

Chloe bit her bottom lip and leaned over to get a better look at the screen. "Yeah, I did."

"Do you remember if she met up with anyone that night?"

"No, she came alone, left alone. Probably why I remember her so clearly. Most people hook up with someone."

"She didn't?" Madison asked.

Chloe shook her head. "And she even looked sad, ya know? Not the right word really." She screwed up her mouth. "Hardened. Yeah, that's it. She stood out, too, because she was in her forties when most people in here on Friday are college age."

"Okay," Madison started. "But did she seem interested in anyone?"

"One regular, but all the ladies like him." Chloe twisted a strand of her hair around a finger.

Apparently, the waitress was included in *all the ladies.*

Terry held his phone across the table, and Madison caught the image on the screen. Jake Elliott. "This the guy?"

"Hey, you know him?" Chloe's smile quickly turned sour. "Why are you asking about Saul?"

So Elliott had also presented himself to the waitress using his alias. Curious that he tossed the name around so casually. He took a serious risk by doing so, but maybe he was too cocky to think he'd be found out. "What was your relationship with him?"

Chloe licked her lips, glanced away.

"Just a guess, but I'm thinking you know him rather well. You called him by his first name," Madison added.

"As I said, he's a regular, and showing personal interest in customers is a good way to get larger tips."

Madison raised an eyebrow. "That's all it was with Saul?"

Chloe looked away, tucked hair behind an ear this time, then put both elbows on the table and leaned forward. "I slept with him a few weeks ago. Just the one time." She emphasized this with an erect index finger.

Madison sat up straighter and smiled tightly to bury the pain crackling through her. Maybe Chloe could give them something useful in finding him. Madison would play a little role first to relax Chloe. "Hey, he's a good-looking man."

"Oh yeah, and good in bed." Chloe winked at her. "He has money, too, I think. He drives a silver Mercedes SUV. Don't ask me the model, but they're all pricey, aren't they?"

"They're not cheap," Madison consented. But Elliott, a.k.a. Abbott, would have been flush with all the cash he'd defrauded from women over the years. "Did he take you back to his place?" Madison could only hope, but she wasn't banking on it.

"My place, but why would you care?" Chloe pushed her back into the chair and crossed her arms. "And why are you interested in that woman and Saul? She the ol' ball-and-chain or something?"

It would seem Chloe wouldn't care if she were a homewrecker, which had Madison's respect for the server disappearing. She bit back the urge to spit out, "Murder victim." Instead, she said, "Her name was Chantelle Carson, and she was murdered after she was here two Friday nights ago."

"Dear God." Chloe's eyes widened, and she glanced at Terry. "For real?"

"Afraid so," Terry replied.

"Wow. I don't know what to say."

"So when did Saul show up that night?" Madison asked.

"Somewhere between nine and ten."

Considering that Carson had arrived at eight o'clock, she may have come to talk to him but hadn't arranged it beforehand, or she came early. She had been acting strange on the video. "And when did he leave?"

"Around twelve thirty or so? Not a hundred percent sure."

He could have attacked Carson out back. She was stumbling to the street at quarter to one. "Did he leave alone?"

"Ah…" Chloe's forehead bunched in thought. "I think so, yeah."

"And which door did he use when he left?" Madison eyed a narrow hallway at the back of the pub.

"He used the one in the rear."

Terry leaned forward. "When did you last see him?"

"Come to think of it, that night you're asking about. He's all right, isn't he?" She scrunched up her brow. "You mentioned that lady was murdered. What does that have to do with—" She slapped a hand over her mouth, slowly lowered it.

Madison looked at her and stated calmly, "We both appreciate your cooperation, Ms. Summers, but we have a few more questions."

Chloe nodded.

"You said that Saul was a regular," Madison started. "How long has he been coming here?"

"For a few months now. Usually on Fridays and Saturdays."

"And just to clarify, you slept with him when?" Madison recalled Chloe had said a few weeks ago, but the day of the week might prove useful.

"It was three Fridays ago. I got off early."

The week before Carson's murder. Madison squirreled that fact away and returned her mind to the regularity with which Abbott had come to the pub. Carson's photos and documents testified that she had gathered intel on Elliott, and his coming here on a predictable schedule would have be helpful in tracking him down. Madison couldn't recall a picture that was taken outside the pub, but that didn't mean Carson hadn't known about his habitual Friday night outing. "How often did the woman come here?"

"I only saw her that one time."

Carson could have followed Elliott here in the past and just not entered the bar. "I see,"

Madison said. "And how did Saul react to her staring at him?"

"Just ignored her, from what I could tell."

That must have made Carson crazy with rage after what he'd done to her. "Did you see when she left?"

Chloe shook her head. "Honestly? I don't know. I went to get a drink order for another table, and she was gone. A few quarters for my trouble on the table. And she stayed for a long time." She rolled her eyes.

"When did you go to this other table? Just after Saul left?" Madison was trying to piece together if Carson had followed Saul out of the bar.

"That's about right. Yeah."

"And you're certain you never saw the woman and Saul interact?" Terry asked.

"Nope. Doesn't mean they didn't. Just that I didn't see it." Chloe moved to stand. "I really should get back to work."

"Just one more question," Madison said. "Did Saul ever come here with a date?" She was curious if he brought his next marks to the pub.

"No. He always came alone. Usually he left with someone." Chloe's gaze went past Terry, and Madison followed the direction of it and realized the bartender was waving her over.

"Well, thanks for your help," Madison said.

Chloe didn't make a move to walk away. Instead, she locked eyes with Madison and said, "Do you really think Saul killed that woman?"

"We're trying to figure that out," Madison said.

"And trying to find him, I take it. Given all your questions."

"We are," Madison confirmed. "You don't happen to have a way of reaching him, do you?"

"No. It was just a one-nighter. Not sure if this will help, but I heard him on the phone after we...ah.... He was in my bathroom, but it's not exactly soundproof."

"What did you hear?" Madison asked.

"He told the person he was talking to they needed to keep calm, not that he sounded calm. Panicked, maybe scared even."

The conversation might not have anything to do with a perceived threat in reference in Carson, but it might. And if it did, were they to assume he had a partner? Carl Long or someone else?

Again, Chloe's gaze snapped across the room to the bar. "I'm sorry, but I really need to get back to work."

The server gone, Madison turned to Terry. "We need to find out who he was talking to."

"I agree but have no idea how we're going to do that."

Madison considered the possibilities. "We need Elliott's phone history."

"Hard when you don't have his number."

"No, but we have Carson's. You know, the ones you haven't looked at yet." She paused as

Terry glared at her. "So we call the outgoing numbers that come up repeatedly and ask for Saul Abbott."

"Sounds like a job for you."

"Why me?"

"He has a thing for women."

"Or you could do the calling and say you're from Southern Life about a will. Tell him he stands to inherit, which he does if he didn't kill her, so it's not a lie."

"Ah, sure."

"Assuming one of the numbers she called ties back to him, we'll get a subpoena to trace."

"Sure. But consider that the 'calm down' comment might have had nothing to do with Carson."

"Considered. And we need to find that Mercedes. Is it registered to him or someone else? Maybe even a woman he's currently conning?"

"Any ideas how to find out?"

"Must I think of everything?"

"Why not?" He grinned.

Madison got up with care and stood to full height without her ribs hurting too badly. "Chloe also said that Elliott—or as she knew him, Saul Abbott—came here regularly for months, but hasn't been in since Carson was murdered. Seems suspicious to me, like he's hiding out."

"Me too."

She walked toward the back door, passing an entrance to the kitchen. She peeked in, and the staff was busy fulfilling orders, but she was looking for one man in particular and spotted him. It was the smoker from the back stoop they'd talked to last Saturday. He was pinching green garnish onto a plate of pasta. "Excuse me," she called out. The other five people in the kitchen looked at her before the man did. When he saw her, he held up a finger to indicate a minute, then headed over.

"Detectives," he said, wiping his hands on his apron and letting his gaze go from her to Terry, back to her. "What can I do for you?"

"You often take your smoke breaks out back?" she asked him.

"All the time."

"On a set schedule?"

"Not necessarily." He glanced back at the bustling staff and bellowed, "Stepping away for a minute!"

The three of them shimmied down the hall toward the back door but remained inside.

"You ever see this woman before?" Madison pulled out her phone and showed him a picture of Carson.

"A few times."

That didn't coincide with the server's story. "Where? Inside the bar, out back?"

"Out back. Usually standing at the edge of the parking lot under the oak tree."

Madison recalled the tree that hung over the lot at the back side. "But she never came in?"

The man smiled. "In the kitchen, remember?"

"Right." Madison put her phone away. "Is there anything else you can tell us about her? Did she ever approach any of the pub's customers maybe?"

"Not that I saw. When you were here… When was it?"

"Last Saturday," Madison confirmed.

"You mentioned something had happened to a woman. That her?" He pointed in the general area of the pocket where she'd tucked her phone.

"Yes."

"Well, I definitely know her, to see her anyway. She was often out back like she was waiting for someone, but she was twitchy. I assumed she was high and just left her alone because I didn't want any trouble. She was hugging her purse to her chest and mumbling… She made me uneasy."

"She could have been on her phone, using earphones," Terry suggested.

"Possibly, but I don't think so. She seemed to figure out I was watching her sometimes and would leave through the opening onto Napoleon Avenue."

That was the street that ran north of Burnham behind the pub.

"She was in quite the hurry too. Almost like I spooked her."

It would seem Carson had been hanging out back waiting on Elliott several times. Stalking him? Building up courage? Madison showed him the picture of Jake Elliott. "You ever see this man talking to her?"

He leaned in. "I recognize the guy, but I never saw them talk."

This man had already told them last week he hadn't witnessed any altercations in their lot, so no point going down that road again. They probably should question everyone on staff though, just in case someone saw something. But if Elliott was such a regular, maybe this guy got the plate on the Mercedes. "Did you ever see a silver Mercedes SUV parked in the lot?"

"Yeah."

"Did you happen to notice a plate number?" The meat of her reason for asking him about the Mercedes.

He smiled and shook his head.

"Thought I'd try. But thank you for your help. What's your name if we need to speak to you again?"

"Glenn Donnelly."

Madison dipped her head in thanks and stepped outside with Terry.

"I'm almost starting to wonder if Carson intended to physically harm Elliott," she said, feeling the truth of her instinct send chills through her. "Donnelly mentioned her mumbling and hugging her purse. Like in the video from the night she was murdered. Twitchy too? Sounds like she was up to no good. What if she didn't plan to expose Elliott but to kill him? She could have pulled the knife on him, but she wound up the one on the blade's stabbing end."

Forty-Seven

Madison and Terry stood on the back stoop of Luck of the Irish for a few minutes. She looked to the oak tree and the opening to Napoleon Avenue. She considered doing a little tour of the area, but she'd made a promise to Troy. Besides whenever Cynthia and Mark arrived, they could handle that along with Terry.

"Listen, I've gotta go," she said.

"You're in pain?"

"No…yes, but that's not why."

"You want me to drop you off?"

"I'll call a cab. I need you to stay here. Question all the staff about Carson and Elliott, the Mercedes SUV. See if anyone saw the two of them interact or caught a plate."

"Okay. Might take all night."

"You know I'd help if I could."

Terry slowly nodded. "Go. I'll fill you in later."

"Also, arrange to have officers watch the pub tonight in case Elliott shows up."

"Will do."

"Oh, and run our thought about Carson past Cynthia. Maybe there was a knife missing from Carson's kitchen that was a match to the stainless pulled from her stab wound?"

"Carson could have purchased one just for confronting Elliott. Maybe just as a means of threatening him."

"Could be, but I have the feeling she planned more. He'd destroyed her, and it was cumulative. Every man in her life had let her down. Her husband, her new lover, that being Elliott, and her boss. And if she only wanted justice, why didn't she report him?"

"You said before if she didn't know Abbott's real name, that would have been tough to do. Look how hard it's proved to be for us. We still haven't found him. You really think she had cold, premeditated murder on her mind?"

"Wouldn't shock me."

Terry returned inside the pub, and she called for a cab. It showed up five minutes later, just after she'd gotten rather comfortable on one of the stairs at the front of the pub. She had the driver take her straight home, even though she felt like a dog dragging its ass along the ground. She was queasy just thinking about what Troy wanted to discuss.

With early-evening traffic starting to pick up, the drive took twenty minutes as opposed to fifteen. She paid her fare and let herself inside.

Troy was on the couch, watching something on television.

Hershey barked and jumped off the couch, hurtling toward her.

"Hey, baby." She ruffled his ears and bent over and kissed the top of his head. "You broke him out of jail?" she said to Troy.

He flicked the TV off and got up to meet her at the door. "Surprise." He'd said the word rather drily, and she couldn't touch on the reason why. Disappointment she hadn't been there when he came home with Hershey?

He hugged her gently and kissed her. "Happy you're home." He tapped another kiss to her forehead.

She smiled, a little more at ease by his reaction to seeing her. They'd made peace before she went to Luck of the Irish, but his hanging up on her earlier still wasn't far from mind. Troy didn't typically get worked up and terminate their phone conversations like that. "Happy too."

She slipped out of her coat and placed it on a hanger in the front closet. Troy didn't say anything, but Madison didn't miss the expression of surprise on his face at her doing so. She would normally toss it on the back of a chair or hook it on the closet handle. She slipped off her shoes and let out a deep breath.

"How are you doing?"

"Please don't ask." She attempted a smile, and he swept a hand over her head.

"Want a drink or something to eat? I can get it for you if you want to sit down."

"Do I want a drink?" She laughed. "A glass of water, I guess."

"Coming right up."

She settled on the couch, getting semi-comfortable. Hershey laid his head across her lap, and she rubbed behind his ears.

"So how's your murder case coming along?" Troy returned to the living room with her water.

"Think we're making some headway. Finally. Thanks." She took the glass from Troy and took a greedy sip, imagining it was wine instead. "Not sure how Terry kept himself busy without me though."

"Ah, you're too hard on the guy. I'm sure he followed a lot of leads."

She grinned. "He did. I'm just kidding around." She hated herself for how awkward she was feeling.

"I was thinking a chicken casserole would be our safest bet. Sound good?"

They smiled when they met each other's eyes.

"We can risk it," she said.

Silence wormed in, the tension crackling in the air. She would take a stab at easing it.

"I'm happy that you understand why I left the house today." Definitely wishful thinking, but phrasing it that way might help him see things from her perspective and put off what he wanted to talk about.

He sat in a chair, seeing as Hershey was taking up the rest of the couch and seemed quite content all spread out.

"You know that when I get a case, I need to see it through," she added.

"That's why you're Bulldog."

"Right. But you do understand?" She wished she could retract the question the instant it came out. She was quite sure she didn't want to hear his answer.

"I know what you're like. I know you have a hard time letting go."

She could puff out her chest and become all indignant about how she took her badge and the responsibility that came with it seriously, but there was no need, and she in no way wanted to imply that Troy didn't.

Troy went on. "I just want what's best for you. I always have."

The urge to cry rushed over her. Likely the cursed pregnancy hormones at work. Could she blame them yet? "I know you do. But I'm fine."

"I know you are, but I don't want you to just be fine. I want you happy, good, great even. I don't know if you realize how often you say you're fine." His green eyes locked with hers. "Are you happy, Maddy? With me, us, I mean?"

"Yes, I…" She gulped as her heart raced. "I love you. I love my life with you."

"It's just things have been strained lately."

So he had noticed. "I've been busy with work."

"Is that all?" His question was short but potent and heavy as concrete. He let it sit there for some time, and she considered bringing up the ring and how she thought he was going to propose, but he continued. "I told you I tracked the partial plate you gave me to Joel Phelps, Dustin's brother. Well, I spoke with Joel. He said his truck was in his driveway all week, including Monday night."

"He's lying," she burst out.

Troy's gaze hardened.

"I'm telling you his truck was the one that rammed me." Looking at him, she decided to hell with holding anything back. Maybe he was more understanding than she ever gave him credit for. He had understood when it came to her interest in Dustin Phelps and had even stood by her side to set things right.

"Why would he?"

And we're back to that! "You're treating me like I've done something wrong." She detected the screech to her voice and hated herself for it. "I know what I saw. Murphy behind the wheel and the partial plate. Murphy must have been driving Joel Phelps's truck, I swear to you. Talk to Joel's neighbors, ask around, verify that the truck was in his driveway all week—because I'm telling you it was not." She stiffened, about ready to pull out her phone and show him the pictures she'd taken of the grille guard, but she had a feeling that would just make everything worse.

"I'm not saying that you're making it up or—"

"No? You aren't? Then you're telling me I'm crazy?"

"That's not my intention." He clenched his jaw. "I want to find who did this just as badly as you do."

She resisted the urge to say, "You could have fooled me." It would have been a rash, impulsive, and completely unfair reaction. Troy did care—about her and their baby. "Troy," she started, speaking softly, "what happened to me wasn't an accident. I know it, and I'm sure you do."

"Not denying that," he countered stiffly.

"I have no doubt Murphy's intention was to hurt me, maybe even kill me."

His face transformed from concentration to anger and became chiseled granite. He leaned forward, putting his elbows on his knees. "Why? Just answer me that."

He was giving her every opportunity to open up, but how would he react? Would he leave her to raise their child on her own? Her chest became heavy. "They almost succeeded in killing me and our baby, Troy."

"Murphy, or *they*, which is it?"

"I think you know who *they* are." She paused as the revelation electrified his green eyes.

"The Mafia," he ground out.

"Yes."

Nothing was said for several minutes. Troy sat back and rubbed his jaw.

"I'm…" She cleared her throat. "I'm looking into them and the corrupt cops of the Stiles PD. They need to be flushed out, Troy. You must see that."

Troy just held her gaze.

"Tell me you do."

"You know what I see?" His imposed silence was long enough to drive a stake into her heart.

The solitaire. Princess cut. She'd never see it on her finger. She was losing him. "What?" The single word barely scraped from her throat.

"I see a woman who is obsessed—" He quickly held up his hand to keep her from saying anything. "I see a woman who is willing to risk everything, including her own life, to purify the city and the department. You know what else?"

"No." She was afraid to talk for fear her voice would be laden with emotion, including anger.

"I see a woman who is foolish." He squeezed his eyes shut and pushed off his chair.

Hershey got off the couch and curled up on his bed in the corner of the room.

"How dare you!" She choked on a sob.

"Why can't you just leave them the hell alone? What's with the obsession? Is bringing them down worth dying over? I get your drive—"

"You obviously don't." She panted for breath despite the pain. Rage and heartbreak were fighting for dominance. "And I didn't know I was pregnant."

"Why can't you understand that I'd be ruined if something happened to you?" He snapped his mouth shut and turned away.

"So I'm just supposed to look away and let the bad guys win?"

"I've gotta…" He raked a hand through his hair.

She recalled his reaction to the pregnancy, how happy he'd been, how celebratory. "Troy?" she squeaked out. She'd gone and given her heart to this man, and now she had to pay for that vulnerability. "Is that it, then? Are we… done?"

His eyes steeled over. "I just need time to think."

"I found the ring," she blurted out.

His gaze was fierce when it aligned with hers. "You what?"

"I'm sorry. I shouldn't have…"

Hershey got up from his bed and left the room.

"You were going to propose to me at Cynthia's wedding, weren't you?" She couldn't bring herself to look at him, but she had to know if she was losing her mind, her ability to read people, her instinct.

He didn't respond, and seconds later, she looked over at him. He was staring straight ahead, his jaw tight.

"Troy, please, talk to me."

"So you want me to talk to you, but you're obviously keeping secrets and running around behind my back." He clenched his teeth, his nostrils flaring.

"To protect you."

"I don't need your protection. When are you going to accept that? Fuck, I'm a SWAT team leader."

"A bullet would still take you down."

"What might take me down is being made a target in the first place." He grabbed his coat from the front closet and slammed the door on his way out.

She couldn't get herself to respond, even to open her mouth. She was paralyzed from the throat up. All she could think was she'd lost the man she loved because of her tenacity and need to right wrongs. Maybe she'd be better off if she could just let the mob be someone else's problem. But that wasn't who she was. It wasn't even normally who Troy was, and one of the qualities she admired about him the most was that he didn't back down. She'd always seen him as strong and impenetrable. He had to be acting like this because of the baby.

Forty-Eight

Madison had taken the department laptop to bed after Troy left, skipping the casserole because she wasn't even hungry. Last time she looked at the time, it was two in the morning, and Troy still hadn't returned home. She shuffled through the surveillance photos Carson had taken of Elliott, not that it seemed she knew his real name. Madison had read all her research, and the name Jake Elliott hadn't surfaced once.

Most of the photos were at a distance. She'd wager they were taken with Carson's phone given the fuzziness of some of the zoomed-in shots. Madison's phone was much better taking one-ratio pictures then enlarging and cropping compared to magnifying and then clicking the shutter button.

Another thing she noticed was quite a few of them were taken outside the same brownstone. Unfortunately, the street number wasn't in focus, and she didn't think that Cynthia could work her magic on what was there. That's even if Cynthia was speaking to her. Maybe she'd finagle things so Terry could ask.

In some pictures, it looked like Elliott was looking straight into the camera lens, as if he saw Carson. Surely he had to know she was tailing him. Waiting outside Luck of the Irish, for one thing.

As she stirred awake, all of this felt like a dream more than something that had taken place. But she smelled bacon. Maybe she was still dreaming. Troy didn't cook or eat bacon.

She looked beside her, and the bed was empty, but the pulled-down comforter and ruffled sheets confirmed they'd been slept in. At least Troy had come home last night. Still, there was an ache in her chest, like something had broken between them.

The bedroom door slowly opened, and Troy entered holding a tray of food. "You're awake. Good." He advanced on the bed, and she shuffled into a seated position. He pulled out the legs on the tray and set it over her lap. She never even knew they had one of these things.

She wasn't much in the mood to talk to him just yet, but him bringing her breakfast in bed was a smart move.

He sat on the edge of the mattress. "I'm so sorry about last night." He peered into her eyes, and his apology sliced her open.

"You really hurt me." *And pissed me off!*

"I know, and I'm mad at myself for that. I never wanted to hurt you. I never *want* to hurt you. I love you, Madison." He placed a gentle hand on her cheek.

"Why did you…" She couldn't bring herself to speak the word *leave*. Something about saying it out loud would make what had transpired between them last night more real. As it was, the persistent hurt in her heart told her it had happened.

"I was upset."

"Yeah, well, guys act like absolute assholes when they're upset."

He laughed and gestured to the spread of food on the tray. "Hopefully, that will help make up for my asshole behavior."

Bacon and scrambled eggs, a couple small pancakes drenched in syrup, a few strawberries, a glass of orange juice, and a coffee. She pointed to the latter. "Decaf?"

"You know it."

"Where did you get the bacon?"

"I picked it up at a twenty-four-hour grocery store on my way home last night. Along with pretty much everything else you see."

"For me? To make up for your asshole behavior?" She was probably having a little too much fun with this.

"Yes." A few beats passed, and he continued. "Enjoy your breakfast while it's hot, and then we'll talk. Okay?" He touched the hair at her temple, his fingertips grazing the area for the briefest of moments before he got up.

"Oh, please stay." Her invitation was impulsive.

"I was hoping you'd say that." He sat back down. "But eat up."

She went for the coffee first and took a sip. "You know this stuff really isn't that bad. I might even be able to fool myself into thinking it's the real deal."

"Until you nod off in the middle of the afternoon."

"Thanks for pointing that out." She shoved him gently in the shoulder. "Speaking of nodding off in the afternoon, what time did you get up? What time is it now?" He blocked her view of the alarm clock. She took a bite of bacon. He'd cooked it to perfection—crispy, but it didn't shatter into bits when chewed.

"I was up at six. Slept like crap."

"I didn't sleep well either." She polished off the first slice and lifted her fork and dug into the eggs.

"Not that one could tell given your snoring."

"Hey!" She swallowed her mouthful. "I don't snore."

He laughed. "Oh, yes you do."

"Whatever. I'd like proof." She made a show of rolling her eyes but smiled. They met each other's eyes, and it was clear to Madison there was still love between them, but last night had hurt them both. "So the time is…"

"Ten thirty."

"Ten thirty! I haven't slept that late for—I can't remember how long."

"And how does it feel?"

"Like I'm a lazy toad." She laughed, then reeled back. Blasted ribs.

"Well, you've been through a lot this week and need your rest." He put a hand on her thigh, his touch not evoking thoughts of sleeping. She put her right hand over his, and they held that position as she ate every bite of what he'd prepared.

She set her fork down and burped. "Excuse me."

He laughed. "Someone was hungry."

"Very." She was going to jest she was eating for two now, but it would be blaming the baby, and it was far too young to be responsible for an increased appetite. "I just realized that my stomach's feeling pretty okay this morning."

"That's good, considering." He indicated her empty plate and cleared the tray so she could get out of bed. "The bacon will probably help."

"How?"

"Fatty foods sometimes sit well on an upset stomach."

Unless it's a greasy burger.

She got out of bed and was going to just wrap a robe around herself and go to the living room, but decided she'd rather get dressed for the day, even if it was putting off the conversation Troy obviously wanted to have with her. He'd brought her breakfast in bed, but was that a sign that he'd come around to her point of view or a way of buttering her up so she could see his?

"I'm just going to have a shower and get human," she said. "Then I'll be out."

"Okay." He pecked a kiss on her forehead and left the room ahead of her.

She stopped to pick up her cell phone off her nightstand. Terry had texted a message last night at eight thirty. She hadn't heard it come in because she'd silenced her phone. She was so angry at Troy for leaving, but she didn't trust herself to ignore him if he called. As it turned out, he hadn't.

She read Terry's message now.

> *Interviewed all pub employees. No one saw anything. No murder weapon found or purse. And dumpster out back emptied on Mondays. Cyn will review video closer. Looking into Carson/knife. Lipstick and scrap of fabric found. Will compare to Carson*

She fired back a quick, *Thanks for the update*, and headed down the hall.

She ran a shower, turning the faucet to as hot as her flesh could stand, and stood under the stream. The ache in her chest was still there, but it had dulled. Now it was more like a scar, a reminder that she'd been wounded, that she was vulnerable, that she was not invincible. She closed her eyes and let the water pour over her face and down her body. She heard the hooks on the shower curtain sliding along the bar and turned to see Troy stepping in behind her.

"I'm so sorry, Madison. I really am." He closed the distance between them.

They put their foreheads together, but it wasn't long before their mouths met, their tongues darting and hungry. Hands searching, cupping, kneading, caressing. Panting and gasping.

Forty-Nine

Making love to Troy had been long overdue. Madison sat on the couch afterward, feeling euphoric, and cuddled with Hershey. Her bruised ribs and tender stomach were far from her mind.

"Want anything?" Troy called from the kitchen.

"Actually, I'd love another one of those decaf coffees."

"You got it."

He joined her a few minutes later, shooing Hershey off the couch and sitting next to her. He handed her the coffee, and she thanked him.

There was a wave of anxiousness that lapped over her, just anticipating the conversation to come.

Troy blew out a deep breath, his cheeks swelling like a chipmunk's stuffed with peanuts, then deflating. "I left last night because I just needed to think everything through."

She was afraid to really probe what *everything* was. "We can't just walk out when we want to think, Troy. We're a couple. We should work things out together."

"I know. I was wrong. Hence breakfast in bed..." He smiled in his typical fashion that barely curved his lips. "This is hard to say, but sometimes it feels like..." He met her eyes and seemed hesitant to continue.

"Feels like?" she prompted.

"You've been intent on bringing down the Russians for so long, and now on taking out corrupt cops, that I feel...I don't know, second place."

His words chipped at her heart. "Never," she said, but she was deceiving herself. That's exactly where she'd been placing him—if not in third place. Her job, her side mission, then Troy. She inched along the cushions and tucked herself close to him.

"It's just how it feels sometimes."

"I'm sorry for that."

He dipped his head, accepting her apology. "I don't like feeling second."

"No one would."

"I do know why you're—I don't want to say obsessed again—but why you're determined to clean up Stiles, the city and the police department. It's who you are, and I'd never want you to change. It's just...now you're carrying our baby."

"Trust me. I'm aware."

He took her hand. "I never actually asked you how you feel about us having a kid."

She could tell he was still excited, and she wished she could say the same, but if they were being honest with each other… "I'm adjusting."

"I know being a mother's not really where you saw yourself."

She shook her head and put a hand on her stomach. "I'm sure I'll love the child, Troy. I just need to get used to the idea of becoming a mother."

He nodded. "I can appreciate that. Came as a shock to me, too, but I think we're ready for this."

She bit her bottom lip, thinking, *Ready for a baby but not marriage?*

"And just for the record," he started, "I'm still angry, but not at you. At the Russians and Murphy for ramming your car."

She shifted straighter. "You believe me now?"

He sighed. "Maybe I did from the start? I just didn't want to. He's a fellow officer, and he stood up for Cynthia's husband at the wedding."

"Again, I'm well aware." She filled him on the confrontation she'd had with her best friend. "It's killing me that she's mad at me, but I get her side too."

"It will probably take some hard proof, but she'll come around. In the end, Cynthia's a good person."

"She is."

"If you're going to continue to pursue this—" he rolled his hand as if to summon the right word "—operation of yours, can we do it together?"

She scanned his face and pulled back. "I don't want you involved. They almost killed me."

"And our baby," he fired back. "Probably why I reacted so strongly yesterday. I trust that you can handle yourself, Madison, though I still fear for your safety, but our baby makes me need to get involved. Not just for what they did to you, but the mob and the corrupt cops need to be exposed. I'm prepared to stand by you, but I want to do this by the book. Legit. We bring in Andrea."

There was some relief that would come from working with him. She'd have someone watching her back. It still didn't change the fact she was pregnant—not that she needed to be put in bubble wrap, but she had to think of the baby's welfare. "Maybe we step back before something happens that can't be reversed," she started. "Murphy didn't know I was pregnant."

"If he did this to protect himself, do you think he'd have cared if he had known?" There was a level of conviction in his voice that hadn't been there before.

"Probably not," she said solemnly. "What you're saying is…you're in whether I am or not?"

"Yeah. In the least they need to answer for the hit-and-run."

She held his gaze and blinked slowly. "Okay, then let's do this." She proceeded to fill him in about Club Sophisticated, her stakeout, and the storage unit. With every new tidbit, his eyes widened, and his brows raised.

"You're like a female James Bond."

"I just want to end this."

"So do I, but it's not going to be something that happens overnight."

"You don't have to tell me. I have no idea just how deep the Mafia reaches into the department yet."

"I can tell you that my sister can be trusted."

She was just about to tell him about Tatiana Ivanova and Roman Petrov's miraculous resurrection when there was a knock on the door. She looked at Troy. "You expecting someone?"

He gave her raised shoulders and a funny face. "But maybe you should get the door."

"Ah, it's probably Terry. He texted last night, and I just responded this morning." She got up and answered the door.

A woman was standing there with a huge smile, holding a vase wrapped with a red ribbon, and Hershey's bars were poking out.

She turned to Troy and raised a brow.

"Madison Knight?" the woman said.

"Yes."

"Here you go. Have a great day." The woman left, and Madison returned to the living room.

"You like?" Troy smiled.

"Like? Love! Who told you Hershey's is my favorite flower?" She chuckled and set it on the coffee table.

"Just don't mow them all down in one sitting."

"Please, I'll show some restraint." She snatched one of the larger bars and tore through the wrapper.

"Oh, right now? We're doing this right now?"

She bit off a chunk and swallowed. "You must have been feeling really bad about walking out last night."

He pressed his lips and gestured to the bouquet. "Believe that says it all."

"I love you, too." She plastered a huge, wet, chocolatey kiss on his cheek.

Fifty

"**I'm never going to eat again,**" Madison moaned. She hadn't eaten the entire jumbo bar, but she'd inflicted some damage.

Troy laughed. "Just because the Hershey's bouquet arrived didn't mean you had to sample it right away."

"You're kidding, right? It's Hershey's." All the explanation needed. She'd always find room in her stomach for chocolate.

"So…" Troy's expression had become serious, and his tone further reflected that sentiment. "We need to discuss our next steps, but should we give this mission of ours a code name?" The suggestion was an obvious attempt at lightening the somberness of the conversation.

"Sure. If you'd like." She smiled at him.

"All right, then. How about Stiles Clean Sweep?"

"Fine, but I don't really care what we call it, honestly. I just want Murphy held accountable for what he did. We'll start there."

"I can get behind that."

"I'd also like to out any and all corrupt cops."

"Who do you suspect so far?"

"Two, and both you know about. Dustin Phelps and Garrett Murphy. There's probably more. I'm just getting started. As I told you, I've staked out at Club Sophisticated a couple times. I want to identify all the players involved with the mob and do whatever we can to stop any criminal activity." The fact one of those "players" was her ex-boyfriend Blake Golden might complicate things a bit. She went on. "There's this woman… I had no idea who she was at the time, but I followed her from the club last weekend."

"Two Saturdays ago when you said you were working late?"

Her gaze flicked to his. "I did go to the club that night, yes. What made you think—"

"Just the way Terry looked at you in the hospital when I made some comment to the effect of you working all the time."

"Can't pull much over on you, can I?"

"Remember that."

"Yes, I went there that night, but I also returned on Sunday."

"When I was at work."

She nodded. "That's when I followed that woman. She was driven to a house in Deer Glen. The property is registered to a numbered corporation. I could only find one name associated. Roman Petrov."

"Roman? I thought he was dead."

"Me too. But I've got it on good authority that he staged his death."

"Good authority?"

She took a deep breath. "Leland King."

"He's involved with this war against the Mafia too?"

"Not anymore. His advice is that I leave it alone."

"It's probably wiser than either of us want to admit."

Silence spanned between them for a while.

She took a few deep breaths. "He also told me her name is Tatiana Ivanova, and she's Roman Petrov's second cousin and star assassin."

Troy sat on the edge of the couch cushion. "Shit."

"Yeah, we don't need her attention until it's time for her to go behind bars."

"Wow." Troy rubbed his jaw and sank back into the couch again. "Do you think she ordered Murphy to hit you?"

"I hope not, but who knows? Murphy and the Phelps brothers could have acted of their own volition, but I have a feeling it goes deeper."

"Let's just start by focusing on Garrett Murphy. If we're running with the assumption he drove Joel Phelps's truck, how do we prove that?"

"Talk to his neighbors and see if they give the same story about the truck not leaving the driveway all week."

"And if they do?"

She didn't want to go this route, but now it seemed she had no choice. Besides, she came clean about so much else. "I have proof that his truck was used." She'd pushed the admission out quickly, but if she and Troy were going to be a team, she had to come forward with all she had.

"Proof?" His eyes darkened.

"Pictures." She got up and went down the hall for her cell phone. She brought up the spread of photos she took.

"Where did you get these?"

"From his driveway."

"Saturday morning when you slipped out in my truck." Not a question.

"Yes."

"I should—" He clenched his jaw and stared in the distance for a few seconds. "You know what? Never mind. You'll telling me now, and I appreciate that. But why not come to me with this sooner?"

"I didn't know how to handle it." The truth was she wanted to avoid confrontation and bringing her little op into the light.

Eventually he said, "Fair enough. We just need to get that indisputable proof that Joel Phelps let Garrett Murphy borrow his truck and they conspired to kill you. But what gets me is why be so blatant about it? Why would Murphy let you see his face?"

She considered his question, one she hadn't thought of before. "Maybe he thought I'd have been unconscious. Or it was a warning. He might not have intended to kill me at all. It could have just been to deliver the message that I need to back off and stop snooping around."

Troy balled a hand into a fist. "Intention aside, he almost succeeded in killing you."

"Maybe we could appeal to Murphy's humanity. He wouldn't have known I was pregnant."

"Do you think knowing would be enough for him to confess to dealings with the mob or to expose their presence in Stiles?"

"I guess not. How do you propose getting Murphy to talk?"

His eyes glazed over with concentration. "I have an idea."

"I'm listening."

"I'll call Garrett and invite him over for beers and a barbecue. I'll try to get him to open up."

"So you think burgers and beers will do that?" She still wasn't seeing where he was headed.

"Uh-huh, and I'm going to use the fact I'd questioned him about the accident to my advantage. The meal will be an apology of sorts, setting things right between us."

"Ah, so you'll present yourself as his friend."

"Yes, but I'll be wired. Andrea will be brought up to speed ahead of time. You and Andrea can listen in, and whoever else she wants present as a witness."

"Which would probably be good as we're all practically family."

Troy smiled. "We are family, I agree. Maybe we'll want to include Sergeant Winston."

"Not sure I can trust him. What about Terry? And—" She stopped. Maybe suggesting who she had in mind wasn't a good idea.

"Who, Maddy?"

"Cynthia. But I need to talk to her before this all goes down. Let her know. It's the right thing to do."

"Except you can't risk her tipping off Murphy, or Lou finding out and warning his friend."

"If I tell Cynthia in confidence, I can't see her passing any of this along to Lou. I do trust her, but just as a preventative measure, we could time it so I'm telling her when Murphy's already on his way to our place."

"Now, that sounds like a plan."

Fifty-One

I t was six thirty, and Madison was holed up in a communications trailer parked a block over from her and Troy's house. Andrea was there, along with Cynthia and Terry and Nick, one of Troy's best friends, who was also from his SWAT team.

Madison wasn't quite sure that Cynthia was talking to her anymore, but she'd agreed to come along with the words, "What the hell?"

When Madison approached Terry, she did her best to lay everything out. She'd started with, "There is something I'm involved in that I prefer to keep you out of, but it turns out, it's best to get you involved."

"Now you have me intrigued."

"Before you get too excited, what I'm asking could be dangerous. First, you should know the Russian Mafia is still operating in Stiles—" She held up her hand to stop him from interrupting. "And they have corrupt cops on their payroll."

"Hate to sound dismissive, but there are probably cops on the take in every police department around the world. What do they have to do with you?"

It had been a good question, but the answer was simple if not vague. She had an inexplicable drive to clean up her city.

"So?" Terry pressed.

"It's just who I am, Terry. Corrupt cops need to be taken off the streets."

"And you're going to do that all on your own?"

"I like to think others in the department would support my efforts and that people have my back."

"You have people, Maddy," Terry eventually said. "You just don't let us in."

She responded at the risk of her voice cracking. "I'm working on that."

"All right, then. In that case, I'm in. I'll do whatever I can."

She went on to explain what she and Troy had planned, how she needed a neutral party, and Terry was just one part of that team.

At first, he'd hesitated. He'd expressed concern about the night going sideways and tried to place doubts in her mind. What if she was mistaken and had seen it all wrong? But she didn't think he questioned her sanity as much as he would have loved for her to back off.

"It's one thing if it's Garrett and Joel in on this. Another if the mob ordered them to do it," Terry had said.

"Trust me, I know," she'd responded, and Terry hadn't said anymore except that he had her back, *even if he regretted it.*

There was enough room in the trailer for all of them to sit. Nick would ensure that the wire was working, and he was recording the conversation, which played at a low volume in the trailer so they didn't all have to wear earbuds.

Troy had spoken to some of Joel Phelps's neighbors that afternoon, and there were a few who couldn't vouch for the truck being in his driveway Monday night.

"Here you go," Troy's voice came over the comms. Madison wished there was some way to watch what was happening, too, but she imagined Troy handing Murphy a beer.

There was a bit of silence. Both probably drinking.

"So where's that girlfriend of yours?" Murphy asked.

Madison noted how Murphy avoided using her name. *Detective* when face-to-face, and *girlfriend* now.

"She's spending some time with Cynthia."

Madison glanced over at her friend, but she seemed to be looking everywhere but at her.

"Women." Murphy laughed.

"Yeah, I just wanted to have you over because I feel bad," Troy said. "You know about yesterday. It wasn't cool that I questioned you."

"I appreciate that."

"It's just…well, you know Maddy gets stuff in her head sometimes, and it's hard to convince her otherwise." She and Troy had discussed how he was going to approach the conversation and playing her up as a little zany and obsessive was agreed upon ahead of time.

"Uh-huh," Murphy mumbled.

Madison noticed how Troy planted the subliminal *you know Maddy* into his statement, and Murphy's lackluster response indicated that he knew what she was like. But they had never spent time around each other so unless he poked into her business, he'd have no idea about her personality or her motivations.

"Anyway, I've spoken with her, and she's backing off."

"That's good, man."

Another stretch of silence.

Cynthia sighed loudly and shook her head.

Troy went on. "She's just obsessed, you know."

"Obsessed?" Murphy's voice was tentative.

"Yeah, with the mob. She swears they're still active in Stiles."

"Oh, please."

The hairs rose on Madison's arms, and her earlobes heated. She could strangle the man. Troy deserved credit for sitting across from the guy without knocking him out.

"You don't think they are?" Troy asked.

"Nah. They're gone."

"You're probably right."

A span of silence, Murphy broke it.

"Why would she even think the Russians are still in town?"

Madison noted the small victory. Murphy was curious, which meant he was on the defensive.

"She's quite sure some Stiles PD cops are on their payroll too."

"Huh." Murphy scoffed laughter. "She really has an active imagination." It was apparent he made the comment as a throwaway, but there was more to his tone of voice. Fear? Dismissal? Misdirection?

"She does."

"So do you have any idea who might have run into her car?"

Troy was doing great at getting Murphy relaxed and open. Murphy probably had no clue that he was being duped.

"We have a vehicle make and model and a partial plate."

A few seconds passed in which Madison could picture Murphy leaning forward, eager to know where that had led Troy.

"Any hits?" Murphy asked.

"Yeah."

"Well, that's good, right? Who owns the vehicle?"

"Ah, don't concern yourself with it. I don't even know if it's going to stick."

"What's gonna stick?"

"The pending charges against the driver."

"And who—"

"Like I said, don't concern yourself with it."

"You thought it was me yesterday, so I am." There was an edge to Murphy's voice. He'd probably heard from Joel Phelps that Troy was asking questions about his truck.

Cynthia looked at Madison now, just briefly.

"Guy's name is Joel Phelps," Troy laid out.

"Phelps?" Murphy seemed to be experiencing a period of amnesia—all a show.

"He's Dustin Phelps's brother."

"Ah, that's why I know the name."

"So you've never met him? Joel?"

"Not that I remember."

"Wow, that's rich," Madison exclaimed.

Andrea laid a calming hand on her shoulder. Terry and Nick glanced over and offered pressed-lip expressions that communicated support. Cynthia crossed her arms.

"Huh, I thought you might have met," Troy began. "You and Dustin pull some shifts together, don't you?"

"Sure, but we're not buddies."

"He's a real lying sack of shit!" Madison fumed and paced the trailer.

Cynthia bolted to her feet and moved in front of her. "Do you even know Garrett?"

"Not personally—"

"Then how would you know who he knows?" With that, Cynthia stormed from the trailer.

Madison balled her fists and looked up the ceiling.

Andrea went to her and put her hands on Madison's forearms. "This has gotta be rough on her. She probably thought she knew Garrett. Give her time. She'll probably come around."

"I hope you're right."

"I think it's obvious to all of us here that Officer Murphy is hiding something," Andrea declared.

"I agree, Maddy," Terry told her.

Nick nodded.

She sat down at the table, and so did Andrea and Terry. They listened as Troy made more small talk and cooked him and Murphy dinner. During the couple hours they spent together, there were no admissions—not that this was expected—but it laid the groundwork.

The next step would be more fun, but it was one that she promised to leave in Troy's hands. He'd commissioned a couple other men from his SWAT team to follow Murphy. Troy had said enough that if Murphy was involved with the mob, he'd be running back to warn his partners in crime. It was also pretty much guaranteed that he'd be paying Joel Phelps a visit.

Fifty-Two

Monday. And there wasn't one good thing about it. Murphy hadn't led Troy's men anywhere. Not even to Joel Phelps's house. But Troy and Nick were back to tailing Murphy. She was pouring herself a second decaf coffee when there was a knock on the door. That would be Terry picking her up for work.

"Any progress?" he asked when she let him inside.

"With Murphy?"

He nodded.

"Not yet, but it's only a matter of time." She just wished they had enough to warrant tapping his phone. Unfortunately, the pictures she had of Murphy at Club Sophisticated weren't enough for a subpoena as they weren't acquired during an official police investigation.

She put on her shoes and coat, said goodbye to Hershey, who looked content on his bed, and locked the door behind her and Terry.

"I heard back from the bank on Keller's rent check."

"Really? It's only nine forty-five. Someone's up early."

"Someone's a fan of cops."

"Guess there are a few left."

"Cheery and optimistic this morning, I see." Terry laughed and loaded into his van. She got into the passenger seat.

"And?"

"The name attached to the account is Morgan Palmer, female. And I have an address."

"Someone else paid her rent or is Shannon Keller a fake name too?"

"Guess we'll find out."

"After, we exchange this thing for a department car."

"Sounds like a plan."

As Terry drove them to the station, her mind kept drifting to the vehicle they were in. Would a van be her next vehicle?

"I assume you pulled a background on Morgan Palmer," she said.

"Yep. She's thirty-five, a brunette, five-ten."

"Okay, but I'm more interested in her criminal record."

"Doesn't have one," he said.

"Hopefully, this Palmer lady can give us a lead on Keller. Again, that's if she's not Keller. Let's face it, this wouldn't be the first time we ran into a fake name with this case."

Terry grinned. "Want to make a bet?"

"Really?"

"It also wouldn't be the first time."

She considered then said, "Okay, the regular twenty?"

"I'm in."

"All right. I say that Morgan Palmer and Shannon Keller are the same person."

"Don't cry when you lose."

"Don't you." This friendly bet was lifting her spirits, and she was ready to collect.

He got them to the station, and they signed out a department car, swapped seats so she was driving, and they headed to Palmer's address.

Her phone rang on the way. Caller ID told her it was Cynthia. Madison answered, prepared for a lashing—from her friend *and* Terry, who usually freaked out when she spoke on the phone while driving.

"How are you?" Cynthia asked.

"Fine." Madison hadn't expected that to be the first thing out of her friend's mouth.

"I should have known you'd come back with that." There was the teeniest hint of a smile to her friend's voice.

Then there was an awkward silence.

Cynthia offered, "I'm sorry if I hurt you yesterday. I've had all night to sleep on what I heard between Troy and Garrett. I think he's shady as hell. But I haven't said a word of this to Lou. As far as he knows, it was just you and I hanging out last night."

"I appreciate that. Listen, maybe we could meet up and talk in person?"

"I'd love that, but work first, right?"

"Always. Actually, Terry and I are following a lead in the Carson case at this minute."

"Oh, well, I have some news for you. I watched more of the video from the city."

"You got the plate on the Mercedes?"

"Why do you always do that? Jump in and try to steal my thunder?"

Madison felt tingles run through her body. "So you got a plate?"

"Not exactly. And I can't zoom in and clean up the tag enough to read it."

"Why give me a hard time, then? What's your news?"

"Just that I saw a silver Mercedes SUV enter the pub lot at nine fifteen the Friday Carson was attacked."

"You saw who was behind the wheel?"

"Not yet."

"Okay… That's all?"

"And I wanted to apologize."

Madison shut her eyes briefly and opened them. "Thank you."

"You're welcome. Now, go catch a killer."

Cynthia beat Madison to hanging up.

Terry looked over at her from the passenger seat. "What was all that about?"

"Cynthia has a silver Mercedes on the city's video but no plate."

"Hmph. Hardly worth a call."

Madison smiled and pulled in front of a brick bungalow. "You said number two thirty-four?"

"Yep. This is it." Terry beat her getting out of the car, which wasn't much of an accomplishment as she was still in discomfort.

She noted the vehicle in the driveway as she walked to the front door. It was a newer model sedan, but no Mercedes.

Terry rang the doorbell before she got there, and footsteps padded toward them.

"Yes?" A woman in her thirties, brown hair, approximately five-ten, stood there, dressed in jeans and a blue T-shirt.

Terry held up his badge, Madison followed his lead.

"We'd like to speak with Shannon Keller," Terry said. "Or should I say Morgan Palmer?"

The woman smiled and let her expression carry from Terry to Madison, then bolted into the house and down a long hallway. Terry tore after her. Madison wasn't running anywhere for anyone. She calmly stepped inside and thought of ways she was going to spend the twenty bucks she'd made off the bet.

Terry's shoes clamored on the wood floor as he chased Keller—or rather, Palmer. It wasn't long before there was a loud thud, followed by a string of expletives and Terry yelling, "Get to your feet!"

He hauled Palmer back toward the front door.

"Why run? Unless you're guilty of something." Madison scanned Palmer's eyes.

Palmer balled up her face like she was going to spit or scream, but the ugliness washed away as quickly as it appeared. She shrugged free of Terry, and he let her go.

"Tell us about Jake Elliott," Madison demanded.

"He's a douche bag."

So she knew him by his real name. "That part we figured out already. Now we're trying to figure out if he's also a killer."

"A killer?" Palmer pushed out. Not so much from shock, but amusement. Her eyes lit.

"Uh-huh." Madison closed the front door, encasing the three of them in a shadowy entry. She found a light switch and flicked it on. "Where can we find him?"

Palmer wiped her cheek on her shoulder.

"Want to clam up? Really?" Madison huffed out. "You operate under an alias. Only criminals do that. And I'm sure you were in on the cons Jake pulled."

Palmer's gaze flicked to Madison's.

The fact Palmer knew Elliott's real name was enough to verify for Madison, but the eye contact at her accusation sealed it. "So that's a yes," Madison concluded. "Do you know or have you heard of Chantelle Carson?"

"Maybe."

Terry nudged Palmer in the back. "A yes or no would work nicely."

"Yes," Palmer hissed.

"Well, she's dead. Murdered." Madison delivered the news without tact to get a reaction. Palmer's shoulders sagged—that's all.

"Well, I can't see Jake killing anyone."

"Let us determine that," Madison said. "Tell us where we can find him."

"I've fallen out of touch with him in the last several months."

"That's convenient," Madison said drily and thought it was probably a lie.

"I mean it, but he's probably in his mother's basement."

"And where would that be?" Madison was losing patience with this woman.

"She has some nerve, I'll tell you that. She just showed up one day, kicked me out, and she moved in. Said her son didn't need me anymore, and with him being the douche bag he is—an effing momma's boy—he didn't say anything."

Kicked me out, and she moved in... "What's the mother's name?"

"Mary Smith."

"That her real name?" Madison tossed back.

"Probably a fair question. Don't really know, come to think of it. I was told her last name was different than Jake's because she'd remarried after he was born."

Madison was having a hard time reconciling the sweet, little, unassuming Mary Smith she and Terry had met with the vindictive mother

Palmer was painting. "Does she know what her son does to unsuspecting women?"

"Know?" she scoffed. "She's like the kingpin. Always telling him that he's got to use what God gave him. It would be disrespectful not to. Yadda, yadda."

"And that translates to…?" Madison was hoping for some clarity.

"Using his looks to rope in women and then rip them off. Mother and son have no conscience. But murder? I was his girlfriend for eight years. I can't see Jake killing someone."

"Even if someone threatened to expose him?" Madison countered.

Palmer worried her lip, met Madison's gaze. "Maybe, I suppose."

"We've been told Jake drives a gray Mercedes SUV," Madison began. "We don't show any vehicles registered to him. Do you know whose it might be?" They had been thinking it belonged to his latest mark.

"That would be Mommy Dearest's."

Madison was trying to picture the elderly woman at the wheel. "Do you have a number for Jake?"

"Yeah." Palmer rattled it off, and Terry pecked it into his phone.

"All right, well, we've got to go. Detective Grant." Madison nudged her head toward the door and opened it.

"Wait. You're not arresting me?" Palmer called out behind them.

"Should we be?" Madison volleyed back.

She looked down at the floor.

Palmer probably had information she could provide on Elliott's other cons. Heck, she was likely in on them herself, but Madison wasn't with the fraud department. Not that she'd let her walk but solving Carson's murder was her priority. "Just stick around Stiles. You will be questioned further about the extent of your relationship with Mr. Elliott and your involvement with the cons he ran. But who knows? If he's behind Ms. Carson's murder, you may provide useful testimony for the prosecution and secure yourself a deal."

"Okay."

Madison hurried back to the car, Terry close behind her, and she settled behind the wheel.

Terry pulled his phone and said, "I'm going to give that number a try."

"Hold up, and say what?"

"What I was going to say when I called the numbers on Carson's outgoing list. That I'm looking for Jake Elliott because he stands to inherit."

"Okay, but use Saul Abbott, not his real name, in this case." It felt like a lot had happened since that conversation.

A few seconds later, Terry shook his head. "Didn't ring, and there's no voicemail."

"So it's off but still in service. That's good news. Maybe Cynthia could track the phone. Can you call her?"

"Sure, and you'll be…"

"Driving us to Mary Poppins."

"You mean Mary Smith?"

"Well, it's possible she's just as fictional as the nanny who descends from the sky holding an umbrella. Wait. You don't happen to remember the name on file for Jake Elliott's birth mother, do you?"

"Nope." He gestured to the on-board computer. "Take a look."

She did and the results were there in black-and-white. "Mary Smith is his mother's name."

"There you go."

Terry might have been convinced everything was on the up and up, but she wasn't. It just seemed strange that after eight years of Palmer being with Elliott, his mother would show up out of the seeming blue one day and kick her out. Madison was determined to get to the bottom of it.

Fifty-Three

Madison **pulled a report through the** on-board computer, and no Mary Smith lived at the rental address. A reverse-address search proved useless. Next, she tried a quick DMV search, but no Mercedes SUVs tied back to the rental property or Smith. But she wasn't sure if that meant anything or not.

Madison parked in front of the house, and no vehicles were in the drive, but there was a garage. She walked around the side, and there was a window.

"What are you doing?" Terry said.

"Just trying to get a peek inside." She pressed her hand to the glass to cut the glare and said, "No car at all."

"Maybe no one's home?"

Madison knocked on the front door. She was braced to knock again when it opened.

"Hello, Detectives." Smith smiled at Madison and Terry.

If this woman was the devil that Palmer had painted her out to be, then she deserved acting awards, but there were holes that needed filling. "Do you have a minute to talk?" Madison plastered on sweetness herself, but she'd never claimed to be a good actress.

"Sure. Come on in. I was just making tea."

Smith set them up in the living room that was tastefully decorated but sparse with no personal touches or pictures of Jake Elliott. Sort of odd for a mother who was supposedly so infatuated with her son.

They waited several minutes for Smith to get herself a tea and return to the room.

"Ms. Smith," Madison started. "We understand that Jake Elliott is your son. Is that correct?"

Smith sat straight in a cushioned chair, her tea in a teacup on top of a saucer, held primly in her right hand. "That's correct, dear."

"We're trying to reach him about some important news." She was going to stick to the plan of saying that he stood to inherit. Smith might be willing to part with her son's whereabouts if there was money at stake.

"Oh? What would that be?"

"Well, it would be best if we could tell him in person, but we're having a hard time reaching him," Madison said. "Would you know where we could find him?"

Smith's eyes narrowed just a fraction. "Whatever you have to tell him, you can tell me."

"Yeah? You're sure?" Madison smiled, calling upon acting skills once again.

"Of course, dear."

"Okay, well, we have come into the knowledge that he is the beneficiary of a substantial life insurance policy." Half of that was true; they didn't know the amount.

"Wow. Really?" Her voice took on a high pitch that was seemingly uncharacteristic of the older lady. She set her plate and teacup on a nearby table.

"But as I mentioned, we will need to speak with him," Madison started. "If there's some way you could put us in touch?"

"He's actually out of town on a job."

"Okay, well, what about a phone number for him?" They had one, assuming the one Palmer had provided belonged to Elliott, but Madison was getting a feeling in her gut Mary Smith was stalling.

"I'd love to, but...dang." Smith slapped her leg. "Just before you got here, I was looking for my phone. That's the problem with all these high-tech, finagled gadgets. The numbers go in them and straight out of the noggin'. But maybe you could help me understand something, dear. Why are two detectives here about something like this?"

This woman was as shady as a downtown alley at night. "The deceased was a woman he was involved with, and she was murdered." Madison paused to insert a frown. "I'm sure your son had deep feelings for Ms. Carson, too, so it's best that we break the news about her death to him. I'm sure you can understand that."

"Ms. Carson, you say?"

"Uh-huh," Madison replied. "You knew her?"

"I met her once." Smith put her teacup to her lips. "Such a shame."

Madison's skin crawled. Something wasn't quite right here. She'd just told Smith that Carson was murdered. Most people inquired as to what happened to cause the death. Smith hadn't. But what was Madison thinking—that this older lady stabbed Carson? Was that even physically possible?

"Well, we should go. But please have your son call us." She handed Smith her business card, and she and Terry left.

Back in the department car, she said, "That woman gives me the creeps."

"I think something's off, too, but she's an old lady. Hard to imagine her killing Carson."

"I thought the same. Let's just hope she bought what we said." She drove down the street, turned around in someone's driveway, and parked facing the direction of the rental house. "And now we wait."

Terry shifted his body toward her. "For what? Elliott? He could be home and inside."

"Sure he could, but I think he's out in the Mercedes. It's not in the driveway or the garage."

"So we're just going to sit here?"

"Yep."

"I hate stakeouts," Terry mumbled. "Especially ones without food or coffee."

His complaint made her stomach rumble. She could do another Hershey's bar, but when couldn't she? And now chocolate made her think of Troy and how he was making out at that very moment. Was Murphy doing or saying anything to implicate himself?

She pulled out her phone and fired Troy a quick text. *Thinking of you. R U ok? Having any luck?*

A few seconds later, her phone bleeped back. *Nope. Doing OK. Hope ur taking it easy.*

She'd told him she planned to work today, and pecked off, *With Terry, following lead.*

Nothing for a bit, then, *Ok.*

Her phone rang, and it was Cynthia. She put her on speaker.

"Okay, so I spoke to Judge Myers, and he gave me verbal approval. But no luck tracking the phone."

"Knew not to get too excited," Madison mumbled.

"Wish I had better news." With that, Cynthia disconnected.

Terry looked over at Madison. "You want to keep hanging out and see what happens?"

"Not sure what other choice we have."

"Okay." He clasped his hands on his lap and put his head against the rest.

She was quite sure he'd closed his eyes. Terry wasn't exactly the prize stakeout partner.

A couple hours passed, and her butt was beyond numb. She got out of the car to stretch and wasn't sure if her back was going to straighten. By two in the afternoon, still no visible activity on the rental property, but she called Cynthia and begged for a favor.

She dropped off the Greek salads and gyros Madison asked for, and Terry dug right in.

"Thank God," he said. "I was about to die."

Madison laughed and took small forkfuls to gauge how the food was settling. The smell was intoxicating, so she took that as a positive sign.

The afternoon turned to evening, and she sent a quick message to Troy to let him know she was on a stakeout with Terry and wasn't sure when she'd be home. He responded with, *Just be safe.*

The sun sank in the sky, and the clock on the dash read *9:10 PM.*

Terry had dozed off at least an hour ago and was snoring. Probably more boredom than anything. Madison was pretty much right there herself.

Headlights caught her attention, and she sat up straighter. The vehicle pulled into the rental house driveway. It was an SUV. A Mercedes? Elliott behind the wheel?

"Terry," she said. He didn't stir. "Psst. Terry." She nudged him.

"Yeah, yeah." He inclined his chair.

"What's wrong with you anyway? It's only after nine, and you've been asleep for a bit."

"Dani's keeping us up."

Eight months later… Add sleep to the list of what she'd have to give up. "Well, it's time to move." She pointed out the windshield.

Someone got out of the SUV, dressed in black from head to toe, and went in the front door. Madison crept the department car past the rental. Definitely a Mercedes SUV. She said to Terry, "Grab the plate."

Then she drove down the street and parked several driveways from the rental. She keyed the plate Terry read off to her into the system. "Registered to a Gloria Barker." She paused there. The name sounded familiar. She shook that aside, unable to place why. "She's twenty-eight, but look at the address." She swiveled the laptop as much as she could toward Terry.

"That's down by the harbor. High-priced condos."

"Brownstones," she blurted out. "I should have remembered." The Mafia used to have a warehouse down by the water. She would have driven past the homes a lot of times. "The bulk of Carson's pictures were taken of Elliott outside a brownstone." Her stomach flopped. "And her initials, Terry. GB. Could Gloria Barker be who Carson meant when she wrote the letters in blood?"

"We're gonna find out," Terry affirmed.

"You bet we are." Madison started into a U-turn, and sweat trickled down her back as she remembered the last time she'd intended this maneuver. Today, it was executed without issue.

She parked out front of the rental, blocking the driveway. "It's time to get some answers. Starting with: who is Gloria Barker, and how does she fit into all this?" She turned the car off and headed down the driveway with Terry behind her.

"Shouldn't we call for backup? Just in case this turns sideways?"

"Let's see what we're dealing with—"

A shot rang out. He ducked around the side of the house.

"That came from inside," she hissed, crouch-walking to join him.

Another shot was fired and blasted out the front window of the house.

Shit! She hadn't expected things to go this way. And who was firing on whom? "That backup you mentioned? Now would be a good time."

Terry was already on his phone. "I request backup to—" He prattled off the address. "Shots fired." He hung up and said to her, "We're to hang back and wait for SWAT."

She wanted to run in there, and she might have in the past, but not now with the baby. She put a hand on her stomach.

"Now's not the time to be feeling sick."

"I'm fine."

He pointed a finger at where her hand rested. "Doesn't look like it."

There was nothing but silence now, a deafening bookend to the thunderous reports.

"Did they say how long they'd be?"

"Dispatch knows it's urgent."

It would still take them precious time though, and she and Terry were right there, armed and trained to handle the situation. "Maybe we should just—"

"No," Terry said firmly. "And there's no way in hell I'm going in there with a partner who's still on the mend."

Hell was a swear word to Terry, and he meant business if he pulled it out, but he was right. She was in no condition to go in there and had no right to put her baby at risk.

Terry's phone rang, and he filled his caller in on the details—two shots fired; he and Madison were on the north exterior side of the building; the occupants were suspected to be a Mary Smith and Jake Elliott, allegedly mother and son; or it was Gloria Barker with Smith, relationship unknown.

The sound of vehicle traffic intensified, and she caught the sight of colored lights reflecting off neighboring buildings. No sirens.

Madison poked her head around the bend, saw the SWAT command vehicle, and watched as the men unloaded. It was Troy's men, which meant he would be there.

The SWAT team moved up the driveway toward the house. Nick Benson led the way and held up a large bulletproof shield to cover the rest of the men who followed. All of them kept their focus on the house, as one distraction could prove deadly.

Troy spoke through a megaphone. "Stiles PD. Put down your weapon and come out with your hands on your head."

Madison heard the distinct creaking of the front door opening, then Mary Smith appeared.

"Please, please. She's hurt."

"She?" Madison turned to Terry, who shook his head, also confused.

"Stay there, ma'am," Troy commanded. "Drop the weapon and put your hands on your head."

"Please…there was an accident. She shot herself." Smith was crying, but there was an insincere edge to her voice.

Had Gloria Barker been the one to arrive in the Mercedes and get shot?

"Gun down," Troy barked.

"Yes, yes, sorry."

"Hands on your head," Troy repeated.

"Please help her."

Footsteps advanced to the front door. Troy was likely securing the weapon. "Tell us where she is, ma'am."

Smith directed Troy to the dining room.

"Hurry! She's bleeding out!" Smith cried. "Why, God?"

Just hearing that woman say *God* made Madison bristle.

A few minutes later, the all-clear was given, and the paramedics from the waiting ambulance were allowed to go inside.

Troy rounded the corner of the house. "I can't leave you alone for one minute," he said to Madison.

She stiffened. "I couldn't have anticipated this."

"Trouble follows you wherever you go."

She angled her head. "Guess you better get out of Dodge, then."

"You kidding me? Do you think I joined SWAT because I can't handle trouble?" He held her gaze and was the first to smile. "*Trouble* can just be another word for *excitement*, and you give me that in spades."

Terry put a hand on her shoulder and left her with Troy.

"I should have taken the day off and gotten some rest," she volunteered.

"You have a hard time doing what you know you should."

"I do." Verbalizing the two words tugged on her heart. She would love to say them to Troy in a different context, and if he wasn't going to ask... Her heart sped up, and she couldn't believe she was even considering doing what fired through her mind. She had to be insane. She was a feminist, but she still clung to the old-fashioned tradition that the man should be the one to ask. And here and now really wasn't the time... "Will you marry me?" She slapped a hand over her mouth, lowered it, peacocked her stance, unapologetic.

He hesitated just long enough to make her want to disappear into the earth.

"Never mind, it was stupid of me to—" She turned to walk away, but he caught her hand on a backswing.

"I'd love to marry you."

"You...you..." No more words would form.

"Yes, Madison, and I should have answered you when you asked if I was going to propose at Cynthia's wedding."

"Were you?"

"Yes."

Her stomach clenched. "Why didn't you?"

"It wasn't the time or the place. I didn't want you to think I'd just made the decision impulsively."

"You get caught up in your emotions and make impulsive decisions? Not a chance I'd think that." It was the opposite of his character—unless he was pissed off.

"Truth is I was planning it for a few weeks. Been thinking about it for a lot longer than that."

Troy's men shuffled down the driveway, and the paramedics loaded up the injured woman. Gloria Barker? Madison hadn't seen her face.

The ambulance drove off, lights flashing and sirens blaring.

"You still haven't asked though," she said timidly, not used to this feeling. "Why? Because of what you said to me earlier about feeling second place?" Her voice caught.

"Yes. I just need to know that we're in this together—all the time. No more secrets. I know your job's important to you, and it will always be a priority for you. That's who you are. It's one of the things I love about you. I just want to be a priority too."

"Always." She fell against his chest. To hell with making a "scene" at a crime scene. Let the neighbors see two cops hugging and— She put her mouth on his, and he cupped her face.

She pulled back and said, "I love you, Troy."

"I love you."

"Do you guys have a job to do, or are you going to stand around all night making kissy-face?" Nick had come around the corner and was sticking out his lips.

"Hey, man, we just got engaged," Troy announced proudly and swung an arm around Madison.

"Congratulations!" Nick sauntered off, and Madison was confident the rest of the team would know before Troy returned to the command vehicle.

"You think right now was the best time to make it public?" she asked.

"I'd shout it through the megaphone," he said. "Just dare me." He winked at her, then slapped her on the behind. "I'll see you at home." He walked a few steps and turned around. "I will, right?"

"You will."

At that time, one of Troy's men came down the driveway with Smith. She'd be taken downtown to make a statement of events, and Madison had her own questions.

Smith noticed Madison, and her eyes widened, then she smiled. And it was there: the spacing between the eyes, the bridge of the nose, the knobby chin. Madison didn't know who had been shot, but she was quite certain Mary Smith wasn't who she claimed to be.

Madison trudged toward Smith and grabbed her white hair and yanked.

Smith screeched.

Madison was left holding a wig and the "old lady" had blond hair wound in pins. "Well, hello, Gloria Barker."

Fifty-Four

Nothing in this case **was** straightforward, but rarely was solving a murder easy. There were still questions that needed answers, but they found out the woman shot in the rental house was Morgan Palmer. Why Palmer had been driving Barker's Mercedes was unanswered at this point, as was the relationship between the two women. But Madison would guess the two were working together and benefiting from Elliott's cons.

Crime Scene was combing the rental house and the harbor-front condo owned by Gloria Barker for any forensic evidence tying her to Carson's murder. A picture Cynthia sent over confirmed that it was the same building Elliott had been captured in front of in Carson's photos. In the meantime, Madison was at the station with Terry, getting ready to question Gloria Barker.

Madison had finally remembered where she'd seen the name Barker. It had been in Carson's files. A Maria Barker was defrauded by Jake Elliott ten years ago. A deeper look showed that she had a daughter, Gloria, who was eighteen at the time. As for why she'd latched on to Jake Elliott, that answer wasn't going to come from a file, but Madison had her suspicions that Gloria had tracked Jake down and blackmailed him in exchange for her silence.

"How did you know that Mary Smith was actually Gloria Barker?" Terry asked. "And does anyone go by their real name anymore?"

"It was in her eyes. And that smile. Why smile at me after someone just got shot? It was because she was feeling cocky, like she got away with everything. What happened to Palmer wasn't an accident, and I intend to prove that."

"You sure you want to stay? I can handle the interrogation."

"Troy understands I want to see this through. Besides, there's no way I'm leaving now."

"You sure about that?"

"Why?" She angled her head. "You trying to get rid of me?"

"I might have heard something…" Terry grinned.

"Ah, of course you did." Cops had loose lips.

"You and Troy are going to tie the knot? I heard it from Nick. Guy gossips worse than a girl, louder than a girl."

Madison wound up and punched him in the shoulder.

"Hey." Terry laughed and rubbed where she'd impacted him.

"That one's been a long time coming," she teased.

"Where's the ring?" Terry exaggerated a search of her wedding finger.

"He didn't have the ring at the crime scene."

"You're telling me that man acted on a whim, in the moment? Huh, never would have pegged him the type."

"He's been wanting to ask for a while; it was just the right time." Terry didn't need to know that she'd been the one to pop the question.

"Well, I'm happy for both of you. And it's about time."

She made like she was going to hit him again but started laughing.

"Congratulations," he added.

"Thank you." She leaned in and hugged Terry, then pulled back. "Okay, okay, now we've got that mushy stuff out of the way, let's get in there." She pointed through the two-way mirror into the interrogation room where Gloria Barker was seated at a table.

"Gloria Barker." Madison sat across from her.

"So what? You know my name? Congratulations."

The sweet, old lady act was gone like her wig. In its place were long blond locks released from the pins.

Madison made a display of looking inside a folder full of papers.

"I haven't done anything wrong."

Madison ignored her claim and said, "You graduated True Talent with a diploma in theatrical makeup." Madison flicked a finger toward Barker's face to indicate the wrinkles and crow's feet around the eyes. "Almost had me fooled."

She shrugged.

"Tell us what really happened tonight."

Terry walked to the back of the room behind Madison, facing Barker, and proceeded to jangle the change in his pocket.

"You know what happened. I already gave my statement. Shannon—"

"Nope," Madison cut in. "Try again."

Barker scowled. "Morgan tripped and fell, and the gun went off."

"Nope."

"What the—" She stopped, her gaze going past Madison, likely to a corrective look on Terry's face.

"To start with, the gun was fired twice. Once into the front window and once into Ms. Palmer. Her injuries were inconsistent with being self-inflicted. It's probably a good time to get talking because I guarantee you as soon as Morgan's out of surgery she'll be talking." Something that would never happen, not that Gloria would know that, because on the way to the station

Madison got the call that Morgan Palmer had died before reaching the hospital.

"She's just going to tell you what I did."

Terry jingled his change louder, and Barker glanced at him again. Her obvious irritation had no impact on Terry as he carried on.

"She won't get that chance. She's dead, and I'd like to know why you killed her," Madison tossed out now.

"She's—" Her chin quivered and tears formed in her eyes.

Madison wagged a finger at her. "Man, you're good. Tears on command. You might have had a future in acting."

Barker's chin quivered. "I didn't kill her. I told you—"

"You're not too broken up that she's dead. Not really." Madison leaned across the table. "Am I right?"

"She tripped! She brought this on herself. What was she doing carrying a gun anyway?"

"I think it was your gun, and I think you called her to your house. Why she had your car I don't fully understand, but I'm sure we'll get to that."

Barker held out her hands. "Test them for GSR if you want."

Madison smiled. "We'll find it, and you'll have justification for its presence. You answered the door with the gun, so you'd have deniability. It's the other pertinents working against you— angle of entry and—"

Barker scowled.

"Why don't you just tell me what really happened tonight?"

Barker clamped her mouth shut.

"Fine, you don't want to talk about that. What about your mother's bankruptcy ten years ago?"

"What about it? It has nothing to do with me."

"Who paid for your schooling? Couldn't have been cheap."

"Dad did."

"Huh. Well, I'm quite sure that Jake Elliott was the reason for your mother's financial ruin and that you found him and threatened to expose him unless he gave you money."

Barker slid down in her chair and shrugged.

Madison went on. "But you didn't just want one payoff; you wanted to be set for life or as long as he could pull off the con."

"Whatever." Barker wiped at her face with a tissue, but the makeup remained unaffected. She still had the wrinkles of an older woman.

Madison relaxed in her chair, and Terry stopped jingling the change.

Madison continued. "More recently, you showed up at Jake's door under the guise of being his mother and kicked out Morgan Palmer."

"Whatever."

"Why after all this time? Was he becoming harder to control?" She paused but Barker wasn't talking. "And why kick Ms. Palmer out of the rental? Quite sure you two were benefiting from Jake's cons. That sound right?"

Barker's gaze danced to Madison's.

Madison had struck on something there. "Where is Jake Elliott?"

She knotted her arms. "How would I know?"

"Fine." Madison went into the folder to pull the photo from the crime scene of the GB written in blood, and there was a knock on the door. "Occupied," Madison called out.

"There's something you need to know." It was Cynthia.

Madison stepped into the hall. "What is it? Why aren't you at the rental or the condo?"

"I came back because I wanted to tell you this to your face. We found Jake Elliott."

"Where is he? We'll need to speak with him."

Cynthia's face went grim. "His body was in a large chest freezer in the basement of the rental. He was shot."

Madison stumbled back and leaned against the wall. "Morgan Palmer said he was probably living in his mother's basement."

"Interesting."

A picture was forming in Madison's mind, and it wasn't a pretty one. "I wonder if the two women killed him," she said. "But why?"

"Don't know, but there are a couple other things you should know. You were interested in the call history on Elliott's phone from a few weeks back—Terry asked for my help," she clarified. "Anyway, one of the calls placed on that Friday evening was to a number tied to Gloria Barker."

"Okay, confirms again that Elliott and Barker were working together," Madison said. "And with Barker's and Palmer's phones, I'm sure we'll get all we need to prove their alliance."

"Yes. And there's something else you need to know. I looked at the city's video again with a real close eye for who was behind the wheel of the Mercedes SUV. It was a woman with long blond hair." Cynthia pulled out a photo from a folder she held and gave it to Madison.

Long blond locks. "Gloria Barker."

"Could be. I haven't seen her."

"Oh, no, it's her. She was at the bar that night because she knew Carson was getting ready to expose Elliott and maybe they'd arranged to meet. Gloria did what she had to in order to protect the free ride she had going. Gloria Barker is GB, I have no doubt."

"Crazy." Cynthia shook her head. "But, like you said, why kill Elliott? Carson was out of the way."

"Could be that Elliott found out what Barker had done. Or he was there." She felt herself pale and added, "He could con women, but murder might have panged his conscience. He could have become a liability that needed to be silenced." Madison would be asking Barker, but whether she'd get a straight answer was another thing.

"And you have to wonder what Jake thought of all this. The two women pairing up behind his back."

"It's too late to ask him, but it's fair game, if you ask me. What about the knife that stabbed Carson—have you found it?"

Cynthia smiled. "Someone's a little greedy."

"Never hurts to ask. Take that as a no?"

"It's a no."

"Thanks for everything, and this." Madison held up the picture and returned to the room. She slapped the photo in front of Barker.

Barker tensed but recovered her composure quickly. "That's me. So what? Is there a law against a person driving their own car?"

Madison smiled.

"What?" Barker snapped.

"You're coming out of Luck of the Irish, a pub on Burnham Street."

"I know the place. So what?"

"I'm quite sure you attacked this woman outside the pub. Her injuries killed her." Madison pulled a photo of Chantelle Carson lying just as they'd found her in that shed and smacked it on the table.

"Who's that?"

Not so much as a glimmer of remorse or even a stab of shock at the sight of a dead body. Gloria Barker was a psychopath. "Ah, too late for denial. You told us you knew her when you were playing your role as Mary Smith."

A smile that had been playing on the edge of Barker's lips disappeared.

"But I'll remind you. Her name was Chantelle Carson." Madison slapped a photo of GB written in blood in front of Barker. "Chantelle even identified her murderer."

Barker swallowed roughly, fidgeted, and cried out, "She came at me! Waving a knife around. I just defended myself."

Madison leaned toward believing that Carson had gone to Luck of the Irish that fateful night with murder on her mind, just not her own. She never did hear if there was any forensic proof to back that suspicion. "You could have called for help, but you didn't."

Barker looked at the tabletop. "I was in shock."

"Uh-huh." Madison didn't believe that for one second. She probably didn't want an investigation that would expose the little operation she had going or for the police to find Jake Elliott. She leaned forward. "Tell me this— was it self-defense when you shot Jake Elliott?"

Terry stopped jingling change and stepped up beside Madison.

"Jake Elliott's body was discovered in a chest freezer in the basement of the rental house," she explained to Terry.

"What?" Barker cried out. "I…I don't know what you're talking about."

"Excuse me if I don't believe you. Doubt a jury will either. You'll be going to prison for a very long time. You probably shot Morgan with the same gun that you used to shoot Jake."

"Morgan did that!"

"Easy to blame dead people."

"I'm telling you the truth." Tears sprung to her eyes.

"And I guess you two were friends, eh. Probably why she had your car tonight. But tell me, why did you two kill Jake? Did he find out what you did to Chantelle and threaten to turn you in?"

"Last I saw her, she was still alive."

Madison remained silent.

Barker's tears dried, and her gaze steeled. "All this is his fault! He was a stupid idiot who didn't cover his tracks. That's how Chantelle found us, and she was going to bring a stop to everything."

"By everything, you mean your payday."

Barker dramatically rolled her eyes.

"But why kill Jake?" Madison asked. "You stopped the threat."

Barker's nostrils flared, and she clenched her jaw.

"He *was* going to turn you in for what you did to Chantelle," Madison concluded.

"I don't need to talk to you anymore."

No denial, and Madison took that as confirmation. "Well, it was nice of you to hand over the gun. But if you could just tell us where you put the knife you stabbed Chantelle with, that would be helpful."

"Go to hell. And I want that lawyer!"

Madison smiled as the left the room. Another case closed, and the killer apprehended. Definitely worth the utter exhaustion seeping in her bones.

Fifty-Five

It had been a long ten days. If only people could be their authentic selves instead of hiding behind lies, secrets, and false identities. All Madison wanted was to go home, hug her fiancé—now, that had a nice ring to it—and fall into bed. And with her mind on *ring*, she lifted her left hand. She couldn't wait until their engagement was truly official.

She stepped through the door just after midnight. She'd taken a cab from the station and cursed the entire way home about how slow the driver was going. She tried to tell him if he got pulled over, she'd make the ticket disappear, but he wasn't having any of it. Probably a good thing, since she didn't really have that authority.

The house smelled like vanilla, and candles flickered throughout the living room.

The TV was on at a low volume. Hershey lifted his head and padded over to greet her. He barked, and Troy stirred on the couch but didn't get up. *He must be asleep.*

She grabbed a throw from a chair and started to drape it over him. He reached up and snatched her wrist. It scared the crap out of her, and she squealed.

"Sorry." Troy laughed. "I didn't mean to..." He shuffled into a seated position. "Do you like the ambiance?"

"I might be a little tired to truly appreciate it, but, yes, it's nice." She sank onto the couch beside him. "What's the occasion?"

He got onto one knee in front of her. "There's something I should have done a long time ago."

She winced. "If this is a proposal, you're too late. I'm already spoken for."

"Just let me do my thing."

She smiled, held up her hands, and said, "Sorry, go ahead."

He reached into a back pocket and came out with the ring box. "I just want to be clear on something."

"Oh yeah? And what's that?"

"I want to spend the rest of my life with you. Will you marry me?" He opened the box, and tears sprang to her eyes.

"Yes, I'll marry you."

He slipped the diamond ring on her finger and leaned over to kiss her, sealing the deal and making it official. She was ready to tell the world. But it was after midnight...

"I would have enjoyed seeing your expression when you first saw your ring, but do you love it?"

"I do, but not as much as I love you."

She let him lead her to their bedroom where they made love, and time seemed to stand still. They fell asleep in each other's arms, and she enjoyed blissful dreams only to wake with intense cramping.

She slipped out of bed, careful not to wake Troy. The alarm told her it was five thirty in the morning.

She padded down the hall toward the bathroom. She had to stop twice as cramps stole her breath. Once she made it to the bathroom, she pulled down her underwear and screamed out, "Troy!"

The emergency room doctor came to the end of her bed. He didn't have to say a word as his face said it all, but he put it out loud anyway. "I'm sorry to inform you that you've lost your baby."

Madison cried, the sobs taking over of their own accord. She'd bucked against the idea of being a mother most of the pregnancy. Had she willed it from her womb? Was this her fault? She'd only started to truly accept that she was going to have a baby in the past twenty-four hours. It was because of Troy. Whenever she was with him, she felt confident enough to take on this new chapter in life. Somehow, she felt she'd be able to adjust, still make her job work.

Troy was squeezing her hand and kneading it, and rubbing her shoulders, his arm around her. "I'm sorry, baby."

She couldn't bring herself to speak. She was such a jumble of emotions. She hated that among them was also relief. Her life would mostly go back to the way it was—other than being engaged—but this wasn't how she ever would have wanted things to play out. She was angry. "I was in an accident earlier in the week." She paused, sniffled. "The doctor said the baby was fine afterward. Could it have been due to that? Did the accident hurt the baby?"

"There's no absolute way of knowing," the doctor said. "But sometimes these things happen, and there's no way of knowing why."

Had she stressed the baby with her refusal to rest? She should have just stayed home and watched TV. "Is it because I didn't stay in bed? I mean I didn't do anything…" But she had. She'd tracked down leads, orchestrated efforts to get corrupt cops off the street and to identify the mystery woman, and faced off with a killer. "Could stress have done this?"

"It's possible, but very, very unlikely. Sadly, many women lose their first baby. I'm sorry I don't have better news, and I'm truly sorry for your loss."

The doctor left the room, and she was numb. Troy was balling his hands into fists and then unfurling them.

"I'm so sorry." She swallowed roughly, and he stared in her eyes. "If you want to call off the engagement, I'll understand."

"Madison, when are you ever going to get it through your thick, stubborn-ass skull that I love you? I want to be neck-deep in your trouble. Besides, if I was going to propose because of Peanut, I would have done that at the hospital when we first found out."

"Peanut, huh?" She recalled thinking of the baby that way too. A fresh batch of tears came. Maybe her becoming a mother wasn't too far out there, but it was several years away.

"You're angry," she said, stating the obvious. His neck was red, and he was still making fists.

"Damn right, I'm angry, and I'm going to—" He started off toward the door. She jumped from the bed and snagged his arm. "Madison, let me go." His nostrils were flaring.

"No."

"Just let me—"

"No," she repeated with more force. "We're in this together. Remember? That's what you told me."

He held her gaze, then pulled her to him and hugged her tight. He wasn't crying outright, but she was quite sure he was in his heart. And for that alone—her own grief aside—the Mafia would pay dearly, and so would every corrupt cop in the city of Stiles.

Fifty-Six

I t took the better part of four days from the time Troy had his conversation with Murphy, but eventually he'd found his way to Joel Phelps in a coffeeshop outside of town.

Madison stood in the observation room with Troy and Police Chief Fletcher while Terry handled the interrogation next door. She watched and listened as the conversation came over speakers.

The subject being questioned was Joel Phelps.

"When first asked about your GMC Sierra, you said that it was in your driveway for the entire week of…" Terry went on to provide the date of the hit-and-run, which was part of the week Phelps had referenced.

"It was."

"You sure about that?" Terry paced the room, jingling the change in his pocket.

"Obviously, you think you know something."

"I'll get to that." Terry stopped moving. "Now, you often lend out your truck to your brother, Dustin. Is that right?"

"And if I do?"

"So you're not denying that?"

"Why would I?"

"Okay, then. And you for sure didn't lend it out to him on that day I asked you about?"

"Nope." Joel shook his head.

"Well, I have witnesses who can testify to seeing no vehicles in your driveway that day."

"Who?"

"Yeah, it doesn't work that way."

"Well, they got it wrong."

"See, I don't think they did." Terry pulled a photo from a folder. Madison knew it would be the one she took of his chrome grille guard, showing the blue paint speck.

"What's that?"

"I'm quite sure you know, but to clear it up, it's the chrome grille guard from the front of your pickup."

"Uh, no. I showed my truck to Detective Matthews."

In the observation room, Madison squeezed Troy's hand, and he reciprocated.

"He saw there was nothing wrong with my grille guard."

"So? You had it fixed by then."

"Not quite sure whose grille guard that is, but it's not mine."

"Want to look closer at the picture?"

Joel squirmed in his chair. "What about it?"

"This is your license number?" Terry rattled it off. "You can make out some of it in the picture there."

"Yes," Joel seethed.

"And that—" Terry pointed at the picture "—is a fleck of blue paint." He spoke as if he had a piece of paper from some lab confirming that information.

"If you say so." Joel's forehead was coated in a sheen of sweat.

"Oh, it's paint. Matches perfectly with Madison Knight's Mazda 3."

The play here was the picture of the grille guard and partial plate should have been enough to unnerve him. Then when presented with the blue fleck and a lie, it would hopefully get Joel to start talking.

"Coincidence." His Adam's apple bobbed. "I told you my truck was in my driveway all day."

"You know something interesting?"

Joel extended a hand as if to say, *By all means, continue. You're going to anyway.*

"You have one neighbor who even remembers seeing your brother leave in your pickup that afternoon." An outright lie, but again Terry was convincing. Madison rarely got to see her partner's interrogation skills, but she was impressed.

"What? No, that's not right."

"They ID'd him from a photo array." Terry shrugged nonchalantly, carrying on the charade.

"They're mistaken."

"Your brother's looking at jail time. He'll lose his badge."

"On one person's say-so?"

"Turns out your brother's not exactly true blue. There's been other infractions. Not that I'll be getting into them with you."

Madison had revealed to Troy, Terry, and the chief that evidence had gone "missing" under Dustin Phelps's watch in a previous investigation and that was part of what had started her digging into him.

Joel snarled.

"Now, if there's something you'd like to tell me that might help your brother, I'm listening."

Madison was smiling as she watched Terry work over Joel Phelps. They'd decided that if they could play to the brothers' loyalty, they'd be able to use it against Murphy. It was apparent to Madison the bond between the brothers was a strong one, since it seemed obvious it had been Joel who'd put an end to Leland King's nosing around Dustin's affairs.

Joel remained quiet.

"Fine. We'll bring your brother in." Terry swept the pictures into the folder and went to stand.

"Stop. My brother had nothing to do with this, and neither did I." Joel thrust a pointed finger toward Terry. "I want that on the record."

Madison put her head on Troy's shoulder. "It's working," she whispered.

"Consider it on record," Terry said.

"I lent my truck to Garrett Murphy because he said he was working on a home renovation project and needed to pick up some lumber. He brought my truck back, and I noticed the damage to the grille guard. I asked him about it, and he said it must have happened in the parking lot."

"And you believed him?"

"I did. Then Detective Matthews started asking questions. I realized something serious might have happened while he had it."

"Why not come forward?"

Madison winced at Terry's question, hoping it wouldn't prevent Joel from replying.

"I was just in denial, I guess. I mean, Garrett's a friend."

"So you're ready to go on record that he was driving?"

"I am."

"I'm going to need some proof," Terry laid out, speaking to Joel as if he were a friend now.

Joel fished his phone out of his pocket and keyed on it, then handed it to Terry. "It's a text from my wife."

Terry read it out loud. "*Garrett just dropped off the truck.*"

"See the time stamp?"

"Huh. It's about half an hour after the accident happened." Terry looked toward the glass. They had Murphy, but they had yet to prove motive.

Terry relaxed in his chair. "Do you have any idea why Murphy would ram Detective Knight's car?"

"I can't imagine what was going on in his head."

"I see."

Seconds passed.

Terry continued. "Maybe he was pressed into it."

Joel's eyes flicked to Terry's face. "Someone forced him to? Nah." Joel shook his head.

"I just know there are a lot of powerful people in Stiles. People who aren't a fan of Detective Knight."

Joel crossed his arms. "The mob?"

"Funny how you went right there."

"I know her suspicions about them, about us—me, my brother, and Murphy."

"How?" Terry pushed back.

Joel's gaze met Terry's. "It's just— Maybe I should get a lawyer."

"Was the mob behind the accident?" Terry put a photo on the table.

Joel's face became shadows. "Where did you get this?"

"That's your brother there, right? And Murphy? Also, this guy is Jonathan Wright. This woman here was a mystery at first, but her name's Tatiana Ivanova, isn't it? And I'm quite sure she's involved with the Russian Mafia."

"I'll take that lawyer now."

"Have it your way."

Terry left and joined everyone in the observation room.

"You did great in there," Madison told her partner. "Thank you. Murphy will be going away now because of you."

"It pains me to say this, but your accident was premeditated. Still don't know if the mob ordered it or not. I think he peed his pants when I showed him that picture with Ivanova though."

Tatiana Ivanova was why Madison leaned toward the trio acting on their own to protect their secrets and not following mob orders. A star assassin of the mob didn't *attempt* to take life; she succeeded. She turned to Troy. "Thank you for your help, too, and believing in me."

"Of course."

Andrea went over to them. "So this is how it's going to play out. Murphy will be brought in, and a thorough investigation conducted. I'm going to request that Internal Affairs opens investigations into him as well as Dustin Phelps."

"Thank you." Madison smiled at her.

"That's not all. The intel you've gathered may be extremely useful, and we might need more before this is all over. Are you sure you're up for it?"

Madison looked at Troy, and he put his arm around her.

"We're in this together," she said, peering in his eyes.

"Very well. The road ahead won't be easy, but if all works out, justice will be served." Andrea addressed Terry. "And she's right. Great job in there." She shook his hand and left the room.

"I'm gonna head out too," Terry said. "Nice ring, by the way." He smirked before turning to leave.

Madison held out her hand and splayed her fingers. "Yes. Yes, it is."

Madison and Troy were curled up on the couch after dinner, and there was a knock at the front door.

Madison answered, and it was Cynthia.

"Do you have a minute?"

"For you, always."

Cynthia shivered as she stepped inside. "That wind's bitter tonight."

Madison gestured to the couch. "That's why we're cozied up in front of the TV."

"Wait a minute." Cynthia reached out and grabbed Madison's hand. She grinned at the sight of the ring on her finger. "Troy," she called out, and he walked to the entryway. "It's about time you made an honest woman out of her. Congratulations, you two."

"Thank you." Troy wrapped an arm around Madison.

"And you," Cynthia directed at Madison, "will need to fill me in on everything, but I don't want to interrupt your evening."

"Too late for that," Troy said, and Madison pushed him in the chest.

"I just came to quickly say—in person—that I'm appalled by Garrett's actions and so is Lou. He's having a hard time accepting that his friend rammed your car, Maddy. But he said that he's been different in the past few months. More secretive and seemed to find amusement in abusing his power as a police officer. I just wanted to let you know there are no hard feelings on this end. Hope you can forgive me." Cynthia reeled her in for a hug. "I'm so happy you're okay."

Madison swallowed the urge to cry. Cynthia hugging her, Troy rubbing her back.

"Me too," is what she said, but there were moments in the past few days she didn't feel okay; she didn't even feel fine. She felt sad. But as long as she had Troy and her other loved ones, she'd get through her grief, and she could feel the warmth of hope. She also felt like today she made it at least one step closer to her goal of ridding Stiles of corrupt cops. Maybe one day they'd all be behind bars—would be if she had a say. But who really knows what the future holds?

Catch the next book in the Detective Madison Knight Series!

Sign up at the weblink listed below
to be notified when new Madison Knight titles
are available for pre-order:

CarolynArnold.net/MKUpdates

By joining this newsletter, you will also receive
exclusive first looks at the following:

Updates pertaining to upcoming releases in the
series, such as cover reveals, book descriptions,
and firm release dates

Sneak peeks of teasers and special content

Behind-the-Tape™ insights that give you an
inside look at Carolyn's research and creative
process

Read on for an exciting preview of
Carolyn Arnold's FBI thriller
featuring Brandon Fisher

ELEVEN

One

Nothing in the twenty weeks at Quantico had prepared me for this.

A crime scene investigator, who had identified himself as Earl Royster when we'd first arrived, addressed my boss, FBI Supervisory Special Agent Jack Harper, "All of the victims were buried—" He held up a finger, his eyes squeezed shut, and he sneezed. "Sorry 'bout that. My allergies don't like it down here. They were all buried the same way."

This was my first case with the FBI Behavioral Analysis Unit, and it had brought me and the three other members of my team to Salt Lick, Kentucky. The discovery was made this morning, and we were briefed and flown in from Quantico to the Louisville field office where we picked up a couple of SUVs. We drove from there and arrived in Salt Lick at about four in the afternoon.

We were in an underground bunker illuminated by portable lights brought in by the local investigative team. The space was eleven feet beneath the cellar of a house that was the size of a mobile trailer. We stood in a central hub from which four tunnels spread out like a root system. The space was fifteen feet by seven and a half feet and six and a half feet tall.

The walls were packed dirt, and an electrical cord ran along the ceiling and down the tunnels with pigtail light fixtures dangling every few feet. The bulbs cut into the height of the tunnels by eight inches.

I pulled on my shirt collar wishing for a smaller frame than my six foot two inches. As it was, the three of us could have reached out and touched each other if we were so inclined. The tunnels were even narrower at three feet wide.

"It's believed each victim had the same cuts inflicted," Royster began, "although most of the remains are skeletal, so it's not as easy to know for sure, but based on burial method alone, this guy obviously adhered to some sort of ritual. The most recent victim is only a few years old and was preserved by the soil. The oldest remains are estimated to date back twenty-five to thirty years. Bingham moved in twenty-six years ago."

Lance Bingham was the property owner, age sixty-two, and was currently serving three to five years in a correctional facility for killing two cows and assaulting a neighbor. If he had moved in twenty-six years ago, that would put

Bingham at thirty-six years old at the time. The statistical age for a serial killer to start out is early to mid-thirties.

The CSI continued to relay more information about how the tunnels branched out in various directions, likely extending beneath a neighboring cornfield, and the ends came to bulbous tips, like subterranean cul-de-sacs.

"There are eleven rooms and only ten bodies," Jack summarized with impatience and pulled a cigarette out of a shirt pocket. He didn't light up, but his mouth was clamped down on it as if it were a lifeline.

Royster's gaze went from the cigarette to Jack's eyes. "Yes. There's one tunnel that leads to a dead end, and there's one empty grave."

Jack turned to me. "What do you make of it?" he asked, the cigarette bobbing on his lips as he spoke.

Everyone looked at me expectantly. "Of the empty grave?" I squeaked out.

Jack squinted and removed the cigarette from his mouth. "That and the latest victim."

"Well…" My collar felt tighter, and I cleared my throat, then continued. "Bingham had been in prison for the last three years. The elaborate tunnel system he had going would have taken years to plan and dig, and it would have taken a lot of strength. My guess would be that Bingham wasn't working alone. He had help and, after he went to prison, someone followed in his footsteps."

Jack perched the unlit smoke back between his lips. "Hmm."

I wasn't sure how to read *Hmm*, but the way his gaze scrutinized me, I was thinking he wasn't necessarily impressed.

"Anyway, you'll want to see it for yourself." Royster gestured down one of the tunnels and took a step toward it. "I know I haven't seen anything like—" Royster didn't catch his sneeze in time, and snot sprayed through the air.

Ick. I stepped back.

More sniffles. "Again, sorry 'bout that. Anyway, this way."

Jack motioned for me to follow behind Royster, ahead of him.

I took a deep breath, anticipating the tight quarters of the tunnel.

Sweat dripped down my back, and I pulled on my collar again.

"Go ahead, Kid," Jack directed.

He'd adopted the pet name for me from the moment we'd met, and I wished he'd just call me by my name.

Both Jack and the CSI were watching me.

The CSI said, "We'll look at the most recent victim first. Now, as you know, the victims alternated male and female. The tenth victim was female so we believe the next is going to be—"

"Let me guess, male," Jack interrupted him.

"Yeah." Royster took off down the third tunnel that fed off from the bottom right of the hub.

I followed behind him, tracing the walls with my hands. My heart palpitated. I ducked to miss the bulbs just as I knew I'd have to and worked at focusing on the positive. Above ground, the humidity sucked air from the lungs; in the tunnels, the air was cool but still suffocating.

I counted my paces—five, six. The further we went, the heavier my chest became, making the next breath less taken for granted.

Despite my extreme discomfort, this was my first case, and I had to be strong. The rumor was you either survived Jack and the two years of probationary service and became a certified special agent or your next job would be security detail at a mall.

Five more paces and we entered an offshoot from the main tunnel. According to Royster, three burial chambers were in this tunnel. He described these as branches on a tree. Each branch came off the main trunk for the length of about ten feet and ended in a circular space of about eleven feet in diameter. The idea of more space seemed welcoming until we reached it.

A circular grave took up most of the space and was a couple of feet deep. Chicken wire rimmed the grave to help it retain its shape. With her wrists and ankles tied to metal stakes, her arms and legs formed the human equivalent of a star.

As her body had dried from decomposition, the constraints had kept her positioned in the manner the killer had intended.

"And what made them dig?" Jack asked the CSI.

Jack was searching for specifics. We knew Bingham had entrusted his financials to his sister, but when she passed away a year ago, the back taxes had built up, and the county had come to reclaim the property.

Royster answered, "X marked the spot." Neither Jack nor I displayed any amusement. The CSI continued. "He etched into the dirt, probably with a stick."

"Why assume a stick?" Jack asked the question, and it resulted in an awkward silence.

My eyes settled on the body of the female who was estimated to be in her early twenties. It's not that I had an aversion to a dead body, but looking at her made my stomach toss. She still had flesh on her bones. As the CSI had said, *Preserved by the soil.*

Her torso had eleven incisions. They were marked in the linear way to keep count. Two sets of four vertical cuts with one diagonal slash through each of them. The eleventh cut was the largest and was above the belly button.

"You realize the number eleven is believed to be a sign of purity?" Zach's voice seemed to strike me from thin air, and my chest compressed further, knowing another person was going to share the limited space.

Zachery Miles was a member of our team, but unlike Jack's reputation, Zach's hadn't preceded him. Any information I had, I'd gathered from his file that showed a flawless service record and the IQ of a genius. It also disclosed that he was thirty-seven, eight years older than I was.

Jack stuck the cigarette he had been sucking on back into his shirt pocket. "Purity, huh?"

I looked down at the body of the woman in the shallow grave beside me. Nothing seemed too pure about any of this.

"I'm going to go," Royster excused himself.

"That's if you really dig into the numerology and spiritualistic meaning of the number," Zachery said, disregarding the CSI entirely.

Jack stretched his neck side to side and looked at me. "I hate it when he gets into that shit." He pointed a bony index finger at me. "Don't let me catch you talking about it either."

I just nodded. I felt I had just been admonished as if I were his child—not that he needed to zero in on me like that. Sure, I believed in the existence of God and angels, despite the evil in the world, but I didn't have any avid interest in the unseen.

Zachery continued, "The primary understanding is the number one is that of new beginnings and purity. This is emphasized with the existence of two ones."

My eyes scanned Zachery's face. While his intelligence scoring revealed a genius, physically, he was of average looks. If anything, he was slightly taller than Jack and I, probably coming in at about six foot four. His hair was dark and trimmed short. He had a high brow line and brown eyes.

"Zachery here reads something once—" Jack tapped his head "—it's there."

Jack and I spent the next few hours making our way to every room where Jack insisted on standing beside all the bodies. He studied each of them carefully, even if only part of their remains had been uncovered. I'd pass him glances, but he seemed oblivious to my presence. We ended up back beside the most recent victim where we stayed for twenty minutes, not moving, not talking, just standing.

I understood what he saw. There was a different feel to this room, nothing quantifiable, but it was discernible. The killer had a lot to say. He was organized and immaculate. He was precise and disciplined. He acted with a purpose, and, like most killers, he had a message to relay. We were looking for a controlled, highly intelligent unsub.

The intestines had been removed from nine of the victims, but Harold Jones, the coroner—who also came backed with a doctorate unlike most of his profession—wouldn't conclude it as the cause of death before conducting more tests. The last victim's intestines were intact, and, even though the cause of death needed confirmation, the talk that permeated the corridors of the bunker was that the men who did this were scary sons of bitches.

Zachery entered the room. "I find it fascinating he would bury his victims in circular graves."

Fascinating?

I looked up at Jack, and he flicked his lighter.

He held out his hands as if to say he wouldn't light up inside the burial chamber. His craving was getting desperate, though, which meant he'd be getting cranky. He said, "Continue, Zachery, by all means. The kid wants to hear."

"By combining both the number eleven and the circle, it makes me think of the coinherence symbol. Even the way the victims are laid out."

"Elaborate," Jack directed.

"It's a circle which combines a total of eleven inner points to complete it. As eleven means purity, so the coinherence symbol is related to religious traditions—at minimum thirteen, but some people can discern more, and each symbol is understood in different ways. The circle itself stands for completion and can symbolize eternity."

I cocked my head to the side. Zachery noticed.

"We have a skeptic here, Jack."

Jack faced me and spoke with the unlit cigarette having resumed its perch between his lips. "What do you make of it?"

Is this a trap? "You want to know what I think?"

"By all means, Slingshot."

There it was, the other dreaded nickname, no doubt his way of reminding me that I didn't score perfectly on handguns at the academy. "Makes me think of the medical symbol. Maybe our guy has a background in medicine. It could explain the incisions being deep enough to inflict pain but not deep enough to cause them to bleed out. It would explain how he managed to take out their intestines."

Was this what I signed up for?

"Hmm," Jack mumbled. Zachery remained silent. Seconds later, Jack said, "You're assuming they didn't bleed out. Continue."

"The murders happened over a period of time. This one—" I gestured to the woman, and for a moment, realized how this job transformed the life of a person into an object "—she's recent. Bingham's been in prison for about three years now."

Jack flicked the lighter again. "So you're saying he had an apprentice?"

Zachery's lips lifted upward, and his eyes read, *Like* Star Wars.

I got it. I was the youngest on the team, twenty-nine this August, next month, and I was the new guy, but I didn't make it through four years of university studying mechanics and endure twenty weeks of the academy, coming out at the top of the class, to be treated like a child. "Not like an apprentice."

"Like what then—"

"Jack, the sheriff wants to speak with you." Paige Dawson, another member of our team, came into the burial chamber. She had come to Quantico from the New York field office claiming she wanted out of the big city. I met her when she was an instructor at the FBI Academy.

I pulled on my collar. Four of us were in here now. Dust caused me to cough and warranted a judgmental glare from Jack.

"How did you make out with the guy who discovered everything?"

"He's clean. I mean we had his background already, and he lives up to it. I really don't think he's involved at all."

Jack nodded and left the room.

I turned to Zachery. "I think he hates me."

"If he hated you, you'd know it." Zachery followed behind Jack.

Two

S alt Lick, Kentucky was right in the middle of nowhere and had a population shy of three hundred and fifty. Just as the town's name implied, underground mineral deposits were the craving of livestock, and due to this, it had originally attracted farmers to the area. I was surprised the village was large enough to boast a Journey's End Lodge and a Frosty Freeze.

I stepped into the main hub to see Jack in a heated conversation with Sheriff Harris. From an earlier meeting with him, I knew he covered all of Bath County which included three municipalities and a combined population of about twelve thousand.

"Ah, I'm doing the best I can, Agent, but, um, we've never seen the likes of this before." A born and raised Kentucky man, the sheriff was in his mid-fifties, had a bald head and carried about an extra sixty pounds that came to rest on his front. Both of his hands were braced on his hips, a stance of confidence, but the flicking up and down of his right index finger gave his insecurities away.

"It has nothing to do with what you've seen before, Sheriff. What matters is catching the unsub."

"Well, the property owner is in p-pri-prison," the Kentucky accent broke through.

"The bodies date back two to three decades with the newest one being within the last few years."

Harris's face brightened a reddish hue as he took a deep breath and exhaled loud enough to be heard.

Jack had the ability to make a lot of people nervous. His dark hair, which was dusted with silver at the sideburns, gave him a look of distinction, but deeply-etched creases in his face exposed his trying past.

Harris shook his head. "So much violence, and it's tourist season 'round here." Harris paused. His eyes said, *You city folks wouldn't understand.* "Cave Run Lake is manmade but set in the middle of nature. People love coming here to get away. Word gets out about this, there go the tourists."

"Ten people have been murdered, and you're worried about tourists?"

"Course not, but—"

"It sounds like you were."

"Then you misunderstood, Agent. Besides, the counties around here are peaceful, law-abidin' citizens."

"Churchgoers?" Zachery came up from a tunnel.

"Well, ah, I wouldn't necessarily say that. There are probably about thirty churches or so throughout the county, and right here in Salt Lick there are three."

"That's quite a few considering the population here."

"S'pose so."

"Sheriff." A deputy came up to the group of them and pulled up his pants.

"Yes, White."

The deputy's face was the shade of his name. "The in-investigators found somethin' you should see." He passed glances among all of us.

Jack held out a hand as if to say, *By all means.*

We followed the deputy up the ramp that led to the cellar. With each step taking me closer to the surface, my chest allowed for more satisfying breaths. Jack glanced over at me. I guessed he was wondering if I was going to make it.

"This way, sir."

The deputy spoke from the front of the line, as he kept moving. His boots hit the wooden stairs that joined the cellar to the first floor.

I inhaled deeply as I came through the opening into the confined space Bingham had at one time called home. Sunlight made its way through tattered sheets that served as curtains, even though the time of day was now seven, and the sun would be sinking in the sky.

The deputy led us to Bingham's bedroom where there were two CSIs. I heard footsteps behind me: Paige. She smiled at me, but it quickly faded.

"They found it in the closet," the deputy said, pointing our focus in its direction.

The investigators moved aside, exposing an empty space. A shelf that ran the width of the closet sat perched at a forty-five-degree angle. The inside had been painted white at one time but now resembled an antiqued paint pattern the modern age went for. It was what I saw when my eyes followed the walls to the floor that held more interest.

Jack stepped in front of me; Zachery came up behind him and gave me a look that said, *Pull up the rear, Pending.* Pending being the nickname Zach had saddled me with to remind me of my twenty-four-month probationary period—as if I'd forget.

"We found it when we noticed the loose floorboard," one of the CSIs said. He held a clipboard wedged between an arm and his chest. The other hand held a pen which he clicked repeatedly. Jack looked at it, and the man stopped. The CSI went on. "Really, it's what's inside that's, well, what nightmares are made of."

I didn't know the man. In fact, I had never seen him before, but the reflection in his eyes told me he had witnessed something that even paled the gruesome find in the bunkers.

"You first, Kid." Jack stepped back.

Floorboards were hinged back and exposed a hole about two and a half feet square. My stomach tossed thinking of the CSI's words, *what nightmares are made of.*

"Come on, Brandon. I'll follow behind you." Paige's soft voice of encouragement was accompanied by a strategically placed hand on my right shoulder.

I glanced at her. I could do this. *God, I hated small spaces.* But I had wanted to be an FBI special agent and, well, that wish had been granted. Maybe the saying, *Be careful what you wish for, it might come true,* held merit.

I hunched over and looked into the hole. A wooden ladder went down at least twenty feet. The space below was lit.

Maybe if I just took it one step at a time.

"What are you waiting for, Pending?" Zachery taunted me. I didn't look at him but picked up on the amusement in his voice.

I took a deep breath and lowered myself down.

Jack never said a word, but I could feel his energy. He didn't think I was ready for this, but I would prove him wrong—somehow. The claustrophobia I had experienced in the underground passageways was nothing compared to the anxiety squeezing my chest now. At least the tunnels were the width of three feet. Here, four sides of packed earth hugged me, as if a substantial inhale would expand me to the confines of the space.

"I'm coming." Again, Paige's soft voice had a way of soothing me despite the tight quarters threatening to take my last breath and smother me alive.

I looked up. Paige's face filled the opening, and her red wavy hair framed her face. The vision was replaced by the bottom of her shoes.

I continued my descent, one rung at a time, slowly, methodically. I tried to place myself somewhere else, but no images came despite my best efforts to conjure them—and what did I have waiting for me at the bottom? *What nightmares are made of.*

Minutes passed before my shoes reached the soil. I took a deep breath when I realized the height down here was about seven feet and looked around. The room was about five by five, and there was a doorway at the backside.

One pigtail fixture with a light bulb dangled from an electrical wire. It must have fed to the same circuit as the underground passageways and been connected to the power generator as it cast dim light, creating darkened shadows in the corners.

I looked up the ladder. Paige was about halfway down. There was movement behind her, and it was likely Jack and Zachery following behind her.

"You're almost there," I coached them.

By the time the rest of the team made it to the bottom, along with the deputy and a CSI, I had my breathing and my nerves under control.

Paige was the first to head around the bend in the wall.

"The sheriff is going to stay up there an' take care of things." The deputy pointed in the direction Paige went. "What they found is in here."

Jack and Zachery had already headed around the bend. I followed.

Inside the room, Paige raised her hand to cover her mouth. It dropped when she noticed us.

A stainless steel table measuring ten feet by three feet was placed against the back wall. A commercial meat grinder sat on the table. Everything was pristine, and light from a bulb reflected off the surfaces.

To the left of the table was a chest freezer, plain white, one owned by the average consumer. I had one similar, but it was the smaller version because it was only Deb and me.

My stomach tossed thinking about the contents of this one. Paige's feet were planted to where she had first entered the room. Zachery's eyes fixed on Jack, who moved toward the freezer and, with a gloved hand, opened the lid.

Paige gasped, and Jack turned to face her. Disappointment was manifested in the way his eyes narrowed. "It's empty." Jack patted his shirt pocket again.

"If you're thinking we found people's remains in there, we haven't," the CSI said, "but tests have shown positive for human blood."

"So he chopped up his victim's intestines? Put them in the freezer? But where are they?" Paige wrapped her arms around her torso and bent over to look into the opening of the grinder.

"There are many cultures, the Korowai tribe of Papua New Guinea, for example, who have been reported to practice cannibalism even in this modern day," Zachery said. "It can also be involved in religious rituals."

Maybe my eyes should have been fixed on the freezer, on the horror that transpired underground in Salt Lick of Bath County, Kentucky. Instead, I found my training allowing me to focus, analyze, and be objective. In order to benefit the investigation, it would demand these three things, and I wouldn't disappoint. My attention was on the size of the table, the size of the meat grinder, and the size of the freezer. "Anyone think to ask how this all got down here in the first place?"

All five of them faced me.

"The opening down here is only, what, two feet square at the most? Now maybe the meat grinder would fit down, hoisted on a rope, but the table and the freezer? No way."

"What are you saying, Slingshot?"

My eyes darted to Jack's. "I'm saying there has to be another way in." I addressed the CSI, "Did you look for any other hidden passageways? I mean the guy obviously had a thing for them."

"We didn't find anything."

"Well, that doesn't make sense. Where are the burial sites in relation to here?"

"It would be that way." Zachery pointed at the freezer.

We connected eyes, and both of us moved toward it. It slid easily. As we shoved it to the side, it revealed an opening behind it. I looked down into it. Another light bulb spawned eerie shadows. I rose to full height. This find should at least garner some praise from Jack Harper.

"Nothing like Hogan's Alley is it, Kid?"

Also available from
International Bestselling Author
Carolyn Arnold

ELEVEN

Book 1 in the Brandon Fisher FBI series

Eleven Rooms. Ten Bodies. One Empty Grave.

When Brandon Fisher joined the FBI Behavioral Analysis Unit, he knew he'd come up against psychopaths, sociopaths, pathological liars, and more. But when his first case takes him and the team to Salt Lick, Kentucky, to hunt down a ritualistic serial killer, he learns what nightmares are truly made of.

Beneath a residential property, local law enforcement discovered an underground bunker with circular graves that house the remains of ten victims. But that's not all: there's an empty eleventh grave, just waiting for a corpse. The killing clearly hasn't come to an end yet, and with the property owner already behind bars, Brandon is certain there's an apprentice who roams free.

As the FBI follows the evidence across the United States, Brandon starts to struggle with the deranged nature of his job description. And if the case itself isn't going to be enough to push Brandon over the edge, he's working in the shadow of Supervisory Special Agent Jack Harper, who expects nothing short of perfection from his team. To make matters even worse, it seems Brandon has become the target of a psychotic serial killer who wants to make him— or his wife—victim number eleven.

**Available from popular book retailers or
at CarolynArnold.net**

CAROLYN ARNOLD is an international bestselling and award-winning author, as well as a speaker, teacher, and inspirational mentor. She has four continuing fiction series—Detective Madison Knight, Brandon Fisher FBI, McKinley Mysteries, and Matthew Connor Adventures—and has written nearly thirty books. Her genre diversity offers her readers everything from cozy to hard-boiled mysteries, and thrillers to action adventures.

Both her female detective and FBI profiler series have been praised by those in law enforcement as being accurate and entertaining, leading her to adopt the trademark: POLICE PROCEDURALS RESPECTED BY LAW ENFORCEMENT™.

Carolyn was born in a small town and enjoys spending time outdoors, but she also loves the lights of a big city. Grounded by her roots and lifted by her dreams, her overactive imagination insists that she tell her stories. Her intention is to touch the hearts of millions with her books, to entertain, inspire, and empower.

She currently lives near London, Ontario with her husband and beagles and is a member of Crime Writers of Canada and Sisters in Crime.

CONNECT ONLINE
Carolynarnold.net
Facebook.com/AuthorCarolynArnold
Twitter.com/Carolyn_Arnold

And don't forget to sign up for her newsletter for up-to-date information on release and special offers
at
CarolynArnold.net/Newsletters.